PRAISE FOR ABBY JIMENEZ

"I've loved this author since her debut…Abby Jimenez [has a] talent for layering complex, realistic themes with the sweetest of romances."
—Ali Hazelwood

Jimenez writes "romance for the ages!"
—Tessa Bailey

"Abby Jimenez tackles heavy subjects with humor and care in her exquisitely written novels."
—Farrah Rochon

"Put me in the Abby Jimenez fan club."
—Katherine Center

"Jimenez masterfully blends heavy issues and humor."
—*Publishers Weekly*

"Jimenez is an excellent storyteller."
—*BookPage*

"A dangerously addictive sense of humor."
—*Booklist*

YOURS TRULY

"This heartfelt romantic comedy deals respectfully with mental health issues…The protagonists are also beautifully developed and authentic. Fans of Jimenez will clamor for this book, and first-time readers will want to explore her backlist."
—*Library Journal*, starred review

"Sparkling prose, skillful plotting…contemporary romance gold."
—*Publishers Weekly*

"Abby Jimenez once again flexes her ability to tackle big feelings and sensitive topics in this slow-burn romance." —*Elle Canada*

PART OF YOUR WORLD

"The perfect embodiment of romantic joy...This book is an emotional experience that will tick all the boxes for passionate romance fans. A must-read." —*Kirkus,* starred review

A "layered, soul-stirring romance...Jimenez dexterously tackles class difference and shades her endearing side characters with as much care as her lovable leads. The result is an emotional roller coaster centered on love as a source of empowerment." —*Publishers Weekly,* starred review

LIFE'S TOO SHORT

"A hilarious, tender, and altogether life-affirming gem of a book. This is the kind of novel that leaves you a little better than when it found you. Jimenez is a true talent." —Emily Henry, *New York Times* bestselling author

"Jimenez continues to burnish her well-deserved reputation for delivering truly unforgettable love stories." —*Booklist*

THE HAPPY EVER AFTER PLAYLIST

"*The Happy Ever After Playlist* tackles love after loss with fierce humor and fiercer heart." —Casey McQuiston, *New York Times* bestselling author of *Red, White & Royal Blue*

ALSO BY ABBY JIMENEZ

Yours Truly
Part of Your World
Life's Too Short
The Happy Ever After Playlist
The Friend Zone

JUST FOR
THE *SUMMER*

ABBY JIMENEZ

FOREVER

New York Boston

Forever
Hachette Book Group
1290 Avenue of the Americas, New York, NY 10104
read-forever.com
@readforeverpub

First Edition: April 2024

Forever is an imprint of Grand Central Publishing. The Forever name and logo are trademarks of Hachette Book Group, Inc.

The publisher is not responsible for websites (or their content) that are not owned by the publisher.

Forever books may be purchased in bulk for business, educational, or promotional use. For information, please contact your local bookseller or the Hachette Book Group Special Markets Department at special.markets@hbgusa.com.

Library of Congress Cataloging-in-Publication Data

Names: Jimenez, Abby, author.
Title: Just for the summer / Abby Jimenez.
Description: First edition. | New York ; Boston : Forever, 2024.
Identifiers: LCCN 2023046026 | ISBN 9781538704431 (trade paperback) |
    ISBN 9781538768631 | ISBN 9781538768648 | ISBN 9781538704448 (ebook)
Subjects: LCSH: Dating (Social customs)—Fiction. | LCGFT: Romance fiction.
    | Novels.
Classification: LCC PS3610.I47 J87 2024 | DDC 813/.6—dc23/eng/20231003
LC record available at https://lccn.loc.gov/2023046026

ISBN: 9781538704431 (trade paperback), 9781538704448 (ebook), 9781538768648 (signed edition), 9781538769409 (special edition), 9781538768631 (special signed edition), 9781538769423 (special edition), 9781538769171 (large print)

Printed in the United States of America

CW

10 9 8 7 6 5 4 3 2

This book is for my wonderful readers. I started writing just for me. I never thought it would go anywhere or that anyone would see it. Now I write for you.
It's way better with company.

Dear Reader,

While my books are all rom-coms, some themes in this story may be triggering for some readers. If you feel trigger warnings are spoilers and you don't need them, please skip the next paragraph and jump right into the book.

This book has scenes containing panic attacks, anxiety, PTSD, depression, depictions of undiagnosed mental health issues, a toxic mother, and past child neglect. Please visit my website or Goodreads page for a full list of content guidance.

Posted by just_in_267

AITA for naming my ugly dog after my ex best friend?

I [29m] have been friends with Chad [32m] since we were born. Our moms are best friends and we grew up together and were roommates for the last 10 years, up until the incident that set our current situation into motion.

A little backstory. I have this...streak if you will? Basically every woman I date more than a few times ends up finding her soulmate after we break up. It's a thing. It started three years ago and it's now happened five times. We break things off and the very next person they date ends up being The One.

My friends think this is hilarious. I always part ways with the women on good terms, and I'm happy they're happy. But my buddies tease me mercilessly about it. They call me the good luck charm.

Anyway, forward to five months ago. I dated Hope [28f] for a few weeks. Not a big deal. We decided we weren't feeling it, no chemistry, so we called it quits. And then lo and behold she hits it off with Chad. Of course in true Good Luck Charm fashion, this means Chad is her soulmate. Chad is all googly-eyed over her, they've met the parents, they're ring shopping—and they want to move in together. Immediately.

The only problem is that Chad has six more months on our lease but found a perfect new house for him and Hope, and he can't afford to pay rent on two places at the same time. So he had to make the difficult decision to screw me over or screw her over—and he picked me. Now I have to find a way to cover his rent until the lease is up.

I spent several weeks stressing. I really didn't want to find a new roommate, and the landlord wouldn't let me out of the lease completely, but he did say I could move to a less expensive apartment. The only available unit in the entire complex was a studio. A little small, but it's just temporary, and it's cheap. I jumped at the chance and agreed to it sight unseen. Then I found out WHY this studio was cheap and available—it directly faces one of those Toilet King plumber billboards. The one where he's dressed like Henry Tudor and holding a plunger over a giant poop-filled toilet bowl? It should be illegal for a billboard to be this close to a building. It's like the only person meant to see it is the poor soul who lives in this apartment—who is now me. Seriously. It's all you can see. No sky, no water—just the Toilet King. All day. All night. Lit up when the sun goes down, it shines through the blinds. I work from home. I am in hell.

Chad thinks this is the funniest thing that's ever happened and he trolls me constantly, despite this being mostly his fault. He keeps sending me pictures of every Toilet King billboard, bus bench, and airplane banner he sees, which if you live in the Minneapolis/St. Paul area, you understand exactly how often this happens.

I'm annoyed, but I decided to try to find a reason to spend

more time outside so I don't have to stare out my window. I've always wanted a dog, but Chad would never agree to it. So I went to a rescue and found the ugliest animal there. The one so hideous, nobody else wanted it. This dog's got an underbite and mange, and he's missing half an ear. He's a little Brussels Griffon, so he's got that deep frown—he looks like a judgmental gremlin. I adopted him and named him Chad since the dog is now my new best friend. If you're reading this, you're dead to me, human Chad. (Not really, I still love the guy.) But I tag him in the captions of every Chad the Dog Instagram post with "Look, a loyal Chad!"

Chad laughs it all off, but Hope is upset and says I should rename the dog. Chad's mom agrees and says I'm not allowed to come over until I change the name, which kind of sucks because she's my mom's best friend and I end up there a lot for family stuff. I'm still not doing it.

Am I petty? Yes. But am I the asshole?

CHAPTER 1

EMMA

Have you seen this?"

My best friend tilted her phone so I could see what she was talking about. There was a black Reddit "Am I the Asshole" thread taking up the screen.

We were in the hospital cafeteria on our lunch break.

"What is it?" I asked, squeezing ketchup on my fries.

"Just read it," she said. "I'm sending you the link."

She thumbed it in and it came through.

I picked up my drink and held the straw of my iced tea between my teeth while I read. The moment I hit the second paragraph my eyes went wide. "Oh my God..." I breathed.

"*Right?* And here I thought you were the only one with that good luck charm thing."

"It's a gift," I said. "Not for *me*, but my exes are happy." I sipped my drink and kept reading. When I finished, I set my phone down. "Not the asshole."

"Totally agree," she said. "Have you seen that billboard?"

"No."

"I googled it. Look."

She held her phone out again and I almost choked on my laugh. "That poor guy."

"I would never do you dirty like that," Maddy said.

"I hope not. I couldn't live without you."

She grinned and took a bite of her veggie wrap.

"It's weird you guys both have the same thing going on," she said, after she swallowed. "All your exes, just riding off into the sunset."

"Ha. I wonder how many weddings he's had to be in," I said, pulling the pickles out of my chicken sandwich and putting them on her plate.

She nodded at my phone. "You should ask him."

I gave her a look. "Just DM him?"

She shrugged. "Yeah, why not? Guys love it when girls slide into their DMs," she said. "Seriously. Ask him. Lunch is boring. It'll give us something to do."

I sighed. "All right. *One* message." I wiped my fingers on a napkin, picked up my phone, and swiped open my Reddit DMs.

His handle was just_in_267. I wondered if his name was Justin. My handle was Emma16_dilemma. I hadn't changed it since tenth grade. I probably should.

I started typing.

> I have the same problem you have. It's happened seven times in the last four years. We break up and the guy is married within six months. Do they ask you to be in their weddings too? I've been asked to be a bridesmaid three times 😄

I hit send. "There. I sent it, a message to a complete stranger." I set my phone down. "It sort of feels like something my mom would do."

Maddy scoffed. "If this were Amber, she'd spend all her rent money on a psychic who paints portraits of your soulmate and then sends you the same painting she sends everyone else. *That's* what Amber would do."

I didn't laugh. It was too true to be funny.

My cell pinged. "That Reddit guy just replied," I said.

Maddy stopped with her wrap halfway to her mouth. "What'd he say?"

I clicked on the message.

Justin: Excuse me if this isn't the case, but you're not a reporter trying to figure out my identity for another article about the Reddit thread, are you? You have to tell me. It's like when you're an undercover cop and someone asks you if you're a cop and you can't lie about it.

I laughed.

"What?" Maddy asked.

"He thinks I'm a reporter trying to figure out who he is."

"Is that a problem he has?"

"Apparently."

I started typing.

Me: I am not a reporter.

Justin: That's exactly what an undercover reporter would say.

I shook my head with a smile.

Me: I'm a nurse.

He sent me a narrow-eyed emoji.

I got an idea.

Me: Tell me how many fingers to hold up.

A few seconds passed.

Justin: Four

"Maddy, take a picture of me."

She gawked. "You're gonna send this dude a *picture*?"

"Yeah, why not?"

"Uh, because he could be a serial killer?"

"A serial killer with a sense of humor, a rescue dog, lifelong friends, and a relationship with his mom?" I handed her my phone. "It's no different than what he'd see if he'd matched with me on Tinder and anyway, we'll be in Hawaii in a few weeks. He's in Minnesota. Even if he could figure out who I am, he'd never track me down."

"What if he's some gross dude who doesn't floss and now he's got a picture for his spank bank?"

I rolled my eyes. "Oh *stop*."

I tilted my head so my braid fell to one side and held up four fingers. Maddy didn't look happy, but she took the picture with my phone, then handed it back to me.

I was in scrubs and my hospital badge was clipped to my pocket. I opened the edit feature, scribbled out the identifying information, and sent the pic.

Me: I'm at work. Do reporters wear scrubs? And how many times have you been catfished by reporters?

Justin: This week? Or like, in total?

I sent a laughing emoji.

Justin: Now that we've established you are who you say you are, I will answer your question. I've been asked only once to be in a wedding for someone who benefited from my little streak. But I was best man and it was Beetlejuice themed.

I laughed and read it out loud to Maddy.

"Pictures or it didn't happen," she said.

I typed "Pictures or it didn't happen. 😊 "

I set my phone back down. "You're right. This is fun."

"I have good ideas," she said.

I was almost done eating my sandwich when my DMs pinged.

"He just replied," I said. "There's a picture."

Maddy jumped from her seat to stand over my shoulder.

When I clicked it, I started cracking up. The bride and groom were dressed as Beetlejuice and Lydia, in her red wedding dress from the movie. The maid of honor and best man were dressed like the Maitlands, only with the scary faces they put on in the beginning to frighten the new residents. He was wearing a long cone-shaped nose and buggy eyes. I sent a row of laughing emojis.

"You're right, he *does* have a sense of humor," Maddy said.

I tilted my head. "Too bad I can't see his face."

"Send me that."

"Why?"

"I'll reverse image search it."

"Oh, good thinking. Okay, hold on."

I sent it to her. She sat back down and started thumbing into her phone, and I went back to finish my food.

"Found him," Maddy said, after about forty-five seconds.

I gawked. "*That* fast???"

"The FBI should hire more women. We're natural investigators. It's on his Instagram. And it's definitely him, I see the billboard. I'll send you the link."

My phone chirped with the incoming text, but I paused. "Wait. Should we be looking at this? It feels like a violation of his privacy."

She gave me a look over the top of her phone. "When men stop assaulting women they meet on the internet, we'll stop creeping on them to make sure they pass the vibe check. And anyway, if he wanted privacy, his account would be *private*."

I bobbed my head. "Okay. Good point."

I clicked on the link, and we both pored over his wall at the same time from our respective phones. He had brown hair, brown eyes, he was clean-shaven. White, dimples. A nice smile, fit—and he was *cute*. Super cute.

"Are you seeing this?" Maddy said. "This guy *definitely* flosses."

"Oh my God, the dog."

She gasped. "Wow. He really *is* ugly. Like a tiny gargoyle."

I tilted my head. "I don't know. He's so ugly he's almost adorable." The small brown dog was shaggy with floppy ears, a pushed-in snout, and a hard frown. His watery eyes bulged a little. In the picture, Justin was holding him and smiling like a kid who just got what he'd always wanted for Christmas. The caption read: *Well, Dog Brad's got a tapeworm, but at least he didn't stiff me on rent.*

"Brad?" I asked, looking up. "I thought his friend's name was Chad."

"He probably changed the names to protect their privacy. Classy. Did you see the comments?" she asked. "Go look."

I clicked to expand them. Laughing emojis, laughing emojis. Someone named Faith said, "Really, Justin? SMH." And then a guy named Brad commented, "The next time I come over I'm stealing the stick to your blinds."

I was laughing over my phone.

"Check out the way the dog looks," Maddy said.

"What about him?"

"The dog looks comfortable with him. I always look at the animals in pictures, it tells you a lot about the person. Like, I can totally tell when someone borrowed someone's dog for their profile pic. The dog's like, 'Okay, don't know you but I guess.' Scroll down," she said. "See? Look at the one of him on the sofa."

There was a shot of Justin on a couch. On one side he had an arm wrapped around a little girl who was sleeping curled up against him with her head on his chest. The dog was sleeping on the other side with his chin on Justin's thigh. The picture was adorable.

"That dog trusts him," Maddy said. "And that's a rescue dog, so that means something. They're usually all skittish and freaked out." She went quiet again looking at his wall. "Go down further," Maddy said. "The billboard."

I scrolled a few pictures down and there it was. The infamous sign. And Justin hadn't been kidding, it was *bad*. I already knew what it looked like from Maddy's Google search but seeing it from the apartment was a whole different thing. It consumed the entire window. "Oh wow. Yeah, Justin's definitely not the asshole. That's a *lot*."

The picture had been taken from the kitchen, so he could get the entire view. Since it was a studio, it only had the one large sliding glass door, and the whole thing was filled with a grinning, bearded middle-aged man dressed like a king, holding a plunger over a clogged toilet.

"He's got a bed frame," Maddy said.

"So?"

"So that's a green flag. The closer to the floor the bed is, the worse humans they are. Every guy who pretends to forget his wallet on a date a thousand percent sleeps on a futon or a mattress on the floor. I make them send me a picture of their bed before I show up. *And* I deduct points for sleeping bags as blankets, even if they *do* have a headboard."

"Why?"

"Because sleeping bags have floor energy?"

"What if it's a bunk bed?" I said.

"That is the *only* circumstance in which my theory doesn't hold up, but that is also why I require bedroom photos before I meet them."

"You kill me."

I zoomed around the photo at the rest of the room. His bed was made with a beige duvet. A neat desk with an elaborate computer set up on it. Three large screens and a keypad and wireless mouse in the middle. There was a tiny dog bed next to the desk and a potted plant in the corner. Artwork on the walls. It was a nice apartment—minus the view. He was obviously clean and had good enough taste.

I scrolled down to look at the rest of his photos. None with girls. Several with what appeared to be his family—a teenage boy who looked like a fifteen-year-old version of Justin, same dimples. A girl who was probably eleven or twelve, and then the little sleeping girl from the couch photo, who couldn't be more than five. He'd tagged who I assumed was his mom in the pictures and I clicked on her profile, but it was private.

"I found him on LinkedIn," Maddy said. "His full name is Justin Dahl. He's a software engineer." She went quiet again for a few moments. "His dad died a few years ago. I just found an obituary that mentions him. Yup. That's him. Same kids from his Instagram. He's got three siblings. Alex, Chelsea, and Sarah."

"How did his dad die?" I asked.

"It just says 'unexpectedly.' He was only forty-five. Sucks. Hold on, I'm checking the sex-offender registry." She typed into her phone for a minute. "He's clear." She set her phone down and picked up her wrap. "I don't see any red flags here, other than he's got a J name. J-named men are the *worst*. I'm following him on Instagram from my throwaway account to keep up surveillance. You may proceed."

I looked at her, amused. "Proceed to do *what*?"

"I don't know. Keep talking to him. See if he's normal."

"He seems normal," I said, looking back at the phone. "We're the ones who aren't normal," I muttered.

He'd sent the Beetlejuice photo nine minutes ago and we'd already deconstructed his entire life. I'd seen his face, his family, his apartment, his dad's obituary, and I knew where he worked.

Then I looked at the time. "Oh, crap, we gotta go."

Maddy checked her watch. "Shit." She took one last bite and got to her feet. We cleared our table and ran to the ICU. Justin didn't reply before I went back to my shift.

That night after work Maddy made dinner. Grilled portobello mushrooms and rice pilaf. I did the dishes and cleaned the kitchen, then took a shower and blew out my hair.

I was in my pajamas and in bed when I finally saw the DM from Justin. It was from right after I'd gone back to work from my lunch break.

He sent me a picture of himself. It wasn't one on Instagram. He was in his living room and the billboard was behind him over his shoulder. He was holding the dog.

Justin: So you know that I'm not actually a Beetlejuice character. Please don't be an undercover reporter trying to blow the lid off the Good Luck Charm story.

I laughed and started typing.

Me: So this is Chad?

Justin: Brad. I changed the names on Reddit. Hope is actually named Faith.

Me: Ah. And how does Brad feel about being internet famous for being an asshole?

Justin: He thinks it's funny. Because he *is* an asshole.

I made an amused noise.

Me: You weren't kidding about that billboard.

Justin: Believe me when I tell you it is so much worse in person.

Me: For the record I don't think your dog's that ugly.

Justin: I'm disappointed to hear that. Takes some of the thunder out of the name. Do you have any pets?

Me: No. I'm a travel nurse. It would be too hard. But I buy a plant at every new city.

Justin: You take it with you?

Me: No, I can't. I leave it.

Justin: *gasp* murderer.

I shook my head with a smile.

Me: I leave it with someone. No plants are injured in the pursuit of my career.

Justin: Why a plant? Do u like to garden?

I sat up and crossed my legs under me.

Me: Plants brighten a room. And yes, I like to garden. I move too much for it though.

Justin: So the same thing really happens to you? The good luck charm thing?

Me: It does. So why are reporters trying to figure out your secret identity?

He typed for a minute, and I dabbed on some lip balm while I waited.

Justin: Because everyone wants to know who the guy who can guarantee you a happy ever after is. I don't think anyone even cared about the rest of the story. The good luck charm part was what made it viral.

Me: I could see that.

Justin: My DMs are off the hook. I had to turn off notifications, it was driving me bonkers. I only answered you because you said the same thing happens to you and I figured you weren't trying to date me just to break up with me.

I laughed. Again.

I looked at the time. It was late.

Me: I have to go to bed. I have another twelve-hour shift tomorrow.

Justin: 👍 Okay. Nice chatting with you.

I smiled.

Yeah, you too.

CHAPTER 2

JUSTIN

I spotted Brad and Benny at the back of the restaurant and made my way over.

"Finally," Brad said as I slid into the maroon booth. "You know some of us have limited lunch breaks, dick."

"Sorry, I had to give Brad his dewormer. I brought some for you too. Faith said you've been dragging your ass on the carpet?"

Benny snorted and Brad tried to keep his face serious, but he couldn't.

My best friend was in a Hawaiian shirt and pink cargo shorts. He was a general manager at Trader Joe's. I missed not having to go to the grocery store now that he had moved out. Actually, I missed a lot of things now that Brad had moved out. Like having another human to talk to, even if it *was* this one.

I plucked a mozzarella stick off the appetizer platter they'd ordered and dipped it in marinara. "What's good here?"

"The wings," Brad said.

"How did I know you were going to say that?"

Brad got wings at every restaurant we went to, without fail. He'd get wings at a sushi place if they had them.

Benny nodded at the menu. "The burgers are good. They make their own buns."

"Oh cool," I said, taking off my jacket. "How's Jane?"

"Good. She says hi."

Brad put an arm over the back of the booth. "Yeah, Faith says hi too. And to rename your fucking dog."

"Nope." I made a popping noise on the *P* while I grabbed the menu. "It's viral. I can't back down now, where would my principles be?"

"That Reddit thing's still going?" Benny asked.

"Yeah, pretty much," I said, talking while I looked at the menu. "I think it hit TikTok the other day, so it started up again. It's been nonstop all week."

"What are people saying?" Benny asked.

I laughed a little. "Mostly that *I'm* not the asshole." I looked directly at Brad, and he smirked.

"A few people told me I should have sued you for breach of contract." I laughed at this. Never. "A bunch of comments said we're both assholes."

"This is true," Brad said, looking at his phone. "We are assholes. But only to each other. It's the foundation of our friendship."

"I had a bunch of girls ask if I'd date them and break up with them so they can find their soulmate," I said, amused, perusing the burger options.

"Are you gonna do it?" Brad asked. "Offer your services?"

I scoffed. "No."

"Why not?" he asked.

"They only want to date me to break up with me. I have like two hundred messages right now and they're all the same."

"What if there's someone cool in there?" Benny chimed in.

I gave him a look. "Someone cool who wants to break up with me? Before we've even met? I'm a novelty. A fun story to tell their friends. They got to date the good luck charm guy from Reddit. No thank you. Besides, my streak's not even a real thing."

"As someone on the benefiting end of it, I'm gonna tell you, it's real," Brad said.

"It's a series of coincidences," I said. "There is nothing magical about any of it."

Brad shook his head. "Look, you can believe whatever the heck you want. But when I met Faith, and I mean the *second* I laid eyes on her, it was like I got hit by a truck. It was the same way for her. You're ferrying women to their happily ever afters. You could charge for this shit."

"Oh, now you tell me," I said, slapping the menu shut. "I could have used the extra twelve hundred bucks last month."

He flipped me off.

I grabbed another mozzarella stick. "You know, I actually did sort of meet somebody from it."

Benny looked interested. "You did? Who?"

"Just some girl. A nurse. She messaged me a few days ago. Said she's got the same thing I do."

"The good luck charm thing?" Benny asked.

I nodded. "Yeah."

She was *beautiful*. In her picture she was wearing light blue scrubs and her long brown hair was in a braid. She had hazel eyes, a broad grin. She didn't look like a nurse. She looked like a movie star playing a nurse. She seemed pretty cool too.

"So you gonna hook up with her or what?" Brad said.

"I don't think she lives here. She's a travel nurse."

"Damn. That sucks. Where's she at?" Brad said.

"I don't know. I didn't ask."

"You should ask," Benny said. "What if she's in Vegas or something? We could all go. It'd be fun."

Brad nodded at me. "You know, if she's got the same thing you do, if you guys date each other, you'll both find your soulmates when you break up."

I laughed a little, dipping my mozzarella stick in ranch.

"No, I'm serious," he said. "Think about it. You guys would cancel each other out."

"I don't know about that. She was pretty nice though."

"Did you text her today?" Brad asked.

"No. Why?"

"I don't know. Just getting tired of your ass being single all the time. You're messing up the ratio."

"Bold of you to assume I care about the ratio," I said, taking a bite.

Only lately I sort of *did* care.

Benny and Brad were both in serious relationships now. I didn't like fifth wheeling it when their girlfriends were around— and they usually were.

They were starting to do the couples thing for all the trips and birthdays. They were all going up to Lutsen in October to go hiking. They asked me if I wanted to go, but I didn't. Not alone.

I puffed my cheeks and blew a breath. "I'm just getting burnt out on dating, I think."

"I hated dating," Benny said.

Brad leaned back in the booth. "You lucked out. Met Jane

through your sister. And you know she's ride or die too 'cause she was with you before you even had kidneys."

Benny laughed. He'd had a kidney transplant two years ago, donated by Jane's brother Jacob.

Brad took a swallow of his drink. "Ask that nurse out. Go wherever she is. Pitch the idea to her, she might be into it."

I eyed him. "Pitch the idea?"

"Yeah," Brad said. "She dates you, you guys break up, and *she* rides happily into the sunset too. It's a win-win. Seriously. This is your chance. If you don't do something you're gonna spend the rest of your life sending women on to their forever families and never getting one for you."

"Ha." I finished my mozzarella stick. "You know, it's not a science. Not *every* woman I date goes on to get married."

"No, it only happens with anyone you like enough to ask out more than twice. Look," he said, leaning onto the table. "You know I'm not a superstitious person. I don't believe in magic or hexes or curses, but this thing that's going on with you? It is *real* and it's been happening for three years and it's going to keep happening if you don't do something. Maybe this is the something."

I shook my head. "Why do I care if the women who didn't work out for me go on to be happy? I don't see why I need to put a stop to it."

"Because every girl you're serious enough about to date more than a few weeks is cosmically destined for someone else?"

I paused and stared at him.

Brad looked me in the eye. "You will never find someone as long as all the women you date aren't actually meant for you. You're not their soulmate. Their soulmate is the person they meet *after* you. It's decided the minute it starts. They are literally fated *not* to be The One. Think about it."

But I didn't have to think about it. Because the second he said it, I knew it was true.

He was right. Ever since I noticed the streak, there was always something…missing. Nobody ever felt right. Not enough chemistry or I just lost interest after a few dates. I didn't think much of it. Just figured it wasn't a fit. But now that he mentioned it…

"Message her," Brad said, going on. "Try it. What can it hurt?"

Benny was nodding.

I *had* actually thought about her. I'd checked once or twice to see if she'd messaged me again. She hadn't. The last message was me telling her it was nice chatting with her, three days ago. Trying to keep talking to her was a dead end if she lived somewhere else. But I don't know. Maybe Brad had a point. What could it hurt to try? Worst-case scenario, I'd spend some time and money and have no connection with her. What was new? I was already doing that with every date that didn't pan out anyway.

Screw it. I opened my phone and started typing a message to Emma16_dilemma.

CHAPTER 3

EMMA

Justin just messaged me."

Maddy was driving us home from the grocery store.

I hadn't heard from him in three days and sort of figured we were done talking.

"What'd he say?" she asked.

I read it out loud.

Justin: Can I ask you a medical question?

Maddy glanced at me from behind the wheel. "You're either about to get a rash or a dick pic."

"Should I take my chances?" I asked.

"Yes. I'm actually interested in seeing the size of both."

I laughed and typed in a reply.

Me: I'm here to answer any of your burning questions. And if it's actually burning, you should see a doctor.

Justin: 😂

And then: "Is there any truth to the q-tip thing being bad for you or do doctors just not want me to be happy?"

I laughed. Then I read it to Maddy.

"You know, for someone that cute, he's pretty funny," she said.

I looked at her over my phone. "What, they can't be cute *and* funny?"

"No. When they're that attractive or over six feet tall, they usually have the personality of a sexy palm tree."

I was cracking up when I typed in my reply.

Me: Sadly, the q-tip thing is true. I have flushed many, many impacted ears.

Justin: I'll never stop.

Me: Me either. #qtipsforlife

Justin: Lol

I waited a few minutes, but he didn't send me anything after that.

This was the place in a back-and-forth to either make an effort to keep it going or let it die.

I was a little bored. I opted for life support.

Me: so what do u do for a living?

I already knew what he did for a living because Maddy had cyberstalked him. Of course I couldn't tell him that, so I had to ask questions.

Almost immediately he replied.

Justin: I'm a software engineer. I build out websites. Can I ask you another question?

Me: yes

Justin: Where do u live?

Me: Why?

Justin: I was thinking maybe we could go for coffee or something. Exchange good luck charm war stories.

I looked up at Maddy. "He just asked me out."

"What took him so long," she said flatly. "Are you gonna go?"

I shook my head. "No."

"Why not?"

"He's in Minnesota," I said.

"Maybe he'll come to you."

"You think some guy I met three days ago is going to fly all the way to Colorado just to take me to Starbucks? Why would he do that?"

"Uh, because you're hot? Your mom didn't give you much, but she did give you her face."

I rolled my eyes and typed into my phone.

Me: I would love to go for coffee, but I'm in Colorado. Then in three weeks I go to Hawaii for three months.

We pulled into our driveway right after that, and I got busy unloading the car and putting away the groceries. When we were done, Maddy went to take a shower and I plopped on my bed to check my phone. Justin had responded half an hour ago.

Justin: Where are you going after Hawaii?

I typed.

Me: Not sure yet. I live with my best friend Maddy and we alternate who chooses where we'll go next. She picked Hawaii, and I haven't decided where to go after that.

I figured he wouldn't reply right away. He'd said he had to turn off his notifications because of all the messages he was getting, and after half an hour I was sure he wasn't sitting there watching his inbox waiting for me to respond, but I got a message within thirty seconds.

Justin: May I suggest Minnesota?

Me: Lol why?

Justin: Fall in Minnesota is beautiful. We have Mayo Clinic and Royaume Northwestern. Two of the best hospitals in the world…

I smiled and started typing.

Me: Wow, you want to have coffee with me that bad huh?

Justin: 💀

A small pause and then…

Justin: You know, in theory, if we date each other, when we break up we'd both find our soulmates after.

I narrowed my eyes.

Me: I thought you didn't want to date anyone who only wanted to break up with you??

Justin: This is different. This is mutually beneficial. Seriously, what are your thoughts? Cause I gotta be honest, I could be down for this.

And then a second later:

> Nothing inappropriate, a purely professional
> arrangement.

I sat up against my headboard, amused.

Me: Can I call you?

Justin: I mean, yeah. 651-314-4444

For a moment I debated calling from a blocked number. He was nice, but I still didn't know him. But I figured it was just as easy to block him later if he got creepy. I dialed and he picked up on the first ring. "Emma."

I don't know why, but his deep voice gave me a little flutter in my stomach for some reason.

"I don't believe in this whole magical good luck charm thing," I said without preamble.

"Neither do I."

"I'm not superstitious."

I heard him suck air through his teeth. "I'm a little stitious."

I let a laugh out through my nose. "It's just a coincidence," I said. "You realize that, right?"

"I agree." He paused. "But…"

"But? But what?"

"But what if it isn't? I'm just playing devil's advocate here. What if it isn't? Brad said that everyone I'm serious enough to date more than twice is cosmically destined for someone else." He went quiet for a beat. "Does nobody feel right to you? Like, there's just enough there to give it a little go, but then the bottom falls out? Is that just me? Or is it like that for you also?"

I shrugged. "Yeah, it's like that for me too. But I just don't think I'm meeting the right people."

"Yeah, but maybe this is why," he said. "It's exhausting, starting over all the time, again and again. Like there's no point. Like I'm trapped in some loop, partnered over and over with people I'm just supposed to redistribute down the line to someone else. I'm starting to wonder why I even bother. You know what Brad said that made me think? That when he saw Faith for the first time, it was like he got hit by a truck. It was that big." He paused. "I haven't had that moment. With anyone. I'm twenty-nine. I should have had that with someone by now, right?"

"I'm twenty-eight and I've never had a truck moment either," I admitted.

"Do you want that?"

"Of course I want that. Who wouldn't want to get hit by a love truck?"

"Look," he said. "I know the idea's a little out there. But if this is actually a thing, we're in a pretty low-risk/high-reward situation. We'd just have to hang out a few times and then stop. That's it. If what Brad said is true and we can't find our person because everyone we're interested in is meant for someone else, I would actually really like it if it stopped."

I bobbed my head. "Okay, I'll bite. So we what?"

I pictured a shrug. "I don't know. We go on some dates, split up after. See if we can't break the cycle. How many dates trigger the thing for you? It's three for me."

"It's not dates for me. It's length of time."

"What do you mean?"

"I have to be seeing someone for at least a month for it to happen," I said.

"Okay. And what does that look like? Do you have to see them every day?"

I shook my head. "No. It's having contact every day. Texting or talking on the phone. And seeing each other at least once a week."

He seemed to think about this.

"So me going out there wouldn't work unless I stayed a month or I flew back and forth every week."

"I think so."

"That's not really doable for me. Hawaii's pretty far and I've got some family stuff going on. I can't take off for that long."

"Well," I said. "I'll be back on the mainland in three and a half months."

"Yeah. Maybe then?"

"Sure. Sounds like fun."

I couldn't be sure, but I thought there was disappointment in the silence.

Maddy knocked on my doorframe. "Ready?"

I nodded and put up a finger. "I've got to go," I said into the phone. "Maddy wants to watch a movie."

Justin and I hung up, and I went out to the living room to watch *Forrest Gump*.

This movie always bugged me. Maybe because watching Jenny—Forrest's beautiful, tortured love interest—reminded me too much of Mom.

Maddy must have been thinking the same thing. When the credits began to roll, she put the TV on mute and looked over at me. "Have you talked to Amber recently?" she asked.

"No," I said.

"Do you know where she is?"

I paused a moment. "No. Her phone's disconnected. Again."

Maddy looked annoyed. "Probably didn't pay the bill. You know, for someone who asks you for as much money as she does, she sure ends up in collections a lot. God, I hate her."

I looked away from her. My relationship with my mother was complicated. It wasn't complicated for Maddy though, she knew *exactly* how she felt about it.

"I called the cafe," I said. "They said she quit three months ago. Just stopped showing up for work."

She rolled her eyes. "Of course."

I'd stopped calling jails and hospitals years ago when this kind of thing happened. Filing a missing person's report was a waste of time. Amber moved too fast, was too impulsive. She'd go to a concert and climb onto a tour bus and end up across the US. Or she'd meet a guy at a bar and get invited to live on his boat for four months in Florida.

The only time I knew for sure where my mother went was when she'd resurface suddenly. Then I'd get a little peace of mind for a few weeks until she vanished again.

Maddy shook her head. "I wouldn't worry about it. She's like black mold, she always comes back."

She was right. She always did.

But I'd call her landlord anyway. Just in case.

Just in case she left someone behind when she went...

"I don't understand how that woman made this," Maddy said, going on, waving a hand over my face. "A fully functional member of society."

"She had a very different life than I did, Maddy. I don't think all of it's her fault."

"The hell it isn't. You're too nice. Try being pissed off for a change."

I sighed.

This is where we always landed with Mom. Maddy being furious on my behalf and me reminding her that Mom wasn't all bad. Sometimes she was wonderful.

When my mother was at her best, you could meet her and walk away thinking you'd been in the presence of a Muse or an angel. This witty, enchanting woman who made you feel interesting and special.

When she was at her worst...

Anyway.

I don't believe anyone is black or white. Amber had been a single parent at eighteen with no family, no money, no support. Maybe her childhood had been like Jenny's in *Forrest Gump*, full of abuse and instability. Did she have issues? Yes. Did I believe that there were some people not meant for parenthood—also yes. But who knew what made Amber Amber? I couldn't begin to guess the demons she fought. I just knew that she did.

When Maddy got up to put the popcorn bowl into the sink, I

pulled out my phone like I expected a text from Mom to be waiting for me. There wasn't. I saw Justin's number instead, the last call I'd placed. I saved it in my contacts.

I did like his idea, and not just for the good luck charm thing. It would be fun to try it. He seemed nice. I probably would have swiped right and dated him if I'd met him on an app. Minnesota was a problem though. Definitely not one of the states on our list to visit.

Maddy came back and flopped onto the sofa. "So have you given the anniversary thing any thought?"

"What?"

"Janet and Beth's thirtieth. They're trying to get an RSVP."

"I don't know. I think I'm going to sit this one out."

Maddy pressed her lips together.

"What?" I said. "It's hard for both of us to get a week off when we're under assignment. I'll stay so you can go."

"It's not impossible. You should ask. They want you there. You're their daughter too."

I had to look away from her.

Maddy's moms were my foster parents. They'd wanted to be my real parents, but it just never felt right. I had a mom. And I was fourteen when they got me. The imprinting didn't take. That's all I could say about it, it just didn't take. I cared about them. I called on their birthdays and came back with Maddy for Christmas when we could get it off. They just weren't...*mine*. And Maddy knew it. It bothered her. She couldn't wrap her brain around it and I couldn't explain it to her in any way that she found acceptable.

She sighed and stood up. "I think I'm gonna meet that IT guy from Tinder for drinks again. Want to come? I can see if he's got a friend."

"Nah. I want to finish my book."

"All right. Don't wait up. I'm probably going to his place after."

I arched an eyebrow.

"What?" she said. "This nomad life isn't exactly conducive to relationships and I'm getting sick of DJing my own party."

"I'm assuming he's got a bed frame?"

"You know it." She started for her room.

"Maddy?"

She stopped in the doorway. "Yeah?"

"I will ask for the time off. Okay?"

Her face softened a little. "Okay."

I would. But I secretly hoped I wouldn't get it.

* * *

Maddy hadn't come back last night, as promised, and I guess the date went well because he was taking her to breakfast and then some art exhibit. She wouldn't be home until dinner. I was off and had nothing to do and nowhere to be.

I was in a robe in my room, fresh out of the shower, getting ready to paint my nails when Justin texted me a picture.

I clicked on it and burst into laughter. It was a selfie of him wearing a long red wig and crooked lipstick. The text said, "I babysat my little sister Chelsea this morning. I had to be Princess Anna. She got to be Elsa."

Me: You look good as a redhead.

My phone rang.

I smiled and hit the speakerphone button. "Princess Anna?"

"Princess Emma," he said back.

"Just a reminder, you can't marry a man you just met."

"You can if it's true love," he replied seriously.

I had to stifle my giggle.

"Chelsea made me stand frozen solid for fifteen minutes," he said. "She wouldn't let me move. It was that part from the end—I don't remember that scene taking that long in the movie."

"Ha."

"That would kill me, right?" he asked. "Like if I was really frozen solid."

I grabbed my red polish from the bathroom and shook the bottle on my way to the bed. "Maybe. We'd warm you up first to try and revive you. You're not dead until you're warm and dead."

I sat down on the mattress and heard the sound of keys and the click of a bolt lock on the other end of the phone. Then excited dog noises.

"Are you with your dog?" I asked.

"Yeah, I just got home," he said. "He wants to go on a walk."

"Oh," I said. "I'll let you go then."

"I don't need to hang up. Unless you need to," he added.

I gave a one-shoulder shrug. "I'm not doing anything. Just ran an errand. Back at home."

I heard the jingle of a leash attaching to a collar and the clickety-click sound of nails on tile.

"Oh yeah?" he said. "What kind of errand? Tell me your day today from start to finish."

"Why do you want to know?" I asked.

"Why wouldn't I want to know? I'm curious. Unless you're a reporter and you're afraid to let it slip."

"Ha *ha*."

I heard a door closing and echoey footsteps in a hallway.

"Call me old-fashioned," he said, "but we're talking about undertaking the exhaustive, extremely intimate, time-honored tradition of breaking a curse together. We can't start until you come back from Hawaii, but we *can* prepare by getting to know each other."

"Oh, so it's a curse now?"

"I mean, isn't it? It's keeping us from being happy."

I scoffed to myself. He wasn't wrong.

"What do you think we did to deserve it?" he asked.

"I don't know," I said, putting in my earbuds and grabbing lotion off the nightstand. "I think I'm a good person. I don't think I do deserve it."

"Me either. I can't for the life of me think of why someone would waste a perfectly good hex on *me*."

I heard elevator doors opening.

"So your day," he said, getting back on topic. "Tell me."

"Well, I woke up and had my coffee—"

"What's your coffee?"

"Just regular coffee with sweet cream in it," I said, putting lotion on my legs.

"And where'd you drink it?" I heard the ping of an elevator.

"On the sofa in the living room while I scrolled through my phone."

"So day off today then," he said.

"Day off. No nursing until tomorrow."

"Why'd you become a nurse? Did you always want to do it?"

"Yeah. Always. Since I was ten."

"Really? Why?" he asked.

"I have the right temperament for it. I'm patient. I'm not easily frustrated or grossed out. I have a high threshold for stress—"

"And you knew this at ten years old?" he asked.

"I did. I mean, I knew I wanted to take care of people at ten years old. I was already good at it."

"Who did you take care of at *ten*?"

"My mom."

"I see…" he said. "Was she sick or something?"

"Or something."

He must have sensed my disinterest because he changed the subject. "So is there a view from your living room? What's your house like?"

"We have a fully furnished two-bedroom A-frame cabin," I said, leaning over to grab the red nail polish off my nightstand. "We always try to find someplace fun. A beach house or a loft in a big city where we can walk to things. We stayed in a converted grain silo once, it was really neat. Oh, and a tree house."

"A tree house?" He sounded impressed.

"Yeah, it had rope bridges and everything. We were on a quick two-week assignment to Atlanta. Maddy and I had to share a bed, but it was so cool."

"Wow."

"In Hawaii we're staying in a condo," I said, my chin to my knees while I painted my toes. "It's not that exciting. But we can walk to the beach."

"Nice. So you drank your coffee. Then what?"

"Then I made breakfast," I said. "Scrambled eggs and cheese on an English muffin. Grapes."

"Seedless?"

"Of course. I'm not a sadist."

"So you know how to cook," he said.

"Yeah. Do you?"

"Yeah. I'm a good cook," he said.

"What's the last thing you cooked?" I asked.

"Well, the last thing I cooked was mac and cheese with hot dogs in it for Chelsea. She's four. The last *good* thing I cooked was slow cooker ribs. I have a Crock-pot in my kitchen, under the watchful eye of the Toilet King."

I laughed.

"So then what?" he asked. "What else did you do today?"

I smiled. I had to admit, it was refreshing that he was asking about me. I found that most men I dated just liked to talk about themselves.

"Well, then I went to Target for nail polish remover—"

"And you went to Starbucks."

"Yes, I went to Starbucks. I had to, it was right there."

"The absolute *chokehold* that Starbucks has on us. What do you get there?" he asked.

"I get a salted caramel cold foam cold brew, but as a decaf Americana since I already had regular today. What do *you* get there?"

"In the winter I get a grande triple caramel macchiato. In the summer I do the iced tea infusion thingy. The dragon fruit one."

"So you drink caramel macchiatos nine months out of the year?"

"Hey, don't poke fun at Minnesota," he said good-naturedly. "It's not that bad."

I paused in my toenail painting. "I saw on the news that it was negative thirty for a week a few months ago. How is that not that bad?"

"You just do the door-to-door sprint. It's thirty seconds of cold, tops. Like getting something from a walk-in freezer. Half the time I don't even put on a jacket. And you get the right clothes for when you do need to be outside longer. The summers are great, fall's beautiful. Travel vlogger Vanessa Price lives here and she could live anywhere."

"Hmm, I do like her. So I told you my day," I said. "What did *you* do today?"

"Well, I woke up and made my coffee—Nespresso machine. Used my frother to make a cappuccino. Two percent milk. Opened the blinds and stood there with my mug in my hand, staring at the billboard, questioning all my life choices. I took Brad out, came back, took a shower. Watched Chelsea for an hour, then went to meet Benny and best friend Brad for lunch."

"Where did you go?" I asked.

"It's a little restaurant Brad found."

"What did you order?"

"A peanut butter burger," he said.

I made a face. "Was it good?"

"It was, actually. It had caramelized onions on it and this grape jelly chutney thing."

"So did anything happen at lunch with your friends?"

"Not today. But when I had lunch with them yesterday we talked about the Reddit thread. I told them about you, obviously," he said. "That's when Brad gave me his prophecy about you and I being able to break the curse."

"Ah, so *that's* why you texted me," I said with my chin to my knees, blowing the paint dry on my toes.

"No. I really needed to know about the Q-tip thing."

"I see," I said, smiling. "Then you went home?"

"I stopped for gas and then I went home. I texted you my Princess Anna picture. Here we are."

"And where are we exactly?" I asked. "What do you see on your walk?"

"Hold on, I'll show you."

I had a tiny moment of panic thinking he was about to video call me, but instead a picture came through.

"This is where I'm walking right now. I took this the other day at sunset."

It was a picture of a city skyline taken from the middle of a wide concrete walking bridge with a rust-colored railing.

"This is the Stone Arch Bridge." Another picture came through. "That's the Mississippi."

The river was tree-lined. It was really pretty, urban but naturey at the same time.

I exited and googled the bridge and hit Images. "I'm looking at the bridge online. There are a lot of engagement photos."

"I see about one proposal a week," he said. "It's a very popular spot to pop the question."

"Public proposals are hostage situations," I said, going back to his picture and zooming in. I could see the back of a billboard and I wondered if that was his apartment building just beyond it.

"You wouldn't want to be proposed to in public?" he asked.

"Noooo."

"Yeah, I never really got that whole concept. It feels like something that should be intimate, right? Doing it in front of a bunch of strangers just feels so performative."

"That is *exactly* what I was telling Maddy a few weeks ago. Some guy proposed in front of a whole stadium at this game we went to—and the girl said no."

He sucked air through his teeth. "Talk about not knowing your audience."

I heard barking. "Brad?" I asked.

"No, a husky barking at Brad. Do you like dogs?"

"Who doesn't like dogs?"

He was smiling in the pause. "So back to Minnesota being the greatest state in the nation—"

I sighed. "Okay. You're making a small case for visiting Minnesota, I will give you that. But it's probably never going to happen. It's not in our top twenty-five list of states to visit."

"How do you get a state bumped up the list?"

"You don't." I slid off the bed to brush my hair. "It's never happened."

"Hmmm. So how do you decide which state to go to next? Are they in order?"

"No. We look at all the determining factors. What time of year it is, the weather during our stay, if there's any concerts or festivals that will be there, what kind of house we can get, what hospital we'd get to work in and what positions they're looking to fill." I pulled off my towel and my long, wet hair tumbled out. I was brushing it when Justin gasped.

"Oh my God. Someone's proposing on the bridge," he said. "Seriously. Hold on, I'll get you a picture."

I smiled and started working my damp hair into a bun.

"Okay," he said. "I just sent it."

I leaned over my screen and laughed. The woman had her hands on her mouth and the man was on one knee, tall buildings looming in the backdrop. "Wow. That is a really great picture spot though. I kinda get why they do it there."

"It's a nice walk too. Brad likes it. Want to see it in real time? I can video chat you—"

"Uh, no. I'm not dressed."

"Well just accept the video call but don't turn on your camera."

I thought about it a second. "Okay. But I'm really not going to turn on my camera."

"Totally understand."

A moment later a video call came through. When I accepted the call, the screen faced the long concrete bridge. There were people on bikes and a woman jogging with headphones in. "Say hi, Brad." The camera angled down and Brad looked up at it with his frown, wearing a red leash and collar. "Can you see okay?" Justin asked, coming back to the bridge.

I pulled my phone closer. "Yeah. Wow, it's really pretty."

"Look at this."

He brought the camera over to the side of the railing and panned over the Mississippi. There was a waterfall churning in the distance.

"The bridge is part of a two-mile historic walking loop. I try to do it once a day when the weather's good."

He started walking again, the camera forward so I could see what he did.

"Are there shops on the loop?" I asked, seeing buildings with outdoor seating off in the distance.

"Yeah, there's some cool coffee shops, a couple of restaurants. I have to drive to get my favorite food though. Ecuadorian from this little hole-in-the-wall place called Chimborazo. I'll take you if you come down here."

Then he turned the camera on himself and beamed into the frame. I sucked in a little breath of air.

My *God* was he cute.

It was even better when he was live action. Or maybe it was even better because he had a good personality to match? I think his sense of humor made him more attractive.

He was wearing a gray T-shirt and had a black earbud in his ear. His hair was messy. His dimples were popping and he had the nicest brown eyes. They were kind eyes.

Justin looked like that quintessential TV show boyfriend that the main character always has in high school. The super sweet one who lives next door and takes her to prom and lets her wear his hoodies and they only break up because he has to go to college out of state and it's her idea. There was just something so easy and grounding about him.

I realized I was smiling at my phone. I let out a breath and tightened my robe. Then I turned my camera on too.

When my face popped up on the screen, he grinned. "Hey."

"I figured you should have a right to know you're not getting catfished," I said. "Still not a reporter."

He laughed. He was still walking, but he kept the camera on himself.

"So," I said, sliding back onto my bed. "You have a captive audience. You're on a scenic walking path. Show me your town."

CHAPTER 4

JUSTIN

I pulled up to the high school pickup line and put the car in park, then grabbed my phone to look at the picture of Emma. Again.

We'd talked for three hours last night. She stayed on the phone with me for my whole walk, then another two hours after I'd gotten back to my apartment. She was cool. She was *really* cool. I liked her. This curse-breaking thing was turning out to be way more interesting than I had anticipated.

A bell rang and kids started pouring out. The last day of summer school. When I saw my brother, Alex, walking with a group of his friends toward the buses, I rolled down the passenger side window and leaned across the seat. "Hey! Need a ride?"

He looked over and his whole face lit up. He said an excited goodbye to his friends and jogged toward me, backpack bouncing. I got out just as he made it to the car, and I tossed him the keys. He caught them against his stomach and stared at me with wide eyes. "Seriously?"

"Mom says you need behind-the-wheel hours. You're driving."

His face ripped into a grin. "Yesssss!" He fist pumped.

We drove for thirty minutes, then stopped at a drive-thru, got food, and headed back to Mom's. He clipped a curb and almost missed a stop sign on the way home, but we survived.

"Hey, we're here," I announced, shutting the front door behind me. "I got McDonald's."

"In the kitchen!" Mom called.

I came in and Mom was there loading the dishwasher. Leigh, Mom's best friend and Brad's mother, sat at the kitchen table.

"Hey, Leigh." I set the food down. "I didn't know you were here or I would have gotten you something."

She waved me off from her chair at the table, bracelets clinking on her wrist. "I've got a Bumble date in a half an hour. Let him buy me food."

I pulled my face back. "A date? What happened to George?"

"He's gone, Justin. May God rest his soul."

I blinked at her. "Your boyfriend *died*?"

"He's dead to *me*."

Mom laughed and I shook my head at my honorary aunt.

Leigh was a character. Forty-eight like Mom, but her polar opposite in every way. She'd been married four times and had been engaged twice as many times as that. Leigh's single periods were always a lot of fun for the family. Highly entertaining.

I could hear Chelsea running down the stairs. I pulled out her food right as my little sister tore into the room.

"Jussin!" She hugged my legs for a split second, then launched off me and climbed into a chair. "Yay!" she squealed, seeing the Happy Meal.

I started setting her up, opening her box of nuggets and peeling the top off the sweet-and-sour sauce.

Mom looked up from loading the dishwasher right as I was putting a straw into Chelsea's apple juice. She made a face. "Justin, why did you get drinks? We have juice here, you didn't need to waste the money."

"If I don't get her the Happy Meal, she won't get the toy."

My tone came off drier than I intended. Mom ignored it.

"I got you a chicken sandwich," I said to Mom. "Where's Sarah?" I asked, looking around.

Mom dried her hands on a kitchen towel and sat down at the table next to Leigh. "She's in her room. You're not eating?" she asked, noticing I didn't have anything in front of me.

"No, I gotta go soon," I said. "I need to walk Brad."

Leigh rolled her eyes. "Still on that, huh? Christine, tell your son to rename his dog, please."

"He's a grown man," Mom said, tiredly. "I can't tell him to do anything."

"You know, I've been thinking long and hard about it and you're right, Leigh, I'm being unreasonable," I said, setting out Chelsea's fries. "If Brad agrees to pay the seven thousand dollars he intended to stiff me, I'll rename the dog."

Leigh made an exasperated noise. "Seven thousand—you got a new apartment, Justin. Your rent is lower than before, how is it that he owes you seven thousand dollars?"

"It's for pain and suffering now."

Leigh cackled, despite herself.

"So how did he do?" Leigh asked, nodding at Alex. She was still tittering.

"He did great," I said.

Alex beamed, shoving fries in his mouth.

"Thanks for taking him," Mom said, rubbing her wrist.

Leigh eyed her. "How's work?" she asked.

Mom gave a one-shoulder shrug. "It's okay. I did four houses yesterday. The Klein house has three sets of bunk beds. It's hard to make them. Wears me out. But I'm taking as many jobs as I can before I go."

Before I go.

My jaw ticced and I had to look away from her.

Mom cleaned houses now.

There was nothing wrong with being a housekeeper. What made me upset was *why* she was a housekeeper.

She had a bachelor's degree in accounting. She'd been a CFO. But her degree and the last twelve years at her old company were worthless now. She wouldn't get jobs like that again. The repercussions for what she'd done had already begun, and she hadn't even left yet.

My mother was going to prison.

My brain just couldn't wrap around it, it didn't feel real. But it *was* real. It was coming. And my whole life was about to be turned upside down so that everyone else's life could stay the same. In a few weeks, I was taking custody of my siblings. I had to move back in here. Give up my apartment—not that it was much to give up, but still.

If I didn't, Chelsea, Alex, and Sarah would have to go with Leigh. They'd have to change schools, leave the neighborhood they'd grown up in. It was bad enough they lost their dad, now they were losing their mom too. I couldn't let the rest of their world disintegrate. And I couldn't even contemplate what this meant for me and *my* life because thinking about it made me feel like I couldn't breathe.

I got up. "I gotta get going," I said flatly. "Want me to run this up to Sarah?" I nodded at the bag of food for my sister.

"Yeah, can you?" Mom said.

I left the kitchen without saying goodbye.

When I got to Sarah's room, I had to shout over the music. A moment later she pulled the door open and went back to her bed without saying hello.

I came in and looked around. "This is new," I said. She had red LED string lights along the walls. The whole bedroom was bathed in red. It was sort of depressing. "I got you McDonald's."

"Thanks," she muttered without looking up from her phone.

I put her food on the desk. "So what have you been up to?"

No answer.

"Are you watching any cool shows?"

She glared up at me, annoyed.

"Oookay," I said. "Well. I'll see you later then."

"Bye," she said, irritated.

I left.

This was another thing that worried me. Alex was easy. Chelsea was too, in her own way. But Sarah? I didn't know what her deal was recently. She was moody and pissed off, and *I* would be the one who had to figure it out.

I felt preemptively exhausted.

The kids probably needed therapy. I would have to find someone, at least for the older two who knew what was going on. One more thing to add to the long-ass list of stuff I would now be responsible for.

A few hours later I'd gone for a run and come back to my apartment and put some Buffalo chicken into the slow cooker for tomorrow. I looked up some options for family counseling and sent a few emails, which at the very least made me feel like I was heading in the right direction. I was thinking of dropping in on Brad or Benny or something, just to stay busy, but something better came up. Emma texted me "WYD."

Right now Emma was my favorite distraction. Honestly, she was the only thing going on that *didn't* suck.

I didn't text her back. I called.

"Hey," she said, picking up.

"Hey."

I heard the long sound of a zipper closing on luggage.

"What are you doing?" I asked. "Packing for Hawaii?"

"No. Not yet. I'm just throwing something in there. I don't pack until the morning I leave."

"Really?" I sat in front of my monitor. "I need like a whole day to pack."

"That's because you're deciding what to bring. I know what to bring. I just bring everything I came with."

I smiled, pulling up the spreadsheet I'd started working on last night. "So do you have a second?" I asked.

"Yes, or I wouldn't have answered."

"I know we're not doing this thing until you're back on the mainland somewhere, but I was thinking we should probably work out the baseline. You know, so we're ready when we meet."

"A baseline?" she said. "For what?"

"For the dating thing. So we do it right. This has to be a controlled experiment. We need to replicate the pattern that leads to the outcome we keep getting. How long the dates need to be, what we need to do on the dates, where we need to go. We have to make sure we hit all the common denominators."

"Oh," she said. "Good idea. You're so organized."

"I need to be in my line of work. I started a spreadsheet. I can send it to you when I'm done."

"Okay."

"All right, so we have to do a minimum of four dates," I said, "over the course of one month. Does the length of time matter for each date?"

"I think it has to be at least two hours."

"Maybe we should shoot for three hours, just to be safe?"

"Okay. Three hours works."

"Or longer. The dates could definitely be longer. You know, if that feels organic of course."

"Sure."

I smiled. "Is there anything that we absolutely have to do?" I asked. "Something that's been the same for all the qualifying dates? Like they've all been dinner dates or something?"

"They've all been different."

"Okay. Mine too," I said.

"Do we have to kiss?" she asked.

"I did kiss all my dates at least once," I said.

"Me too," she said. "And they always kiss me first."

"Okay. So we have to kiss once, and I have to initiate it. Open-mouthed or -closed? Either has been enough for me."

"Open. So you kissed Brad's girlfriend? Is that weird now?"

"Not really. It was a closed-mouthed kiss and I don't think either of us particularly enjoyed it. It was sort of like kissing my sister?"

"Ha."

"So I'm assuming since you only kissed a few of them once, sex isn't a prerequisite?" I asked, as professionally as possible.

"If it was, I would not agree to it for the sake of this experiment. Just so you know."

"Just being thorough. It's not a prerequisite for me either. And same. Gross." I made a shiver noise. "I'm a sex-on-the-fifth-date kind of guy," I said. "So you've lucked out."

She was laughing.

"All right," I said. "So we have to have four dates over the course of a month, one a week, a minimum of three hours each, we can do any activity, we have to text or talk daily, and I have to kiss you at least once."

"Yes. I think that's everything."

"So four dates, one kiss, and a breakup."

"Four dates, one kiss, and a breakup," she agreed.

"I'll get this typed up. Let me know if you think of anything else."

"Okay."

This felt like the moment the call could have ended, but instead she said, "So what did you do today?"

I grinned. She didn't want to hang up.

I leaned back in my chair. "Well, I did the same exact thing I did when I woke up yesterday—drank my coffee while staring morosely at my personal billboard. Walked Brad. Worked for a few hours, then I took my little brother for driving lessons— Oh, I forgot. I also made you something."

"You did? What?"

I leaned over my keyboard and hit send on the draft I had waiting.

"I'm going to hang up so you can look at it. Check your phone."

CHAPTER 5

EMMA

Justin sent me a picture of a graphic. The second I opened it I almost choked on my laugh.

So Justin Dahl has invited you to break a curse with him. Congratulations!

We know that you have many options when it comes to curse breaking and choosing the right partner can be difficult, which is why we've gone the extra step and provided you with some reviews.

» *"Justin was a wonderful gentleman. And I met my husband Mike after we broke up! 10/10 would break up with him again. —Sabrina B."*

» *"Justin smells very nice and even my cat liked him, and my cat doesn't like anyone. Highly recommend. —Karina S."*

» *"Justin made all my wildest dreams come true,
which was to get married to someone who wasn't
him at Disneyland! If I could give six stars I
would.* —Kimberly R."

» *"Justin saved my dog and my grandma from
a burning building. He's my hero.* —A Real
Person."

And then finally:

» *"I'm only writing this because I'm assuming if
he gets a girlfriend she'll tell him how stupid he
is for naming his dog Brad and she'll convince
him to change it. Justin was very polite and has
excellent personal hygiene. You should date him.*
—Faith."

I shook my head at the screen, laughing.

I texted him.

Me: Nerd

He replied with laughing emojis.

I had to admit, he'd piqued my interest in Minnesota after
our marathon call yesterday. He'd piqued my interest in *him*,
which is why I'd spent the day making phone calls and sending
emails and putting together a presentation for Maddy. It was time
sensitive and I had to do it tonight, and it was *not* going to be
pretty. I blew air through pursed lips and got up to go find her.

She was in the living room on the sofa in front of the
wood-burning stove on her phone. I came into the doorway. "Hey,
do you have a second? I want to talk to you about something."

Maddy looked up. Then her eyes dropped to the laptop I

was holding and she somehow immediately knew what was about to happen. "No." She shook her head. "No. No, no, no, no, no. NO."

I came into the room and slid onto the couch next to her. "Hear me out."

"We are going to *Hawaii*, Emma. It was my turn to pick. I bought a new bathing suit—"

"You can wear it here too."

"I am *not* going to Minnesota. It's a flyover state. It's not in our top twenty-five—"

"How did you know I was going to say Minnesota?"

"Uh, because you're all twitterpated over what's-his-face? Listen to me, you don't really like him. You're only feeling this way because he's six-three."

I laughed. "He is *not* six-three."

"Well how tall is he then?"

"I don't know. I didn't ask, I don't care."

"Well he looks six-three to me and I think that's clouding your judgment. You are not swapping *Hawaii* for Minnesota."

"Why not?" I asked. "It is a beautiful state, we could day-trip up to Canada. Remember that cupcake shop you saw on Food Network? Nadia Cakes? They have two locations there. And the top twenty-five is more of a guideline than a rule."

She crossed her arms. "A rule we've never broken? Not once in three years? And how dare you try and lure me off a tropical island with cupcakes. Exactly how spectacular is this man's penis?"

"Maddy!"

"What?! You are not selling me on your sudden love for the Upper Midwest. Do not sit here and pretend like this isn't a hundred percent about the guy."

"Justin. And yes, it's a little about him. But this is purely logistical."

"Oh yeah? How?"

I tucked my leg under me. "Okay, so I know how this is going to sound. But if Justin and I date for a month, then break up, in theory"—I put my fingers in quotes—"the next guy I meet will be The One."

She gave me a look.

"What? It sounds like fun," I said. "You're telling me you don't want to see if it works?"

"Have him fly to Hawaii to see if it works. We do not go out of our way for *men*. We do not inconvenience ourselves for men, we do not change our well-laid plans for men. No."

"Tickets to Hawaii are like a thousand bucks round trip right now. I can't ask him to do that once a week for a month, that makes no sense. Look."

I opened the laptop. "Look at the place I found for us—"

"There is no place cool enough for me to—"

"It's a historic cottage on an island in the middle of a lake."

She paused in the way that I knew meant I'd gotten her attention.

I tapped on the tab and turned the screen toward her. "It's two bedrooms. It's super cute. Look at the porch. We could have our coffee there every morning, overlooking the water. It has a beach, with sand and a firepit."

She peered over and pressed her lips together while she studied the pictures. Then she looked up and narrowed her eyes at me. "If it's on an island, how are we supposed to get to it?"

"It comes with a boat."

She arched an eyebrow. "A boat?"

"A pontoon."

She paused. "I get to be a sea captain?"

I nodded. "You get to be a sea captain. It's only fifteen minutes from the hospital. And guess which one it is? Royaume Northwestern."

Her eyebrow went higher. "Royaume?"

"Yup."

Minnesota had never been on our top twenty-five, but Royaume Northwestern was one of the best hospitals in the world. It was a huge selling point. Hospitals like Royaume had excellent certified-nursing-assistant-to-nurse ratios, nice lounges, lots of perks.

She seemed to think about it for a second. Then she shook her head again. "We'll piss off the agency if we bail on Hawaii."

"Nope. We haven't signed contracts yet. They really need nurses at Royaume, they said they're more than happy to make the switch. And it's only a six-week assignment, we'll be in and out. Just for the summer."

She sat back against the sofa. "What department?" She looked at me.

I closed the lid of the laptop and mumbled it under my breath without looking at her.

She leaned in. "What? I couldn't hear you. I thought for a second there you said Med Surg."

I glanced at her. "I did. It's Med Surg."

She slapped her hands on her thighs and got up. "NOPE."

"Come on!" I said, watching her walk to the door. "It can't be that bad!"

She turned. "Med Surg and it can't be that bad? Are you kidding me? Surgeons are assholes. They are assholes in direct proportion to how good they are. Can you imagine the absolute *audacity* of the doctors working there? The abuse we will be subjected to on a daily— No." She shook her head. "I'm not doing it. Absolutely not."

"They're only assholes if you suck at your job—"

"They draw their energy from making nurses cry. We'll be sacrificial lambs. And you know we'll get all the crap assignments because we're the newbies, they'll float us three times a shift— No."

I let out a slow breath. Then I set the laptop gently next to me. "I didn't want to have to do this..."

She crossed her arms again. "Do *what*?"

"The trailer park."

I let it hang there between us.

Her arms dropped. "You said you were never going to bring that up again," she breathed.

"No, I said I was going to drop it. But I guess now I'm picking it up because you've given me no choice."

"That was three years ago, Emma—"

"I agreed to a three-month stay in a *luxury* trailer home in a *luxury* trailer park in Utah with allllll the amenities—"

"Emma—"

"And when we got there, it was a two-thousand-year-old camper with no working AC, mice, a drained pool, and a creepy laundry room. No long-term rentals in sight because it was peak tourist season, so we were trapped in the RV from *Breaking Bad* for three *months*—"

"I found us a different place and you didn't want it!"

"Really? The spare bedroom from the drunk guy you met in the ER who kept telling me I'd be prettier if I smiled more? *That* guy?"

She looked away from me. "I can't believe you're bringing this up," she muttered.

I stood and walked slowly toward her, knowing I had her. "All I'm asking is to put off Hawaii for six more weeks. We get to stay in a gorgeous cottage on a lake, we have a boat for the summer, we get to cross Royaume off the bucket list. Yes, I realize Med Surg is less than ideal, but we'll be working with some of the best surgeons in the world. And then I get to try this thing with this Justin guy—it'll be an adventure."

She didn't reply.

"You can pick where we go for the following six months. You get two turns back-to-back."

Her eyes slid to mine. "Can I pick the same place the whole time?"

This caught me by surprise. "We never stay at the same place for six months," I said.

"Yeah, well we also never chose from a state not on our top twenty-five and we never skip turns."

My heart started to pound. I don't know why the thought of not moving made me feel slightly panicky. Maybe it was just the change in routine? We always moved on once a contract was up.

But I wanted this. It sounded fun. And if we waited until after Hawaii, we'd get to Minnesota when it started to get cold, and no way was I doing Minnesota in the winter no matter how cool Justin made it sound.

"Fine," I said. "We can stay someplace for six months. Wherever you want."

She drew in a deep breath and let it out before looking reluctantly at me. "Fine," she mumbled. "We'll go to Minnesota."

I started bouncing all over the living room.

She jabbed a finger at me. "But you're not allowed to bring up the trailer. Ever again. We are even. And you're buying me cupcakes when we get there or the deal's off."

I bounced back to her and hugged her.

She shook her head. "Med Surg and no Hawaii, just so you can break up with some guy."

"We've done stranger things."

"Yes," she said. "Yes, we have."

* * *

I didn't tell Justin about Minnesota. I wanted to surprise him. We talked and texted on and off for the next week and a half until Maddy and I packed up to make the two-day drive to our new state.

Our contact for the cottage was a woman named Maria. She worked for the owner, who had a full-time residence on the mainland of the lake. We'd be parking our car in his driveway and using his dock to come and go to our cottage.

When we pulled up to this house, five minutes early, we sat in our car and stared. It was *huge*. A mansion.

"What the hell does this guy do?" Maddy asked, shaking her head.

"I don't know," I breathed.

She looked at me. "How'd you find this place again?"

"The agency. The lady seemed like she knew someone. I think it was luck."

I got out and shaded my eyes as I looked up at the house. I'd never seen anything like this in real life. It reminded me of a castle. Stone walls and minarets. I could see at least four chimneys.

"Maybe he's a famous rapper?" Maddy said, "Or like, some big executive?"

"Jeff Bezos maybe?" I joked.

"He probably has a helipad on the roof."

"He probably does…"

As we started pulling our bags from the trunk, a brown-haired middle-aged woman came out of the side of the three-car garage. "Are you Emma?" she said in a thick Mexican accent.

"Yes, hi." I smiled.

"Hello. I'm Maria," she said. "I'll take you to the cottage. Is this all you have?" she asked, looking at my two bags and Maddy's three.

"This is it," I said. "Are we okay to park here?"

"No," she said, taking one of Maddy's bags. She handed us a garage door opener and pointed to the bay on the far left. "You can park in there. Mister doesn't like to see cars in the courtyard. I'll wait while you move it."

We moved the car into the garage—which had a lift inside to double-stack vehicles. Maddy mouthed *What the fuck?* to me while Maria wasn't watching. And then we followed Maria across an enormous backyard to the lake, dragging our luggage through the perfect grass.

The back of the mansion was even grander than the front. The backyard had a pool and an enclosed gazebo. White Adirondack chairs lined up on a huge sandy shoreline and beyond that a yacht was parked under a cover off the dock.

Farther down, an old pontoon so dilapidated it looked like it had washed up in a storm was tethered to a pole.

"This is your boat," Maria said. "It's old, so you beat it up all you want, Mister won't care. Do you know how to drive a boat?"

"No," I admitted.

She opened a door on the side of the pontoon and started loading our bags. "I'll show you. It's easy. Just like a car."

We stood behind her as she gave us a quick tutorial on how to start it and raise and lower the prop. Then she untied it, pushed off the dock, cranked it into reverse, and backed out expertly into the open water. She turned us around and started for a large island toward the center of the lake.

Maria spoke over her shoulder as we drove. "The radio doesn't work and it doesn't go fast. There's life jackets and a paddle under the seats. You have to put gas at the marina, I'll show you on a map. Look at the house so you remember where to go when you come back."

Maddy scoffed quietly. "Yeah, I don't think we're going to lose the house. They can probably see it from space."

My hair whipped around in the warm late-July breeze, and I had to hold it at the nape of my neck to keep it out of my face. The sun beat down on us. The boat didn't have a canopy over it. Like an ancient, nautical convertible with no top. It was just wide open to the elements.

Maddy must have been thinking the same thing I was. "Does it rain a lot in Minnesota?" she asked, raising her voice over the sound of the old motor.

"All the time," Maria said. "I'm so happy he did this. This is the first time Mister's ever rented the cottage."

"Why did he decide to rent it?" I shouted.

She waved her hand. "He never uses it. His girlfriend left him a few years ago and he never came after that. Too sad because he always came with her, you know? This has been in the family for fifty years, and now it sits empty. You will like it, it's very nice." She nodded ahead of us. "You see the dock with the owl?"

We strained to look. There was a small dock on the island ahead with a plastic owl perched on the end. "That's it. Very easy to find. And you can see the house from here. See? Very easy."

I was relieved it was such a short trip. I'd looked at a map of Lake Minnetonka and it was *huge*. I'd been a little worried we'd get lost trying to go back and forth, but you could see one dock from the other.

When we pulled up, which took a lot longer than the short distance implied—Maria was right, the boat did *not* go fast—Maddy grabbed on to the pole and pulled us in as Maria showed me how to kill the motor. She showed us how to tether the boat and turn off the battery, and then we grabbed our bags.

We started walking toward the property, the wheels of our luggage thunking on the planks of the dock. There was a tiny sand beach, just big enough for the firepit and four beach chairs. At the top of a zigzagging flight of wooden steps I could see a small white cottage nestled in the trees. We had neighbors on both sides, but they were far enough for privacy.

We lugged our bags up the stairs and were sweating by the time we made it to the door. We came in through a screened-in porch that overlooked the lake. Maddy and I shared a glance. It was adorable. White wicker rocking chairs and a small matching loveseat with thick floral cushions. A cute coffee table and plastic ferns in wrought-iron planters and hanging baskets.

"This is it," Maria said, unlocking the front door. "No candles allowed, but you can use the fireplace. It doesn't have a heater." She pushed open the door and we followed her into a gorgeous, bright, cozy living room. Maddy and I looked around smiling. "Oh wow. It's even better than the pictures," I said.

Maria looked pleased.

The house was vintage rustic. Colorful area rugs covered the weathered hardwood floors. In front of a stone fireplace, there was a chunky white couch with a heavy knitted throw blanket draped over the side and plaid throw pillows at each end. There were mismatched armchairs that looked lived in, a hope chest turned coffee table, and a chandelier made of driftwood over the four-person table in the kitchen. The kitchen had a large white farm sink, white cabinets with glass panes with mason jar cups and handmade bowls and plates behind them. No dishwasher, but we'd live.

Maria sighed at the house and shook her head. "Every year I come, I clean and dust. He never comes. Finally I said, 'Why don't you make someone happy with this place? You rent it.' I'm glad he listened."

"Me too," Maddy said.

"A place like this should have laughter in it," Maria said, taking us to the bedrooms. "Memories."

The bedrooms were off the living room on either side of a short hallway with a single bathroom shared in the middle. The bathroom had a white claw-foot tub, pale blue tile, and an old pedestal sink. I took the room with the cushioned reading nook in the window and Maddy picked the one with the hanging swing chair in the corner.

"Where's the washer and dryer?" Maddy asked, looking around after the tour was over.

"No washer," Maria said. "If you bring it to me, I'll wash your clothes for you. It's an extra charge or you can go to the laundromat, but it's not close. Also you have to bring out all your trash. There's no trash service. You can throw it in the bins in the garage when you get back to the house."

We both nodded.

"Use the house address for mail," she said, going on. "I'll leave it for you in the garage. Any problems you call me."

Maria gave us the cottage key and her number. Then we drove her back to the mansion to drop her off. Maria had made it look easy, but I was glad the boat was old and junky, because it was actually pretty hard to maneuver and I had a feeling we'd be bumping into the dock more than we liked.

We decided to go into town and get groceries since we were already docked.

"It's great, right?" I asked Maddy as I pulled out of the mansion's garage.

"Yes, it's great."

"Did you see the cute wall art? All the Minnesota lake-life stuff?"

"Yes." She let her flip-flop fall off and put her bare foot on the seat to put her chin to her knee. "It's like we just went back in time to 1950."

I smiled.

"Who do you think owns that house?" I asked.

"Mister."

I laughed. "Kind of sad he stopped using it," I said, pulling out of the neighborhood.

"Sounds like it had too many painful memories."

"Yeah. We'll appreciate it though."

We drove about a mile away from the lake to a more commercial side of town that Google Maps said had a grocery store. That's when I saw it.

"Oh my God," I said. "I have to pull over."

Maddy looked out the window. "What?"

"Something for Justin."

I turned into the mini mall and parked.

Maddy looked around. "What do you need to get for Justin *here?*"

"Hold on."

I texted him.

Me: Tell me how many fingers to hold up.

A second later:

Justin: Hey, did you make it to Hawaii? How was your flight? Did you get in okay?

I gave my phone a twisted smile.

Me: I did. How many fingers? I have a surprise for you.

He replied with a smiling emoji and the number 3.

"Let's go." I got out.

"What the heck are we doing?" Maddy asked, following me.

"Get a picture of me on this bus bench. Help me make it look good."

She eyed the bench. "I don't think *anything* can make this look good."

She took the picture and handed me back my phone. I cropped the photo so it was just me and the ad on the seatback. Then I sent it through.

It was a solid fifteen seconds before my phone started to ring.

CHAPTER 6

JUSTIN

When the picture of her came through, I stood up so fast my chair fell behind me, and Brad got scared and ran under the bed.

No fucking way. No. Fucking. *Way.*

My heart was pounding in my throat. She was sitting on a bus bench. A Toilet King bus bench. She was *here*.

I called her immediately.

"Justin…"

"Are you serious? You're here?"

I could hear her smiling before she said a word.

I was pacing across my apartment. "Are you just stopping here on your way to Hawaii? Can we meet? I could take you to dinner, I can leave now."

She started laughing. "Justin."

"Yeah?"

"I'm here for six weeks."

I stopped, and a grin ripped across my face. "You skipped Hawaii?"

"Are you surprised?" she asked.

I bit my knuckle and did a silent fist pump in the middle of my kitchen. "Are you kidding me? Where are you staying? When can I see you?"

"I'm on Lake Minnetonka, in a cottage on an island. And I think...tomorrow? Does that work for you?"

I nodded. "Yes. Definitely. That definitely works."

"Okay. Justin?"

I was beaming. "Yeah?"

"You're right. Minnesota is beautiful."

CHAPTER 7

EMMA

Four hours later, Maddy and I were back at the cottage sitting in the screened-in porch. We'd had dinner in town and then boated back. The fridge was stocked up and we'd unpacked.

Maddy came out of the house and handed me an iced tea. "No caffeine."

"Thanks."

There was a party going on somewhere on the island. We could hear music and shouting and the air smelled faintly of a charcoal grill. The sun was setting over the water.

This was going to be an amazing summer.

Maddy sat down with a can of Sprite. "So...Justin tomorrow."

I looked at her. "Is it strange that I'm this excited?"

"Uh yeah, for you it is."

"What if he smells weird?" I asked. "Have you ever had that happen? You meet someone and everything about them is perfect but the way they smell? Like, they don't smell bad or anything, they just don't smell...attractive?"

"Yes! Why is that a thing?" She opened her soda with a *pith*.

"I don't know. Pheromones maybe? I hope he smells good. I have to kiss him."

"Look at you, doing charity work," she said sarcastically.

Even Maddy with all her cynicism couldn't deny that Justin was *very* attractive.

"Would you do more with him?" she asked.

I shrugged. "I don't know. I don't even know if he smells good."

"Well, do you like him? Like, like him like him?"

"Yeah I like him. I wouldn't be here if I didn't."

"But?"

I glanced at her. "But we're dating to break up? I'm not really sure what the rules are. He might just want to get through the dates and be done with it."

She made a *Come On* face. "Really? You don't think he's going to try and see if there's something there with you two?"

I laughed. "Why would he? I mean, the next girl is supposed to be The One. He probably wants to get to that. And I'm only here six weeks anyway."

"I think if you like him you should give him a fair shot. Don't just treat him like a checklist."

I gave her a look. "We're just doing this for fun, Maddy. He's not giving me a fair shot either."

My phone started to vibrate.

I pulled it out expecting Justin, but I didn't recognize the number—and when I didn't recognize the number, I *always* answered. "Hold on, I have to take this. Hello?"

"Emma, you will not *believe* who I found."

I bolted up straight. "Mom? Where have you been?"

Maddy rolled her eyes before pulling out her phone.

"Boston," Mom said. "I told you."

I shook my head. "No. You didn't. And your phone's discon-nected. I was worried—"

"I gave you the new number weeks ago, remember? I was still on Jeff's plan and he canceled my line, can you believe that POS? God, J-named men are the *worst*."

I put my forehead into my palm, feeling the wave of relief I always got when I finally knew where she was.

"Anyway," she went on, "guess who I found? You won't believe it." She paused for dramatic effect. "Stuffie."

I lifted my head. "Stuffie?"

"Yeah. That little unicorn doll you used to carry around every-where? I went to visit Renee. Remember her? We stayed with her for two months back when you were in the fourth grade? She divorced that guy she was married to, the electrician? Finally. I don't know why she thought a Libra was a good idea—and a Taurus Moon of all things, can you imagine? She's selling dream catchers on Etsy now, I got you one. Anyway, she still had our boxes in her garage. Opened a few up and there he was, just sitting on top of a bunch of board games."

Stuffie. I couldn't even breathe.

There were very few things that I cherished. I wasn't a senti-mental person, at all. But I *loved* Stuffie. I'd thought he was gone.

"Give me your address and I'll send him to you," she said.

"Do you need me to Venmo you for the shipping?" I asked, a little too quickly. But I didn't want her to put it off because she couldn't afford to send it. She'd lose him, or damage him, or get distracted and forget.

"No, I got it. Got a job as a cart girl on a golf course, tips are good. So how have you been? Where are you? Tell me everything!"

"I'm in Minnesota. We just got here today, actually."

"Minnesota…" she said, her voice going a little flat.

For some reason it wasn't until just this moment that I remembered that this was where Mom had grown up. She didn't talk about it, hardly ever. She'd left when she was eighteen.

"Where?" she asked.

"Lake Minnetonka."

"Oh, it's such a party lake!" she said, bursting back to life. "You're going to have so much fun! Make someone grill you a walleye. Hold on." Then she started talking to someone muffled in the background. She came back on and sighed dramatically. "I gotta go. Text me that address. Love you!"

And then she was gone.

I slumped back against my seat and Maddy raised her eyes from her phone and we shared a silent exchange. She was letting me know that Amber exasperated her, and I was letting her know that I was aware.

I sent the address of the mansion to Mom and saved her new number in my phone and set it down on the seat next to me.

Maddy set her phone down too. "So I got you something," she said.

"You did?"

"Yeah. And I really want you to be open to it. Can you promise me you will?"

I eyed her. "What."

"Just keep an open mind. Promise me."

She waited.

"Fine," I said. "I will keep an open mind. What is it?"

She pulled a box out from under the wicker chair she was in. The second I saw it I shook my head.

"No. I'm not doing a DNA test."

"Why?"

"Because I don't want to mess up someone's life. My dad doesn't even know I exist—"

"And don't you think he has a right to know? Anyone who runs their DNA through these things knows they might get surprises. So someone might find out they have a kid. They *do* have a kid. You exist and it's not your fault and anyone who finds out they're related to you would be lucky."

"*No.*"

"I'm sorry, but Amber cannot be the only family you ever have. I literally forbid it."

"She's not the only family I have. I have you."

Maddy studied me for a moment. "And our moms. Right? They're your family too."

I licked my lips. "Yeah. Of course." But even the way I said it came out disingenuous.

She looked away from me. "Emma…" Her eyes came back to mine. "Please. *Please* do it. Do it now before you lose the chance to meet them altogether. People don't live forever."

I knew who she was talking about. My grandparents died before I was born. Not getting to know them had always made me deeply sad. My mom had no siblings, no cousins, nobody else. There would only be my dad.

Mom said my conception had been a passionate one-night stand with a handsome, charming *married* stranger on a beach in Miami. She didn't know his name—or she didn't want to tell me.

I'd talked to Mom once about taking a DNA test. She got extremely upset. She said the only family I might find would be his, and she'd made it very clear that me popping up would ruin a marriage. She also said he'd told her he didn't have kids and didn't want any. I would not be a welcome surprise.

So if I wasn't likely to find any siblings and my dad was someone who'd rather not know I exist, what was the point?

Only what if things were different?

What if he *did* have other kids now? People change their minds. What if I had a sister? Or a brother? What if I was an aunt, or somebody's cousin—and *they* wanted to know me? What if he had a medical condition I should know about? Something genetic? Something I should be screened for?

I chewed on my lip.

"How about this," Maddy said. "Run your DNA and make your account private. We'll change your privacy settings for a few minutes, poke around. If you have any relatives out there, we'll screenshot it and go back to private. Then I'll go and find them online and tell you if they seem like people worth knowing."

"I don't know…"

"Aren't you curious?"

I blew a breath through my nose. I was. I always had been.

"Okay," I said. "*Fine.*"

She squealed and tore the box open.

We did the test. I set up my profile on the website and Maddy said she'd mail it in the morning.

She went back to scrolling on her phone and I sat looking out over the water as the sun set. When my cell pinged next to me, I half expected Mom again, but this time it was Justin.

It was a link to SurveyMonkey.

"Huh," I said.

Maddy nodded at my phone. "Amber?"

"Justin."

"What is it?"

I clicked on it and a survey popped up titled "Your Date With Justin." I had to cover my smile with a hand.

Congratulations on your upcoming date with Justin! Your preferences are important, so he'd like to know what you think. Please complete this questionnaire by 9:00 tonight.

"Oh my God," I breathed. "He *didn't*."

It was multiple choice.

PREFERRED TIME OF DAY FOR OUR DATE:

- ☐ Breakfast
- ☐ Lunch
- ☐ Dinner

WHAT ACTIVITIES INTEREST YOU?

- ☐ Hiking
- ☐ Dinner and a movie
- ☐ A museum or aquarium
- ☐ Day on the lake
- ☐ Escape room
- ☐ Wildcard (Justin's choice)
- ☐ Other:

FOOD PREFERENCES:

- ☐ Thai
- ☐ American

- ☐ BBQ
- ☐ Vegetarian or vegan
- ☐ Steakhouse
- ☐ Indian
- ☐ Italian
- ☐ Justin's pick
- ☐ Other:

FANCINESS LEVEL:

- ☐ Pajamas
- ☐ Activewear
- ☐ Everyday casual
- ☐ Business casual
- ☐ James Bond movie

PREFERRED GREETING:

- ☐ Contactless
- ☐ Victorian greeting (small curtsey and a slight nod)
- ☐ Handshake
- ☐ Hug
- ☐ Air kiss on both cheeks
- ☐ High five

PREFERRED MODE OF TRANSPORTATION:

- ☐ Please have Justin pick me up at the following address:
- ☐ I would like to transport myself (destination to be provided no later than two hours before the start of the date)

I was cracking up. "He sent me a pre-date questionnaire."

"What? Let me see that," Maddy said. She took my phone. Then her eyes raised to mine. "I like this."

"So do I."

She handed me back my phone and I bit my lip. I really, *really* hoped he smelled good.

I started filling out the form. I picked Lunch, Wildcard (Justin's choice) for the activity, Justin's pick for the food since I figured he'd know the best places to eat and I wasn't picky. I almost went with James Bond for the fanciness level, just to see what he'd do, but I went with Everyday casual instead since I didn't have anything James Bond level to wear. I picked Hug for the preferred greeting, and I opted for him to pick me up so Maddy would have the car.

I hit enter and sent it through.

The next morning I woke up to an Evite invitation.

It was floral and it was titled "Casual Date With Justin":

JULY 28TH, 11:00 A.M.

PLEASE JOIN JUSTIN AT THE ADDRESS YOU PROVIDED AT 11:00 A.M. SHARP FOR A SURPRISE ACTIVITY, LUNCH AND CONVERSATION. PLEASE WEAR LONG PANTS.

I laughed and scrambled out of bed and let myself into Maddy's room. "Look at this," I said, climbing onto her comforter while she yawned and took my phone.

She looked at the invite. "I gotta give it to him, he's putting in the work." She handed my cell back and stretched. "Too bad he's just your future ex-boyfriend."

I bit my lip and beamed at the invite.

"Hey," she said. "Try and find a way to reject him on this date."

I looked up. "Huh?"

"Tell him no. See how he reacts. Or beat him at a game. If he takes you bowling or to miniature golf or something, destroy him. You can tell a lot about a guy by how they deal with rejection and getting their asses handed to them."

I laughed a little. "Okay…"

She threw the blanket off. "I'll start breakfast. You should get ready."

"Right." I hopped up and hurried to my room to pick out something to wear. I settled on olive leggings and a slouchy white T-shirt and gold sandals, gold dangly earrings and a matching bracelet. Then I went to take a shower.

The water smelled weird. Like rust. Maybe the house was on a well? When I got out and brushed my hair, it felt like I hadn't conditioned it.

I opened the bathroom door and leaned out. "Is the water weird to you?" I called. "My hair feels all gross."

"I think it's hard water," she called back from the kitchen. "We're in the iron range."

I made an unhappy noise and wrestled the brush through my stiff knots. We started work tomorrow and I was going to shower at the hospital locker rooms whenever I could. This was awful.

I finally got through it and plugged in my hair dryer, and when I turned it on, the whole house turned off.

"Uh…what just happened?" Maddy called from the kitchen.

I tipped my head back. "I think we blew a fuse."

"What did you do?"

"Nothing, I just turned on the hair dryer."

We spent ten minutes looking for the breaker panel until we finally gave up and called Maria.

"Oh, it's very sensitive," she said. "You can't use the toaster and hairdryer at the same time. When I vacuum, I have to unplug *everything*."

She told us where to find the panel. We reset the breaker and started a twenty-minute trial and error of what we could and could not use while I dried my hair. The answer was nothing. We couldn't even use the coffee maker with the hair dryer on without tripping the breaker.

We prioritized power for the coffee maker first and we brewed a pot while I sat in the kitchen with a towel wrapped around my head. When it was done, Maddy poured me a cup and handed it to me.

"The house is old," I said. "What are you gonna do?"

She leaned against the counter with her mug in her hand. "I bet it's hard to even get a repair guy out here. You gotta go pick him up."

I cocked my head at her. "I just realized we can't get DoorDash."

"Or Shipt," she said, like it just occurred to her. She looked at me. "What if we need to call the cops? Do they have boat police?"

I wrinkled my forehead. "I think so. Don't they pull people over on the lake? But do they work at night? And what if we need to call an ambulance? Do they have boat ambulances?"

"I don't know."

I thought about this for a bit. "Our boat is *really* old."

"Yeah."

"And if it breaks down, we're kinda trapped here."

"Or dead in the water."

We sat there, contemplating this. Maddy was going to have to ferry me to the shore for my date and then come back alone and pick me up when Justin dropped me off. She was going to have to dock the pontoon by herself.

I don't think I really realized the logistics of this one-boat thing until just now. I mean, we only had the one car, and that always worked for us. But that's because we always had Lyft and Uber to fall back on, or public transit—or the ability to walk. But the only way on and off this island was that boat.

That rickety, ancient, canopyless boat.

"Remind me to buy rain ponchos," I said.

"Yeah." She took a sip of her coffee.

I took my mug and went back to do my hair.

I had breakfast while my curlers set. Then I washed the dishes, did my makeup, let my hair down, spritzed myself with perfume, and I was ready to go.

At 10:45, we set off for shore.

I couldn't see if he was here yet. He'd be waiting in his car parked in front of the house. I probably wouldn't see him until I walked around the garage.

"I'm going to wait until I know he's here," Maddy said as we approached the dock.

It was windy today. She kept having to correct the boat because we were being pushed off course by the gusts.

"Maybe if you give it more throttle?" I said over the sound of the motor and wind.

"I'm giving it throttle. This is all the throttle it has."

I think she was worried about drifting too far off the path, so she didn't cut the engine until we were really close. We overshot and headed right for the shore.

"Reverse! Put it in reverse!" I yelled.

The snail's-pace speed the pontoon put out somehow seemed faster with the beach approaching. Maddy threw it in reverse. The engine downshifted miserably, but we started to slow. Then to my horror we began to move backward, motor first, right into the dock.

The sides of the boat had bumpers. Large air-filled rubber balls that keep the body of the pontoon from making contact and causing damage when it hits. But the motor had no protection. It was prop blades and the engine, heading straight into the dock.

"We're gonna back into it!" I shouted.

"Well push me off!" she said, throwing it frantically into drive. The weak engine fought against the inertia—and lost.

I sprinted to the end of the boat, pulled up the bench seat, grabbed the paddle, and leaned over the side just as we were about to make impact. I stretched out and used the paddle to push us off the dock inches before the hit. It was just enough and we started to float back to the lake.

Both of us were panting. We stood there, hearts pounding, drifting aimlessly in the water for a moment like astronauts ejected into space.

When we were safely away from anything we could crash into, Maddy killed the engine and slumped in the captain's seat. "If we'd been on the other side of the dock, we could have hit the yacht," she said, looking shaken.

I let my eyes slide over to the boat that probably cost more than both of us made in five years. I had a retroactive heart attack.

"Are you gonna be okay to dock this by yourself back at the cottage?" I asked.

She was still catching her breath. "I mean, what choice do I have?"

We looked back at the shore. We had to try this again. We'd have to get good at this. We'd have to drive and dock this boat, at a minimum, twice a day on days we worked.

We'd have to do it at night. In the rain. During heatwaves and maybe even during hailstorms—if we had to get to work, we had to get to work.

I hadn't really anticipated it being this hard or there being this many variables. When you drive a car, you don't have to worry about the wind.

"Do you want me to try?" I asked.

She nodded. We switched.

I lined the nose of the boat up with the side of the dock and started for it again, only this time I killed the thrust earlier. We coasted along the side and I put us into reverse to slow us down while Maddy grabbed one of the dock poles and we came to a stop.

"Don't tie it up," I said. "I'll just get off and push you back out."

We switched again, I grabbed my bag, stepped off the boat, gave it a steady push back toward the lake, and watched her drift until she was clear.

I had no idea how she was going to dock this by herself back on the island. I was actually really worried about it.

"Call me when you're docked!" I shouted.

She gave me a thumbs-up.

I was completely frazzled. Rattled by the near accident. My hair was windblown and I felt like I was starting to get a little burnt too. This was *not* how I wanted to start this date.

I watched Maddy for a moment. Then I turned and made my way across the lawn toward the side of the mansion and around the garage. When I got to the top, Justin stood there in the courtyard, leaning against his car.

CHAPTER 8

JUSTIN

The moment Emma came into view, my entire world slipped into slow motion. My brain took a screenshot. I felt the moment freeze and save.

She was *beautiful*.

I'd seen pictures, we'd video called, but it didn't even begin to make me ready for this.

Long brown hair, a white top, leggings. She was smiling at me, this easy, comfortable smile, and the closer she got, the more paralyzed I felt. I couldn't even will my legs to walk to meet her. I wasn't standing by my car, waiting for my date. I was in the middle of a road, watching the headlights of a Mack truck coming right at me.

I liked to consider myself a pretty level, confident, easygoing person. I didn't get flustered or anxious about dates. But everything I knew about myself prior to the moment I laid eyes on *her* was no longer true.

I was a nervous wreck. Instantly.

She closed the distance between us. "Hey."

"Hey," I said a little breathlessly, hoping that I didn't actually sound breathless.

Then I was just staring. Wide-eyed and mute, like a human Justin wax figurine.

She didn't seem to notice. She came in for a hug. The hug we'd agreed upon in the survey. But I was *not* prepared.

She wrapped her arms around me, and I processed her in split seconds. Shorter than me. Soft. Warm. Her hair smelled like flowers. This is what she feels like. This is *her...*

"You smell good," she said, breaking away.

"Thanks. You too," I managed.

"God, I'm so frazzled," she said. "You should have seen us trying to dock the boat."

My mouth was dry. "What happened?" I asked.

"We almost beached it. It was like a comedy skit."

Her phone rang. "Oh, hold on. I have to leave my ringer on in case Maddy gets in trouble trying to get back." She looked at it. "It's her." She swiped and put the phone to her ear. "Maddy? Are you okay?" She listened for a second and then glanced at me. "Okay." Then she hung up. She nodded over her shoulder. "Can we go down there really quick?"

"Sure."

She turned and started back the way she came. We made our way around the side of the enormous house until we had a view of the lake.

There was a short brown-haired woman in a pontoon just off-shore. She raised binoculars to watch us.

"Is that her?" I asked.

"Yeah, that's her," she said, looking amused. "She must have found those in the boat. Go!" She made a shooing motion with her hands. "Call me when you're docked!"

She turned back to me shaking her head. "I think she wanted to see you."

I gave Maddy a wave over Emma's shoulder and the woman's smile vanished. Then she dragged a finger across her neck in the universal sign for *I'll kill you*.

I blinked.

Emma saw my face and turned back around to see what I was looking at, and Maddy beamed and waved enthusiastically at her best friend.

Okay…

Emma came back to me with a smile. "So. Ready to go?"

"Uh, sure?"

We walked to the car and I jogged ahead of her and opened her door. After she got in I went around the back to the driver's side, too self-conscious to walk in front of her.

"I like your car," she said when I got in. "I can't believe you let Alex drive it."

I let out a laugh that was probably too loud and turned on the engine.

She peered down at my drink holder. "You went to Starbucks."

"Oh, yeah. I got us drinks. Here." I picked up her salted caramel cold foam to hand it to her—and dropped it. It kerplunked in her lap and she caught it before it tipped sideways. The lid stayed on, but a little coffee splashed up out of the sipping hole onto her white shirt.

"Shit!" I breathed, looking around frantically for napkins. "Shit shit shit shit shit."

"It's okay, I'm fine," she said, brushing the droplets off with her fingers.

Not a single napkin in the whole car. Nothing. I went to open the glove box and look in there and my hand grazed her knee. She jerked it out of the way.

Literally everything I'd done in the last sixteen hours since the minute I realized she was here was in preparation for this date. I'd made the questionnaire, typed up the invite, made plans and phone calls. I'd even cleaned my apartment—not that I thought she was coming back to my apartment. But on the off chance she wanted to see the billboard up close or meet Brad or something, I wanted it spotless. And now I wondered why I even bothered since none of the other stuff even mattered if I was just gonna come off as a fucking weirdo because I was so flustered.

I wanted to say, "I'm sorry, I'm so nervous." But then I didn't want her to know I was nervous. I wanted her to think I was calm and collected like I usually was on dates. But this date wasn't like my usual dates, and not for the reason it should have been. The fact that this wasn't really real, we were just trying some stupid experiment for the fun of it, should have made this less stressful. It wasn't like I had to actually impress her. We were collaborators, she didn't have to like me or even be attracted to me. But now I suddenly *really* wanted her to like me and be attracted to me, and even after all the things I did to make today special, I worried it wasn't enough to compensate for *me*.

I rummaged through my glove box and cursed under my breath when I didn't find anything.

"Justin, it's okay," she said, laughing a little. "I have wipes in my purse."

Then I realized she'd moved her legs not because I'd accidentally touched her knee, but because she was getting her purse off the floor. She pulled out a baby wipe and started to blot the little stain. "See?

Almost gone." She finished and balled the wipe up and put it back into her bag. Then she picked up her drink. "Thanks for the coffee." She took a sip. "I can't believe you remembered. I can never remember anybody's drink. I was a waitress once—I was so bad at it."

I felt the corner of my lip twitch up, despite myself. I cleared my throat. "Let me text her and tell her we're on our way," I said, pulling out my phone.

"Her? Who?" she asked.

"My friend Jane. Benny's girlfriend."

I hit send and put on my seat belt.

"So what's this activity?" she asked.

"Can't tell you. Top secret. So," I said, changing the subject, "has Maddy ever killed anyone?"

She pretended to think about it. "Nobody I can prove."

I laughed nervously as I pulled away from the curb.

I felt like I was buffering with her sitting next to me. Like all I could do was loop around and around over the fact that she was here. I was physically willing myself to act normal. *Be cool, Justin. Be. COOL. She's just a regular person.*

I glanced at her. She was definitely not just a regular person.

Thankfully *she* was not a nervous mess and she carried the conversation the next few minutes. Emma acting so comfortable and normal made me think she didn't notice that *I* wasn't comfortable and normal, and this helped me get ahold of myself. By the time we got to Benny and Jane's, we'd fallen into the easy back-and-forth that we had on the phone, thank God, and I was mostly recovered.

We got out of the car, and Jane opened the front door before we knocked.

Jane beamed. "Hi, so nice to meet you!" She shook Emma's hand.

"Nice to meet you too," Emma said.

"Benny still at work?" I asked.

Jane put out a bottom lip. "Yeah, he thought he might be able to get away for lunch but he can't. Sorry."

I hadn't really cared too much that Benny might not be here today. He wasn't the point of this visit. But all that had changed in the last ten minutes. Now I *wanted* my friends to meet her so I had someone to talk to about her.

Jane led us through their living room and down a hall and stopped by a closed door. "Everything's ready. You guys can go in when you want."

"And what's everything?" Emma asked, looking at me.

"I think I'm going to save it until you see it." I put up a hand. "Now remember, no matter what's behind that door, don't fall in love with me. That's not what we're doing here."

Emma laughed, and I felt relieved that I'd regained enough composure to be funny.

I leaned over and opened the door and she gasped. "Kittens?" She beamed.

"Yup."

The five six-week-old kittens Jane was fostering came mewing up to us, tails in the air. We shuffled in and I shut the door behind us before any escaped.

Emma scooped one up. "Oh, Justin, look! It's so cute!"

I grinned. "Do you want to sit? They climb all over you if you do. That's why I said to wear pants."

Emma set her purse down and sat cross-legged next to it, and I took a seat opposite her. The kittens began to scale us immediately. One clawed up Emma's back and popped out over her shoulder under her hair while two more played in her lap.

Her whole face lit up.

I was glad we did this first. She was so busy looking at the kittens, it gave me the chance to look at her without her noticing I was staring—and I *was* staring. Tiny freckles on her cheeks. Bronze woven into her hair. Her hazel eyes were a kaleidoscope of green with flecks of gold. They were different in person.

Everything was different in person.

I think if I'd known she was coming, if she'd told me her plans to switch Hawaii out for Minnesota, none of this would feel so unbelievable. But then something told me this would feel unbelievable no matter what.

"Did her cat have babies?" she asked.

"No. She fosters for Bitty Kitty Brigade. I've done it a few times too. I like cats. We had one when we were in college, Cooter. Benny took him when he moved out a few years ago. He's probably here somewhere."

She talked to a kitten but was speaking to me. "We're only twenty minutes in and this is already the best date I've ever been on. I don't know how you're going to top this, Justin."

"I've got a lot of ideas."

She glanced at me. "Oh yeah? Am I getting your top four?"

"You're only giving me four dates?" I asked. "You're here for six weeks. We could have more."

"I don't want to take advantage."

"Please. Take advantage." *Please.*

She gave me a wry smile that I hoped was flirting.

"Seriously," I said. "I'd like to see you more than that. To show you Minnesota," I added quickly, worrying I sounded too eager.

"Well, you *did* talk up a good game about this place. It would be a shame if I didn't have a guide to show me the highlights."

"Agree. One hundred percent. I consider it my duty, it's purely obligatory, I won't enjoy it at all."

She laughed.

"So where are we going for lunch?" she asked, snuggling her baby.

"A breakfast place actually. Unless you prefer pizza."

"I *love* breakfast food," she said.

"It is far superior to any other kind," I agreed.

"I do like pizza though," she said.

"Do you eat the crust?" I asked, petting a passing kitten.

"I *love* the crust on pizza," she said.

"I *hate* the crust."

"Maddy hates the crust too and I get to eat hers," she said. "It's part of why we're so compatible."

"Brad likes them too. He eats all my crusts. You know, I bet if they did a study about relationships, romantic and platonic, the ones where two people have alternating crust preferences are the ones that work the best."

"Imagine putting that on a dating app," she said.

I made my voice serious. "Must be willing to eat my discarded pizza crusts, no weirdos."

She burst into laughter. The relief I felt that this seemed to be going well was insurmountable.

"What food don't you like?" I asked, still smiling.

"Carrots. You?"

"Pappardelle," I said. "Can't stand it."

"That thin, flat pasta?"

"Yeah. It feels like you're eating a tongue," I said, getting my arm tackled by an orange tabby. "Okay, all right, that's enough, Murder Mittens." I pulled the cat off me one claw at a time and Emma beamed at me.

Her phone rang and she picked it up and looked at it. "Oh, hold on, it's Maddy. Hello?" She listened for a moment. Then she sucked air through her teeth. "That's what the bumpers are for. Well I'm glad you made it, I was worried. Okay. Okay. I will. Bye." She hung up.

"She docked it okay?" I asked.

"Yeah, she rammed it kind of hard, but she says the boat is fine."

"You two are going to be professionals by the time this summer is over."

"I hope so. It's been a little stressful." She picked up Murder Mittens. "I don't think I really thought this island thing through. It sounded like a good idea at the time but it's kind of inconvenient. Anyway, it's only for six weeks and Maddy likes the cottage, so…"

"Where'd you and Maddy meet?" I asked.

She rubbed noses with the kitten. "She's my foster sister. Her moms took me in when I was fourteen. They were amazing. Put me through nursing school and everything."

"They adopted you?" I asked.

She shook her head. "No."

"Why not? Actually, you know what, no. You don't have to answer that. That's personal."

"I don't mind. I didn't want to be adopted," she said. "I wanted my mom to be able to come back for me if she wanted to."

"Annnnd…did she?"

She paused for a moment. "No. She did not."

Another kitten crept toward me on its belly. I wiggled my fingers and it pounced on my hand and I picked it up and cradled it while it bit my knuckle.

She tilted her head. "That is adorable. I need to get a picture," she said, grabbing her phone.

"Hey, you should find me on Instagram," I said after she took the shot.

"Um…" she said as she set her phone down. "I have a little confession to make. I've already seen your Instagram."

"You have?"

"Yeah. Maddy found you."

"When?"

"About four minutes into our first Reddit DMs?"

"Okay…" I chuckled. "Well, follow me then so I can follow you back."

"All right. Also, Maddy found you on LinkedIn too," she said. "And your dad's obituary. I'm sorry."

I paused. "I can't tell if I should feel violated."

"She just wanted to make sure you weren't creepy."

"Did it help you decide to talk to me?"

"It did, actually."

"Then I'm glad she did it."

She smiled. Murder Mittens draped over her arm, languidly. "God, cats are just liquid, aren't they? I always wanted a cat but we moved too much."

"Moved for work?"

"Sometimes. Sometimes we couldn't pay the rent or she was tired of the city we were in. My mom wasn't really good at sitting still," she said.

"So why the foster care? Do you mind me asking?"

She shook her head. "No. She'd leave me. It was neglect."

She said this matter-of-factly, like it didn't bother her and she was talking about someone else.

Then she laughed a little. "One time when I was eight, my mom left for the weekend, but she didn't come back. She'd left me twenty dollars, and there was some food in the pantry. But a week went by. Then another week. Then three and the food ran out. When she did this in the winter or the fall, I'd eat at school. I'd always save some of my lunch and take it home so I had something to eat on the weekend, but this time it was the summer. The neighbor had this garden in her yard and I was so hungry that I couldn't sleep and I went over there in the middle of the night and I dug up her carrots. All of them. I took them home and I ate them for days. I turned orange." She laughed. "The beta-carotene gave me carotenemia. I thought I was dying. I went to the neighbors and they called 911. That's how I ended up in foster care the first time. That's also why I hate carrots."

I just stared at her. "Where *was* she?" I asked.

She shrugged, petting the kitten. "I don't know. She'd gotten a job as a flight attendant, and I'd spent lots of nights alone. But this time she just didn't come home. I think something happened. Not really sure what. The hospital. Jail."

"*Jail??*"

"I think she struggles with some mental health issues sometimes. It gets her in trouble. Anyway, she'd forgotten to pay the phone bill so the phone got shut off a few days after she left and I think she didn't know how to get in touch with me without telling someone she'd left me alone. She was always really afraid I'd get taken from her."

"You *should* have been taken from her," I said, incredulous.

"She was a single mom, Justin, doing the best she could. She couldn't afford overnight daycare and I was really independent. Honestly, it was fine 99 percent of the time."

I shook my head. "Emma...That's fucked up."

"I genuinely don't believe she meant to hurt me. She was doing what she had to do. It was what it was. I'm fine. I turned out okay. I'm happy and I have a good life."

I blinked at her. "I don't know how you could forgive someone like that."

She shrugged again and looked up at me. "Why not forgive? In a world where you can choose anger or empathy, always choose empathy, Justin. I don't know what it was like to be her. A single mom at eighteen, no money, no family. She struggled. She *still* struggles. But she loves me and I never doubted that for a second no matter what she did."

She went back to playing with the kitten in her arms and I just sat there studying her.

Always choose empathy...

I wish I could do that. I wish I could go on with my life and not hold a grudge against Mom. But I couldn't forgive her. At least not right now.

After an hour with the kittens, we wrapped things up to eat.

I'd wanted to bring her somewhere special, so I carefully selected where to go. It had to be somewhere uniquely Minnesota, the food had to be amazing, and it had to be memorable. I picked a small family-run place called Hot Plate. When she walked in and smiled around the little cafe, I knew I'd chosen correctly.

The walls were covered in hundreds of completed paint by numbers. Figurines sat on every surface, and eclectic lamps and chandeliers hung over the booths, and there was a whole shelf of games to play at your table while you ate.

"Wow," she said, looking around. I was rewarded with a grin.

There was a fifteen-minute wait, so we stood outside talking. I was more than happy to draw the date out, it was already going way too fast. I was taking her to Minnehaha Falls after we ate, but I wanted to ask her if she'd like to check out the Minneapolis Sculpture Garden or go get ice cream after that, just to make it last, but she said she started work tomorrow and she needed to get back. I was hoping the table would take longer than they said, to give us more time, but after ten minutes they called my name. I was holding the door open for her when she put a hand on my arm.

"Let's just hang here for a bit," she said.

I looked at her confused. "Why, what's up?"

She was peering past me at a middle-aged woman sitting on a Toilet King bus bench across the street, rummaging through a purse on her lap.

I looked back and forth between them. "What's wrong?"

She didn't answer me. She studied the lady for another moment, then crossed the street. I let go of the door and followed her.

Emma sat on the bench next to the woman. "Hi."

The woman looked at Emma and then back inside her purse.

"Do you know what time the bus comes?" Emma asked her.

The woman didn't answer.

"I'm going to see my mom," Emma said. "Who are you going to see?"

"Samantha," the lady said, not looking up. "I'm waiting for my Uber. We're going to Santa Monica."

"Oh. What time's your flight?"

The woman stayed busy digging in her purse. "No flight, it's a half-an-hour drive."

Emma made split-second eye contact with me.

"So it looks like the Uber app is down," Emma said. "I talked to Samantha, and she told me to take you to get some coffee in the restaurant over there until she can pick you up. Are you ready?"

The woman's eyes moved back and forth over the mouth of her open Coach bag. Emma took her gently by the elbow. "I'm Emma. What's your name?"

The woman looked up at her. "Lisa."

"Nice to meet you," Emma said, helping her to her feet. "Can I see your phone for a second? Unlock it for me? I want to see if Samantha is almost here." When Lisa gave it over, Emma slipped it into my hand. "Justin, can you make a call for me?" she whispered. "Let Samantha know Lisa is having coffee with us?"

I found Samantha in her contacts and called.

Ten minutes later a tearful twentysomething woman ran through the restaurant to our booth to get her mother. Emma had sat with Lisa the whole time talking about an imaginary day at the beach she was going to have in a city two thousand miles from here.

"How did you know?" I asked, once we were alone again. The woman seemed perfectly normal to me. At first glance anyway.

"Her shirt was buttoned wrong," she said. "I used to work in memory care. She seemed off. Disoriented."

"Was it dementia? She seems too young."

"Dementia can happen young. Could be early-onset Alzheimer's, head injury. Could be a lot of things."

The waitress stopped by and filled our coffee cups. Emma grabbed some sugar packets, tore them, and spilled them into her mug.

"Why didn't you tell her the truth? That we're not in California," I asked.

"It's too confusing. The truth scares them. Sometimes the best way to show love or be kind to someone is to meet them where they are."

"Literally? Or figuratively?"

She paused with the spoon in her hand. "Both."

I watched her while she stirred her coffee. I liked that she helped. I liked that she noticed she had to.

We ordered our food, then we went to go check out the games.

"What about chess?" I asked.

"I like chess," she said, looking the game shelf up and down. "You don't want to do one that's more fun though? Uno or something?"

I arched an eyebrow. "You think we're ready for Uno? That game has torn entire families apart."

She laughed. "Okay. Chess then."

We brought it back to the table and set it up. I knew ten minutes in that this wasn't going to go well for me. I was good at chess, but she was better. A *lot* better.

"So, why travel nursing?" I asked, watching her take my rook.

"The money is nice," she said. "We want to see the US. We take an international trip once a year too."

"So you fly a lot," I said, studying the board.

"I do."

"Do you clap when the airplane lands?" I asked.

"Absolutely not."

"Do you run on the fasty-fast moving sidewalks at the airport?" I slid my bishop over.

"I *walk* fast on the fasty-fast moving sidewalks. Do *you* run on the fasty-fast sidewalks?"

"No. Why? Did someone say something?"

She laughed with a hand on her queen. "I bet you're that guy that stands in the walking lane and I have to clear my throat really loudly to get you to move."

I made eye contact with her. "Do I strike you as the kind of man to obliviously impede the flow of traffic? I am a *very* considerate person," I said. "I will have you know that I do not monopolize the armrests and I help little old ladies get their bags down from the overhead."

Her expression was an amused one. "Wow. And I suppose next you're going to tell me that you wash your dishes before there's mold on them?" She knocked out my knight.

"Of *course* I wash them," I said.

"And when's the last time you washed your pillowcase?"

"Wait…you have pillowcases??"

"And there it is."

I was chuckling over the board game and she was smiling. Big time.

"What kind of men are you going out with?" I asked, managing to get one of her pawns. "I take pride in my apartment."

"I could see that about you."

"Why? Because you've cyberstalked me and you've already seen all the pictures of it?" I grinned at her.

She moved her queen. "I didn't see *everything* online. There is stuff I don't know about you."

"Like?" I moved *my* queen.

She raised her eyes to me. "Like what happened to your dad."

I went quiet for a beat.

"A drunk driver hit him on his way to work," I said.

Her eyes went soft. "I'm sorry…"

I kept my gaze fixed on the game. "I never get used to explaining it—which I have to do every time I start dating somebody new. So it'll be great once we break this curse," I said, laughing a little.

"I get that. I don't really like explaining my mom to people either."

"Yeah. I understand."

We studied the board quietly.

"You know what I think about sometimes?" she said, raising her eyes to mine.

"What?"

"You know how when something bad happens to someone you love, and you wish you could take it from them instead?"

"Yeah."

"What if the universe listened? What if you or your mom or the kids were supposed to die in a car crash and your dad said 'Take me instead'—and the universe did. And nobody remembers the way it was supposed to be because that's the deal. You never get to know that he's a hero. The fates are reversed and the tribute takes the thing he asked for to save someone he loves. If you think of it that way, instead of being sad that he's gone, be happy that he got what he wanted. And that somebody loved you enough to take your place."

I nodded slowly. "That is actually oddly comforting."

Her eyes focused on the board. "I've had a lot of bad things happen to me, Justin. I think sometimes the key to happiness is framing those things in a different way."

"It would mean magic exists," I said.

"It might. Isn't that why we're here?" Her lips quirked up. "Checkmate." She knocked my piece over.

I stared at my fallen king. "I'm already out?"

She shrugged playfully.

I sat back. "You are *really* good at chess."

"Are you surprised?" she asked.

"I'm not actually."

"One of my foster homes had a chessboard and a broken TV."

"So I got hustled," I deadpanned.

"Am I the asshole?" She batted her eyes at me.

"No. It was a privilege to see you work."

She laughed and I folded the board in half just in time for our food.

After breakfast we went to the falls. An hour later I drove her home. I didn't want to drop her off. It didn't feel like we'd gotten enough time, but to be fair the whole day wouldn't have been enough time.

When we got to the mansion, I walked her to the dock, where Maddy was waiting in the pontoon.

Emma and I stopped on the lawn just short of the beach. "So you work the rest of the week?" I asked.

"Yeah. I work the next four days straight. Orientation tomorrow, then right into it the day after."

"So I won't be able to see you at all? Can I have lunch with you maybe?"

"I never know when I'm getting my lunches. But that's sweet that you want to." She smiled up at me. "It was a very nice date. Can I make a request for the next one though?"

"Of course."

"Can I meet your dog?"

I smiled. "Absolutely."

She reached up and gave me a hug. When she broke away, she paused for a moment like maybe I'd kiss her. I was supposed to kiss her, but it didn't feel right just yet, especially with Maddy standing there watching. But when Emma's eyes flickered to my lips for a split second, I started to consider it anyway. Then she glanced over my shoulder and sucked in a breath. I turned to see what she was looking at.

A yacht was pulling up to a slip in the dock, a woman waving from the bow.

"Oh my God…" Emma whispered.

"What?" I asked, looking back and forth. "Who is that?"

A long, disbelieving pause. "That's my *mom*."

CHAPTER 9

EMMA

I watched in disbelief as the yacht docked.

Maddy was already off the pontoon and running toward me across the beach. She skidded to a halt in front of me, still catching her breath from the sprint. "This *bitch*," she managed.

Justin stood next to me. "You didn't invite her?"

"No the fuck we did not," Maddy said, glaring over her shoulder at Mom getting off the boat.

Amber was in a flowing white-and-peach chiffon summer dress with a slit up the thigh. Her long brown hair was down, she had on a floppy wide-brimmed hat and huge sunglasses. She was carrying a bottle of champagne in one hand and her sandals in the other, dangling off the tips of her fingers. She was beaming, running toward us across the beach, kicking up sand. "Emma!" She laughed.

Despite my shock and the lasers I could feel coming out of Maddy's eyes, I smiled. *Mom...*

That old thrill ran through me. The one I always got when

she showed up again unexpectedly, to rescue me, or surprise me, or finally take me home. I ran toward her. And when I met her in the middle of the lawn and she hugged me, I was so overwhelmed with relief, I started to cry.

I was a little girl again. Catapulted back to eight years old, in the arms of my mother. She smelled the way she always did during good times. Like roses. The smell was strong and fresh and I felt myself reset back to zero.

That scent was a barometer. When she stopped putting it on, it meant she was getting closer to disappearing again. When she started losing interest in self-care, she'd start losing interest in everything. Her job, her responsibilities.

Me.

It was strange how I realized I knew this, without ever consciously knowing it. The fading scent of roses would make me brace. Make me hyperaware of her comings and goings. Make me try harder to be less of a burden so maybe she wouldn't feel the need to put me down again and go.

Do well in school. Do my own laundry. Make my own food. Don't ask for anything. Don't *need* anything. Clean up after myself. Then after her. Be helpful. Be invisible. Be small.

She broke away from me and smiled.

I wiped under my eyes and her hat blew off and she laughed with a hand to her hair as it tumbled toward the water. The man who'd been driving the yacht was coming up the beach. He leaned over and grabbed it on his way.

He was good looking. Maybe early fifties. Strong jaw, a full head of gray hair, chin dimple, tall. He wore a pink polo and white shorts. Mom gave him one of her dazzling grins as he came up next to her.

"Emma, you won't *believe* my day," she said, looking back at me. "So I wanted to surprise you. I flew all the way over here on a red-eye, got an Uber, and came out to the address you gave me, but when I knocked on the door this handsome man answered instead."

The handsome man put a hand out. "Neil."

I shook it, realizing I was meeting our landlord. Maddy must have realized it too, because she came over with Justin following right behind her.

"This is Maddy," I said. "And that's Justin."

Mom smiled at Maddy, who gave her a stiff "hey." My date extended a hand to Neil. "Nice to meet you." They shook and Justin tipped his head at Mom, who was putting her hat back on.

"What a day," Neil said, looking at Mom. "Here I thought it was going to be just another boring Tuesday and then there's a beautiful woman standing on my porch."

She peered up at him with stars in her eyes, and he grinned.

She talked to me but looked at him. "After a minute or two we realized that you're renting his *cottage*." She turned back to me. "It was still early and I didn't want to call you and wake you up, so he invited me in for a coffee and we just couldn't stop talking. Then he got the idea to drive me out to the island and drop me off, so we got on the boat, and we just ended up cruising around instead. We spent the whole day on the water. We stopped at Lord Fletcher's and had drinks—"

"Thanks for taking care of her," Maddy said flatly.

"We were going to grill some lobsters," Neil said, putting a thumb over his shoulder toward the pool. "Would you like to join us?"

Mom gasped happily. "Yes! You should all join us! I was going to make a Bloody Mary bar!"

Maddy started shaking her head. "We're still unpacking—"

"Oh, you can do that later," Mom said, waving her off. "What's one more hour? Neil's having Maine lobsters delivered!"

"It's settled then," Neil said, rubbing his hands together. "I'll get some appetizers started."

Mom smiled up at him. "If you aren't the best host I've ever met."

He beamed and nodded to the back of the house. "Let's all head to the pool and find some shade." Then he and Mom left us standing there while they laughed and chatted on their way to the outdoor bar.

I turned stiffly back to Maddy and Justin.

"Are you kidding me with this?" Maddy hissed as soon as they were out of earshot. "She's here for what? Six hours? And she's already hypnotized our landlord?"

I chewed my lip. "We don't know that." I watched Maddy scowl at something over my shoulder and when I turned around Neil had a palm on Mom's lower back. She leaned into him in a way that definitely didn't look like this was the first time he'd touched her.

Shit.

"That woman scorches the earth," Maddy whispered. "This is so fucked."

"She'll probably only stay a few days," I said, my voice low. "It's not that big of a deal."

She scoffed. "Come on. You know *exactly* why she's here. You gave her the address, she googled it, she saw this big-ass house, and she caught the very next plane to get in on whatever you had going on. And now she's boning that guy and it's gonna be alllll the drama."

"What is she going to do?" Justin asked, looking back and forth between us.

Maddy crossed her arms. "What she always does? Show up and leave a path of destruction in her wake? She's not staying with us," she said in her end-of-discussion voice.

But it was pretty clear Mom had her eyes on a much more comfortable house than ours.

"You need to tell her to leave," Maddy said.

My head jerked back. "No!"

"What the hell do you mean no?"

"I haven't seen her in almost two years, Maddy."

"So?" She threw up a hand. "See her. But make her get a hotel room. We don't need to burn bridges with the man we're renting from. It's going to be a shitshow."

"She's not going to listen to me," I said, lowering my voice. "You know that."

Maddy rolled her eyes in the way that I knew meant she was aware. "Please tell me I don't have to stay and watch you eat crustaceans with that woman. Let's just go back to the island and you see her tomorrow or something when she's done with what's-his-face."

"I want to have dinner with my mom, Maddy."

She put a thumb to her chest. "If you stay *I* have to stay. I'm not leaving you alone to third wheel it on whatever the hell that is."

"I'll stay," Justin said.

We both looked at him.

"It's no problem," he said. "I can stay as late as you need. I can get Brad to run over and walk the dog. I don't mind."

I looked back the way Mom and Neil had gone. "The couples

thing probably *would* be a better dynamic." Considering they're on a date.

"Excellent," Maddy said. "Deal. Call me when you need me to pick you up. Justin, come push me off the dock." She turned and stomped toward the lake.

I looked back at Justin tiredly as Maddy made her way down the lawn.

"She's…intense?" he said.

I blew a breath through my nose. "She's protective. We've been through a lot together. She doesn't want to see me get hurt."

"Are you going to get hurt?"

Yes, I thought. "No," I said. "Are you sure you don't mind being here?"

Justin shook his head. "I don't mind. I like crustaceans."

"If you need to go, you totally can. Just wait until Maddy leaves so she doesn't think she's leaving me here alone."

"I wouldn't dream of leaving you." He gave me that cute, dimpled smile he'd been giving me all day.

Maddy shouted from the dock. "Justin! Are you coming or what?"

Justin grinned good-naturedly. "I'll be right back."

I watched him walk to the beach and I let out a long breath. Maddy was right. This was bad. Mom never left anywhere on good terms. Not jobs, or apartments, or relationships. *Especially* relationships.

I felt so tired all of a sudden. Seeing Mom was great, a wonderful surprise. But at the same time, I wished she wasn't here.

But then I'd just be worried about where she was.

It was like there was no peaceful place to exist, no emotional safe space. I could have chaos, or I could have worry. I could be in the tornado, or I could be in the eye. But I could never be out of the storm. It was so, *so* exhausting to live this way and I had *always* lived this way because when it came to my mother, I didn't know how to not care. I never felt calm except for the fleeting time her perfume was strong and I knew she was okay.

But *I* am never really okay.

Justin pushed Maddy off the dock and started back up the beach.

I felt relieved the instant he said he would stay with me because it let Maddy off the hook. She would walk through hell for me—and this cookout was her hell. I was glad she didn't have to be here. Sometimes her reaction to Mom was more stressful than Mom herself.

"Emma, your drink!" Mom sang, coming down from the pool with two Bloody Marys with celery, an olive, and a carrot stick poking out of the top. She made it to me the same time Justin did.

Mom gave me my glass and turned her attention on my date. "Justin." She tried to hand him his drink, but he put up a hand. "I'm not a fan of tomato juice."

"Oh. Okay. How about a beer?"

He nodded. "Sure. Thank you."

"Any requests? He's got a full bar."

"Surprise me."

"You got it." She winked at him.

Mom turned and made her way back drinking his Bloody Mary. Justin plucked the carrot out of my glass and tossed it in a bush.

"Thanks." I looked back at the lake, at Maddy fading into the distance on the pontoon. "And thanks for pushing her off."

"Yeah, I think she had an ulterior motive in asking."

I looked back at him. "Which was?"

"Uh, she threatened my life, actually. Told me if I hurt you, she'd kill me. Said they'd never find my body." He looked back at the pontoon for a second and then back to me. "I kinda believe her."

"Ugh. I'm sorry."

"It's fine. The good news is, I'm not going to hurt you, so I get to live." He nodded toward the pool. "Are you really worried about this situation?"

I chewed on my lip. "I don't know. Maybe she's doing better? She looks good."

He peered over in the direction Mom had gone. "You look just like her."

"I know."

"It's kind of hard to imagine her in jail."

I let out a sigh. "I know," I said again.

But then this was Mom at her best. Charming and fun. When she was at her worst, it wasn't hard to imagine at all.

* * *

Three hours later, we were in the pool.

It had gotten so hot, Neil offered us some spare swim trunks and bathing suits that he had in the pool house. I was in a slightly too tight tropical-looking two-piece halter with green palm fronds on it. Justin had on black trunks that fit him perfectly.

In addition to being handsome, Justin also had a *very* nice body.

Maddy had been right about his height. He was probably

about six-one. He was on the leaner side, but toned. I'd had to put sunblock on him and there was not a single part of that that I disliked.

I felt a little bad that he'd stayed. I was only able to half listen to whatever Justin and I were talking about because I was so focused on Mom, which was funny because she was *not* focused on me.

Maddy's impulse not to leave me as a third wheel had been right. Mom was so busy fawning over Neil, she was practically ignoring me.

"So what does she do for a living?" Justin asked, watching Mom laugh a little too loudly at something Neil said over by the outdoor grill. The lobsters had just been brought out and Neil was holding one up, showing it to her.

"She waits tables or bartends. She was a drink cart girl at a golf course until…today I guess."

He peered over at her. "You said you haven't seen her in almost two years?"

"Yeah."

"Weird she isn't spending more time with you."

The tiniest twinge of…I don't know what…pecked at me. Hurt? Jealousy maybe? Embarrassment that Justin noticed this— all three?

A part of me wished she hadn't met Neil so I could have more of her attention. But there was another part of me that was glad she had a distraction. That I wasn't going to have to entertain her or be fully responsible for her while she was here. But then I was simultaneously worried that she was going to do something to upset Neil and I'd have to deal with that and the Maddy fallout afterward.

My anxiety pitched around inside me, and I kept trying to bring it back to the fact that at least Mom was safe and I knew where she was and I was getting to see her—even if she didn't seem that interested in seeing me at the moment.

"It's okay," I said to Justin. "Gives me more time to hang out with you." I smiled at him, but it didn't feel like it reached my eyes.

"So why did she come anyway?" he asked.

Then suddenly I remembered. *Stuffie.* I stood up. "Mom?" I called. "Where's Stuffie?"

Mom looked over at me from her seat by the grill. "He's in my luggage. Just wait, I'll grab him."

I started climbing out of the pool. "No, I'll get him. I don't want to forget him." I picked up my towel from the recliner where I'd left it, and Justin started getting out after me.

"My bags are still in the yacht," Mom said.

Neil nodded at us. "It's open. Actually, Justin, would you mind pulling Amber's luggage down for me? She'll be staying with me."

"Sure," Justin said, toweling off.

Mom beamed up at Neil and he gave her a smitten look that I had to turn away from as I walked barefoot to the dock.

CHAPTER 10

JUSTIN

Damn," I breathed, looking around. "Have you ever been in a boat like this?"

This thing was loaded. Besides the upper deck with its full bar and lounge area, the cabin had a kitchen, two bathrooms, a primary bedroom with a king-size bed, and another room with twin beds in it. It was bigger and nicer than my apartment—and the view was better too.

Emma shook her head. "No. I've only ever seen something like this on TV. How much do you think this cost?"

"I don't know, but I'm gonna google it."

Amber's luggage sat in the middle of a spacious living room. Two large Louis Vuitton bags. Emma walked around them and flopped down on the sleek white leather couch. "Can we just hide in here for a few minutes?"

"You don't think he minds?"

"He'll probably completely forget we even exist," she

mumbled, resting her head on the cushion. "Amber has a way of making people do that," she said tiredly.

I sat down next to her. She'd sat in the middle so no matter which side I took I was going to be just slightly inside her personal space. My heart completely lost its shit.

We were both still in our borrowed bathing suits, wrapped in towels. She'd closed her eyes and I peered at her. Her skin was sun kissed. She smelled like the sunblock we were both wearing and her long hair was wet, over her shoulder.

I didn't mind staying behind with her one bit. I was glad I was asked. I hadn't been ready for the date to end three hours ago and something told me I wouldn't be ready for it to end later either.

"Kittens feel like a million years ago," she said, opening one eye to look at me. "I miss the kitten part of the day."

"We can go back tomorrow if you want. We can go after work. Or before. I'm sure Jane wouldn't mind."

She turned away from me and went quiet for a moment. "I should probably try to spend some time with my mom. I don't know how long she'll be here."

I nodded. "Right. I didn't think about that." *Damn.* "If Neil's coming, I could always go as your plus one," I offered.

"All right. I might take you up on that."

"So how long is she staying?" I asked.

"I honestly don't know."

"Well, where does she live?"

"Nowhere. Anywhere."

She stared out into the galley, deep in thought. "You know what I wish?" She paused. "I wish I could ask questions and always get the truth."

"You don't get the truth from her?"

She scoffed. "No."

I peered into the galley too. "How about we make a deal. If you ever ask me what I'm thinking, I'll always tell you the truth."

She looked at me with a raised eyebrow. "What if it's embarrassing?"

"The truth isn't supposed to be pretty, right? It's the truth."

She smiled. The first real smile I'd seen since her mom showed up. "Okay," she said. "What are you thinking right now?"

I laughed. "Wow, just coming in hot."

"Well, you said I could."

I smiled at her. Then I looked away when I realized what the answer to the What Are You Thinking question was. I glanced back at her. "This is going to be harder than I thought."

"Oh, it's that bad, is it?" She looked amused.

"It's not bad. It's just, you know, *my thoughts*."

"Okay." She tucked her leg under her. "How about this. I'll do it too."

Now I arched *my* eyebrow. "You're going to tell me what you're thinking when I ask?"

"Yup."

"So you and I are never going to bullshit each other. The stone-cold truth, on demand, no filter, whenever we want it. That's what we're agreeing on?"

"Yes. The truth, whenever we want it," she said.

"I guess we'll always know where we stand, right?"

"Right."

"We have a deal then," I said.

"We have a deal. So what are you thinking?"

I puffed my cheeks. "Damn. All right. Here we go." I looked her in the eye. "You know, this exercise is a flawed experiment because the second you asked me, my brain started to catalog all the things I'd rather you *didn't* know and now that's the stuff I'm thinking about."

She smiled.

I paused for a moment. "I'm thinking that I like you a lot more than I thought I would. I'm thinking that I probably smell because it's hot and all my deodorant washed off in the pool, and that this place would be the perfect place to kiss you like I'm supposed to, but I wouldn't because of the deodorant thing. I'm thinking that this whole thing with your mom and Neil feels weird and I can't put my finger on why. I'm thinking that I don't like her because she's ignoring you for some guy she just met, and I feel bad that I don't like her because I know you do. And then I'm wondering if I'm too hard on people, because I can't stop thinking about what you said earlier, that you should always choose empathy, and if you can choose empathy with someone like that, I should be able to do it with people I love—but I can't. I'm thinking your bathing suit looks too tight and it looks uncomfortable like it's going to leave lines on your skin. I'm thinking about what those lines would look like when you take it off—not in a sexual way, but also sort of in a sexual way." I felt my face starting to heat up a little. "Aaaaand now I'm wondering if I've said too much and what *you're* thinking."

She was grinning. "Wow. That's...a lot."

"Yeah. I agree."

"Do you regret this deal?"

"Right now, in this moment, a little bit, yeah."

She laughed.

"Now you," I said. "What are you thinking?"

She looked at me thoughtfully. "I'm thinking that I'm

embarrassed that you noticed my mom is ignoring me. I'm worried you think something's weird about Neil and her, because what if you're right? I'm thinking that you do smell a little like sweat, but that I like it for some reason. And I'm also thinking this would be a good place for you to kiss me, but now that I know you're self-conscious, I hope you don't because you'll be uncomfortable. And I also think my bathing suit is too tight, and I'll have lines when I take it off, and that I really, really want to take it off because it's starting to hurt."

"You like the way I smell?" I grinned.

"I do. Also, I'm sorry you have to kiss me. It sounds like a tough job," she said, putting out her bottom lip. "But you might want to."

She was flirting? I beamed. "I might *not* want to," I said.

"*I* might not want to."

"Oh, you will."

She twisted her lips. "Hmmmmm. Well, I do love a man with confidence."

"I've never kissed someone for the sake of breaking a curse before," I said.

"Me either."

"Good. We'll be unencumbered by technique."

She laughed. It was a loose, tinkling sound and I loved that I got it from her. When she came down from it, she sighed. "I just hope she doesn't do anything bad to him."

"Is that why you're worried about this?" I nodded in the general direction of the pool.

"There are only two types of relationships my mom gets into. The ones where they ruin her life and the ones where she ruins theirs."

"And which kind is this?"

"Definitely the second one."

I shook my head. "I don't know. He seems like a smart guy. He can probably handle himself."

"Yeah," she said, but it didn't sound like she believed it. She peered over at me. "Tell me about your mom, Justin. What's she like?"

Now *I* blew out a long breath. "Well, she's funny. Hardworking. She reads any book she can get her hands on and she remembers everything she reads, even years later. She had me really young. Same age Amber had you, actually. She's a good mom, always shows up for us—school stuff, birthdays. She makes these Italian cookies every Christmas and Easter that make me think of my childhood."

She smiled softly. "She sounds really great."

"Yeah. She is."

"But?"

So she sensed the "but." "You know, if you would have told me yesterday that today I'd be sitting half naked in a million-dollar yacht with you, I wouldn't have believed it," I said, changing the subject.

She laughed. Then she gazed at me with those kaleidoscope eyes. "I'm glad you're here."

"You are?"

"Yeah. I am."

The corner of my lip twitched.

"You know, I just realized you're the first boyfriend my mom has ever met," she said.

I grinned. "*Boyfriend?*"

"You know what I mean." She gave my knee a little push.

"No, I'll be your boyfriend. Sign me up. I mean, we're not

supposed to be dating anyone else, so we are technically exclusive. It's not far off," I said.

"Isn't this whole thing so weird? What we're doing?" she asked.

"I don't really care if it's weird. I'm just glad it's happening. And not because I want to break a curse either."

She smiled.

I cleared my throat. "So how does the boyfriend thing even work for you?" I asked. "You know, with you moving so much. If you get into a relationship, is it just long distance or…?"

"Well, right now relationships *aren't* working. That's why we're doing this, right?"

"I mean, yeah. But if you did like someone. You know, in theory."

She shrugged. "It hasn't happened yet. By the time I'm ready to move on to the next assignment, it's usually just sort of petered out."

"And if it didn't peter out?"

"I don't know. It's never happened."

She looked back into the room at Amber's bags. "I should probably look for Stuffie," she said. But she didn't get up. She peered at the luggage like she dreaded opening it and I wondered if she might find something in there she didn't want to see.

"Are you unpacked yet?" I asked, changing the subject.

"Yeah. All done the day we got here. It was just two bags."

I raised my head to look at her. "*Two?* What about all the stuff you accumulate?"

"I don't accumulate. I don't get attached."

"To what?"

She shrugged. "To anything. You know how you get a new phone and you save the box? I don't do that."

"You don't save your phone box? What if you need it?"

She gave me an amused look. "Have you ever actually needed your phone box, Justin?"

"Well, no—"

"There you go. I bet you have a whole closet full of clothes you never wear anymore. A bin full of random wires and chargers that don't go to anything—"

"They go to *something*."

"You'll never use it. Most of the stuff we hang on to we don't actually need. My entire life packs into two large suitcases. And if it doesn't, I leave whatever doesn't fit."

"That is almost terrifying," I said. "No wonder you abandon plants."

"I prefer the word 're-home.'"

"You don't want to live somewhere? Like, find a forever home where you can plant things in the earth?"

She looked back at her mom's luggage. "Maybe one day. But so far I haven't found a home I'd want to stay at forever."

"Maybe home isn't a place. Maybe it's a person."

She blew a soft breath through her nose. "Maybe it is."

She got up and went to the first bag and laid it on its side to unzip it.

"What exactly are you looking for?" I asked.

"A stuffed animal," she said, rummaging around the clothes. When she didn't find it in the first bag, she went to the second one. I knew exactly when she spotted it because she made a little happy gasp.

I watched her from behind, clutching something to her chest. "You got it?"

She nodded. "I never thought I was going to see him again."

Her voice was a little thick. She turned with a bright smile and showed me a droopy, gray, dirty unicorn with a floppy horn and a missing eye.

"Wow," I said. "He looks...old."

She looked down at him like he was a baby. "Yeah. Have you ever seen those YouTube channels where they restore dolls like this? I want to do that one day. Have his stuffing replaced and have him cleaned. Get his eye sewn back on." She brushed a gentle thumb across his forehead.

I watched her looking at this doll lovingly and just smiled softly at her.

I knew that feeling. The feeling that you're getting back a piece of your childhood. Like at Christmas when Mom would hand me a tin of her cookies and I'd be catapulted back to six years old eating them with Dad in front of the fireplace.

I deflated again, remembering what this Christmas was going to look like. And the Christmas after that, and the Christmas after that...

Amber's voice floated up from the deck. "Emma? Justin? Lobsters are ready!"

We made eye contact. Like maybe neither of us wanted to go back to the real world. But we did.

The real world doesn't like to wait.

CHAPTER 11

EMMA

When I got back to the cottage an hour later, Maddy was in the screened-in porch, reading. She wore shorts and flip-flops, and she was drinking a beer. She set down her book when I came in.

"Hey," I said, flopping into a chair. "Neil dropped me off in the yacht. He wanted to take Mom for a sunset cruise."

She rolled her eyes. "I wonder how long the honeymoon's gonna last. I give it a week."

I didn't answer. Though a week sounded about right.

"So, how was it?" she asked. She seemed de-escalated now that a few hours had passed.

"Fine. She seems okay."

"Did you get Stuffie?"

I got my purse from the floor and pulled him out to show her.

In looking at him I wondered if you see things differently in childhood. If innocence can make anything beautiful. Because he looked like he always had, but I didn't remember him being this tattered. His eye was gone and his fur was matted and dirty. His stuffing was flat and his neck hung limply.

"Wow," Maddy said. "That's him, huh?"

I set him on my thighs and sighed. "Maybe I can clean him up?"

"Maybe." She didn't sound hopeful. "And the date?" she asked.

I smiled. "He took me to play with kittens. Then we went to a cool breakfast place and then to a park with a waterfall. It was fun."

"Did you tell him no to something?"

"I did—*and* I beat him in chess. He passed both of your tests."

"Nice." She took a sip of her beer. "Does he smell good?"

"He smells *really* good."

"Did you make out with him?"

I shook my head. "No. Mom and Neil were there. It would have been weird." I looked at her. "Did you really threaten to kill him?"

"It wasn't a threat. It was a promise."

I laughed dryly. "*God.*"

"There's a chance you might actually like this guy enough for him to hurt you, and I need him to know there will be repercussions if he does."

"Wow. You've never threatened anyone before, he should feel special."

"Well, I've never seen you chase someone before."

I gasped. "I am *not* chasing Justin."

She sat up and looked dramatically around the porch. "Are we not in Minnesota right now? You have never, in the entire time

I've known you, put this much effort into a guy. You are aloof to a fault. You don't even get attached after sex. You're like a dude."

I made an indignant noise.

"I'm serious," she said. "This feels different from your normal MO and there's only so much trauma you can handle. You've met your lifetime maximum already. If he fucks with you and you unravel, I'm going to unalive him with a can opener."

I was laughing. "I don't have trauma."

She looked at me like I had two heads. "Uh yeah, you do. Your entire childhood was traumatic. You should be in therapy working out the shit that woman put you through—"

"I went to therapy. For four years. Your parents made me go all through high school. I have *resolved* trauma, there is nothing wrong with me."

"Oh yeah? Then why did you live out of a suitcase the entire time we were at home?"

"I didn't live out of a suitcase—" I said defensively.

"Yeah you did."

"I kept my suitcase under my bed and I used it to store things."

"Yup. The things you cared about. The stuff you'd take in a fire, or if Amber showed up to get you. You never once unpacked. Not really."

"So?"

"So you don't think that's weird? That you can't ever act like you actually live somewhere? That you're always ready to take off on a moment's notice?"

I shook my head at her. "I think you're reading way too much into this."

"I don't think you're reading enough into it." She sat back into her chair. "So when do you see Justin again?" she asked.

I shrugged. "Next week maybe?"

"You didn't want to see him sooner? You dragged me all the way to Minnesota, extorted me and everything to get here."

"I just feel kind of bad taking up his time when I know it's not going to lead anywhere and I'm leaving in a few weeks."

"Maybe he wants you to take up his time."

I looked down at Stuffie. "He *did* say he wanted to show me around. I don't know. I might take him up on it."

My phone vibrated, and I pulled it out to look at it. I couldn't help but note that the thought that it might be Mom made me feel preemptively exhausted.

But it wasn't Mom. It was Justin. "Oh my God…"

"What?" Maddy said. "What is it?"

"Justin sent me an exit interview."

"He *didn't.*"

I scanned it, laughing. Then I read it out loud.

1. On a scale from Awkward to Charming, how would you rate Justin's performance?

2. At any point during the date did you experience the following symptoms:

   ☐ Butterflies in your stomach
   ☐ Flushing and heating of the cheeks
   ☐ Ringing in the ears
   ☐ Unexplained arousal
   ☐ Uncontrollable laughter
   ☐ Fluttering of the heart

3. On a Scale from 1–10, how likely would you be to date Justin again if the breaking the curse thing wasn't a factor?

4. What words would you use to describe your date with Justin?

5. Any further comments?

Maddy was cracking up. "I've gotta give it to him, he does put in the effort."

I was smiling at my screen. "Yeah, he does."

"That was nice of him to stay with you."

It was nice. Justin had impressed me. He was a little more than I'd expected, in more ways than one.

"So?" Maddy said. "If you weren't breaking a curse together, how likely would you be to date him again?"

I twisted my lips thinking about it. Then I checked 10.

CHAPTER 12

JUSTIN

When I got to my apartment, Brad was in my kitchen eating leftovers out of my fridge.

"Hey," I said, coming in, my dog jumping at my feet. "You didn't have to wait for me."

"I'm not. I'm having dinner." He took a bite out of the pulled pork sandwich he'd put together. He nodded at it while he chewed. "I don't miss your ass much, but I do miss your cooking," he said.

I smirked. "I had grilled lobster for dinner. In the backyard of a mansion on Lake Minnetonka."

"Daaaamn, you are pulling out all the stops for that girl."

I sat down on my office chair and my dog hopped in my lap. "No, it's a long story."

He took another bite, leaning on the counter. "How was it? Do you like her?"

"I don't think 'like' covers it," I said, petting my dog.

"Reeeallly?"

"Yeah. Really."

"Aren't you guys supposed to break up though?" Brad asked.

That whole thing felt so unimportant to me at the moment, I'd almost entirely forgotten about the reason she'd come here. My goal had officially shifted. This was *not* a woman I wanted to end things with after four dates. I was already thinking of ways I could make our dates more special, things I could bring her or places I could take her.

I set Brad down on the floor and leaned over my keypad to send Emma an exit interview I made for her. "Hey, what do you think about Glensheen Mansion in Duluth," I asked. "You think she'd like it? Should I take her there?"

Brad ate the rest of his sandwich. "Sure. That place is cool. So what does she think of you taking the kids in a few weeks?"

I felt the high from today evaporate. She didn't know about the kids.

I didn't tell her at first because I didn't like to talk about it. And anyway, it wasn't really going to matter since it wasn't going to affect her. I never thought she'd come to Minnesota. In fact, I'd been pretty sure I wasn't ever going to meet her at all. And now I had, and meeting her was bigger than I thought and I did have to tell her.

I wouldn't have the kids forever, but it'd be long enough to matter. I wondered if that would change things for her.

I was getting ahead of myself. We'd been on one date. I didn't even know if she liked me, and as of right now she was scheduled to leave in six weeks. I just had to focus on showing her a good time and getting to know her, and maybe, possibly, getting her to stay a little longer than she planned. I'd worry about the rest when I had to.

"I haven't told her yet," I said. "I haven't gotten around to it."

"Well, you better hurry. That shit's coming up."

"Yeah," I said. "I know."

He wiped his fingers with a napkin. "Hey, I saw your mom earlier."

I kept my eyes to the screen. "Oh yeah?"

"Yeah. I actually wanted to talk to you about that. I think you need to spend more time with her," he said.

My jaw flexed. "No."

"Why?" he asked.

I turned to him. "Because I don't want to?"

He shook his head. "I don't think she's doing great, man. She's your mom. She needs your support."

"I *do* support her. I'm dropping my whole life in a week to pick up the pieces she's leaving. There's not one thing she's asked me to do that I haven't done."

"That's not what I'm talking about and you know it."

I looked away from him.

"Look, I get that it's hard," he said. "It's shitty and fucked up. *Nobody* likes it. But she can't undo it, man. She would if she could."

"Yeah, well she can't."

Brad let the silence stretch out between us. It was useless arguing about this. Nothing he said would change how I felt. I could *not* forgive her for this. I didn't want to spend more time with her or pretend like any of this was okay.

"I'm playing nice," I said. "I do what she needs me to do. I'm polite and I'm speaking to her. And frankly that's more than she deserves."

I saw him give up the argument. He knew me well enough to know the conversation was over.

He pulled away from the counter. "All right. You're gonna do what you're gonna do." He knocked a knuckle on the granite. "I'll see you."

"Yeah. I'll see you."

He let himself out.

I dragged a hand down my mouth and swiveled to face the balcony. The Toilet King leered into my apartment.

If you can choose anger or empathy, always choose empathy.

I couldn't. At this point anger was all I had.

I got up and closed the blinds.

CHAPTER 13

EMMA

I swear to God, I smell like rust," Maddy whispered, sniffing her arm. "Do I smell like rust? That water at the cottage is so gross."

We were walking through the halls of the surgical floor of Royaume Northwestern behind the charge nurse, Hector, assigned to give us a tour. We'd done paperwork, gotten our badges, trained on Royaume's electronic medical record system. The tour was the last part of the day, then we'd get our schedules and go home. Our first real shift was tomorrow.

"I can't tell if you smell like rust because I probably smell like it too," I whispered.

"We need a third party to confirm. Do you think Justin would have told you if you smelled?"

I thought about it, and our new agreement to be brutally honest with each other. "Yeah, I actually do." I sniffed the inside of my shirt. I couldn't smell it, but maybe I was used to it? "We're probably okay. Though I'm showering in the locker room whenever I can."

"Ick. Same. Probably better to wash up in the lake."

Hector's shoes squeaked ahead of us. "Pyxis is in there, cafeteria's on the ground floor. The chief of surgery is Dr. Rasmus-
sen," he said in a Mexican accent. "Stay out of his way, and hope
to God he never notices you enough to make direct eye contact
with you."

Maddy gave me a face that meant to remind me she'd called
this when we signed up for Med Surg.

"He's that bad?" I asked.

He scoffed and looked over his shoulder at me. "There's a reason we need travel nurses in this department, people quit left and
right. He is craaaaanky. Super smart but he does *not* like anyone
who doesn't do their job, so don't be messing anything up. He's
in a good mood today though. Maybe he won his game of golf
yesterday." He laughed at his own joke.

Maddy gave me a look.

"What's your favorite thing from the cafeteria?" I asked,
changing the subject.

"The chicken and wild rice soup," he said. He glanced at us.
"Where are you guys originally from anyway?"

"California," Maddy said.

"Glendale," I clarified.

"Hmmm. Nice. Warm. Not like here. A couple of months
from now, that lake you're stayin' at will be so frozen you can
walk across it." He stopped talking and came to attention. "There
he is," he said, lowering his voice.

I peered past him at the doctor in the blue scrubs coming
toward us. I sucked in a shock of air.

Maddy froze. "What in the seventh circle of hell is *this*?" she
breathed.

Neil was making his way down the hall.

He saw us and his serious face broke into a grin. "Emma, Maddy, nice to see you again!"

We were both rendered mute. Even Hector's jaw was open.

"How are you enjoying your first day at Royaume?" he asked, stopping in front of us.

I swallowed. "It's...it's great?"

"Good, good. Happy to see you ended up in my department. I wasn't sure where they'd put you."

"Did...did you know we were working here?" I asked, confused. I hadn't mentioned I was a nurse. Maybe Mom did? But she didn't know I was coming to Royaume either.

"Of course. I gave the agency the info for the cottage. Figured travel nurses would make good renters. If there's anything the cottage needs, you two just let me know. I haven't been out there in years—how's the landscaping?"

I licked my lips. "Um...fine?"

"Just fine?" He crossed his arms. "What does the place need, tell me, don't be shy."

"Uh...some hostas might look nice?" I said cautiously. "Maybe around the sides of the house where it's shady? You could put rock cress along the slopes by the stairs where there's full sun? Pretty ground coverage, deer resistant."

He looked pleasantly surprised. "You garden."

I nodded. "Yeah. My mom taught me, actually. She's got a green thumb."

He shook his head with a grin. "Just when I thought that woman couldn't impress me more. Any interest in doing it for me?"

"Sure?"

"Wonderful. Just get me receipts and I'll take the cost off the rent."

"Okay."

He grinned back and forth between us. "Maybe we can get together for dinner later this week, once you've gotten settled in," he said. "Amber and I would love to have you."

Amber and I. Like they were an item.

I glanced at Maddy. "We can't wait."

He looked at his watch. "Perfect. Well, I'm off. See you at the house."

He moved past us and was gone.

Maddy and I turned to each other, wide-eyed, and Hector crossed his arms. "Something you ladies want to tell me?"

Maddy spoke first. "We're renting his lake house and he knows her mom."

He looked us up and down with pursed lips. "Uh-huh. Well, he must like her. I've never seen him that nice to anyone. Go check in at the nurses' station for your assignments and you can go." Then he left too.

As soon as he was out of earshot, Maddy whirled on me. "Is this a joke? Please tell me this is some prank show. The mood of our boss is dependent on his relationship with *Amber*?"

I licked my lips. "You heard Hector—he's never been this nice."

"Uh yeah, because Amber hasn't unleashed the kraken yet. Do you know how fucked we are?"

"She's doing really well," I said defensively.

"Yeah? And you think she's going to do well for the whole time we have to work with that guy? She's gonna burn his fucking house down and we're gonna be left there with the garden hose.

This is my nightmare," she whispered. "Med Surg, Amber, and *this*?"

"I'll talk to her," I said. "When we get back."

"Good. Make her leave. He'll be upset for a bit, but it's better than the alternative. Just tear off the Band-Aid."

"Yeah."

But I knew Maddy was right. We were fucked.

CHAPTER 14

EMMA

After work, I rang the bell to the mansion and stood there fidgeting. Mom hadn't answered a single text all day.

Maddy was in the pontoon on the dock, playing games on her phone waiting for me. She'd sent me like an ambassador for Rust Water Cottage to try to convince Mom to leave.

It was never going to happen. I knew this. But Maddy wouldn't let it go unless I tried—and really, I *should* try. Maddy was right, this whole situation was a ticking time bomb.

I had this sinking, sickly feeling of being out of control. A gnawing anxiety of what was to come. Mom always made me feel like this, I realized. When she was here, when she wasn't here. A gaping, bottomless impending feeling of doom.

I rang the bell again in quick succession. A few seconds later I heard a bolt lock turn and when the door finally opened, it was Maria.

"Hi, is my—"

"You here for your madre?" she said, annoyed. She pushed the door open and stood with her arms crossed while I peered past her into the house.

The door opened to a large vestibule, and beyond that was a spacious living room. Huge vaulted ceilings, white sofas, a shiny black baby grand piano—and Mom, on a ten-foot ladder with her back to us...painting a wall?

I blinked at her. "What— Mom, what are you doing?" I called.

"She can't hear you," Maria said. "She has to have music for inspiration." She put her fingers in quotes. "Ésta casa se está yendo a la mierda," she mumbled. "Already like she owns the place." She threw up a hand. "Well? Come in."

I walked into the house.

Mom stood at the top of the ladder barefoot in denim capris. She wore a men's button-down shirt knotted in the middle with the sleeves rolled up, probably Neil's. It was too big to be hers. Her long hair was tied back into a red bandana. Half a dozen brushes and paint cans sat open and scattered on a clear plastic sheeting under the ladder. I was practically underneath her before she spotted me. "Emma!" She pulled out her earbuds. "You're back!"

She set her brush on top of the paint can she was using and started down the ladder. "I've been waiting all day. What do you think?" She gestured to the mural she was working on, beaming.

I peered up at it. Large colorful roses. It was a whimsical design. Bold and beautiful.

Mom had always been artistic. I remembered the time she did face painting at a Renaissance fair for a few weeks when I was ten. She'd paint my face first and then let me run loose for the rest of the day to watch the roving performers and pet baby goats in the petting zoo. It was one of the best summers of my life.

This summer was up for debate.

"It's nice," I said, watching her climb down. "But is Neil okay with you doing this to his wall?"

She got to the bottom rung and hopped off. "Who do you think paid for the paint? I pitched the idea to him this morning and he *loved* it." She put her hands on her hips and looked up at it. "I mean of course he did, *look* at this place, it's like living in an asylum. All this white, it's depressing. I'm going to do the whole wall, top to bottom, first thing you see when you come in. It's going to change his *life*, completely different energy."

I studied her while she studied her work. She looked good. Her makeup was done, she seemed rested. She seemed *happy*. The light scent of her rose perfume reached my nose like a gentle whisper telling me to relax.

She snapped her fingers and turned back to me. "Oh!" she said, like she just remembered something. "Come with me to the kitchen. I got you something."

She grabbed me by the hands and walked backward a few steps before turning to lead me through the house. I followed in the wake of her perfume, peering around. The home was enormous. And she was right, it was white—and stark and slate and cold. It was all very...surgical.

"This is old money," she whispered, nodding at an expensive-looking vase on a pedestal. "It just feels different, right? Sort of regal."

"He lives here alone?" I asked.

"I think so. Well, Maria has a room somewhere, but that's it." She looked over her shoulder and gave me a wry look. "Did I tell you what he does? A *surgeon*."

"Uh, I know. I work with him at Royaume."

Mom stopped to gawk at me. "*What?*" She paused for a dramatic moment. Then she burst into sparkling laughter. "Well, I guess it's nice I'm showing him a good time then!"

"Mom, I have to talk to you about that—"

"About what?" She cocked her head.

"I just…he's our landlord and Maddy and I have to work with him and—"

"And?" She blinked at me innocently.

"It just…it feels like a conflict of interest for you to get involved with him." I hoped it came out diplomatically. I didn't want to hurt her feelings, but I also needed her to understand the stakes.

Her expression turned amused. "Emma, we are two grown adults. What does it even have to do with you?"

I licked my lips. "Things don't tend to end well with you and men. I can't afford for this to implode. Please."

She rolled her eyes. "Sweetheart, I know that in the past I've picked some winners. Believe me, I know. But this guy is *different*. He's good at his job, he's got all these awards everywhere. He owns things, no criminal record, he's sweet, and he goes to therapy—"

"He goes to therapy?"

"Yeah. He's *really* focused on self-improvement. Our therapists sound a lot alike actually."

I blinked at her. "You have a therapist?"

"Yeah, I told you."

I shook my head. "No, you didn't."

"I've been going for like two years now. It's virtual."

I shifted on my feet. "Well…well what do they say?"

She shrugged. "I don't know. Lots of stuff. She's expensive as hell. Insurance won't cover a dime. But I haven't missed one session."

I felt a weight on my chest lift. *Therapy.* Never, in my whole life, had she gone to therapy.

"Mom, that's really great," I said, relief in my voice.

"Baby, I am doing *so* well. I have never been this Zen. I'm in a really good place, you'd be so proud of me. And Neil? He likes me. I like him. We're having fun. Nothing bad is going to happen, we're just enjoying each other, I don't want you to worry about it."

I let out a breath. I still didn't feel a hundred percent, but what else could I do? I couldn't make her stop seeing him. All I could do was let her know my concerns and hope she'd behave.

"Okay," I said. "I won't worry."

"Good." She turned and started walking again.

She gave me a tour as we went, showing me all the things Neil must have shown her. Expensive paintings, sculptures he'd picked up during his travels. An office with a view of the pool and about a million framed degrees and diplomas on the walls.

When we got to the kitchen, she stopped in the doorway and held out her arms. "Here we are! Ta-da!"

I looked past her into the room. The large granite island was *covered* in white buckets full of flowers. Every inch.

"What *is* this?" I said.

She left me in the entry and breezed into the kitchen to pluck a peony from the water. "I stopped at a farmers' market on the way back from the paint store and there was a stand with the most beautiful flowers and I thought, *Why not?* We need to brighten this place up." She sniffed the petals.

I shook my head at the room. "How did you afford all these? Did you buy the whole stand?"

"Yup. And paid them fifty bucks to drop them off. Neil gave me his Amex and told me I could get whatever I wanted for the house." She lowered her voice. "What's-her-face is supposed to be putting them in vases, but I swear to God that woman moves like she's being paid by the hour." She rolled her eyes. "Anyway, I'm going to have these all over when he gets home. I got some potted herbs for the kitchen, heirloom tomatoes for a caprese before dinner. And smell this." She put the peony back in water and brought a candle to me and held it under my nose. "Roses." She smiled. "Soy, handmade, organic goat's milk candles. I'm putting them *everywhere*." She leaned in conspiratorially. "I made gem water too. Put rose quartz in a spray bottle, misted all over the bedroom. Enhance the love energy and improve the qi—it is *way* off in this place. I mean, he's a Taurus with Mercury in Aries, so it all makes sense looking around here, but still."

She set the candle down on the counter and peered around the cavernous kitchen. "You know what? This man needed me." She gazed back at me thoughtfully. "I think he's been sleepwalking. I'm going to wake him up."

I felt my face soften, despite myself. *This* was the Mom I loved.

This was my favorite version of her. The vibrant, happy, spiritual one who made my Halloween costumes by hand, and they were always so good the other kids were jealous. The Mom who turned an old shed in the yard of our rental into a beautiful playhouse, the Mom who woke me up on my birthday with confetti pancakes covered in gummy bears and those trick candles that don't blow out.

It was so easy to love this version. Maybe she would *stay* this version. Maybe she *was* doing okay. Getting help. Settling down with age, wanting something steadier.

And maybe she and Neil *were* different. She was right, he wasn't like the men she usually dated. He was stable and educated. He had his own money. He didn't need anything from her but *this*.

For a second, I let myself imagine. Pretended that five years from now I'd be coming here for Christmas. Maybe they'd be married and she'd be comfortable, living with all this wealth and privilege, and he'd be happy because his life had been graced by a beautiful, charming muse.

I wanted it *so* badly. Even though experience and common sense told me not to hope, it burst into life inside me anyway.

"This one's for you," Mom said, turning and reaching into the sea of buckets. She pulled out one filled with red roses. "For the cottage. I know you love them."

The corner of my lip quirked up. "Thanks."

"Are you hungry? I was going to make my garlic lemon shrimp with polenta for dinner. Neil won't be home until late—I guess the guy works a million hours a week or something—but I can start it now and we can crack open a bottle of white. You should see the wine cellar, oh my God, it's *amazing*. You go grab a bottle and I'll start the sauce—I want to hear *all* about Justin." Her eyes sparkled.

I deflated a little. "I can't, Maddy's waiting for me in the boat."

Mom put her lower lip out. "I feel like I haven't even *seen* you. Go get her, she can eat with us."

"No," I said, a little too quickly. "I...it's just we're tired. We worked today. Maybe tomorrow?"

She sighed deeply. "Okay." Then she bounced a little. "This is going to be the best summer! We're together again, we're both in love—"

She came over and hugged me. I breathed her in and my muscles relaxed.

Roses.

* * *

When I came back out to the pontoon, Maddy was lying on her back on one of the ratty vinyl seats with a straw hat over her face that she must have found in a storage compartment.

"Hey," I said.

She whipped the hat off and sat up. "God, finally. What took you so long?" Then she eyed the bucket of roses I was holding. "Uh, what's that?"

"Mom gave them to me," I said, setting them into the boat.

"Okay. Random." She looked back up at me. "Well? What did she say?"

I breathed in deep. "I think it's going to be okay."

She looked skeptical. "Okay. Okay *how*?"

"She's in therapy. I think she's trying to be different," I said.

Her face immediately called bullshit. "Right. So she's what? Going to squat here until she goes off the rails again and Neil throws her out? Then we get to apologize for her and God knows what the fuck else?"

I blinked at her. "Maddy, what do you want me to do? I can't control her. I can't tell her to break it off. And why can't we just give her the benefit of the doubt for once?"

"Because she sucks? We're gonna end up paying for the shit

she steals and then we get to work with him in the aftermath until we leave."

"You don't know that—"

"Yeah, I *do*. You should warn him. Tell him what she is so he can make an educated decision whether to keep messing with her."

My jaw set. "No."

She pulled her face back. "*No?*"

"No. I'm not going to sabotage her relationship."

"So you're okay with him dating a psychopath?"

"Do not call her that!" I snapped.

Maddy looked at me in shock. I never yelled at her.

"You know what?" I said. "Go home without me."

Her mouth dropped open. "What? *Why?*"

"I don't want to see you right now."

She gawked. "You're pissed at me?"

"Yeah, I am." I shook my head at her. "I am so *tired* of this, Maddy."

"Then be mad at *her*! Not at me for pointing her shit out!"

"You think I don't know?! You think I don't fucking see that something is wrong with her?"

She blinked at me. I'd never admitted this. Not like this.

I shook my head at her. "You want to warn him, Maddy? Go ahead. Ruin her chances for a normal life with a normal man, send her back out into the universe where I won't know where she is or if she's even alive. Go ahead. But *I'm* not doing it. I'm not going to undo whatever progress she's made in therapy by throwing her past back in her face and trying to destroy her life when she's trying to be better. Leave her alone."

She stared at me, shocked.

I turned and started for the house.

"Emma!"

I kept walking. My eyes started to tear up. I *hated* fighting with Maddy. We almost never argued. But why wouldn't she just let me have this? This *one* thing?

Mom had never been in therapy before. She'd never met a nice guy like this before. Maybe things could be different, and I just wanted Maddy to see that and let me have my stupid, pitiful fucking hope.

I made my way back through the pool area to the French doors off the kitchen to find Mom. But when I got to the door, I saw Neil through the glass.

He must have come home early. He was standing with Mom by the center island beaming at the flowers. Mom was hugging him and he had his hands under her ass.

I pivoted to put my back to the side of the house before they saw me. I squeezed my eyes shut, willing myself not to cry. When I opened them, I could see Maddy already pushing off the dock and heading to the cottage.

I took in a shuddering breath and went down to the pool. I plopped heavily onto a reclining chair by the cold firepit just as thunder rumbled overhead.

I wanted to sob. For half a dozen different reasons, I wanted to sob. I wasn't going to admit defeat and call Maddy back to come get me. I wasn't going to be the third wheel with Mom and Neil either. I didn't have a car, Maddy had the keys.

I swiped at my tears with the side of my hand. I could feel myself getting small. Shrinking into myself the way I always did when something stressful or awful happened. Retreating into my own brain.

When I got like this, I didn't want to see anyone or talk to anyone. I could shut down for days. Turn off my phone, call out of work, abandon my social media. Not answer the door for anyone or anything, cut off everyone until I felt safe enough to start to let them in again a little at a time. But I had nowhere to vanish.

I wasn't home. I didn't have my wallet *or* my purse—they were in the boat. I was sitting on a pool chair, out in the open, still wearing my scrubs with a storm rolling in. The sun was going down. In a few minutes the mosquitoes would start to come out.

I sat there, feeling overexposed and getting more and more upset and there was nothing I could do to hide from it and no place to bury myself and nowhere to go. My chin quivered.

Then my phone chirped.

Justin: How was your first day at work?

I sniffled and sent a thumbs-down emoji and put my face in my hands.

My phone started to ring. I raised my head and watched it chime for a few long moments. And I don't know what part of me decided to answer before I got too small to do it, but I did.

"Hey," I said. I tried my best not to let him hear the thickness in my throat.

"Hey. What happened? Why was it bad?"

I rubbed my forehead. "It's a lot to explain." I paused. "Do you want to have dinner? My night just freed up."

It wasn't a quiet room behind a closed door, but it was somewhere to go. I'd be with someone safe and removed from what was happening with Mom and Maddy. And at least I wouldn't be outside, sitting by a pool, hoping I didn't set off the motion sensor lights after it got dark.

God.

I had to move the phone away from my mouth because I wanted to cry.

"Yeah, I can totally do dinner," he said. "But I'm babysitting. I didn't think I was going to see you, so I told my mom I'd watch Chelsea."

I felt myself deflate. "Oh. Okay. That's all right. I'll just see you—"

"No, come. I'm making spaghetti. We can watch a movie or something. Can you get over here? If not, I can pick you up."

"Justin…I don't think I should meet your family."

He laughed a little. "Why?"

"Because I don't do that with guys I date."

"Aw, come on." He sounded amused. "She's four. It's not like you're meeting my mom. And anyway, I met your mom. What's the big deal? Besides, I'm not really a guy you're dating, right? What are the rules for curse-breaking arrangements? I feel like there's wiggle room."

I let a small smile crack.

"My dog is here," he added. "You can meet Brad."

I *did* want to meet Brad…

I drew in a long breath through my nose. "You know this isn't going to count as one of our dates, right?"

"I zero percent care about that."

I looked up and peered out at the shrinking image of Maddy boating off into the distance. Behind me I heard Mom shriek with laughter from somewhere in the house. I really didn't want to meet Justin's family. Not even the four-year-old. It was a rule I didn't break. Ever.

But I had nowhere else to go and no one to go to. Nowhere to be small.

"Okay. I'll call an Uber."

* * *

Justin's mom's house was a two-story in a quiet suburban neighborhood. There were little butterfly flags in the planters and a red tricycle by the garage. The driveway next to Justin's car was full of children's chalk drawings.

This was the kind of house that had a bouncy slide in the backyard during birthday parties and Christmas lights on the holidays. I knew without knowing that on Halloween Justin's mom handed out candy dressed in a costume while jack-o'-lanterns flickered on the steps, and on Easter she'd hide pastel eggs around the yard.

It was funny, but seeing this brought Justin full circle for me. This is why he was well balanced and level. He'd had a good childhood. I could tell. And I wondered if it was as obvious that I hadn't.

Justin had come out onto the front porch to meet me when my Uber pulled up. The second I saw him I was glad I came. He wasn't Mom, and he wasn't Maddy. He was a break. And he was happy to see me. It was impossible not to feel better when I saw him as I got out of the car.

"Hey," I said, coming down the walkway.

He went right in and gave me a hug.

It was nothing but friendly. He didn't hold me for longer than he should. But I found myself sort of wishing he would have. I needed the hug, I realized. And Justin was a *really* good hugger. Warm and firm, like he'd given and received a lot of hugs in his life.

He was in a T-shirt and jeans. He hadn't done anything with his hair like he had yesterday. It was shaggy and loose the way it was the day we video called on his walk. I decided I liked this better. It was the kind of hair you wanted to run your fingers through. The kind that came with lazy Sunday mornings and familiarity.

He looked at what I was wearing and smiled. "Scrubs."

"I came right from work."

I heard a dog-crying noise from the door and peered around him. Brad was scratching at the screen.

Justin nodded over his shoulder. "Come on. Meet my dog."

The little Brussels Griffon bounced off my legs in the vestibule, and I knelt down to pet him.

"Justin, he's so cute!" He licked the underside of my chin and I laughed.

"He's better now that the mange is gone," Justin said. "I guess he is pretty cute these days."

Brad lunged to lick me on the lips, and I fell backward on my bottom and burst into laughter. Justin was beaming from his spot by the door. Then I saw the little girl peeking around the corner. She had wispy brown hair and Justin's brown eyes. She was barefoot and wore a light blue nightgown.

"Hello," I said.

She pulled back a little, only one eye visible from the doorframe.

Justin crouched. "Chels, come here." She paused for a moment, like she was thinking about it. Then she darted into his arms. He scooped her up and stood. "This is my friend Emma. Can you say hi?"

She peered at me shyly as I got to my feet. "Hi," she said softly.

I noticed a Band-Aid on her knee. "Oh, did you get a boo-boo?"

She nodded.

"Emma's a nurse," Justin said. "Maybe she can change your Band-Aid for you later."

"An Elsa one," she said, quickly.

"We have those," Justin said, winking at me.

"I can work with that." I smiled.

She put her head on Justin's shoulder and my heart melted a little. He was her safe person. The dog was sitting by his feet now too and I remembered what Maddy said about dogs, that they always tell you who the good people are.

Justin nodded toward the back. "Dinner's ready. Let's go eat."

I followed him through the house. It was a comfortable home—the lived-in kind. The living room had a sofa with a gray tweed slipcover, a multicolored carpet. A dark wood coffee table, a toy bin next to a child-size easel. A backpack was tossed onto a chair, framed family photos sat on a buffet table against the wall.

"Did you ever live here?" I asked.

"Yeah, but not until I was sixteen, so only for a bit. Sarah has my room now."

"So you lived with Brad longer than you lived in this house."

"I did," he said. "We had an almost ten-year streak. There was a three-month period where he was living with his girlfriend Celeste in South Dakota, but it didn't last."

"He couldn't quit you, huh?"

"Not until now."

The kitchen had a stainless fridge with photos and children's drawings stuck to the front. There was a blue backsplash and a wooden table to seat six in the breakfast nook. Justin put his sister in a chair with a booster seat and pulled one out for me. Then he moved to the stove and started plating pasta.

"It's nothing fancy," he said. "It's jarred sauce. I kinda spruced it up a bit, put in some red wine and some ground beef. But I *did* make the garlic bread."

"It smells good." My stomach grumbled, and I realized how hungry I was. I'd barely eaten at work. The anxiety of finding out about Neil had killed my appetite.

"So tell me about your day," he said, over the stove.

I scoffed a little. "Guess who I work with?"

"Who?" He put a red plastic plate of food in front of his sister and gave her a fork.

"Neil."

He stopped to stare at me. "No way."

"Yeah. He's a surgeon. Chief of surgery actually."

"Are you serious? He's your boss?"

"The charge nurse is my boss, but Neil could still make my life miserable if he wanted to. So yeah."

Justin set a cup of juice with a lid in front of Chelsea and put a piece of garlic bread on the plate he was serving and placed it in front of me. The garlic bread was a half of a toasted hot dog bun that he'd smeared with butter and sprinkled with dill and garlic salt. It made me smile. The meal was the kind of thrown-together one Mom used to make. It was comfort food.

It was exactly what I needed.

"Thanks," I said.

"So are you still worried about the Amber thing?" He handed me a Starbucks napkin and a glass of V8 fruit punch and then sat with his own food.

"I don't know," I said, looking at the napkin. "It's not great."

He nodded at the napkin. "My mom," he explained. "I never, in my entire childhood, used a store-bought paper napkin. They were all from fast-food places. Not that we'd eaten out a lot. One or two times a month if we were lucky. But Mom was *very* good at coaxing extra napkins out of cashiers."

"Where is she tonight?"

He twirled his pasta in his fork. "Cleaning an office building. Sarah's at a sleepover, and Alex is at an amusement park with a friend. He'll get home before Mom and then we can leave. He can watch Chelsea. No meeting the parents, as requested." He smirked and took a bite.

I gave him a look. "It's not personal. I just don't do that."

He swallowed. "No, I get it. I get the full Amber/Neil/Maddy death-threat submersion experience and you just get to vibe."

I snorted. "I'm sorry. Am I the a-hole?"

He smiled. "Nah. You're all right."

We ate dinner and I told him about the whole day while I helped Chelsea color a picture of Elsa. I told him about Mom painting the wall, the flowers, the fight with Maddy. He mostly listened. When I finished the spaghetti, I asked for seconds and he got up and served me more.

"Do you think Maddy's right?" I asked. "Should I tell him?"

He sucked air through his teeth. "That's hard," he said, putting my plate in front of me and sitting back down. "If she's turned over a new leaf, I can see why you wouldn't want to get involved. It's kind of messed up to bring up old stuff. And it's not like he's marrying her or something, they're just having fun, right?"

"Yeah."

"Then let them have fun. Let him make his own decision about her. The guy's not an idiot."

I nodded, feeling a little better about my decision.

Chelsea squirmed in her seat. "Jussin, I'm done."

He set his fork down and got up again. "Okay. Let me clean your face and then you can go watch *Frozen* until bedtime."

I watched him take a wipe and get the sauce off her mouth and her hands. When he let her go, she ran out of the kitchen toward the living room. He followed her to put on her movie. I smiled after them.

When he came back, I was washing dishes.

"You didn't have to do that," he said, coming up next to me as I set the pot in the drying rack.

"It's no problem, *Jussin*."

He grinned and picked up a towel to start drying. I'd already loaded the dishwasher and started it, it was just the big stuff left to wash.

"Do you babysit a lot?" I asked.

He laughed dryly, but he didn't get to reply. The sound of a door slamming came from the front of the house. Justin checked his watch and leaned back to peer down the hall. "Alex? You home? You're early."

But it wasn't a teenage boy who came down the hallway, it was a young girl with a pink backpack slung over her shoulder.

He wrinkled his forehead. "Sarah. I thought you were spending the night at Josie's."

She looked around the kitchen, bored. "She's being a bitch. I don't want to hang out with her."

"Uh, does Mom let you talk like that?" Justin said.

She rolled her eyes. "You asked me."

"How did you get home?"

"I walked?"

He shook his head. "I don't want you walking alone at night. You need to call me next time."

"It's like three blocks—"

"I don't care. It's late."

She looked annoyed. "Fine. Whatever." Then she looked at me. "Who are you?"

"This is Emma," Justin said.

"Is she your girlfriend?" she said, looking me up and down.

"Yes."

The corner of my lip twitched. I know we'd agreed on that title, but it still surprised me to hear it out loud.

"Nice to meet you," I said.

I'd never seen someone roll their eyes without actually rolling their eyes, but she somehow managed it anyway.

"There's spaghetti—" Justin said.

"I ate at Josie's. I'll be in my room." And she left.

Justin looked at me with an amused expression while we listened to her stomp up the stairs and slam the door.

"She's twelve and at the hating-everything stage," he said. "Were you like that when you were twelve?" he asked, taking the cookie sheet from me to dry.

"I didn't have the luxury of being like that. I had to be invisible."

He drew his brows down. "What do you mean?"

I shrugged. "I couldn't really be needy or crabby. It just made Mom worse. And then when I was in foster care, I didn't want to draw attention to myself."

"Why?"

"Because being difficult is the best way to get sent back? Or getting the crap beat out of you?"

He stopped and stared at me. "Did anyone ever do that to you?"

I looked at the sink as I scrubbed it out. "I have seen the good, the bad, and the ugly of the foster care system, Justin. And there's definitely all three. Maddy's parents were the good. I got really lucky with them."

A little twinge of guilt stabbed at me suddenly, remembering I wasn't going home for the anniversary party. It didn't stab at me because I felt bad I wasn't going. It stabbed at me because I felt bad that I *didn't* feel bad.

What was *wrong* with me? These people had saved me.

Maybe Maddy was right. Maybe I was aloof to a fault. Except with Mom. With Mom I felt everything, all the time.

"What are you thinking?" Justin asked, snapping me out of it.

I looked up at him. "Was I making a face?"

"A little bit."

I started rinsing the sink. "I'm thinking that my mom takes a lot out of me. And that maybe she doesn't leave anything for anyone else."

He nodded slowly like he understood.

"There's this thing that I do," I said. "It's…never mind. It's hard to explain." I shut off the water.

"No, explain it," he said, handing me the towel. "Tell me."

I leaned my hip on the counter. "I have this thing where I get small," I said, looking at the towel as I dried my hands. "I get really withdrawn and I just want to be alone."

"Everybody feels like that sometimes."

I shook my head. "No. It's bigger than that." I stopped and he waited for me to go on. "When I was little, I couldn't really count on anyone. I mean, really I *couldn't*. My mom was so all over the place and we were always moving. I'd get a friend or a teacher I liked and then they'd just be gone because I'd go live somewhere else. So I became an island—and the island is small. I don't need anyone. And I know that sounds sort of terrible, but it's actually comforting to know that I have this ability to need no one. It feels like a superpower. Like I'm untouchable."

He was studying me quietly, listening.

"Usually Maddy is on the island. And Mom is on the island. Everyone else is on the shore. And sometimes I wish I could go get them, but I just…can't. I don't have the space for them. And I know that it hurts people, but it's just who I am. And it makes me feel like a horrible person."

He shook his head. "I don't think you're a horrible person. I think you went through something horrible and that's who you needed to become to get through it."

"Maybe." I had to look away from him. "I'm sorry. I'm just in a funk today."

He dipped his head to look me in the eye. "You only have two people on your island and you're worried about one and fighting with the other one. I'd be in a funk too."

I gave him a little smile. "You know, I was almost too small to come here tonight."

"I'm glad you did."

The corner of my lip turned up. "I'm glad I did too."

CHAPTER 15

JUSTIN

Emma helped give Chelsea a bath, then changed her Band-Aid afterward. It was just a Band-Aid, but watching how gentle and sweet Emma was with my sister made me smile.

After that we moved to the living room and sat on the sofa to watch *Frozen*, me at one end and Emma at the other because Chelsea wanted to be in the middle curled up against me. Brad jumped into my lap and I was officially buried.

Emma smiled at me from the other end of the couch. "You're like a docking station for small vulnerable dependents."

"Well, we all need a job."

She laughed.

When Chelsea fell asleep, I carried her up to bed. When I came down, I sat back in my corner. I didn't want to assume Emma wanted me closer.

She looked at me, amused. "All the way over there?"

"Well, I don't want to crowd you. Though the docking station is available if you'd like to give it a try."

She made a show of thinking about it. "You know, I *would* like to give it a try. See what all the fuss is about."

I grinned and made a come-here motion with my hand and she scooted over and let me put an arm around her. The highlight of my entire week, hands down.

"So what do you want to watch?" I asked, hoping she couldn't feel my heart racing, though I was pretty sure she could.

She tilted her head up and her mouth was *very* close to mine. "Whatever you want."

"Okay. *Hellraiser* it is."

"Ha."

I picked up the remote and started scrolling. "How about *The Sopranos*?"

"Sure. But from the beginning though. It's been a few years."

"Got it." I was scrolling down to season one when my phone pinged on the coffee table. "Sorry, I leave the ringer up when I'm babysitting," I said.

I looked at my screen and cracked up. "Look what Brad just sent me."

It was a picture of a shirt with the Toilet King on it and a text that said, "Your birthday gift motherfucker."

She laughed. "When is your birthday?" she asked.

"Not until next year. When's your birthday?"

"In a few weeks, actually."

"Oh. Well, do you have plans? Can I take you out?" I asked.

"It'll be after my contract's up."

Her way of saying she wouldn't be here for it. I only got to feel disappointed for a second before my phone pinged again.

"Sorry," I said, looking at it. "It's my mom. I have to reply to this."

I took my arm away from Emma and typed a short message about Sarah being home and Chelsea being in bed.

"What time does she get home?" Emma asked.

"I don't know. Midnight?"

She must have heard the tone in my voice.

"What?" she asked.

"Nothing." I hit send and put my phone away. But when I went to put my arm back around her, she didn't scoot in.

"It doesn't feel like nothing," she said.

I looked away from her. "She's dealing with some pretty serious legal issues at the moment."

"For what?"

I paused, not sure how much I wanted to share. I decided on all of it. Emma was going to be here when it all hit the fan anyway, so there was no point in keeping her in the dark.

"She's going to prison." I stopped because the next part was hard to say out loud. In fact, I had never done it with anyone besides Brad and Benny. "She embezzled money. A lot of money."

Emma just stared at me.

"She wrote herself fake checks. She was doing it for the better part of a year. She got caught."

"Had she ever done anything like that before?" she asked.

"No. Never. She didn't have any priors, not even a speeding ticket," I said. "We hoped for a slap on the wrist, probation, restitution. Even her old boss asked for leniency." I shook my head. "She didn't get it. She worked for a nonprofit and almost put it out of business. It pissed off the judge. He gave her some time to get her affairs in order, then she has to turn herself in. She got six years."

"Oh my God," Emma breathed. "How much did she take?"

"A lot. Flew the kids to Disneyland. Redid the landscaping. Stupid shit. Shit that wasn't worth it. I don't even know why she did it. To be honest I don't even think she knows."

"And who's taking the kids?" Emma asked.

I paused. "I am."

I couldn't read the expression on her face. "Oh."

"I'm sorry I didn't tell you. It only became official a few days before I met you. It was hard to talk about," I said. "Mom's best friend Leigh agreed to take them, but they'd have to move twenty miles away to live with her. Leigh's got horses and she can't board them. Alex and Sarah were having a really hard time with it. I didn't want them to have to change schools. Plus if I move in here, I can keep paying the mortgage so Mom won't lose the house. She already had to liquidate her 401(k) and all the college funds to pay back the money she took. I couldn't let the house end up sold after all that."

"When does she leave?"

"Next week."

The words hung there.

Today I was single. I had my own place, my own life. And next week I'd be the legal guardian of three children.

I still couldn't believe it. No matter how fast it was coming or how many emails Mom sent with instructions and the names of pediatricians and dentists they had to see and sports I had to sign them up for in the fall, I still couldn't accept this was real.

We sat there for a moment in silence and I stared at a photo on the mantel, the last one we took with Dad before he died. The one-eighty our lives had taken since then was truly unbelievable. Some alternate universe. A hellscape.

"She won't be able to chaperone Chelsea's field trips," I said, almost absently.

When she got out, she wouldn't pass the school's background check. All the memories I had of Mom on the bus, on our way to Como Park or Long Lake—Chelsea wouldn't have that. She wouldn't have her dad and she'd lost parts of her mom now too. Alex would be in his twenties when she got out. She was going to miss his graduation. Sarah's too. Chelsea would be ten, a sixth grader. I'd be thirty-five. Maybe I'd be married. Maybe Alex would. She'd miss the weddings. She'd miss our *lives*.

And I was angry.

I'd been angry for years. I was angry when Dad died, and then I slid right into being angry at Mom and angry at what was happening to my life and I just...I couldn't stop. I couldn't forgive it. I couldn't understand it and I couldn't forgive it. And now everyone would pay for it. Alex, Sarah, and Chelsea. *Me.*

Emma watched me quietly.

"I'm trying really hard to not hold on to it," I said. "It's just a lot to accept. It was right after my dad died." I shook my head. "It was so out of character for her, I don't get it."

"Be glad you don't get it. It means your life has been a lot gentler than hers."

I stopped and looked at her.

"How old was Chelsea when your dad died?" she asked.

I wrinkled my forehead. "Five months."

"When did she do this?"

I paused. "That same year."

"She could have been dealing with postpartum depression, PTSD, complicated grief. Any of those things can make you impulsive and reckless. She might have been self-medicating to deal with it, taking things you didn't know about. Trauma changes you."

I set my lips into a line. "So you think she got so depressed she decided to steal two hundred thousand dollars?"

"Justin, people get so depressed they kill themselves."

I blinked at her.

"You have a lot of ice in Minnesota, right?" she asked.

"Yes…"

"What happens when water gets into a crack and it freezes?"

"It expands," I said. "Makes the crack bigger."

"Unhealed trauma is a crack. And all the little hard things that trickle into it that would have rolled off someone else, settle. Then when life gets cold, that crack gets bigger, longer, deeper. It makes new breaks. You don't know how broken she was or what she was trying to do to fill those cracks. Being broken is not an excuse for bad behavior, you still have to make good choices and do the right thing. But it *can* be the reason. And sometimes understanding the reason can be what helps *you* heal."

"I've…I've never thought of it that way," I admitted.

Emma tucked her leg under her. "I think the thing that always got me through the stuff with my mom was knowing that she didn't *want* to be the way she was. Nobody wants to be the villain, Justin. If you start there, it's easier to get how people end up who they are and where they are. My mom put me through a lot. She hurt me. A lot. But she's full of more cracks than I can ever comprehend."

"So how do you reconcile that?" I asked. "How do you learn to forgive her?"

She shrugged. "You don't have to forgive her. You really don't. You can still love someone that you've decided not to speak to anymore. You can still wish them well and hope for the best for them. Choosing a life without them doesn't mean you stop caring about them. It just means that you can't allow them to harm you anymore. But if you don't think your life would be better without them in it, then accept that they have cracks. Try to understand how they got them and help fill them with something that isn't ice." She peered at me. "If you can choose anger or empathy, always choose empathy, Justin. It's so much healthier than anger. For both of you."

I wanted to respond, but I didn't even know what to say.

It was weird but it had never occurred to me that maybe Mom had been changed because of what happened with Dad. I mean, she always seemed to keep it together. She didn't miss work, she didn't stay in bed for days at a time or lose a bunch of weight or stop brushing her hair.

But maybe she *did* fall apart. Maybe she just didn't let us see it. Maybe that was her way of protecting *us* from more cracks.

I felt a small lump form in my throat. Because when I reframed it this way, I started to wonder if I'd failed her. If I hadn't felt like someone safe that she could be honest with and lean on. I hadn't met her where she was.

Emma was right. My life *had* been gentler than hers.

I studied the woman sitting next to me. Imagine someone who went through what she did, turning out the way she had. Able to give grace to someone who'd let her down so badly. Emma was a better person than I was. And my life had been gentler than hers too.

The front door opened and my sweaty, slightly sunburnt teenage brother came in. I was glad for the interruption.

I leaned to look over the back of the couch. "Hey, how was it?"

Alex dropped a gift shop bag on the floor. "It was epic! Mitch barfed on the Corkscrew, we were making fun of him the whole time."

"Nice." I nodded at Emma. "Alex, this is my girlfriend, Emma."

She smiled. "Hi."

"Hey." My brother froze and beamed like he'd never seen a woman before. "So what're you guys doing?" he asked, looking back and forth between us.

I hadn't brought anyone home in years, not since the streak started. This was exciting for everyone apparently.

"We're getting out of here, actually." I looked at my watch, then at her. "Ready to go?"

"Ready." She stood.

I gave Alex the rundown on his sisters. Then I collected Brad and we got in the car.

I wanted to ask her if she'd like to go do something else. Dessert somewhere maybe? But it was already almost 11:00 and she had work in the morning. I figured I'd save myself the letdown of being told no and I'd just drop her off. But I was not ready to end the night, by any stretch.

Something told me I wouldn't be ready for her contract to end either.

CHAPTER 16

EMMA

I'd texted Maddy on the way to ask her to get me at the dock. I wasn't ready to go home when we pulled up in front of Neil's house. I couldn't tell if it was because I wasn't ready to face my best friend, or if I just didn't want to leave Justin.

Maybe a little of both.

I'd liked the docking station. I wanted to see what else I liked.

By now with most guys, even one date in, I was already starting to lose interest. But every time I saw Justin, I was only getting *more* interested, which was unusual for me.

But I didn't love that he had kids.

I never dated men with kids. Ever. It was a hard, *hard* rule for me. And while they weren't technically *his*, for all intents and purposes they were. So, realistically our relationship would just be our fun four dates and maybe, possibly breaking an imaginary curse.

I told Justin he could just drop me off, but he insisted on

walking me to the dock. He left Brad in the car and escorted me to my pickup spot.

It was after 11:00. The mosquitoes were long gone. The sky was crystal clear and the stars were out. The air was perfect. One of those nights where you couldn't even feel it on your skin. The water lapped quietly on the shore and lightning flashed in the distance, some far-off storm, beautiful and ethereal, like the horizon of a different world.

When we got to the sand, Justin gazed at the moon over the water and shook his head. "This view doesn't suck," he said.

I turned to look up at him and his eyes settled on me.

"Thanks for dinner."

"Yeah. I'm glad you came."

The lights of the pontoon pricked the distance. Maddy was coming. Slowly, but she was coming. We had a few minutes. A soft wind blew a lock of hair across my cheek and I dragged it off with a finger. I watched his eyes follow the movement before they came back to mine.

"So when do I get to see you again?" he asked.

"I start full-time tomorrow. I work three days straight, twelve-hour shifts, so I probably won't see you until next week."

He frowned. "You said I can't meet you for lunch or anything, right?"

"No."

He nodded. "Okay. Well, if you have another dinner emergency, call me."

"I will."

Then we just gazed at each other. A comfortable silence. A safe one. And for the second time tonight Justin was inside my personal space.

I didn't mind him there. At all.

"What are you thinking right now?" he asked.

"I'm thinking that you're supposed to kiss me," I said. "What are you thinking?"

"I'm thinking I'm supposed to kiss you."

"Do you think it still counts if you kiss me on a date that's not one of the dates?" I asked.

"I don't care if it counts."

His eyes dropped to my mouth, my heart picked up—and then the lights on the balcony turned on over the pool.

Mom came out and leaned over the railing. "Emma, Justin! Is that you?"

The moment was shattered. A flicker of disappointment flashed across Justin's face. He turned and waved. "Hi, Amber."

Neil came out onto the balcony in his robe and Mom hugged him from the side. "Neil and I are going to goat yoga on Saturday," she called. "Do you two want to come?"

Justin glanced at me. "Goat yoga?" he said, too low for them to hear.

"They climb on you," I said. "Baby ones."

"Hmm."

We gazed at each other.

"Well?" Mom called.

I snapped out of it and turned back to her. "I have work Saturday, Mom."

"Thanks for the invite," Justin said.

"Okay, let us know if you change your mind!"

They went back inside, there was giggling, a playful shriek, and then the balcony door closed.

The motion sensor light stayed on for a few seconds, then

doused us back into soft darkness. Maddy was almost here. Too close now for a kiss to be anything but rushed. Oh well.

Justin put his hands in his pockets and looked around the yard. Then he gave me a playful glance. "You know what this feels like?"

"What?"

"A zombie movie."

I snorted. "I was *just* going to say that. That dark, eerie night, the moon's out and zombies start ambling from the bushes and you have to run for your life."

"We would be pretty screwed if we had to run from zombies here," he said.

"Why?"

He nodded at the lake. "We're trapped on one side by water."

"You just run around them back to the car."

"You can't outrun a zombie horde," he said.

"Yes you can. They're dead, they're not fast."

"Yeah, but they never stop. That's how they get you."

"Uh, I promise you I can outmaneuver a zombie, Justin."

"Well, if you can't, *I* promise to run slower than you."

I smiled and so did he. He was really cute.

Two seconds later the pontoon pulled up to the dock. Justin stepped away from me to go catch it. He said hi to Maddy and secured the boat. Then he hugged me and whispered "Next time…" in a quiet voice that made my stomach do summersaults. He helped me onto the platform, pushed us off, and stood there watching me until he was too small to see while Maddy steered us back to the island.

CHAPTER 17

JUSTIN

I was sitting in the passenger seat of my car with my dog on my lap. Alex was driving. Another lesson. We were on side streets and he was doing well enough that I felt safe checking my texts. This morning Emma and I had swapped Spotify playlists. I just finished hers.

Emma: Well? What do you think?

I keyed into my phone.

Me: Not bad. I like the throwback with More Than Words by Extreme. A little too much of 1975 and Nothing But Thieves, but I think the Lola Simone tracks make it work overall.

I smiled at my screen at the Emma is Typing popup.

Emma: More Than Words is Maddy's favorite song, it's in there for her. I'm still listening to yours. It's three hours long. And you have an almost nine-minute song on there about someone ending up in the belly of a whale? What is actually wrong with you?

Me: The Mariner's Revenge is a cult classic. Chelsea calls it the pirate song, she likes it. Do you ever think about the children, Emma? No. You only think about yourself.

She sent me a long row of laughing emojis and: "Am I the asshole?"

I beamed at my phone.

Our second date would be tonight. It had been six days since dinner at Mom's and I'd been looking forward to seeing her all week. I was taking her to Stillwater, a small town on the St. Croix River. Ice cream shops and antique stores, a river walk. My favorite wine bar for dinner.

I might kiss her tonight. I almost did the other night at the dock, but then Amber showed up. I was looking forward to the do-over.

Alex and I finished the driving lesson and went to Burger King for lunch. I just got food for my brother. Sarah was at Josie's and Chelsea already had dino nuggets. Leigh and Mom were home, but they didn't want anything. They were going out tonight for their last hurrah before Mom went away.

She left tomorrow.

The last week had been a daily countdown of activities Mom planned to make as many memories as she could before she left. She took the kids to the zoo, then up to Duluth. Did a movie night in the living room, spent a day at the lake with everyone. I went to as much of it as I could around work. Tonight was her last night out with her best friend and then tomorrow she got dropped off at the prison.

It was weird how normal today felt against the tectonic shift that would take place twenty-four hours from now.

I was glad I had Emma here. It was a distraction. Something to look forward to when pretty much everything else was awful.

We got to Mom's and I came inside with Alex to say hi. I was in a rush. I had to stop at Brad's, then go home and get ready for my date, then I had to drive to go get Emma. But the opportunities to come in and say hi to Mom were running out, and I didn't want to waste one.

I'd tried to be softer with her the last few days. The energy shift I'd had over Mom after my talk with Emma was almost as bad as being mad at her. At least when I was mad, I didn't feel the guilt I was feeling now.

I thought about Emma's island, the metaphorical one she'd told me about. And it made me wonder if we all have an island sometimes and maybe Mom had been on hers alone and I hadn't known. This ate away at me now.

Mom was at the kitchen table with Leigh already petting my excited dog before I came in. I gave her a small squeeze on her shoulder before I sat down next to her.

"I can't stay long," I said. "Just wanted to come in and say hi. I've got a date."

"Oh? With who?" Mom asked.

"Her name's Emma," I answered.

"She's cool," Alex said, taking a bite of his burger. "I met her the other night. She's like, superhot."

"Sweetie, don't chew with your mouth open," Mom said. "Will I get to meet her?"

The full question hovered between us. Will I get to meet her *before I go*? And no, Mom wouldn't get to meet her.

"She's got a busy schedule at the hospital," I said. "I only get to see her once a week myself."

That was true. But the real reason was that Emma didn't *want* to meet her.

I got it. I guess if you're always a few weeks away from leaving, what's the point in getting to know the family of the people you date? You barely have time to get to know the person you're dating.

This was another thing I was trying not to think about—her leaving. I should be happy that she came at all, that she wasn't in Hawaii. We still had three more dates, maybe more if I could convince her. I'd already gotten a freebie the other night at Mom's. But I dreaded the clock running out. Emma was the only good thing happening to me at the moment and when she was gone, not only would I lose her, I'd be left sitting in my new reality. Dad gone, Mom in prison. Me with all the children.

It was coming. Barreling at me faster and faster and it was almost here.

And now that I'd met Emma, it was more than that.

When she left, I wouldn't be able to just fly out to wherever she was—if she'd let me. And I *would* want to fly out to wherever she was. I knew this, even a week and a half in. And now I wouldn't get to explore it or pursue it the way I wanted to.

This thing with Mom had changed the path of my whole life. Altered my fate, thrown my course off its trajectory.

I could work from anywhere. What would have stopped me from leaving with her in a few weeks if she'd wanted me to? My lease was almost up, Brad had moved on. It was like this was the plan that the universe had set up for me. This was what was *supposed* to happen.

But that alternate reality was gone now. Now I'd just have the What-If. And there wasn't a damn thing I could do about it.

I got up, said my goodbyes, and left. Drove to Brad's.

When I knocked, Faith let me in. "Hey." She pushed the door open and called up the stairs. "Brad, Justin's here." She turned to give me a look. "With his *dog*."

I grinned at her and she made an exasperated noise and left me there.

Brad jogged down the steps and Benny came around the corner from the living room at the same time. The guys were installing a TV and then having a couples dinner tonight. They'd invited me and Emma, but I'd opted for the private date night instead.

I didn't think she wanted to meet my friends for the same reason she didn't want to meet my family, and anyway I wanted to spend time with her alone.

"To what do I owe the honor of this visit?" Brad said.

"I'm here for my shirt."

He pulled his face back. "The Toilet King shirt? You can't ask for it. If you actually want it, it's not funny."

"Not my problem. If she checks the Stupid Shirt option on the what-to-wear part of the surveys I send her, I'm gonna need it."

"Dumbass. Hold on."

Benny came out on the porch and I took a seat while he crouched to pet my dog.

Brad came back out and tossed me the shirt, then he chucked a bag of something at my chest and I caught it in my lap.

"I got you some of those dark chocolate peanut butter cups you like from work. Figured you might be missing the perks of living with me." He dropped into the rocking chair next to mine.

"I do love Trader Joe's," I said, smiling at the bag. "Nothing like a grocery store that makes you have to visit another grocery store right after."

Benny cracked up.

Brad stopped rocking and narrowed his eyes at me. "Take that back."

"I absolutely will not."

He leaned forward. "With as much disrespect as I can manage, Justin, fuck you."

I laughed.

Brad sat back into his chair. "So how's it going with the girl?" he asked.

"It's going," I said. "I like her. A lot."

"How much longer is she here?" Benny asked, taking the seat next to Brad.

I sat with my elbows on my knees. "Four and a half more weeks."

"Can she sign another contract? Stay longer?" Benny asked.

"I mean I guess in theory she could. Though I don't know if she will."

"Have you hooked up with her yet?" Brad asked.

"I haven't even kissed her yet."

"Oh, well there you go," Brad said. "She doesn't know what she's missing if she leaves. You gotta give her the magic peen."

"Ha. I will take that under advisement."

I stared absently at the bag of chocolates in my hand. Brad was studying me. I could feel it. I looked up. "What?"

"Dude. You're fucking *sprung*."

"I said I like her."

He shook his head. "Naw. You're whipped. It's all over your face. Tell him, Benny, he looks whipped."

Benny nodded sagely.

"This is how it starts," Brad said. "They get you by the balls. Next thing you know you're going to musicals."

"Uh, I *like* musicals."

"You would."

I scoffed.

"How you doing with the moving-back-in thing?" Benny asked.

I puffed out my cheeks. "Talked with Mom about how we should do it. We're going to pack up her room and put everything in storage after she leaves, move me into the primary bedroom."

"Yeah, we wanted to talk to you about that," Brad said.

"About what?" I asked.

"We want to fix it up for you," Benny said. "When I got sick and I had to move back into my mom's place, the worst part was how old everything was. We want to replace the blinds, paint."

"We could pull up that old carpet too. Retile the bathroom," Brad said. "Really do it up nice."

I felt my face soften. They got this. They understood what this was like for me.

"Sound good?" Brad said.

"Yeah," I said. "Thank you. There's actually something else you can help me with too," I said, looking at them. "I need help making sure I can still see Emma until she goes."

Benny nodded. "Yeah, of course."

"I might need a sitter," I said. "Or someone to watch the dog last minute."

"Totally," Brad said. "Done. I'm sure Jane and Faith will help too."

"Thanks," I said. "I appreciate it. And I definitely want to retile the bathroom. I will absolutely take you up on that." I looked at my watch. "I have to get going."

"Let's plan something together," Brad said, pushing up on his thighs. "Faith wants to meet her."

"Yeah," I said, though I knew it probably wouldn't happen.

I was barely getting enough of her for me.

CHAPTER 18

EMMA

Maddy and I docked at the mansion for my second date with Justin. It was almost a week since I'd gone to his house for spaghetti. I'd been working nonstop. Maddy was going grocery shopping so she tied the boat up and walked with me across the lawn.

Mom was in a unicorn floatie in the pool.

She wore her wide-brimmed hat and giant sunglasses, drinking something with an umbrella in it.

"Hey!" She waved. "On the way to the hospital?"

"No," Maddy called. "Day off."

"Okay. Well, make good choices girls!" Mom called.

"Will do!" Maddy shouted.

When we got to the side of the garage, Maddy's smile dropped off. "See?" she said. "I told you I would be nice."

"Thank you," I said. "I appreciate it."

We'd had a long talk the night I got back from Justin's. She apologized and promised to give Mom the benefit of the doubt. Then she'd grilled me on Justin for the next hour until I forced her out of my room so I could go to bed.

She was obsessed with the idea of *me* being obsessed with someone. I wasn't, but she would will it into existence if she could.

I *did* like him though. I'd been thinking a lot about the docking station. Then I'd been thinking about *why* I was thinking about it.

Maybe it was because I didn't usually cuddle with anyone? I couldn't actually remember the last time I did. It was really addictive—and I had a feeling I wouldn't like it with any man but him.

I definitely wasn't telling Maddy that.

"What time is he coming?" Maddy asked.

"Another five minutes."

"Want to wait on the porch?"

"Sure."

We plopped into the chairs outside the front door.

"So where's he taking you?" Maddy asked.

"Stillwater. Want to see the invitation he sent?"

"Uh, *yeah.*"

I pulled it up and handed her my phone.

The invite was placed over an old black-and-white photo of loggers standing on a pile of timber.

JUSTIN CORDIALLY INVITES YOU TO DINNER, WINE TASTING AND ANTIQUE SHOPPING IN STILLWATER, THE BIRTHPLACE OF MINNESOTA, AT 5:00, AUGUST 8TH.

PLEASE WEAR WALKING SHOES.

She handed me the phone back. "I swear to God this guy is the epitome of If He Wanted To He Would."

"He definitely makes curse breaking fun," I agreed.

She looked over at me. "So what's up with Amber?"

I shrugged. "Nothing."

"You guys making any plans to hang out?"

"I don't know. She doesn't really answer my texts."

Her expression changed.

"What?" I said.

"Nothing. That's just what my face does when I leave it unattended."

I gave her a look. "She's busy. She's having a good time with Neil. I'm happy for her."

"She didn't look busy a minute ago…" she mumbled.

I didn't get to reply. Justin pulled up.

We watched him get out and go around the back of the car. He got a large potted plant from the trunk and started lugging it to the porch.

"Is that a rosebush?" Maddy asked, squinting.

He came up the walk and greeted Maddy, then he looked at me. "I brought you flowers," he said, around the leaves.

I laughed. "You brought me an entire rosebush?"

He set it down. "You said the ones Amber got you were dead. I wanted to get you some that wouldn't die."

I smiled at it. "Awww. But this needs to be planted."

"Then plant it," he said, grinning. "What's wrong with putting down roots?"

"Absolutely nothing," Maddy said from behind me.

He hugged me hello and kissed me on the cheek. My stomach did a flip.

"I'll put it in the pontoon," he said, letting me go and picking it back up.

"Thank you." I watched him round the corner of the garage.

As soon as he had his back to us, Maddy gave me an *Are You Kidding Me* look. "If he wanted to he would," she said the second he was out of earshot. "Also, if Amber wanted to, she would too. I'm just saying."

I rolled my eyes.

"Where you gonna plant that?" she asked.

"I don't know."

I'd be leaving it behind. So somewhere it could thrive without me.

CHAPTER 19

JUSTIN

Found it!" Emma said.

I put down the antique beer stein I was looking at and came over to the display case she was waiting by. "You definitely did find it. That is the ugliest baby I've ever seen."

She beamed proudly.

We'd just gotten out of dinner. We were on our third antique store and in each one we looked for the creepy baby doll. This one had a half-closed eye, the tufts of what was left of some blond stringy hair, and it was slightly green for some reason.

"I think I love it," Emma said, cocking her head.

I looked back and forth between her and the case. "This. You love *this*."

"I do."

"It's missing an arm."

She peered around the case. "There it is."

I leaned to see what she was pointing at, and she was right, the severed arm was next to the doll on the shelf.

"The arm is missing fingers," I said.

She shrugged. "It gives it character."

I squinted at the tag hanging off the hideous baby. "Eighty-five dollars? For *that*?"

She tried to give me a disapproving look, but she was fighting a smile.

"You think it comes with the arm or is that extra?" I asked.

"That doll was someone's favorite thing once, Justin. Some child probably took it everywhere, slept holding it, cried when it was lost."

"I thought you weren't sentimental about things."

She looked back into the case. "I am about things like that."

I watched her gazing at the doll, and I thought about Stuffie, her decrepit, limp unicorn, and I wondered if her ability to be sentimental got shut off when she was a kid. It stalled out at ancient hideous dolls.

I nudged her with my elbow. "Do you want me to buy it for you?"

"Do you want me to buy it for *you*?"

"Uh, no. I don't need anything that ugly. I already have my dog."

She laughed.

I peered into the glass case. Mom would have thought this was hilarious. She would have really liked Emma.

Emma must have noticed the change in my body language.

"What are you thinking?" she asked.

I breathed out deeply. "I'm thinking that I wish you knew my mom."

Her face went soft. "She goes away tomorrow, right?"

I nodded.

"Should we go back? Do you want to spend time with her?"

I shook my head. "No. I already stopped by earlier and I hung out with her as much as I could this week. She's with Leigh tonight. I see her in the morning. It's how she wants it."

"So you move into the house tomorrow then."

"I do."

"How do you feel about it?" she asked.

"Like I'm in shock," I said, talking to her but staring at the ugly baby. "Like it's not really happening."

"And how are the kids?"

"I think they're in shock and feel like it's not really happening too." I glanced at her. "How did you handle so much change when you were a kid? I mean, that had to mess with you, right?"

She shrugged and looked back at the baby. "Yeah, it messed with me. I think you're doing the best thing for them that anyone can do. Keep them where they are. Minimize the fallout."

I looked ahead. "Yeah."

"What?"

I paused. "What if I mess them up?" I asked quietly.

She smiled at me gently. "What if you save them?"

She looked at me so earnestly she made me believe that maybe I would.

I cleared my throat. "Maddy had less stabby energy today."

"She's a fan of yours," she said.

I raised an eyebrow. "Is she…?"

"Yes. She appreciates that you're willing to endure dinners with Neil and Amber for me. Gets her off the hook."

"And you don't appreciate this?" I grinned.

"Of course I do." Then she reached up, wrapped her arms around my neck, and kissed my cheek. She did it casually. I don't think she had *any* idea the effect it had on me.

She came down from her tiptoes. Her arms were still around my neck and the place where her lips were on my cheek tingled. I was contemplating if kissing her in an antique store in front of a maimed ugly baby doll was tacky when my phone rang. Mom.

"Sorry," I said. "I should take this." I stepped away from her and hit the answer button. "Mom, what's up?"

"Justin! What are you doing right now?" Leigh. Drunk Leigh, by the sound of it.

"I'm just at a store, why—"

Shuffling. Then Mom came on the line. "Justin? Can you give us a ride?" Also drunk.

Mom *never* drank. This was rarer than a solar eclipse. I could hear Leigh roaring with laughter in the background and Mom covered the mouthpiece giggling and hushed her.

"I'm still on my date, Mom."

"Oh! That's right!" she said. "I forgot. I'm sorry I called you, never mind—"

"Justin!" Leigh said in the background. "Give me the phone. Give it to me. No, give it to me—" *Shuffling.* "Justin? It's Aunt Leigh. You need to come pick us up. Your mother and I have been overserved." She slurred on "served."

"You can't call an Uber?" I said.

"Can't." She hiccupped.

"Why not?"

"Banned. Lyft too."

"What? Then use Mom's account."

"We're both banned. We're pariahs."

"How did you *both* get banned from two separate rideshare apps?" I asked.

"It takes commitment and ingenuity." Slurred on "ingenuity."
Mom cracked up in the background.

I took in a deep breath and locked eyes with Emma. She
looked amused.

"It was my ex-husband," Leigh went on. "He works for Lyft.
Did it just to stick it to me one last time and threw Christine in
there just to piss me off—and it did. It did piss me off."

"And your Uber accounts?" I asked.

"Well, that is a very interesting story that I'd love to tell you,
when you pick us up."

I glanced at Emma. I didn't mind picking them up, but
Emma didn't want to meet my mom.

I put the phone to my other ear. "Can you call Brad?"

"Already did. He's at dinner with Benny, and they're drunker
than we are."

I heard Mom whispering. The phone shuffled and they both
giggled. Then Mom was back on the line. "Justin, I don't want to
interrupt your date. We'll figure something out."

"What are we gonna do, Christine?" Leigh said. "Walk? From
here? You only have one shoe! Plus you got prison tomorrow. I
gotta get you back by midnight or you turn into a pumpkin."
They both peeled into giggling.

"Where are you?" I asked, rubbing my forehead.

"Hudson."

Wisconsin. Only fifteen minutes from here. It wasn't even
really out of the way.

Emma must have read my mind. "If it's an emergency, we can
go get them," she said, her voice low.

I put Mom and Leigh on mute.

"You said you don't want to meet my mom."

"It's okay. I'm invested now, I want to hear the story about how they both got banned from Uber."

I snorted.

I took my mom off mute. "Send me your location," I said. "And stay put. Don't make me come looking for you."

I hung up and we went to collect our drunks.

When I pulled up to the bar fifteen minutes later, Mom and Leigh were sitting on the curb with their purses in their laps. Leigh's mascara was running. Mom's sandal was duct-taped and she had leaves in her hair for some reason. They waved and grinned when they saw us and climbed into the back.

Mom leaned in between the front seats. "Hi! I'm Christine!"

"Hi." Emma twisted to shake her hand.

Leigh scooted in next to Mom. "Leigh." She jutted out a hand full of gaudy rings.

"Are either of you going to throw up in this car?" I asked.

"We can hold our liquor," Leigh said, offended.

"We *cannot* hold our liquor," Mom whispered.

Emma pulled two Ziploc bags from her purse. They had Wheat Thins and celery in them. Probably her work snacks. "I trust this zipper seal with my life," she said, turning to hand them to our passengers.

"Thanks," Leigh said. "Can we eat these?" She started eating a cracker before Emma answered.

We made brief eye contact, Emma smiling and me looking exasperated.

"You two smell like you showered in Patrón," I said. I dug in my center console for a water bottle. "Drink some water."

"Water?" Leigh said. "That stuff that killed everyone on the *Titanic*?"

Mom burst into giggles.

"I'll wait for Diet Coke," Leigh said, taking the water and thrusting it into Mom's hands. "Drink this. We don't need you hungover your first day in the clink."

"If you couldn't get a rideshare home, what exactly was the plan?" I asked, pulling away from the curb. "And how'd you get here?"

"My date picked us up," Leigh said. "Supposed to take us home too, but his wife showed up! That son of a bitch said he wasn't married! He looked plenty married to me, getting hauled out by his collar. J-named men are the *worst*."

Emma was laughing now.

"Hey—" I said.

"Not you, you don't count," Leigh said, loudly crunching a celery stick.

Emma leaned over and whispered, "I agree, you don't count. So," she said over her shoulder, "how'd you get banned from Uber?"

"Oh, this is *good*," Leigh said. "Because it was your mom's fault, Justin."

"We had to do it," Mom said. "They were too little, they would have died."

"We found some baby raccoons," Leigh said. "Real young, maybe five, six weeks old. Mama Coon was dead in the street and so Christine's like, 'I can't leave them,' so she gets on her hands and knees and pokes around the bushes until she catches 'em. I told her to put them in her purse and I'd take them to the wildlife rehabilitation center in the morning. So we get in this Uber, and we're not a block from the place and one of 'em gets out and jumps right on the driver. He's hooting and hollering, and he pulls over and kicks us out. So that's how I got banned."

Emma was laughing. "And how did Christine get banned?"

"Same thing, not fifteen minutes later, only this time on her account. We figured out how to keep 'em calm after that. They like sleeping in your shirt. See? Show 'em, Christine."

"Wait, *WHAT?*" I started braking reflexively. "You have raccoons? In this car? Right now?"

"Well yes," Leigh said, like I was being ridiculous. "All this happened tonight."

Emma was *dying*.

I looked at my mother and her wasted best friend in the rearview. "You didn't think to mention this? That you have wild animals in your bras?"

"Only three," Leigh said, like that was better.

"What if they have fleas?" I asked.

"We washed 'em in the sink at the Circle K," Leigh said. "A little Dawn soap, dried 'em with the hand dryer."

Emma looked impressed. "That *does* work."

"Emma, you want to hold one?" Mom asked.

She gasped. "Yes!"

A hand emerged from the back seat with a tiny chittering raccoon in it wrapped in a bar towel. "This is George Cooney."

Emma took it and held it to her chest and looked at me with hearts in her eyes. "Look at his little hands!" she said.

"Oh my God…" I muttered.

"Justin, how can you be mad about this? They're heroes," Emma said, stroking the little gray head. "These sweet babies would have died."

"Thank you," Mom said. "I feel like a hero."

Leigh leaned over the seat. "Now, you just tuck that little trash panda into your cleavage. Quiets him right down."

Emma pulled her shirt open and put the swaddled raccoon inside.

"Are we even sure this is safe?" I asked, glancing at the lump under her shirt.

"If they're not safe, why are they cute, Justin?" Emma said.

"It's the forbidden puppy," Mom said.

All three women started laughing.

I tried to look serious, but I couldn't. Emma was having too good of a time—and Mom and Leigh were actually pretty hilarious drunks.

"Good Lord, these hot flashes," Leigh said, plucking her shirt in my rearview. "Lets me know I can't go to hell because I can *not* take the heat. Justin, you taking us to Culver's or what?"

"You two don't think you've derailed my night enough?" I said, getting onto the freeway.

"I do not appreciate that tone," Leigh said. "I feel like I need to remind you that I used to wipe your butt."

"Uh, you do *not* need to remind me of that," I said.

"He had the cutest little baby butt. Do you remember, Christine? Like a little apple."

"It was soooo cute," Mom said from the back seat.

Leigh tapped Emma on the shoulder. "Is his butt still cute, Emma?"

"It's really cute," Emma said, smiling and waving her raccoon's little hand at me while I shook my head.

She hadn't seen it. Not bare anyway. But I couldn't help but hope that she'd looked.

"Yes, I will take you to Culver's," I said.

"Thank you," Leigh said. "Christine, how we doing on the list?" Leigh asked.

"What's the list?" Emma asked.

"Prison prep," Leigh said. "Memorizing your important phone numbers, dying your hair back to your natural color so you don't see your roots come in, fixing anything wrong with your teeth—I'm gonna put money on your books the second they let me, hon. I'm gonna come every week to visit you," Leigh said. "Press my boob against the glass."

Mom laughed. A deep, tipsy belly laugh. And then the laughter tipped and dwindled into crying. Leigh started crying too. She wrapped her arms around Mom, and Mom sobbed.

"Hon, I'm gonna be there with you every step of the way," Leigh said. "I'm gonna help Justin take care of those babies and I'm gonna send you pictures and we're gonna get through this."

I could see Mom's crumpled face pressed into Leigh's shoulder in the rearview. The tail of a baby raccoon snaked out of Leigh's cleavage and flicked under Mom's chin. She still had leaves in her hair. The whole thing was like some fucked-up sitcom. The plot of a dark comedy.

Emma glanced at me as she pulled tissues from her purse and handed them into the back seat.

I think I would have been embarrassed if I'd been on a date with anyone else. My mother, sobbing drunk the night before she left for prison. But I knew Emma didn't judge. That's just not how she was. She judged this situation less than I did.

When she finished handing out Kleenex, Emma stayed turned in her seat. "You know," she said, "I worked for three months in a women's prison."

Mom raised her head.

"I have never met cooler people than the women in prison," Emma said.

Mom sniffed. "Really?"

"Yeah. You'll make lots of friends. They had a cosmetology school for the inmates. You can get your hair done. And you get to do soooo much reading."

I glanced in the rearview and I could see it. The sudden hope in Mom's eyes that maybe prison wouldn't be as bad as she'd built it up in her mind.

Emma sat back in her seat and twined her fingers in mine between us. Her turn to comfort me.

After that, Mom stopped crying. Leigh and Mom went back to laughing and giggling. They got their Culver's. They held their baby trash pandas and ate their sundaes and Emma chatted with Mom and Leigh. And even though it was the last night Mom would be here and it was awful and sad, it was also sort of all right.

CHAPTER 20

EMMA

We'd dropped off Leigh and Christine and were parked on the curb in front of Neil's house. The front door to the mansion was wide open and Fleetwood Mac was blaring from inside.

Justin lowered his head to get a look at the open door. "Should we go check that out?"

"No," I said. "Probably Amber working on her rose wall. I'm not worried about it."

I got out of the car, and Justin met me on the lawn.

"Sorry for the side quest," Justin said, stopping in front of me.

"They were fun," I said honestly.

"Mom doesn't drink. You were treated to a show." He smiled a little.

So handsome.

I'd been admiring his side profile as we drove. Little glances while his focus was on the road. The way his eyes creased at the corners when his mom and Leigh were laughing from the back seat. The way his jaw ticced slightly when they weren't. The look of gratitude he gave me when I held his hand.

I liked being there to help him through that, the way he helped me the day Mom showed up. Even if it was just a tiny moment in a long lifetime of moments, I was happy to be a part of it.

Justin deserved good things. He deserved for the hard things of his life to be made a little easier, the way he made everyone else's life easier.

"Leigh seems like a good friend," I said.

"She is. She would do anything for Mom. She'd probably take her place if she could."

I nodded. I understood that. Maddy and I had that.

It was weird to think it, especially given the circumstances, but I was glad I met his mom. I wasn't making plans with Justin. We'd be done once I left Minnesota. But for some reason, it was important to me that when he talked about her over the next few weeks, I'd be able to put a face to a name.

That she'd be able to put a face to mine.

I *liked* the idea of Justin talking about me to her, I realized. Of him talking about me to anyone. Being important enough to come up in conversation.

And then I realized that I'd actually feel hurt if I wasn't. If I was just some fling for him that didn't warrant mentioning to his friends and family.

But *why* would that bother me?

That's essentially what this was—a fling.

I couldn't care less about whether the guys I dated previously talked about me. Sometimes I preferred they didn't. What was the point? I was going to move on and drift into their oblivion anyway, why even waste the time to tell their friends my name?

But I wanted Justin to think about me and talk about me. I liked that he planned things for me. That he spent so much time making his surveys and invites and picking out the perfect places to take me.

"Dreams" ended and then Peter Cetera came on with "The Next Time I Fall."

Justin stood there with his hands in his pockets. He was supposed to kiss me.

I thought maybe he'd do it somewhere in Stillwater, but he hadn't.

He took a step toward me, and my heart launched.

"Is it okay if I kiss you good night?" he asked, his eyes flickering to my lips.

"Yes, you may kiss me."

I slid my hands up his chest. He smelled *so* good. I'd been leaning into it the whole evening. Something spicy and warm mixed with the scent of mint. Justin was so...familiar. Like I was dating a boy I grew up with and I hadn't seen him in a few years and when I did, he'd turned into someone irresistible. Obviously that whole scenario was impossible. I knew nobody from my childhood. There was nothing before I moved in with Maddy. Just a smear of people and places and schools and foster homes. But I just knew without knowing that this comparison was the right one.

Maybe a wall that I usually had up was coming down a little—probably because of the circumstances of our arrangement.

Or maybe not.

Maybe it was just *him*.

Something about this made me feel uneasy. Like something scary was happening but I couldn't explain what. But I didn't have time to think about it because Justin was leaning in.

He cupped my cheeks in his hands, looked me in the eye. Then slowly, sensually…kissed me on the forehead.

The forehead.

I waited a moment for the real thing, but he stepped back. "Okay. Good night."

I blinked at him. "That's *it*?"

"You didn't like it?" He smiled.

I gave him a look. "Really, Justin? A forehead kiss?"

"I'm told they're all the rage. The female gaze and all that."

"You are supposed to *kiss* me. On the *mouth*."

He looked thoroughly amused. "We have time. I don't have to do it right away. We have two more dates."

I crossed my arms and his eyes sparkled. He was *messing* with me.

"I'll see you next week," he said. He turned and started around the front of the car.

My arms dropped. "Justin!"

He waved his keys at me over the top of the car as he got in the front seat. I watched with my mouth open as he started the engine and drove off.

I gaped at his taillights until they turned a corner out of view. Un-be*lievable*.

I'm not sure if it was his intention, but the tease made me want him to kiss me a thousand times more than I'd wanted it five minutes ago. Maybe he was right about the female gaze…

I made an exasperated noise at the empty street, then I went to wait for Maddy on the dock, opting not to peek in and bother

Mom. I sat on the bench that overlooked the water and watched the lights of the pontoon beam in the distance.

My heart was still pounding. It was so rare for a man to make my heart pound. I knew my heart *should* pound when I was with a guy I liked. Only mine never had. Everything was always flat for me.

Maybe that's why I was a good nurse. I had the gift of extreme empathy paired with detachment. I could deeply understand someone and anticipate their needs, but also never get close enough to them to feel it when they passed away or suffered or I moved on. I didn't fall in love. Not with people or places. Not with anything, really. I mean, that was the curse we were trying to break, right?

I wondered how I got this way.

Sometimes I felt like I was roaming this earth as a ghost, seeing everything and feeling nothing. These tiny things, a fluttering heart, butterflies in my stomach—the urge to dock. I never got to feel like this. It was *exciting* that Justin made me feel like this. But it didn't really matter. It could never work out with us, at least not now anyway.

I didn't want to raise someone else's kids. I wasn't even sure I ever wanted my *own* kids. I liked my life—the traveling, the money, being spontaneous and always having a new destination to look forward to. I didn't want to stay here. I didn't want to stay anywhere.

Maddy picked me up and we went back to the island.

CHAPTER 21

JUSTIN

The day came. The day all our lives were changing forever.

Mom wanted today to be as normal as possible for everyone. Like she was leaving on a long work trip and would be back before we knew it. She didn't want us to drive her to the intake, she wanted Leigh to take her. She wanted to make us breakfast like it was any other day, do the dishes, kiss us all goodbye, and leave without any fanfare. So Alex, Sarah, and I ate French toast at the breakfast nook and tried our best to pretend what was happening wasn't really happening. We forced ourselves to act normal and watched Mom wash the frying pan with her back to us so we wouldn't see her cry.

I didn't know if this was the best way to deal with her leaving or the worst way, but something told me it would have been fucked up no matter how she did it.

Somewhere in the middle of the surreal fog that was breakfast, Emma texted me.

Emma: I hope you're ok today. Call me if you need anything.

It was amazing how different my life could be from one day to the next.

Last night I'd been with Emma, happy, kissing her on the forehead instead of where I really wanted to kiss her.

I'd been thinking a lot about her since our date last night.

I knew she liked me. She was genuinely attracted to me, I could feel it. But this was still the game for her.

It wasn't a game for me. Not anymore.

I'd hoped before that she'd renew her contract, but now I wanted more. I wanted an actual chance. And to have that, she'd have to meet me where I was. Here, in Minnesota.

She had to stay.

I wanted time to convince her to give me a real shot and we didn't have it. And if she got what she needed from me to complete the agreement we'd made, she might be done. I might never see her again after our fourth date.

Unless I didn't kiss her.

Then she'd have to keep seeing me until I did, or her Minnesota side-trip thing would be for nothing.

It was a flimsy plan. And if it worked, it wouldn't buy me much, just a couple of weeks or a couple more dates. But maybe it would be enough. It had to be. So I couldn't kiss her. But God, I fucking wanted to.

It was funny that two pivotal moments in my life were happening at the exact same time and at complete odds with each other. I didn't know how to balance what was going on with my family and what was going on with my feelings for Emma.

I had four more weeks to convince her not to go, and I had to deal with the fallout of Mom leaving at the same time. I didn't know if I could be spread that thin, mentally, physically, and emotionally, and still give enough of myself to get any of it right.

My siblings would need me. Chelsea had no idea what was going on. That was either going to make this easier or a lot harder in the long run. Mom had been telling her for a few weeks that she was going on a trip, but now that it was happening, nobody knew how Chelsea was going to take it.

Alex was sad but trying to be stoic. Sarah was angrier than usual, and *I* was just taking things one minute at a time. That's all I could do.

When it was time for Mom to go, Leigh hung back in the doorway while Mom walked around the table giving her kids hugs.

Chelsea was the hardest goodbye.

"Baby, can I talk to you for a second?" Mom picked her up.

We all watched Mom explain that she was going away for a while and she was going to miss her but that Justin was going to be here to take care of her.

"Are you going to come back fir my birfday?" Chelsea asked.

This is when everyone lost it. Alex let out a muffled cry over his plate and Sarah got up and ran to her room. I had to turn my head.

"No, baby," Mom said. "But Justin and Leigh are going to make sure you have the best fifth birthday ever, okay? And you can talk to me on the phone and send me pictures and drawings and come see me once in a while."

My sister nodded and then started to wiggle to be put down.

Mom kissed her one more time, fighting tears, and set her on the floor, where she ran off to go watch her cartoons.

Then Leigh and I walked Mom out to the driveway. Mom

stood by the door of Leigh's Jeep, wiping under her eyes. "Give Alex the van when he gets his license."

I nodded. "Okay."

She looked at me with the most shattered expression I'd ever seen. "Justin, I'm so sorry."

I had to muscle down the knot in my throat. "I know."

Her chin quivered. "Please take good care of them."

I brought her in and hugged her. "I will. I'll take good care of them." I paused. "You showed me how."

This broke her. She sobbed and I just held her, feeling helpless. She felt so small. She was always small, a foot shorter than me. But now she felt shrunken. Defeated.

Life had chipped away at her. Filled her cracks with ice. And I just wished I'd recognized what was happening to her before it was too late.

When she got in the car and drove off with Leigh, I wasn't sad. I was angry again, but not at Mom. This time I was angry at the world. The judge who gave her such a long sentence. The manufacturer of the airbag that didn't save my dad, the friends who didn't stop the drunk driver from getting in the car—I was even mad at the nonprofit that didn't notice money was missing until it was so much it meant *this*. And I was angry at the timing. Of all of it. Because none of it was fair and I knew deep down what it meant.

I *would* lose Emma to this.

It was early and it was new between us, but everything in me was shouting that she was important. But I also knew I couldn't make it work now. Not with my life like this. I felt selfish for wishing she would stay, meet me where I was, in the rubble that was my family.

I don't know how she felt about me taking the kids, but she didn't show a lot of interest in getting to know my people, so I didn't think it was a selling point. They meant I couldn't follow her, and if her nomadic history was any indication, she wouldn't stay. And how could I even rationalize asking her to when even *I* didn't want to be here?

What did I have to offer her? I had nothing but baggage. Emotionally damaged, traumatized children that had been catapulted from one tragedy to the next, and me, barely keeping my head above water. Would I even have the time or the bandwidth to be any kind of partner while I was helping my siblings navigate this situation? What was the point in even hoping for anything to be different between Emma and me? To what? Pull her from her glamorous jet-setting life to ground her with me in this fucking mess? I'd feel like apologizing every day. There was no way I could ever be worth it.

Four dates. One kiss. And a breakup.

That's all this would be. And that made me the angriest of all. Because I knew in my gut that's not what this was *supposed* to be.

I sat on the asphalt and put my face in my hands. And I didn't care who drove by and saw me sitting there. The weight of the whole world had just dropped onto my back. A million new responsibilities while I grieved the loss of yet *another* parent and the inevitable end of the only relationship that I'd ever given a shit about.

The house loomed in front of me. The birdbath and new pavers and the flower beds Mom had bought with her ill-gotten gains. The perennials she'd planted that I had no idea how to take care of. The lawn, the gutters, the snow in the winter. The wobbly fence and the loose door handle on the garage. The broken parts and the broken people inside. All mine, all at once.

It was overwhelming. I felt like I couldn't breathe.

Is this how Mom felt when Dad died? Only with a new baby too? This house, like an island, and her, responsible for everyone on it?

At some point Benny and Brad pulled up. And then they were in the driveway with me. I don't know how long we sat there, not saying a word. I didn't really have to say anything. They both knew me well enough.

"How the hell do I do this?" I whispered.

Brad answered. "You go through it. You can't go around it, you have to go through it. And we're here to help you do it."

We all three sat there, staring at the house. Brad wiped at his eyes. He was crying too. Mom was his aunt the same way Leigh was mine. This nightmare was everyone's. An atomic bomb. It affected anyone close enough to be in the blast zone.

After a few minutes Brad got up. "Let's go. Get you guys out of here. You too."

I looked up at him. "What?"

"You're taking the kids to the Mall of America, Great Wolf Lodge for a few days. When you get back, you'll be all moved in, carpet changed out, bathroom done."

I blinked at him. "I thought the kids were going with Jane. I have to help with the move, I can't let you guys do it by yourself—"

"Brad and I talked about it," Benny said. "The kids need to be with you right now. It doesn't make any sense to separate you. We got you a family suite at the water park. Jane and I will take the dog."

Brad put a hand on my shoulder. "They'll have fun. They'll be distracted. It's what everyone needs right now. We'll get your new room set up, make this place feel like home. Benny knows how to put together your computer shit. I know how your room should look. We got it."

I didn't even know what to say. "Thank you" was all I could manage.

"Don't thank us," Brad said. "Just get the hell out of here."

CHAPTER 22

EMMA

Justin's phone rang twice before he picked up. "Emma."

"Hey, Forehead Kiss Guy."

"I'm Forehead Kiss Guy now?" he said. There was a smile in there.

"You are around here," I said. "That's what everyone on the island calls you."

"So you've been telling everyone. My plan worked, you can't stop thinking about it."

"I keep thinking about it because I can't believe you had the nerve. It used to be that you could break a curse with a guy and he'd keep all his promises."

"I'm going to keep my promises. I promise."

He got a laugh out of me.

"What are you doing?" he asked.

I leaned over the railing on the second floor of the mall watching him walk in front of a shoe store with Chelsea. "Nothing. How was it this morning?"

I heard him blow out a breath. "Not great. I'm at the Mall of America with the kids. I have been sent by my best friends and the women who tolerate them, on an all-expense-paid trip while they remodel my new bedroom. We're staying at the water park across the street until they're done."

"Awwww, that's actually really nice of them."

"Yeah. I might have to rename my dog after all."

"Well, I don't know that you need to go *that* far."

He chuckled.

"Hey, would you like to join me?" he asked. "Meet me where I am? Help me forget about my crappy day."

"At the mall?"

"Yeah. We have one of the world's largest malls with an indoor amusement park in it. It's got an aquarium and a mirror maze. One of those giant bean bag places. Every store known to man. There's one that sells nothing but hot sauce. Mini golf, old-timey photos—"

I gasped. "I *love* old-timey photos."

"Great. Come and we'll take some. We can be pirates. Bring Maddy. She can make me walk the plank."

"I want to do the 1920s one with the tommy gun and the bag of money," I said.

"I look *great* in a fedora."

I could see him smiling from all the way up here.

"I can promise you chaste forehead kisses and fine dining at Bubba Gump Shrimp..." he said, trying to sell it.

"You know what? Yeah. I think I would like you to chastely kiss my forehead today. I can be there in...fifteen minutes ago?"

I watched him halt to a dead stop and I grinned.

"You're here?" he asked.

"Jane texted me last week. We've been conspiring to cheer you up for quite some time."

There was a beat of silence.

"Did you just fist pump?" I asked.

Another pause. "How did you know that?"

"You're getting predictable, Justin. Also, I can see you. Look up."

He raised his head and beamed. Maddy popped over the railing next to me and waved.

"I'm on my way down," I said.

Two minutes later I was on the escalator. Justin was waiting at the bottom in a navy Jaxon Waters T-shirt and jeans. He had Chelsea on his shoulders. She was using his forehead to hang on, her little fingers interlocked over his eyebrows. His hair was an absolute mess.

"I find that extremely attractive," Maddy said, too low for him to hear.

"Same," I whispered.

"Hey, Forehead Kiss Guy," Maddy said when we got to the bottom.

He looked at me amused. "Wow. You are *obsessed* with me."

I laughed and smiled up at Chelsea. "Hi, Chelsea."

She gave me a shy hello, and I introduced her to my best friend.

Justin nodded toward the entrance. "I need to rent one of those little car strollers at the entrance. Her legs gave out an hour ago."

"Where are Alex and Sarah?" I asked, looking around.

"On the rides. I got them all-day wristbands. We probably won't see them until they're hungry. I was about to take Chels to the aquarium."

Chelsea leaned over his head. "Jussin, I have to go potty."

"Okay, I'll take you," he said, looking up at her under his eyebrows.

"Want me to take her?" I asked. "You can rent the stroller while we're in there."

"Sure," he said, lifting her off his shoulders. "Thanks."

When we came out of the bathroom, Justin was waiting with the stroller.

I wished I could hug him. I couldn't do it when he had his sister on his shoulders, and it seemed weird to do it now that the hello part was over. I watched him lift his little sister into her seat and turn the stroller to face the mall. But instead of pushing it, he stepped out from behind it, closed the small gap between us, and scooped me into a hug.

I went instantly breathless.

"I didn't get to say hi to you," he whispered, squeezing me.

My heart pounded, and he tightened around the breath I let out.

He held me for just longer and closer than a friend would. Then he kissed my cheek and let me go, and I felt like I'd been twirled around in circles and set back down. I was actually a little flustered.

Maddy was eyeing me.

"Are you hungry?" Justin asked. "Want to get something before we go see the fish?"

"Uh...I'm okay. Maddy?"

"I'm good. Let me push this," she said, walking between us to take the stroller.

I was glad she did because Justin used his freed hand to hold mine.

He led us to the elevator and when he leaned over to push the down button Maddy put her mouth to my ear. "You're blushing," she whispered.

I jerked my head to look at her and mouthed the word *What?*

She gave me a wide-eyed *Oh Yeah, You Are* nod.

I put my free hand on my cheek. It was warm. Knowing I was blushing made me blush harder.

I did not blush. That was *not* a thing I did.

I guess until now.

CHAPTER 23

JUSTIN

Think of how much room there is for activities," Emma said, putting her arms out.

"I *do* like corduroy."

We were sprawled on a giant bean bag at the giant bean bag store on the third level.

I was so glad she was here.

We'd been to the aquarium, then had dinner at the Rainforest Cafe—Chelsea insisted we eat there once she saw the front of it on our way to Bubba Gump Shrimp. Afterward we stopped at a cookie shop and then went to the old-timey photo place. We did pirates *and* the fedoras.

I was using every excuse to touch Emma. My knee against hers under the table at dinner, holding her hand, a palm on her lower back as we walked into a store. And if I didn't know better, I'd say Maddy was wingmanning me. She was attached to the stroller like it was her job to speed push it through the mall five feet in front of me and Emma, and I swear she was doing it to give me alone time with her friend. Right now she was taking Chelsea to the bathroom to wash chocolate off her face while Emma and I tried out different bean bags.

Emma lolled her head to look at me. "Where would you put this thing if you got it?"

"I could probably find a place. The house is a lot bigger than my studio."

"So is your apartment gone?"

I looked back up at the ceiling. "I still have it for another three months. I couldn't get out of the lease. But Mom paid the mortgage on the house through the summer so I'm not paying on two places."

"Will you take me to see it?" she asked.

I looked back at her. "The apartment? Of course. It won't have any furniture though."

"I'm only coming for the Toilet King."

I laughed and we lay there and gazed at each other.

I couldn't help but think that this is what it would be like in bed with her. Talking and laughing, her hair fanned out under her like it was now.

She bit her lip. "I'm glad I came," she said.

"Me too. I wanted to show you all Minnesota has to offer. You would have missed the hairpiece kiosk."

We laughed but it was short-lived. My smile fell and I looked back at the ceiling.

"My life is pretty shitty right now, Emma," I said. "I'm sure you could find much better dates."

She gasped playfully. "Are you breaking up with me?"

"I'm serious."

She sat up and propped her head in her hand, smiling. "I like the dates you take me on. I wanted to come today, and I've had a *very* good time."

I searched her face for something deeper than what she probably meant, but before I could find it, she glanced at something over my shoulder. Alex and Sarah walked into the store. My sister stopped in front of our bean bag, looking disgusted.

"If you guys are done making out, can we go?" Sarah said, crossing her arms.

I sat up on my elbows. "Hey, how was the amusement park?"

They hadn't met us for dinner. Besides a quick thirty seconds when they found me on the bench outside Sephora to get cash for the food court, I hadn't seen them all day.

"It sucked," Sarah said.

"No, it didn't," Alex said. "It was awesome!"

Sarah gave him a look. "Maybe for *you*. Hanging out with my brother isn't my idea of a good time. I'll be outside. I want to go."

She left the store, and Alex threw his hands up in exasperation and went out after her.

I glanced at Emma and sighed.

"She's right, you know," Emma said, sitting up on her elbows too. "You should let her bring a friend next time."

"Alex didn't need a friend."

"Alex is going to have fun no matter what and no matter who he's with."

I bobbed my head. "Okay. True."

She nudged my knee with hers. "You don't remember what it was like to be that age? It doesn't matter how cool the thing is, if they don't have a friend they won't have fun. Trust me. It will save you a ton of grief, it's a teenager hack."

I guess she had a point. I mean, it wasn't much different for me when I thought about it. I didn't want to be at the mall—it had lost its novelty for me about fifteen years ago. I was only here for the kids. But with Emma here, I couldn't think of any place I'd rather be. Even earlier when Maddy was in Sephora and Emma and I sat on the bench outside just talking, Chelsea knocked out in her stroller, it was fun.

It's funny how when you find someone you like as much as I liked her, the destination is suddenly wherever they are. Even if there's someplace better, you wouldn't go if they couldn't come.

I puffed air from my cheeks. "Maybe I should see if Josie can get dropped off at the water park tomorrow."

"You should."

I arched an eyebrow. "I don't suppose *you* want to go to the water park tomorrow. I'll buy your ticket. Maddy's too," I added quickly.

But she shook her head. "No. I promised Neil I'd put in some hostas."

I nodded. "Right. Okay." I tried to keep the disappointment out of my voice. "And where are you putting the rosebush?"

She tilted her head. "I don't know. I have to find a good spot."

"Let me know if you need help planting it."

"I've got Maddy."

"So you're saying she's good at digging holes…"

"I'm telling her you said that."

"Please don't, I'm scared of her."

She laughed.

I peered out into the mall at my brother and sister loitering by the railing, Sarah looking annoyed and Alex texting, laughing at something on his phone.

"If you didn't come today, it probably would have crushed what was left of my fragile spirit," I said, only half kidding.

"Oh yeah? The stakes were that high?"

I looked over at her. "What would you say if I told you you should stay another few weeks? Sign another contract."

She looked up to the side like she was thinking about it before coming back to me. "I would say that it's probably not doable. It's Maddy's turn to pick," she said. "I had to promise her she could pick twice just to get her to agree to come here."

"What if you begged?"

She laughed like I was joking, but really I wasn't.

She propped her head on her hand. "I think I know what you need," she said.

"Oh yeah?"

"Yeah." Then she leaned over and kissed my forehead.

I closed my eyes for the three seconds her lips were pressed to my skin. My heart was in my throat.

She pulled away slowly. "Better?" she whispered. "I hear forehead kisses are all the rage."

"Ha." I tickled her. She squealed and twisted away from me just as an employee approached us. "Hey, sorry guys, we're closing up."

I looked at my watch. Nine p.m. The whole mall was shutting down.

"We should probably go home anyway," Emma said, sliding off the bean bag.

"Yeah," I said, getting off too.

We walked out of the store as they lowered the gate behind us. Maddy was coming back from the bathrooms with Chelsea, a couple of stores down.

"How long are you staying at the water park?" Emma asked.

"Probably a few more days. Until Benny and Brad are done with the house. Can I walk you out to your car?" I asked, trying to buy a few more minutes with her.

She shook her head. "No, no. You have the kids. I'll just say goodbye to you here."

"Oh. Okay."

She leaned over and gave me a hug. I breathed her in, tried to hold it in my lungs. I wouldn't see her until our next date. Another five days at least and too long.

She let me go, and I held Chelsea while I watched Emma leave out the door by Nordstrom without looking back.

Emma had an aloofness to her. Like she was just along for the ride and the ride didn't mean much.

At least not as much as it meant to me.

CHAPTER 24

EMMA

The interrogation started the second we got in the car. "Oh my God, that guy's fucking in love with you," Maddy said, turning on the engine. "It's cute. Honestly, I'm not usually about all that puppy dog stuff, but I liked it."

"He is not in love with me," I said, putting on my seat belt.

"Yeah, he is. And you liiiiike him."

"I do like him," I admitted. "More than I thought I was going to."

She gave me her yay face. "Okay. Awesome. When's the wedding?"

"Maddy!"

"What?"

"I can't date him."

She'd started pulling out of the parking space, but now she hit the brakes and threw the car in park. She pivoted in her seat to look at me straight on. "Why don't you want to date him?"

"He has kids?" I said.

"They're his *siblings*."

"I know. But he's going to be raising them for the next six years."

"So you'd give up someone perfect because his life took a shit turn and he ended up having to raise some kids."

"Uh, I think you're simplifying it a bit."

"You are un*real*." She shook her head at me. "You're just *looking* for a reason, *any* reason, to disqualify him."

I scoffed. "So him having three kids isn't a big enough reason? If I saw that on a dating profile, I would have swiped left. I've never dated men with kids, ever. That's a conscious choice I make."

"You don't want anything that can't fit in your luggage." She stared at me like she'd just had an epiphany. "The lengths you will go to stay living in the chaos you're accustomed to—"

I rolled my eyes. "What *chaos*?"

"The chaos you grew up in! This *whole life* you've made—the travel nursing and the constant moving—you're reliving your childhood," she said. "Doing it in a safe way you can control. You slap the word 'adventure' on it like lipstick on a pig, but it is what it is, just another way to keep you from ever belonging to anywhere or any*one*."

"Really?" I looked at her, amused. "First of all, there is nothing wrong with me liking to travel. It's maybe the *one* thing my childhood set me up for that I *don't* hate. And there's also nothing wrong with me making practical life choices. I've known Justin for like five minutes. So I what? Give up my career and jazz hands my way into his fragile, grieving family hoping it works out between us? Me and this guy I *just* met? And if it doesn't work out? How will that affect these kids, who just lost their mom on the tail end of losing their dad?"

"Keep it separate. Don't go over there. Don't mix your life with theirs until you're sure."

I laughed. "He is a full-time parent now. A full-time *single* parent. He's not going to get weekends when the kids are off with their mom and we can go do things. If I'm not willing to be around the kids, I'll never see him. What would even be the point of staying here? For the once or twice a month when he can get away? Anyone dating him is going to be doing soccer games and pizza nights in the breakfast nook while they help Sarah with homework. I mean, look at today. And honestly, he shouldn't even be dating anyone right now, he should be getting adjusted."

She jabbed a finger at me. "*Not* your decision to make." She looked me in the eye. "That is a *good* man. You are going to fuck up if you let that go."

"What exactly has Justin done to warrant this unwavering support from you? I thought you wanted him dead."

"I think he might be The One."

I cracked up.

"I'm serious," she said. "You're in denial. You're blushing and acting like a lovesick teenager. I've known you half your life. I have never seen you look at someone like that." She started ticking off on her fingers. "First he gets you to come to Minnesota, then you go over there when you're small and you meet his *family*. At this point I'm convinced the man could sell you an MLM."

"I had very rational reasons to do all of those things," I said.

"He's chivalrous," she said, going on. "He stayed with you during the Amber/Neil Lobster Lovefest. He gives you *butterflies*. He's awakened something inside of your cold, dead heart."

"Oh wow, thanks."

"You need to jump on this before it's too late."

"Too late for *what*? What's going to happen? If I don't find someone to love me I shall remain forever a beast?" I made a fake scared face.

She narrowed her eyes at me.

"Do I like him? Yes. Am I attracted to him? Also yes. Did he sort of ask me today to stay in Minnesota longer? He did. But his lifestyle is not for me. It's not a fit. I can acknowledge that I like him while also being practical enough to know it won't work out. That's what dating is for, to see if you're compatible. We're not."

She cocked her head. "He asked you to stay?"

"He asked me to sign another contract. Yes."

"And you said?"

"The truth. That it's your turn to pick and I had to promise you two turns just to get you to come here."

Her eyes went wide. "Oh *hell* no. You're not putting this shit on me."

"Did I *lie*? It is your turn."

She put a hand to her chest. "Let's be very clear here. *I* am not the obstacle in the way of your happiness. That person is you."

"Okay, Maddy. Noted."

She studied me for a moment. Then she looked forward and put the car in drive. She drove out of the mall's parking garage and started to navigate the streets without another word.

"Are you mad?" I asked.

"No."

"You look mad."

"I'm not. It just...sucks. He's a nice guy."

"Yeah," I said. "He is. But it is what it is."

And you know what? It really did suck. Because she was right. I did like him.

Maybe Justin was the right guy, at the wrong time. Maybe if I'd met him a few years ago, or six years from now, when his mom was coming home, it would be a different story. But it wasn't.

In a few weeks I *was* going to leave. It was what we'd agreed upon. Four dates, one kiss, and a breakup. Just for the summer.

We drove on in silence, and I peered out the window. Then we passed the freeway on-ramp and kept driving the side streets.

I turned to Maddy. "Where are we going?"

"Great Wolf Lodge. I forgot my purse."

"Where?"

"In Justin's stroller. In the bag with the shirt he bought."

I pulled my face back. "Why did you put it in his shirt bag?"

My phone started to ring. It was Justin.

I hit the answer button. "Hey," I said, eyeing my best friend.

"Hey," he said. "I think Maddy left her purse in my bag."

"I know, we're heading to the Great Wolf Lodge now."

"Cool, I'll bring it down. Where should I meet you?"

I looked up through the windshield at the parking lot we were driving into. "There's a waterslide that comes out of the side of the building. I think it's the east parking lot? We're pulling in there."

"Okay. I'll be down in a bit." We hung up.

I sat back in my seat and looked at my best friend. "Why do I feel like you did that on purpose?"

She shrugged unapologetically. "He couldn't kiss you good-bye in front of the kids. Figured if we timed it right, he could get them back to the hotel room, then run down by himself. I drove around aimlessly for a few minutes to give him time to get them situated."

I shook my head at her. "You are unbelievable."

"What?" she said, pulling a mint out of the change tray and handing it to me. "You have to manifest your own destiny."

"He's just going to run it to the car," I said, unwrapping it.

"No, he's not, 'cause you're not gonna be in this car. Get out."

"What?"

"Get OUT."

She leaned over and unbuckled me. "Get the fuck out. I mean it."

I put the mint in my mouth and looked at her, amused.

"Emma, go meet him at the door, or I will lose my shit. I didn't push a clunky car stroller around the universe's largest mall for five hours so you could shake hands with this guy on the way out. As soon as he shows up, I'm going to park around the front at the lobby to give you some privacy. Go get your damn forehead kiss."

I was laughing now. "Fine. I'm going."

"Good. Leave."

"I am." I opened the car door. "You are the worst."

"Don't care. Bye."

I shook my head and closed the car door.

The parking lot was empty. It looked like the direct entrance to the water park, which probably closed the same time the mall did. Several large green waterslides snaked out of the building and looped back in. All you could hear was the whir of something electrical and the splattering of dripping water from the slides on the pavement below.

I got to the entrance just as Justin got to the door. He'd changed into a pair of running pants and a hoodie. His hair was wet like he'd taken a shower. Probably getting ready for bed. I noted how snuggly he looked and had to force myself to not think about the docking station.

"Hey," he said, coming out. "Just admit you're obsessed with me, you don't have to plant things in my stuff for excuses to come see me."

I laughed and took the purse he held out.

Justin looked over my shoulder. "Where's she going?"

I turned around to see Maddy in the car, vanishing around the front of the building. I rolled my eyes. "I think we've been set up," I said.

I started to turn back to him, but before I knew what was happening, his hands were on my waist, and I was being pulled against him. I blinked up at him, surprised. His eyes dropped to my mouth, he tipped his head down and *kissed* me. A warm, long soft press of his lips to mine.

I *melted.* My legs lost their bones.

Once when I was twenty I spilled some hot oil on my foot while I was cooking. The searing white pain was so intense it was like everything else vanished. I couldn't see, I couldn't hear. I could only feel.

This was the polar opposite of the same thing.

Every single molecule of my body was in the place where his mouth touched mine. I hadn't even seen it coming and then suddenly it was everything and all there was. The headlights of a truck, so close and fast it's all you can see before it hits you.

I threw my arms around his neck, purse still in hand, half to keep me from buckling and half to get closer. His embrace tightened and he blew a soft breath through his nose and the warm air rolled across my face and all I could think about was some foggy memory of just a few minutes ago of Maddy saying that I was in denial, and me being in denial about it.

Then he pulled away. Just…stopped.

"What happened?" I panted. "Why'd you stop?"

"That's all you get," he said, his voice low.

I blinked at him. "What? *Why?*"

"Because I said so," he said, looking at my lips. "And no means no."

Then he unwrapped my arms from his neck, held my cheeks in his hands, gave me another forehead kiss, and *left*.

I stood there, holding Maddy's purse, staring after him.

"Justin!"

"I'll see you next week. Call Maddy to come pick you up."

I gawked. "Just so you know, that kiss doesn't count!" I yelled. "It has to be open-mouthed."

"Oh, I know." He grinned at me over his shoulder while he scanned his wristband to let himself back into the building.

I crossed my arms. "What exactly is your strategy here? To make me beg?"

He stopped in the open door. "Would you? Beg? It might help."

I gasped. "I *hate* you."

He started laughing. "I don't think so. Good night, Emma."

And then he left me in the side parking lot at Great Wolf Lodge.

CHAPTER 25

JUSTIN

Emma: In case you're wondering, you are the asshole.

I typed into my phone, grinning.

Me: I think what you meant to say was that I am an exceptional kisser and you miss me very much.

She typed for a long time, but only a quick message came through.

Emma: You are an exceptional kisser. But you are still the asshole.

I was in an uncomfortable hotel bed at a water park. My mom went to prison today and I officially took custody of my three siblings. And I *still* smiled myself to sleep.

CHAPTER 26

EMMA

What is it about getting rejected that makes you want them more?" I asked, typing into my charting computer. We were at Royaume at the nurses' station on the Med Surg floor.

"You're still talking about this?" Maddy said from the computer next to me. "It's been over a week. And anyway, he didn't reject you, he just didn't kiss you as much as you wanted, which shouldn't be a big deal since he's not a lifestyle match and all that."

She smirked, and I narrowed my eyes at her.

"That must have been some kiss if you keep thinking about it," she mumbled.

It *was*.

I'd played it over in my head a thousand times. The turn, the pull into his chest, the split second where his eyes had locked with mine before they dropped to my mouth.

His lips were so soft. I'd liked that he'd smelled like toothpaste and Downy, like he'd just washed the hoodie he'd been wearing. I'd liked how tightly he'd held me to him. How his arms had felt wrapped around me. But mostly I kept thinking about it because the way he'd grabbed me and kissed me felt like he'd been waiting all day for a chance to do it. And the more I thought about it, the more I realized I'd been too.

The kiss was a sure thing. I knew it was coming. But it was one thing to expect something, and something very else to long for it. I'd been longing for his kiss. I'd been hoping he'd kiss me the whole time we were at the mall. Every time we were somewhere that gave us a few seconds alone and out of sight, I'd been wishing he'd lean in.

"You okay?" Maddy asked.

I'd stopped typing and was staring blankly at my screen.

"Yeah. Fine," I said, picking up on the chart where I left off. "I just think Justin and I have some sexual tension we need to work out."

"And how you gonna do that?" she asked, giving me a look.

I gave her one back. "How do you think?"

"You think he's gonna be cool with a hookup? I don't get the sense he's a one-night-stand kind of guy."

"All guys are one-night-stand kind of guys," I said, typing.

She grunted. Then she looked up over my shoulder and wrinkled her forehead. "Is that…*Amber*?"

I turned in my chair to see my mom walking down the hallway, a brown paper bag in her hand.

"Did you know she was coming?" Maddy asked.

I smiled. "No."

Mom had never visited me at work before. She spotted me and her face lit up. I watched her make her way over.

She looked like a Greek goddess wearing a dark blue maxi

dress with gold sandals. Ankle bracelets that jingled while she walked.

"Hey, girls!" she said, setting the bag on the counter.

"Hey," I said brightly. "This is such a nice surprise."

"Meeting Neil for lunch," she said, twisting to look around.

I felt myself deflate. "Oh," I said. "He just went into surgery."

Now her face fell. "Oh. Well, how long does that take?"

"Hours," Maddy said. "Depends what it is."

"Huh." Mom chewed on her bottom lip. "He missed dinner last night, and so I just thought—" She looked around like she might see him.

"That's really nice of you to bring him lunch," Maddy said, her tone a little dry.

"Yeah," Mom said distractedly. She put a thumb over her shoulder. "Hey, when I came in, I told that nurse with the blond hair who I was and she didn't know me. Neil talks about me at work, right?"

Maddy glanced at me. "I mean, not really."

"He doesn't really talk to the nurses," I said.

Mom chewed her lip again. "Okay."

There was a moment of silence.

"Do you want me to give this to him when he's done?" I asked, nodding at the bag.

She seemed to snap out of it. "Yeah. Yes. I baked him some zucchini bread. There's a mushroom frittata, a cucumber feta salad—I mean, we're living together. That's a little weird, right? That nobody knows he has a girlfriend?"

Maddy and I looked at each other.

"I bet the other doctors know," I volunteered.

"Oh, totally," Maddy said, nodding.

"I don't think he gets into his personal life with the nurses," I said.

"We're small beans," Maddy added. "The doctors have their own lounge. There's not a lot of mingling."

Mom nodded, but she still looked off.

"Okay. Well, I gotta go," she said. "See you girls at the house."

We watched her walk out.

Maddy took the bag from the counter and peered into it. "Funny she brought him lunch and didn't think to make any for you."

I went back to my keyboard, trying to act like she didn't just say what I'd been thinking.

Maybe it was unfair to expect more from Mom. I was a twenty-eight-year-old woman, capable of making my own lunch. She didn't have to do that for me. Maybe she'd only had enough food for Neil. Maybe she didn't know I'd be here. Yes, she could have texted me to ask, but maybe she thought I'd already packed food and she knew Neil didn't so she only brought enough for him.

It hurt my feelings anyway.

"She hasn't spent any time with you since the Lobsterfest, right?" Maddy asked, breaking into my thoughts.

I shook my head. "No. But she's been trying to get me and Justin to hang out with her and Neil. It just hasn't worked out yet."

"She's inviting you for Neil, just so you know."

I looked at her. "What?"

"It makes her look bad that she ignores you so much. Neil probably mentions it. That's why the only time she invites you anywhere is when Neil's gonna be there."

I stiffened. "No. There was the time she invited me to dinner when he was at work."

"So he would come home and see you there. Or because she was bored and lonely. FYI, Amber only ever calls you when it serves Amber," she said.

"That is *not* true."

She cocked her head. "No? Think about all the times in the last ten years she's reached out to you when it was just for you. She didn't go to your high school graduation. She didn't go to your nursing school graduation. She forgets your birthday almost every year."

"She's forgetful—"

"That woman spends her life asking people what day and time they were born and she can't remember your birthday? Come on. A thousand bucks says she remembers Neil's birthday."

"Well, this year will be different," I said matter-of-factly. "She's here. I'm sure she'll do something nice."

She looked back at her screen. "I hope so."

"And she couldn't afford the time off work for my graduations. She asked for pictures—"

"To show people. Because it doesn't fit the narrative that she's a loving and doting mother if she doesn't even have pictures of you to show people while she's taking credit for your accomplishments." She looked me in the eye. "We've been staying in the cottage for the last three weeks, literally across the way, and how many times has she come to see you there? Had Neil drop her off during one of their many sunset cruises? That would be zero. Everything Amber does is for *Amber*."

"Why are you telling me this?" I said, my tone more clipped than I liked.

"Because you have this thing where you always believe the best in people—especially with her. It shouldn't surprise you that she continues to be disappointing, yet again, but it always does and I'm sick of seeing you get hurt. You need to lower your expectations waaaaaay down. The bar is on the floor and she'll bring a shovel, every time. The sooner you realize that, the happier you'll be."

I looked away from her and stared through the monitor in front of me, my nostrils flaring. I wanted to snap at her. I wanted to tell her to be quiet and to stop making things up.

Only she wasn't making it up.

Maddy was right. I was an afterthought to my mother.

I don't even know why it surprised me. I'd been taught this lesson a thousand times. But it wasn't the slight that hurt. It was the loss of hope.

When I was little, there had been a time I *was* her whole universe. But the older I got, the less interested she seemed to be in me. She left me for longer and longer, and then eventually she didn't come back for me at all. But I never stopped waiting. I never stopped wanting to be what Neil clearly was for her. And if I wasn't now, then I never would be.

I always thought it was a proximity thing. She traveled a lot, she changed jobs all the time, she was busy, she was dealing with whatever Amber dealt with. But now I couldn't rationalize why nothing was different, even though she was right here.

Maddy would gladly give me her thoughts on this, but I didn't want them because it would sound too much like I Told You So. And she had. She *had* told me. I just didn't want to listen.

I felt myself start to get small, my edges drawing inward.

I could handle disappointment. My life had made me very

good at it. But the kind that came from Mom hit me differently. It always had.

My chin started to quiver, and I bit down hard on the inside of my cheek. I could feel the sob welling up inside of me and I desperately, desperately wanted it to stop. I didn't want Maddy to see me upset. If she did, she'd get protective, and Maddy in protect mode was more than I wanted to deal with.

I turned and pretended to be searching for something in a drawer so she wouldn't see me fighting to keep it together. Then Maddy made a surprised little gasp from next to me. "Hey, Justin!"

I whipped around. Justin was there holding Chelsea and smiling at me over the counter.

"Hey," I said, blinking at him. "What are you doing here?"

He lifted a bag onto the counter with his free hand. "I made you lunch. Wanted to surprise you," he said, shifting his sister on his hip. "I know you said you never know when you're getting your breaks, so I figured I'd just drop it off. I made one for you too, Maddy. Vegetarian. You don't eat meat, right?"

I felt my face go soft, and the lump in my throat instantly vanished. "Thank you..." I breathed.

Chelsea started to wiggle to get down. "Emma! Maddy!"

I smiled and came around the counter and picked her up. She hugged my neck and I grinned. Her pigtails were crooked.

Justin saw me looking at them. "I'm still learning how to do it," he said.

"It's cute."

Justin and I stood there, smiling at each other. It was so good to see him. I don't think I realized how much I wanted to until he was in front of me.

On days that I worked, we didn't get to talk much. We mostly texted and sent each other memes and songs we wanted each other to listen to. I was in a Justin deficit, and I hadn't even realized it until just now.

"What are you doing today?" I asked.

"Just errands," he said. "About to drop her off at preschool. I sent you a survey for our date tomorrow."

"I haven't had a chance to check my email."

"Date number three," he said, his dimples popping.

"Date number three."

We held each other's eyes for a long moment.

He nodded over his shoulder. "I should probably let you get back to work. I have to go pick up Alex and take him to a doctor's appointment." He paused. "Am I allowed to hug you goodbye, or...?"

"Yes! Absolutely." I handed Chelsea to Maddy, who was waiting her turn to hold her, and I closed the space between us and hugged him.

The way he folded around me made me think maybe he was in a deficit too. The hug was a warm factory reset. I didn't want out of it. It was the weirdest feeling, like I wanted to leave with him, just walk right out of my job and go. Those cartoons where the character smells something delicious and it puts them in a trance and they float after the scent in a daze.

"I'll see you tomorrow," he said in my ear. He kissed my cheek and let me go.

I was still floating.

He smiled at me another few seconds. Then he took his sister from Maddy and left the way he came.

"Dios mío, he's cute," Hector said, coming up to lean on the counter, watching Justin walk out.

"Yeah," I said absently, watching the double doors close behind him. "He is."

Maddy grabbed the bag Justin had left and started unpacking it. "Let's see what we got here. Some mixed fruit, strawberries and cantaloupe, green grapes, egg salad sandwiches on sourdough. Look, he put dried cranberries and red onions in the sandwich, you're going to love that. Granola bars, Wheat Thins, we've got some celery sticks, cherry tomatoes, snap peas, and a side of ranch, there's a mandarin orange for each of us, Capri Suns— brownies. He baked *brownies*." She looked up at me. "You're right. You should bone him."

I snorted and Hector looked at me like I had two heads. "You're not boning him yet? You better get on it."

Yeah. I should.

* * * * *

When I got home from work that night, all I wanted to do was talk to Justin. I got into my pajamas and texted him. He told me to give him thirty minutes to get Chelsea in bed. I'd just gotten under the covers when he called.

"Hey," I said, picking up.

"Hey."

I smiled into the darkness of my room. I'd missed the tenor of his voice. "What are you doing?" I asked.

"Lying in bed. Finally."

"Long day?"

He blew a breath into the phone. "It's been a long week in a very long couple of months."

I shifted down into my blankets. "Tell me."

"Eh, you don't want to hear it."

"I do. Tell me," I said again.

He sighed. "The kids start school in three weeks. I'm just a little overwhelmed."

My face fell. "Oh. Do you want to cancel our date? If you need the time—"

"Nooooo. No, no, no. I definitely do *not* want to cancel our date."

The corners of my lips quirked up. "So what's going on?" I asked. "Why are you overwhelmed?"

I heard him stretch. "You really want to hear this? It's going to be an info dump."

"Dump away."

He puffed air from his cheeks. "It's like death by a thousand cuts," he said. "Yesterday Alex comes to tell me that I need to refill his ADHD medication. The pharmacy won't do it without a new prescription, so I call the doctor and the doctor won't do it without a physical. The doctor only sees patients Monday through Friday, so I have to take a half day off work to take him. We get there, and they check his eyesight as part of the exam. He needs reading glasses. So then I'm at LensCrafters getting him glasses for three hundred dollars. He still needs behind-the-wheel hours, so he's the one driving us to each of these things, so I'm stressed the whole time because he's still not very good at it. By the time we're done, I've lost most of my workday and spent three hundred dollars plus a copay, and I still haven't done the *one* thing I set out to do—refill his prescription—which I still need to go pick up. It's like one task just bleeds into the next and I'm never done."

"Yikes…"

"I would have to quit my job just to read the amount of emails these kids' schools send. I had to sign Alex up for soccer, Sarah up for dance, I need to load their lunch accounts, prepay for their school photos, take everyone back-to-school shopping. I had to put Chelsea into preschool early so I can work. I thought I could juggle it with her here, but I can't. She needs too much attention and I can't give it to her, and Alex and Sarah aren't much of a help." I pictured him rubbing his eyebrow. "She cried all three days that I dropped her off. She has friends there and she knows the teachers, but she's been clingy lately and crying at night for Mom. I felt like shit leaving her there, but I've already taken as much PTO as I can."

"She's probably just got some separation anxiety with everything going on," I said. "It'll pass."

"That's what her teacher said. It just sucks. I feel bad."

"How's the new house?" I asked.

He scoffed. "A mess. I don't know if it's just because they're home right now? But there's snack wrappers and socks all over the place. I couldn't find any forks, so I went looking and found half the dishes in Alex's room. They leave all the lights on and they throw their crap everywhere. I'm doing two loads of laundry a day. And I'm starting to get why Mom hoarded napkins. I mean, I make good money, but stretching it over three extra people? I'm going to have to start making adjustments. I'd planned to just order takeout if I needed to, but now I'm thinking I can't afford the extra expense. I've been making dinner every night and Sarah won't eat anything I cook. She's pickier than Chelsea. She won't even try it."

"I'd eat your dinners."

"Come over," he said without skipping a beat.

"It's ten o'clock at night," I said.

"I don't care. I want to see you."

The butterflies flittered up.

"How did your room turn out?" I asked, changing the subject.

"Good," he said tiredly. "Great. I'm actually impressed with Brad's interior design skills."

"Do you have any pictures?"

"Nah, I want you to come see it in person." He paused. "I miss you. I want to see you," he said again.

The breath in my lungs stilled.

He was tired and stressed. It was probably making him a little more direct and edgier than usual. But there was something so primal and matter-of-fact about the way he said he wanted to see me. Like seeing me was a need. The way someone says they need to eat or sleep.

"I can't," I said. "I can't ask Maddy to boat me to shore this late."

"What if…" He stopped. "Never mind."

"What?"

"No, it's too much," he said.

"No, tell me."

"I was just going to say, what if you took the boat yourself so she doesn't have to drive you? Come over and just go back in the morning."

I smiled. "You're inviting me to a sleepover? You're going to see me tomorrow anyway for our next date."

"Too long."

I didn't reply. Because I actually agreed.

"Come over," he said again into the silence. "Please."

I didn't reply.

Then the phone beeped to let me know he was video calling me. My heart started racing.

I accepted the call with my own camera on.

He was lying in bed. The room was dim. His hair was messy and he had a gray T-shirt on.

"Hey," he said.

"Hey," I said, softly.

We sat there, looking at each other. I drank him in. I don't know how he pulled it off, but he was somehow completely cuddly looking and adorable but sexy at the same time.

I looked at his lips and my mind flickered to the kiss.

The kiss...

The kiss I couldn't stop thinking about. Maybe he couldn't stop thinking about it either. Maybe that's why he wanted me to come over so bad...

I examined the curve of his collarbone, the hollow at the base of his neck. His brown eyes studied me back and he seemed a little vulnerable lying there, like this last week had taken something from him. And how could it not? He'd lost his mom, and the reality of his new life was hitting him. I knew what it was like to be thrust from one living situation to the next. It's jarring and disruptive—and he didn't have to do it. He could have done the easy thing for him by letting them go with Leigh. She loved them and would have been a great foster mom. It was a good option—but it wasn't the *best* option. He was. So he'd sacrificed his way of life, and I deeply respected him for it—even more now that I saw how hard it was in practice.

"I know I told you this," I said, "but I do think you did the right thing taking them."

He breathed out. "Yeah."

We peered at each other through the screen.

"What would we do if I came over?" I asked.

"Nothing you don't want to do. We could just cuddle."

I smiled. "Cuddle, huh? Every man who's trying to get a woman to come over says he just wants to cuddle."

He looked amused. "Okay. And what if I don't want to just cuddle? Would you blame me?"

I pretended to think about it. "Hmmmm…no."

He laughed quietly. "Seriously, we can just go to sleep," he said. "I'd be happy just to have you here. Be able to talk to you in person. Also I like the way your hair smells."

"I like the way you smell too," I admitted.

He smiled at this.

I pictured what would *really* happen if I went over there.

He'd sneak me upstairs through his dark house to his room, tiptoeing so we wouldn't wake the kids. I'd climb into his bed while he stripped down to his underwear to go to sleep. He'd get in next to me and hug me to that broad chest.

There's no way either of us would sleep.

At some point he'd kiss me, or I'd kiss him. I'd take my shirt off. Maybe I'd slide a hand into the top of his waistband to see if he was hard. He would be. His hands would slide too. Down between my legs, fingers searching. He'd pull my pants down—

I had to shake myself out of it. Going over there was not within the realm of practical things today. But God I really wanted to.

I really, *really* wanted to.

And the weird thing was, I didn't want to go over there for the same reason I usually met a man late at night. I mean yes, I wanted that too. But I wanted to *see* him. Talk to him. Just be around him, even if all we did *was* sleep.

I had never felt like that before.

Something about it scared me. Gave me the urge to pull back, like a hand jerking away from a hot stove. Something told me I should think more on that. Try to figure out why liking him made me nervous, made me feel like something was wrong. Maybe because I knew liking him was pointless? But for now I put it in the same place I put Mom. I'd think about it later.

I cleared my throat. "Where's the dog?" I asked, changing the subject.

He sat up and reached for something off-screen. Then Brad's frown took up the camera.

I grinned. "Hi, Brad."

The dog scowled into the phone.

Justin set him back off to the side and stayed propped against the headboard. "Did you eat your lunch?"

"Yes, it was amazing. Huge, but amazing."

"You work twelve hours. I wanted to make sure you had enough snacks so you don't get crabby."

"Ha. The Go-Gurt was a nice touch."

"I'll send you a lunch survey next time so you can pick your sides." He put a muscular arm behind his head and smiled into the camera. "I want to be clear on your lunch expectations."

"I like clear expectations," I said, distractedly, also liking the view.

"Are mine clear?" he asked. "That I want you to come over?"

I laughed. "Yes, you've been very clear about that."

"Good." He paused. "You are the only thing in my life making me happy right now. And I'm not the least bit afraid to tell you that."

I gazed at him through the phone.

"You know what?" I said. "I will go over there."

His face broke into a grin. "Tonight?"

I was already getting up. "Yeah. I'll have to be back in the morning, but—" Thunder cracked overhead and I froze.

"Was that thunder?" he asked. But before I could answer, another rumbling shook the house and the rain started.

I opened the curtain to my window and looked out. "Ugh. It's pouring." The lake would be choppy and dark, docking would be a nightmare to do alone. "I can't take the boat in this." I was instantly disappointed. God, I hated this island.

"It's okay," he said. "It would have been nice, but…"

"But what?" I flopped back onto the bed.

"Well, the bed's a little crowded anyway." He panned over, and Chelsea was sleeping next to him on top of his comforter, curled up in her *Frozen* blanket. I laughed and he brought the camera back to him.

"Just know that I wish you were here," he said.

I smiled. "I wish I were there too."

CHAPTER 27

JUSTIN

I'd never done drugs before, but I imagined this was what being high felt like. I couldn't wait for our date tonight.

We were doing the historic bridge walk and getting pizza. There was a Music in the Park event in the Nicollet Island Pavilion, which was on the route. It was the last concert of the season. I was bringing a blanket and some bug spray, a bottle of wine and some glasses. Leigh was watching the dog and the kids. I'd planned everything based on Emma's answers to the survey I'd sent and then I made another invite. I used a picture of the Toilet King outside my window as the backdrop for it. Details matter.

Every date with her was sacred to me. I liked spending time with her so much, I brought her lunch yesterday just to have an excuse to see her for five minutes. I thought about the next time I got to see her every second up until she arrived.

I thought about her all the time.

She was getting an Uber to my apartment to meet me. When

she finally knocked on the door, I practically ran to answer it. When I did, I busted up laughing. She was wearing the same shirt as me. The Toilet King, knotted at the waist.

"No way," I said, looking her up and down in the doorway. "Where'd you find it?"

"Like it's hard to find Toilet King anything around here?" she said.

"He's got us as walking advertisements," I said, stepping aside to let her in. "Unbelievable. We look like we're on some twisted team-building exercise," I said, closing the door behind her.

She grinned up at me. "Aren't we?"

I couldn't hide my smile. I didn't know how it was possible she got more beautiful every time I saw her, but she did.

"Hi," I said, my voice low.

"Hi, Kiss And Run Guy."

"Not to be mistaken with Forehead Kiss Guy?"

She scrunched up her face. "Hmmmm. They do look a lot alike."

I laughed and leaned in and kissed her. Just a quick peck, but it got my heart going anyway.

I could have sworn she was blushing when I was done.

"So this is it," she said, tucking her hair behind her ear. "The infamous studio apartment with the view."

I twisted to look over my shoulder. "I'd give you the tour, but you can see everything from here."

She laughed a little and peered around. "Smaller than I expected."

"The room at my mom's house is much bigger," I added.

"And it doesn't have a giant toilet outside."

"Silver lining."

She nodded at the air mattress where my bed used to be. "What's this?"

I rubbed the back of my neck. "The guys left this here. Thought maybe I'd want to use the place from time to time. I'm still paying for it."

"Use it for what?" she asked, blinking at me innocently.

"Uh…naps?"

She nodded wryly. "Right. Naps."

Now *I* was blushing.

I'd be lying if I said I didn't hope we ended up back here after the date. The air mattress wasn't ideal, and Brad put a damn Toilet King blanket on the bed just to be a dick. But still. Aside from getting a hotel room, which I shouldn't be spending money on with all the new expenses, there was no other place for us to have privacy now. She had Maddy at the cottage. My new living arrangement wasn't good with the kids there. An air mattress and the Toilet King was somehow the most reasonable option.

She was standing inside my personal space. Close enough that I could smell her hair. I wanted to pull her to me and put my nose to her head and breathe her in.

I stayed where I was.

"I need to see that billboard up close," she said.

"It's not close enough?"

She laughed and made her way around the foot of my air mattress, dragging a finger on the blanket as she went. She opened the sliding glass door and stepped out onto the tiny balcony into the warm summer air. I followed her and we stood there, hands on the railing, looking up at The King.

"You can see every pore…" she said in wonder. "You know, this would be a really nice view if the billboard wasn't here."

"Don't rub it in."

"Okay, but be honest," she said, turning to me. "He'd be the first person you'd think of if you had a plumbing issue."

"He's been the first thing I think of the minute I wake up, all day long, when I go to bed…"

She laughed, shaking her head at the sign.

"I gotta give it to him," I said. "His marketing *is* effective. He might be some kind of evil genius."

She leaned on the railing. There wasn't much room for two people out here. She was just within my personal space again, and she didn't move to go back into the apartment. The proximity was a tiny intimate sign that even though we hadn't done anything past first base yet, the intention for something past first might be there.

She'd almost come over last night. If she had, I was pretty sure it wasn't going to be just sleeping. It felt like we were inching toward something more serious and I wondered what it meant.

Or if it meant anything at all.

This was a woman who could leave a place and never look back. She kept her life reduced to two suitcases because she didn't get sentimental about anything. Was she sentimental about sex?

She had to know this wasn't just a fling for me. I'd told her I missed her last night. I'd asked her to stay longer and renew her contract. It didn't sound like she was going to do it, but she knew I wanted her to. She wouldn't just come over for a hookup knowing I wanted something more serious. I couldn't picture her doing that.

It felt like we were either going to be all or nothing. We'd kiss, because we were supposed to kiss, and then we wouldn't cross any more lines if she wasn't planning on staying and that would be that.

Or we'd cross all the lines. Many, *many* times. And we'd do it because this was leading somewhere—or she was considering the possibility of that and seeing how it felt. If she wanted to come over last night, maybe it was because she was.

Emma looked over at me and smiled, and I let myself hope.

"You ready to go?" I asked.

She shoved off the railing and we left.

"It's so weird being here with you on the same walk we did that day on the phone," she said, once we were on the bridge. "It's like I teleported into your universe."

"You did," I said, holding her hand. I nodded over the side. "Remember St. Anthony Falls?"

"Yeah."

We stopped to look at the water.

"You liked where you lived, huh?" she said.

"Minnesota? Yes, of course."

"No, I mean you liked living here, near this."

"I did. This is my favorite part of the city. I always dreamed of living within walking distance to the bridge. Didn't dream about having a giant plumber staring into my apartment, but I do love the rest of it. I *did* love the rest of it."

I went quiet.

She nudged me. "What are you thinking?" she asked.

I paused. "I feel like I'm showing you a life that doesn't belong to me anymore."

She looked out over the river. "I understand. I've had a lot of lives too. And none of them belong to me anymore either."

I turned to look at her. "You could make one that does. You could always stay."

I couldn't read the smile she gave me. I wished I could.

I could ask her what she was thinking. She'd have to tell me. But I was as afraid of the answer as I was of not knowing and I didn't want to put a shadow on the night if it wasn't what I wanted to hear.

I cleared my throat. "Come on. Let's go get gelato." I nodded to the other end of the bridge.

A couple walked by, and the guy noticed our outfits. "Cool shirts."

"Thanks, we're employees," Emma said.

I was laughing at this when my phone rang. I pulled it out and checked it. It was Leigh.

I debated just letting it go to voicemail, but she usually texted instead of calling and she had the kids.

"Hold on," I said. "This might be important. Leigh?"

"Justin, I'm sorry, but I need to make you aware of something."

"What's wrong?"

"The kids have head lice."

I squeezed my eyes shut. *Fuck.*

"All of them?" I asked.

"Every last one. Chelsea came home with a letter from the preschool that there's been an outbreak, so I checked 'em and sure enough. I'm gonna get started on shampooing everyone. I gotta comb the eggs out and the girls got long hair. I have to wash all the bedding, all Chelsea's dolls, disinfect the brushes, run to Walgreens and get the treatment—"

I could hear Sarah losing her absolute shit in the background.

"Sarah's having a goddamn fit," Leigh said. "And Alex is no help. Your brother keeps dry heaving when I even mention he pick up a comb."

I rubbed my forehead. "Okay. All right. Can I have a few hours? At least go out to eat with her?"

"You can stay for the whole thing if you want, I can handle it. But if the kids have head lice, *you* probably have head lice. If you're fine with that, continue on."

Fuuuuuuuuuuck.

Sarah screamed again in the background, and Leigh made an exasperated noise. "Hold on. Sarah? You're gonna scare your sister. Zip it."

"It's disgusting!" she shrieked. "We all got this from her. She's so gross, why does she always have to hug everyone?!" She was crying.

"Sarah," Leigh said in a warning voice.

"You don't understand!!!"

"Oh yeah? If I have to pick 'em off you, how is it I don't understand? If you want to help, go strip your bed." Leigh came back to me. "Justin, I gotta go. Let me know what you want to do."

I moved the phone away from my mouth like she could see my disappointed expression through the line. I was going to lose my date with Emma.

I didn't see what choice I had. I couldn't walk around with lice if I had it. I wasn't itchy, but who fucking knew. And I didn't feel good about leaving Leigh to deal with Sarah's meltdown either.

"Okay," I said reluctantly. "I'll be there in a bit."

I hung up and turned to Emma, dragging a hand over my face. "I need to go home."

She looked concerned. "What happened?"

"Chelsea got lice at preschool."

She sucked air through her teeth. "Ohhh."

"The whole house has it. *I* probably have it," I added. "Sarah's having a panic attack. I have to go help. I can't leave them there infested with bugs."

"No, you can't," she agreed.

I let out a long breath. Then I arched an eyebrow. "I don't suppose you'd want to come with me?"

She gave me an amused look. "To pick nits off your family? How romantic."

"You want romance? I thought we were just curse breaking."

"Of course I want romance," she said.

"Well damn, you should have said something. I'll get right on it."

I dropped to one knee.

She sucked in air. "Uh, what are you doing?" she said, her eyes darting around.

"Romance."

"Justin, stop it," she whispered. "Get up! Get *up!*"

I took her hand and did my best to make my face straight. People were already stopping to watch. I made my voice low so only she could hear it. "Emma, would you do me the honor of delousing my family with me?"

She snorted.

I looked at her passionately. "Say yes. Please say yes. I want to spend the rest of my evening with you."

She was trying not to laugh. "You are the *worst...*"

I grinned. "Is this a hostage situation?" I whispered.

"That's *exactly* what this is."

Someone was recording on their phone. Actually, lots of people were recording on their phones. I waited patiently for her answer.

She rolled her eyes. "Yes."

"Yes?"

"Yes, I will comb lice with you."

I stood up and scooped her into my arms and spun her. People started clapping and cheering.

She laughed.

When I set her down, someone shouted congratulations and we both cracked up quietly. Then we stood there, still holding each other, my arms around her waist, hers around mine, the Toilet King pressed between us. I didn't let go.

She didn't let me go either.

"Head lice," she said. "I was wondering how you were going to top kittens." Her eyes moved to my lips. "You should check me too," she said. "Just to be safe."

"Wow. We're checking each other for lice. I guess you could say things are gettin' pretty serious."

I felt her laugh against my chest.

"Are you sure you don't mind coming to help?" I asked. "I know you didn't want to spend time with the kids."

"I got lice once in foster care before Maddy's. It's traumatic and humiliating, especially for teenagers. I don't mind helping someone get it over with sooner."

I smiled a little. If you would have told me a year ago that delousing my family would be a term of endearment for a date, I would have thought you were bullshitting.

You could have told me a lot of things a year ago that I would never have believed.

CHAPTER 28

EMMA

I dragged the lice comb down Sarah's long locks.

She'd been sitting on the sofa when we came in, crying and hugging her legs. I thought maybe she'd prefer Justin or Leigh to do her hair and I would take Alex, but when we came in she scrambled off the sofa and barked "Emma" before stomping to the bathroom. So Justin started on Alex, and I took his sister.

She'd already washed her hair with the shampoo, so we got right to combing.

"This is so embarrassing…" Sarah said.

I shrugged, parting her hair. "Eh, it's not that bad."

Her face called bullshit in the mirror.

"Really, it's not. Trust me, I've seen much worse."

She looked away from me. "Yeah right."

"I pulled a sock off a patient once and the foot came off with it."

Her eyes darted back to mine. "No *way*."

I combed down to the ends. "I've seen things that would keep you up at night. This is not one of them." I made another part in her hair. "Not much fazes me. This isn't even a particularly bad case. There's hardly anything here."

"This is so stupid. Who even gets head lice?" she said.

"I've had lice before."

She blinked at me. "But…but you're so pretty!"

I laughed. "Pretty girls can't have lice? Trust me, they can. Lice are actually attracted to clean scalps, did you know that? It doesn't mean you're dirty."

A flicker of gratitude moved across her expression, but then her face darkened again.

"How have you been doing?" I asked.

She sniffed, but she didn't answer.

"My mom was gone a lot too," I said, wiping the comb on the paper towel. "I was in foster care a couple of times, so I get it."

"You were?"

"I was."

"What'd she do?" she asked.

I shrugged. "She wasn't really good at taking care of me."

She peered at me. "My mom was good at taking care of me," she said, her voice almost too low for me to hear.

"You know who else will be good at that? Justin. And Leigh too."

A long pause. "I guess. It's like, nobody gets it though. Alex is just all *Alex* and Chelsea's so small she doesn't even know. She thinks Mom's at camp."

"Camp's as good of a story as any. Let it be camp."

"Yeah, but it can't be camp for *me*. I have to know."

"She'll be home one day, Sarah. It'll come faster than you

think. You can visit her and write to her and call her. You can stay close to her—you just have to try. I know this is hard, but good things can still come out of it."

She rolled her eyes. "Like what?"

"You find out a lot about yourself during times like this. You realize how resilient you are and what you're capable of."

"I don't want to know any of that," she said.

"Ha. Fair enough." I worked quietly for a moment. "What are you going to miss the most while your mom's gone?" I asked.

She shrugged. "I dunno. Maybe like, her cookies or something."

"Learn to make the cookies, so everyone can still have them. Maybe you can even bring them to your mom when you visit. I bet Justin can help. He's a really good cook. You should try what he makes."

She looked like she didn't believe me.

"He made me this egg salad sandwich that was, I swear to you, the best one I've ever eaten," I said. "He smokes ribs, and he's got a really good Mississippi chicken recipe. Seriously. Try it."

She seemed to consider it. "Yeah. Maybe."

Several minutes passed. I watched her face in the mirror, deep in thought.

"They'll make fun of me at school," she whispered. "'Cause my mom's in jail."

I nodded slowly. "They do that."

"Did they make fun of you?"

"They did." I dragged the comb down to the ends. "My clothes were too small, my hair wasn't brushed. There were a few weeks I had to use a men's briefcase for a backpack because I didn't have anything else. All my clothes were in black trash bags."

She looked horrified.

I shuddered a little thinking about that time. I didn't usually dredge up those memories. Of everything, the trash bags were somehow the worst part. They were so dehumanizing. It made me feel disposable. When I finally had my own money, I bought the most expensive set of luggage I could afford. It was the one thing I never skimped on, the one thing that would always be with me, no matter where I ended up. And every year I bought bags to donate to kids in foster care.

Not everything that comes out of crisis is bad. Sometimes your traumas are the reason you know how to help.

It occurred to me that's why I knew what to say and do now. I guess I had Mom to thank.

"The trick is not letting anyone see you care about anything mean they might say," I said. "Don't react. Don't let them see you cry. They'll get bored when they don't get the reaction they want." I wiped the comb. "And lean on your friends. It helps."

Justin popped into the doorway. "Hey, how's it going in here?"

"Good," I said. "Making progress."

"I just finished Alex," he said. "Want me to take over?"

"I want Emma to do it," Sarah said quickly.

He put his hands up. "Okay."

His hair was tousled. "No lice." He pointed at it. "Leigh checked me."

"Good. Did you check her?"

He paused for a second. Then he disappeared back out the door. I smiled after him. Then I saw how big I was grinning in the mirror and had to make a conscious effort to make my face straight.

Sarah was watching me. "My brother really likes you, I think."

The corner of my lip turned up again. "Oh yeah?"

She nodded. "Yeah. He, like, never talks about girls and he talks about you *all* the time."

"What does he say?"

"Emma this and Emma that. Blah blah blah."

I laughed.

"Do you like him?" she asked.

"Yeah, of course I do."

"Why?"

"He's funny, for one. He's smart. And handsome—"

"Gross," she said.

"He is. Sorry, it's just true."

She wrinkled her nose.

"I also think he's a really good person," I continued. "I like that he's taking care of you guys."

She stared at me through the mirror. Then I nodded at the bag from Sally Beauty on the sink.

"I got you something you might like," I said. "Grab that."

She leaned over and picked it up. I watched her face change instantly the second she saw what it was. Her head shot up. "Hair dye?!" She beamed.

"Yup. I made Justin stop at the beauty supply store on the way over. I already asked your brother, he said it's okay. When we're done with this, you can pick a color."

I'd bought the rainbow. Red, orange, green, blue, and purple.

"The time I got lice, one of the older girls staying in the foster home got me hair dye—stole me hair dye. I'm pretty sure she didn't buy it," I said. "Anyway, I just remembered it turning the whole day around for me. I was so upset and the instant I found out I got to have pink hair at school the next morning, it changed everything. Reframed the memory into something good."

Sarah was practically bouncing. "I can't believe he said yes. Mom never lets me do anything. She won't even let me get my ears pierced."

"Well, it's a new regime," I said, parting her hair again. "We could do two colors if you want. It's semi-permanent, so it'll only last a few weeks."

"I want the purple and blue! Josie's gonna be so jealous. Her mom let her get a henna tattoo and she was bragging about it for forever."

I smiled.

She lined the bottles up on the sink and looked happily at them.

In that moment, maybe for the first time ever for me, she looked like a little girl. She *was* a little girl. I recognized the mask Sarah wore for what it was.

It was easier to pretend to be angry and tough than to admit to being devastated and heartbroken. And by the practiced way she wielded attitude, she'd been devastated and heartbroken for a long time.

Justin's family had been through so much trauma. They had so many cracks.

I wondered if Justin was a docking station because of it or in spite of it. Had he learned to be steady and reliable and safe out of the needs of the people he loved, or did he fight to stay their anchor through all the tragedy? Either way, his family was lucky to have him.

Leigh popped her head in the door. "Hey, Emma," she whispered. She looked over her shoulder and came back to me. "Hey, you think you can convince him to rename the dog? You got that kinda pull yet?"

I grinned. "I don't know."

"Well, work on it, will ya? We've just about given up. He's stubborn as a mule, you're our last hope."

She vanished again. I waited a second to be sure she was gone and then I leaned in over Sarah's shoulder.

"I don't really think he should rename the dog," I whispered.

"Me either," Sarah said, conspiratorially.

Both of us smiled into the mirror.

CHAPTER 29

JUSTIN

Y ou have to drag your leg," Emma said.

"Why?"

"Because you're dead? And you have to amble."

I grinned. "I'm not sure I know what ambling is. Can you show me? Give me your best amble?"

Emma crossed her arms, trying not to smile. "You know how zombies walk, Justin. Walk like that."

"Should I moan? With my arms out? Sort of drool a little bit?"

"Feel free to use any artistic interpretation of a zombie that you want. All I care about is that you walk zombie speed. This has to be an accurate experiment."

Emma bet me that she could survive a zombie apocalypse. She said zombies were slow and easy to outrun. I said they're slow but steady and that's how they get you. She said we should try it, so here we were at almost midnight in front of Neil's mansion getting ready to prove my point.

The night wasn't what I'd planned, but it ended up great anyway.

I don't know what the heck Emma had said to Sarah, but my sister was in a good mood for the first time in—I couldn't even remember how long. She emerged from the bathroom with Emma with blue-and-purple hair and a new attitude. Not the outcome I'd expected after the way the night had started but I'd take it.

After we finished with the lice, I set up the blanket in the backyard. With the landscaping Mom did, it was pretty nice back there with its hanging lights, citronella candles, and magnolia trees. I ordered a pizza, connected my phone to a Bluetooth speaker, and poured the wine I brought, and Emma and I hung out and talked. Mom had a giant Jenga and we set that up and played a few rounds.

One of the onlookers from the fake bridge proposal had offered to send me the picture he got. It was a shot of me on one knee and Emma looking surprised, the Toilet King on her shirt in clear view. It was hilarious. We cracked up about it all night and made it our screensavers.

"Okay. So where do we start?" I asked.

Emma looked around. "How about you start from across the street. I'll be getting out of the car. You have until the dock to catch me."

"All right. I'd just like to point out though that if I do catch you, there's no way you'd outrun a real one in the great uprising."

"Noted. But you won't catch me." She smirked and got into the passenger seat and shut the door.

I smiled and jogged across the street and waited.

When she jumped out of my Acura, I started after her.

She left the door to the car open. Smart. Saved time not closing it and I had to go around it, which bought her a few seconds. She was making good progress and I was beginning to think she might actually get away, until she hit the grass. Her sandal flew off. She looked over her shoulder at me. "Shit! Shit shit shit shit!"

I ambled closer and made a moaning sound, trying not to laugh, and she got frantic. She left it—and then her heel slipped out of the other one. She kicked that off too and started to run again and bolted around the side of the garage.

I thought for sure I'd lost her this time, but when I rounded the corner, I practically crashed right into her. She'd dropped her phone and went back for it. Rookie move.

When she saw me, she abandoned her cell in the grass and spun to get away from me, but I grabbed her by the waist. She shrieked and tried to wiggle out of my arms, but I pulled her closer. Both of us were laughing our asses off. I had her from behind and I put my mouth down on her neck and bit her gently. "You're dead," I whispered.

She giggled and turned in my arms to face me, her hands on my chest, the Toilet King pressed between us. We were both cracking up.

"Look at you," I said. "Thirty seconds into the zompoc and you've already lost your shoes, your phone, and you've been bitten."

She beamed up at me. "So what now?"

"I guess we just wait for you to turn."

She laughed and I felt it rumble against me.

Then her eyes dropped to my lips. My eyes dropped to hers.

"You could always kiss me while we wait," I said, my voice low.

"But it won't count if *I* kiss *you*."

"Well, if you only want to kiss me to check a box," I said, talking to her mouth, "it's better that we don't."

Her eyes came back up to mine. "But we're *supposed* to check a box."

"Call me old-fashioned, but I want to kiss someone who wants to be kissed."

"I want to be kissed," she said.

"By anyone? Or me specifically."

"You." She smiled coyly. "Specifically."

I narrowed my eyes. "No. I don't believe you."

She gasped. "*What?*"

"If you really wanted to kiss me, you wouldn't care who kisses who. You would just do it."

"Well, do you want to kiss *me*?"

"Yes," I said without even thinking about it. "I do. And not to check a box either."

She bit her lip. "Well then?"

"Well nothing. I'm officially deciding not to kiss you. You have to kiss me first. To rule out any ulterior motives."

"Isn't *not* kissing me the ulterior motive? I thought we had an arrangement. You're not going to hold up your end of the bargain?"

She pressed her hips into mine, and I had to suck in a breath. Something mischievous flickered across her face.

She was *teasing* me. And it was working.

Her perfume drifted up between us. Her scent hypnotized me. Absolutely entranced me. Whatever pheromone was made for me, she had it. I felt drunk by the proximity to her.

It was dim on the side of the garage. A motion sensor light

had gone on but it was toward the back of the house. It was quiet and private here. Nobody could see us.

She peered up at me, still smiling, and I wanted to kiss her so bad it made me ache.

Her eyes went to my mouth again. "I don't kiss men first," she said. "They kiss me."

"That is a very stupid rule," I said, a little breathless. "Especially from someone who only has so much time before they're a zombie."

She snorted. Then she bit her lip. "Kiss me, Justin."

"I told you," I said, staring at her mouth. "I don't want to check a box."

She leaned into the erection I had growing between us and I wanted to die.

"Justin…" she said quietly. She was so close she whispered my name across my lips.

She slid a hand up my chest, around the back of my neck, and I felt her fingers curl into my hair.

Fuck…

"Justinnnn…"

I put my forehead to hers and closed my eyes.

I could do this. I could stand my ground. I wouldn't kiss her, not until I knew it was more than just a game for her.

But God, I wanted to. Everything in me screamed to do it.

Everything in me screamed to do everything.

I tipped her chin up and began trailing my mouth down her neck. She sucked in air at the contact and tilted her head. I slid my hands up the back of her shorts and she arched into my body.

"Oh hell," she breathed. Then her face came up and she finally gave me what I asked for.

The second her mouth made contact, I parted her lips, and her tongue plunged against mine and every single thing that mattered in my entire life was somehow happening on the lawn next to Neil's garage.

I liked the way she kissed. I liked the way *I* kissed when I was kissing her. It was that unreal physical chemistry that you never get right on the first try, only it *was* right. We should have been doing this weeks ago. Day one. No way was it this good and we'd only now tried it. What a waste…

"Is it just me, or are we really good at this?" she breathed.

I answered by kissing her again.

She smiled against my mouth and tugged at my belt, pulling me with her until she hit the wall of the garage and I pressed into her.

I was so hard there was no way she didn't feel it.

Her palm slid under my shirt around my lower back and I ran a slow hand up her rib cage under her top. "Is this okay?" I whispered.

She nodded.

"Is this okay?" she asked, fingertips slipping over the front of my pants.

I made a noise in the back of my throat.

My whole body was electric. I could barely breathe.

"Do you want to go back to your place?" she said breathlessly. "Try out the air mattress?"

"Yes," I said. "Fuck yes."

"You're okay with casual sex, right?" she said. "I just want to be sure."

The words powered me down instantly. Everything that was on, shut off. I pulled my face away from hers.

She blinked up at me out of breath. "What?"

I couldn't even speak. I felt like I'd been doused in cold water.

"Justin, what?"

I just stared at her.

"You really don't…" I didn't know how to complete the sentence.

You really don't what? Want it to mean anything? Like me enough to want me for more than just sex? You could really do that with me and then just…go?

I let go of her and took a step back in the grass. I had to turn away. I couldn't even look at her.

So that's really what this was.

But how upset could I be? She'd never said she would stay. In fact, she'd said she wouldn't. It was all me, hoping, thinking that maybe this could be something different than it actually is.

I could feel her study me. "What's wrong? Tell me what you're thinking."

I paused. "I'm thinking I like you a lot more than you like me." I looked over at her, and her expression was an apology.

"Justin…"

"You don't have to explain it. Don't."

She licked her lips. "I'm leaving in a few weeks. I thought we were just having fun—"

"We are. It's fine."

Her eyes roamed my face. "I like you, Justin."

I glanced at her.

"I like you a lot," she said.

"But?"

"You're just in a different place than I am—"

"Then meet me where I *am*."

She held my gaze and I could see by the look in her eye that she wouldn't.

I fixed my stare on the shoe in the grass. "Is it because of the kids?"

I was almost afraid to ask it, but I wanted to be clear.

Her silence was the answer.

"Can I ask you a question?" I looked up at her. "If they weren't a factor, what would be different?"

She shook her head. "I don't know. Maybe if you'd be willing to come with me—"

"So you do feel this between us? I'm not just imagining it."

She was quiet for a long moment. "Yes," she whispered. "I feel it." She peered at me. "I'm sorry," she said. "It's just—"

"Seriously. I don't need to know any more."

And I didn't. She didn't owe me an explanation, and I didn't want one. Because what would it change?

You can't negotiate feelings. You can't convince someone they feel something they don't. She either felt for me strongly enough to stay and accept my situation with my family, or she didn't.

And she didn't.

I didn't think there could be anything worse than her not wanting me like I wanted her. But there was. It was her wanting me and losing her to a circumstance that wasn't my fault and I couldn't change.

I was crushed. Completely crushed.

She stood there in the grass, still barefoot, giving me an expression that looked a lot like pity.

"It's okay," I said. "Thank you for being honest with me."

We heard the garage door opening around the corner, but we didn't move from our sad little standoff. A car rumbled to life, and Neil started to back his Mercedes down the driveway, rolling into our line of sight.

Amber's voice cut through the night. "Fuck you, Neil!"

My head jerked to look at Emma, and her eyes went wide.

A large projectile flew from the direction of the carport and crashed into the grille of the sedan. Neil slammed on the brakes just as Amber darted into view to pick up the thing she threw and vanished back into the garage.

Emma and I bolted around to the grass next to the driveway. Amber stood just inside the carport, barefoot, mascara streaming down her face. "Fuck you, you piece of shit!"

Neil threw the car in park and started to get out. He stood behind his door, using it like a shield. "What the *hell* are you doing?!"

"Oh, so *now* I have your attention!"

"I told you, I was at work!"

"Liar!"

"I'm a surgeon, Amber. I don't have a nine-to-five, I stay until it's done, I can't answer the phone in the middle of an appendectomy—"

Amber drew her arm back and threw the large glass thing again, only this time it bounced off the car's hood, hit the concrete, and broke in half.

Neil stared at it in shock. His jaw flexed. Then he started stalking toward her.

"Oh my God," Emma breathed. "He's gonna hit her. Justin, he's going to hit her!"

I was already in motion, but I wasn't fast enough. Neil got to Amber first. He grabbed her by the shoulders, yanked her toward him—and hugged her.

I stopped in my tracks.

I watched as he wrapped her in his arms and shushed her gently. Then he whispered something in her ear and caressed the back of her hair, and Amber collapsed into the embrace and started to sob.

Emma and I just stood there, hearts racing.

After a few moments Neil looked over and saw us. He whispered something to the woman in his arms, and she nodded into his chest.

"Emma?" Neil called. "I'm going to get your mom some dinner. Can you get her into the bathtub while I order some food?"

Emma's eyes were still wide, but she nodded. Then she padded over in her bare feet, stepping carefully around the glass, took her mother by the shoulders, and led her into the house.

As soon as the door to the garage closed, Neil let out a long breath and closed his eyes. Then he turned to survey the damage. His hood and grille were dented, but he stared the longest at the shattered hunk of glass in the driveway.

"That was my Charles Montgomery Award for Medical Excellence," he said, tiredly.

I didn't answer.

He stood there in silence for a long beat. Then he talked to me but looked at the award. "You know, there was a time when I would have gotten in my car, driven to the nearest five-star hotel, and picked up the first woman who would have me just to teach Amber a lesson. But I'm trying. I'm *really* trying to be the best version of myself."

He stayed for another moment. Then he turned and walked slowly back into the house.

I was alone, standing in the driveway, whiplashed by the last five minutes. The part with Neil and Amber and the part with Emma too.

I began cleaning up the mess. The driveway was full of glass, and Emma's sandals were scattered on the lawn. Her phone was still in the grass. It started to light up right as I reached for it. It was Maddy.

"Hey," I said, answering. Then I told her everything that had just happened with Neil and Amber. A minute later the lights of the pontoon turned on in the distance across the lake.

I closed the door to Neil's car, picked up what was left of the award and set it inside the garage on the deep freezer. Then I swept up the shattered glass and collected Emma's shoes and set them by the garage door to the house. I was done in time to help Maddy dock the boat.

She arrived cursing.

"I fucking knew it," she said, sliding up the dock. "Not even a month and that woman's already losing her shit."

I grabbed the front of the boat and pulled it in. She tossed me a rope and I tied her up and she jumped off, swearing like a sailor while she secured the back. When she was done, she turned to me. "How bad is Emma?" she asked, fixing her windblown hair. "Is she a mess?"

"I don't know," I said. "She went in with Amber before we could talk."

Maddy scowled up at the house. "I *hate* that fucking train wreck. She does this every time."

I slipped my hands into my pockets and stared out past her into the pitch black of the lake.

"What?" Maddy asked, noticing I'd gone quiet.

"Nothing."

She eyed me from the side. I glanced over at her and something moved across her face, like she could read my mind.

Maybe she *could*. Maddy knew Emma inside and out. She probably knew exactly how Emma felt about me—or didn't feel. And she seemed to know that I knew it now too.

"Did something happen?" she asked.

I peered at her quietly. "Just tell me if there's any chance," I said.

I didn't have to explain it.

She looked away from me, like she was trying to figure out how to say what she wanted to say. "I shouldn't be telling you this."

"Tell me anyway."

Her gaze came back to mine. "Justin, you will never get her to love you. You can't. My parents tried with her. For years. They *still* try."

"She loves *you*."

"That's because *I* got in before the doors closed."

I dragged a hand down my mouth. "She said it's because of the kids. That I'm in a different place than she is—"

She shook her head. "It's not because of the kids. I mean it is, but it isn't. If it wasn't that, she would have found something else to be the reason." She held my eyes. "She's not capable of falling in love. Things happened to her and she's..." She blew a breath through her nose. "You seem like a really nice guy, and I genuinely like you. I do. But you should prepare yourself for what's going to happen when it's time for her to go. Because she *will* go."

I had to look away. "I don't think I can give up."

When she didn't reply, I glanced back to her. I couldn't help but notice that she looked sorry for me.

"I thought you might say that." She breathed in deep and looked out over the lake. "Justin, for what it's worth, I really hope this curse thing is real." She peered back at me. "Because I think you deserve your happy ever after when it's over."

The soulmate I'd get once Emma and I broke up. So that was Maddy's prediction: There was no hope.

But my foolish heart would hope anyway. It didn't know how not to.

CHAPTER 30

EMMA

Mom was a mess.

She had glass in her foot. I got her to the bathroom and pulled it out with tweezers, then cleaned and wrapped her wound while she sat at the vanity.

She looked like she hadn't been sleeping. She had circles under her eyes and the robe she was in was stained.

Neil wasn't cheating or lying to her. I knew how busy he'd been at the hospital over the past few days because for the most part I had been with him. But Mom didn't do well with abandonment—even the perceived kind. Which was funny, because it's the very thing she'd subjected me to for most of my life.

Neil brought in a change of clothes, set them on the counter, and bent to kiss her gently on the top of her head. She leaned into it, and I figured the chaos was over for the moment, so I took that as my cue to leave. I left the house to find Maddy waiting and Justin gone.

For the next few days I was small.

Maddy knew it and gave me my space. Justin was also giving me my space, but not for the same reason.

I couldn't even think about what had happened with him by the garage. My brain was too exhausted to revisit it. I didn't have the bandwidth.

I texted him the once-a-day obligatory text to meet the requirements of our curse-breaking agreement, and he matched my energy with a single line back.

Our fourth date was coming up in a few days. Our last date.

I don't know why, but I wasn't looking forward to it. Not because I didn't want to see him, because I did. I just…I didn't know.

Five days after Mom's incident in the driveway, Neil surprised her with a little getaway to Mexico, trying to make up for his long hours at work. They'd left yesterday. Maddy had also left yesterday to her parents' for their anniversary. So I was alone.

I planted the rock cress and hostas I'd recommended to Neil. I didn't plant the rosebush. I couldn't bring myself to leave it on this island where no one would see it or take care of it, but I didn't know what else to do with it. It wasn't like the other plants I'd left behind. This one meant something. I wanted it to be loved and safe. But where?

My mind kept going to Justin's. That's where everything was loved and safe. But would *I* ever go to Justin's again to put it there?

I couldn't deal with thinking about it. So I just left it, sitting on the end of the dock in its pot like it was watching for its lover to come home from a journey at sea.

I navigated the pontoon twice through a miserable rainstorm by myself just to get to work and home. Somewhere in there my

DNA test came back. I'd opened the email and looked at the results. I was Irish and German. Lots of other stuff, but mostly that. It's funny because when I asked Mom what I was, she said she didn't know.

It was always like that with her. Didn't remember, couldn't recall. Like everything's a secret, like my whole past had been smudged with an eraser. She took a broom and brushed the sand behind us so I could never look back and see where I'd been or where I came from. All I had was where I was going and I could never stop moving forward because of it.

I thought for a split second about changing my privacy settings on 23andMe to see if I had family. Then I immediately decided against it. I was feeling too small to handle it right now. Maybe when Maddy came back, I'd let her do it. She could sift through the information for me, tell me if anyone was out there, happy to know I existed.

Sarah had been snapping me. Pictures of her hair, and one with her friend Josie. A few of Chelsea and several of Brad. I guess the Dahl kids had never had a dog before. They were very excited.

I liked the messages. I messaged her back to ask about Alex and Chelsea. Never about her oldest brother though. It was so strange to be barely speaking to Justin but to have a running conversation with someone in the same house.

Sometimes the pictures Sarah sent had traces of Justin in them. His keys on a coffee table. His hoodie on the arm of a sofa.

I was at work, eating my lunch alone, when she sent a picture of Brad in the kitchen. I could see Justin in the background. He was standing at the sink. Probably doing dishes. It was a shot of him from behind, just the waist down.

I stared at that photo for so long, I didn't even finish eating my lunch. I must have studied every inch. Justin's phone in his back pocket, the one he used to send me a generic "good morning" or "good night" reply to my daily obligatory text of the same thing.

He was wearing the same shirt he'd had on that day at the mall. I knew how it smelled. I knew how it would feel if he hugged me against it.

I don't know why, but I had to clutch a hand over my heart. It actually hurt to look at him. Even just part of him.

And the weirdest thing was that while the kids were the biggest reason I didn't want to keep seeing him, I wished I were there with them. I wondered what Justin was making them for dinner. I could picture sitting with him on the couch watching *Frozen*, docked in the docking station, with Chelsea and Brad curled up with us. I wanted to chat with Sarah in person and hear one of Alex's animated stories of what he was up to.

When I went back to work after lunch, I wasn't feeling well.

I stayed two hours later than scheduled, so I was exhausted when I finally got the boat docked. When I got to the cottage, I realized we barely had any groceries. I'd go tomorrow. I was getting a headache and I was too tired to do anything other than peel off my clothes and climb into bed.

A few hours later, the nausea woke me up.

I felt for my phone on the nightstand in the dark. 2:42 a.m. I rolled onto my back, hoping if I lay still enough the feeling would pass.

It didn't.

I barely made it to the bathroom.

I *hated* throwing up. Hated it. Probably something I picked up at the hospital, or maybe something I ate. I retched up everything I had, holding my hair back at the nape of my neck.

When I was done, I rinsed my mouth out and brushed my teeth, tied up my hair. Then I spun and vomited again.

By 6:00 a.m., I'd given up trying to make it back to my room. The stomach upset started a little after the vomiting did. During the short breaks I got from puking and sitting on the toilet, I lay on the semi-damp blue bathroom mat in front of the tub, my head pounding.

I wanted water.

The kitchen felt a million miles away so I pulled myself up to the sink and drank from the tap. It was awful. It tasted like rust and smelled like sulfur.

It was worse on the way out.

I rifled through the medicine cabinet for something, anything, but there was nothing that would help me. Band-Aids, Visine, nail clippers, some NyQuil but that wouldn't stop the vomiting. I moved some peroxide and found an ancient bottle of Pepto. It had separated. The top half was a watery layer of milky-looking liquid. I shook it and the contents came back together a little, but it still looked spoiled. I checked the date. Expired in 1994. I blanched and put it back and slid down on the floor again.

I called in sick to Royaume.

Maddy called around 8:00 a.m. "Hey, just checking in."

"Okay," I croaked.

"You all right? You sound like shit."

I shifted to my back and put an arm across my forehead. "I think I have norovirus. I've been throwing up since last night."

"Ick. Diarrhea too?"

"Yup."

"Ugh. Well at least it passes quick."

"I hope so."

There was a pause. "Janet and Beth asked about you."

I squeezed my eyes shut against another rolling wave of nausea. "Oh. Tell them hi."

"You should come next time."

I nodded, even though she couldn't see me. "Yeah. Sure." I sat up. "I have to go, I think I'm going to throw up again."

After I heaved for another five minutes, I dozed off on the tile with a towel as a pillow. When I woke up, it was noon. Justin had texted good morning three hours ago. I replied with "not feeling great today" and a green-faced emoji. He called immediately, but I didn't answer.

I got up and managed to make it to the kitchen. My legs felt wobbly. I gulped cold water from the Brita in the fridge. It sloshed in my stomach and came back up a few minutes later in the sink.

I couldn't remember ever being this miserable. I was sweating through my pajamas, my ribs hurt.

I pawed around the pantry. I was hungry, but we didn't have soup or broth. I didn't have tea or crackers or anything else that would settle my stomach. I tried to eat a granola bar I found in my purse, but I knew the second I swallowed it, it wasn't staying down.

I decided to try to take a shower and just sat in the tub with the water raining down on me with my head between my knees.

If I could stop using the bathroom and throwing up, then I could take the boat and go get groceries and medicine. But even as I thought it, it felt too hard. I was shaky. I sat in the water until it ran cold and then dragged myself out and managed to get into some clean clothes, but I was too out of it to brush my hair so I just left it in the towel.

I climbed into bed with the bathroom trash can, but the stomach cramps curled me into a fetal position. I lay there, hugging the plastic basket with one arm, willing myself to stop vomiting.

I just needed to sleep. I might be able to keep things down if I was asleep. But I couldn't sleep because I couldn't stop throwing up.

A smoke alarm somewhere in the house started to chirp low battery.

Chirp.

Chirp.

I was too weak to go looking for it.

I threw up again, holding the can on my lap. Nothing came out.

I drifted off. Woke up to vomit. Woke up to run to the bathroom. My stomach was so empty all I could do was dry heave. My head hurt. My throat hurt. My bones ached. The smoke alarm chirped.

It was six o'clock.

I had a fever. I was shivering and freezing. My hair was still wet from the shower. The towel had come off and my head soaked my pillow. It felt soggy and it smelled like wet feathers.

Chirp.

Justin had been texting me all day and he'd called again but I didn't answer.

The sound of the smoke alarm permeated my dreams. Taunted me. Kept me from falling asleep. Like a finger poking me every time I drifted off.

Chirp.

Driving me mad.

Chirp.

Chipping away at me.

Chirp.

By midnight I was starting to become concerned about dehydration. I'd been sick for a full day. It would start to pass soon, right? Maybe I'd feel better in the morning?

But I didn't.

By the time the sun came out again, I was so weak I couldn't even get up to dump the contents of my trash can. The diarrhea had stopped, but only because there was nothing left. All the water I'd tried to drink just came right back out the way it went in. I sat there in my bed, hot and flushed, sweat soaking the sheets.

A creeping sense of panic began to set in. I was really, *really* sick.

And I was alone. On this island. A million miles from shore and nobody was coming. I was in a cottage with no address. What would I say if I called for help? Look for the rosebush? How would they find me? How would they get me to shore?

I started to cry, but no tears came.

Where was Mom? I wanted my mom. I vaguely remembered dialing her. It went to voicemail. She *always* went to voicemail.

Chirp.

I was dizzy. I was awake. I was asleep. I was eight years old and Mom was gone. The food had run out and the smoke alarm was chirping and I was too small to reach it. Couldn't drag the ladder. Couldn't ask for help.

Chirp.

Nobody was going to come.

Do I die here? Do I dig up carrots from the yard? Boulders falling on me in a fever dream. Kittens slipping through my fingers like Slinkys, a truck and headlights, Justin. The docking station. The chirp won't let me sleep. Just be quiet. Be quiet. Be small.

Chirp.

So hungry. My bedroom light was on. Couldn't get up to turn it off. It screamed into my eyes, burned into my brain.

This is why people need people. For flicking switches.

My phone ringing. Justin calling.

Justin...

"Justin, I'm so sick. No, don't call an ambulance. I don't know. I don't know. I can't."

Silence.

Chirp.

Nothing...

CHAPTER 31

JUSTIN

The second I hung up with Emma, I was out the door. She'd sounded bad. Really bad. Disoriented bad.

She'd said not to, but I was a hairbreadth away from calling 911. The only reason I didn't was that she was a nurse and I figured she must know what kind of shape she's in and she didn't think it was an emergency, so at least there was that. But I didn't like the way she'd sounded at *all*. I called Brad to come get the dog, Leigh to ask her to watch the kids, I left Alex in charge until she got there, and I sped to Neil's house.

When I got to the mansion, I rang the bell frantically. Maria opened it. "Dios mío, what is it—"

"Do you have the keys to the yacht?" I said quickly.

"Excuse me?" She put a hand on her hip.

"I need the keys. Emma's really sick and can't come pick me up. I have to check on her."

She shook her head. "I don't have them. Mister keeps them in the safe—"

"Well where is he?"

She crossed her arms. "Like I know? He left with Amber two days ago. He said Cancun, but I don't know where."

"Can you call him?"

"He told me his phone would be off the whole trip."

I cursed under my breath. "Does he have another boat?" I asked. "A canoe? A kayak?"

She shook her head again.

I turned and left her standing there. I jogged around the house down to the beach and paced along the dock.

What was I going to do? It's not like I could call an Uber to take me.

I dialed Emma again. The phone rang and rang. She never picked up.

I had to get to her. I *had* to.

I looked left and right, seeing what the neighbors had. Maybe they knew Neil and would loan me a boat? One dock was empty. The other one had a plane. I eyed a Jet Ski two houses down and ran to knock on their door, hoping Neil's neighbors liked him enough to let me use it. Nobody answered.

I ran back to the house to look for something, anything. And then I saw it. The rainbow unicorn floatie in the pool. I didn't even give it a second thought.

I found a lacquered decorative paddle that hung on the wall over the futon in the pool house and wrenched it free. Then I dragged the unicorn by the tail to the water, straddled the neck, and pushed off.

My progress was painfully slow. If not for the house getting a little smaller behind me, I wouldn't think I was moving at all. I wasn't even entirely sure where I was going. I knew the general direction of the cottage, I'd seen the pontoon come from there half a dozen times, but I'd never been there myself. I figured I'd get close enough and see the boat—but then I saw something even better. The rosebush I gave her was sitting on the end of the dock. It was like a beacon—and I wasn't getting any closer to it. It felt like a nightmare, where you're running in quicksand and you can't move fast enough, can't get to where you're going.

I was fighting the wind and the waves pushing me back to the beach. The sun bore down on me relentlessly. After half an hour my arms burned with the exertion and I was exhausted, but all I could think about was the way she'd sounded on the phone. It drove me. I couldn't quit. I couldn't stop paddling. If the floatie popped and I ended up in the water I'd swim to her even if hers wasn't the nearest shore. I was going to get to her or die trying.

When I got close enough, the island blocked the wind and I started making progress. By the time I finally dragged the unicorn up onto the sand, I was spent and sunburnt and had been on the water over an hour, but I ran up the steps to the house two at a time anyway. The front door was locked. I knocked, but she didn't answer. I went around and knocked on the glass windows. "Emma! Open the door!"

Nothing.

One window was cracked open, but it was also seven feet up. I looked around and spotted a storage chest by the hose and pushed that over to the wall and climbed it. "Emma!"

The sound reverberated around the tiny bathroom. She didn't answer.

The window didn't open more than a few inches. I couldn't get in this way. I'd have to kick in the front door.

This ended up being a lot easier than I anticipated. The frame was so rotten it practically crumbled. I ran through the house and found her in the bedroom, curled up with a trash can next to her in the bed.

The relief I felt at seeing her breathing was unreal.

I crouched next to her. "Hey," I whispered worriedly. "Emma." I shook her gently.

She woke up and looked at me with glazed bloodshot eyes, and her face crumpled in relief. "Justin…"

"I'm here," I said. "Everything's going to be okay."

She was burning up.

"What's going on? What do you have?" I asked.

"I can't stop throwing up," she managed.

"Okay. All right. Let's get you some water."

She shook her head. "I can't keep anything down. It's been thirty-six hours and I can't."

I straightened by the bed and tried to think of what to do.

"I'm gonna call someone, okay? I'll be right back."

I dialed Benny's sister, Briana, from the living room. She was an ER doctor at Royaume and she lived in the same neighborhood as Benny, five minutes to the mansion, tops. I figured I was a solid thirty minutes away from a hospital if I put Emma on the boat right now, and she was in no shape to be moved. And then when I did get her to the hospital, she'd probably sit in the ER for hours until she was seen. If I could get help here, it would be better and probably faster.

Briana answered. She was home and she agreed to meet me at the dock in twenty minutes.

I took the bag out of the trash can Emma was holding and put in a new one. I put a cold washcloth on her forehead, grabbed the keys to the pontoon, and left.

CHAPTER 32

EMMA

There was a strange man in my room.

I tried to blink through the fog of my confusion to make sense of what I was seeing. I didn't recognize him. Reddish brown hair, late thirties. He was taking my blood pressure. A pretty brown-haired woman stood next to him, unpacking a duffel bag full of medical supplies.

Had I called 911? I didn't remember.

They didn't look like EMTs. They were in street clothes.

My head was throbbing. I was so dehydrated I felt withered. My bottom lip had cracked in the middle, and I touched it absently with my dry tongue, my eyes listlessly sweeping the rest of the room trying to figure out what was happening.

Justin was on a ladder changing the batteries on the smoke alarm.

Justin. He *came.*

I would have cried if I'd had enough water in me to make tears.

He finished and started climbing down. "How fast will this help?" he asked the man and woman.

"Pretty fast," the man said. "She should be feeling better soon."

The man took off the blood pressure cuff and smiled at me. "Emma? I'm Jacob. This is my wife, Briana. We're emergency medicine physicians. I'm going to give you some Zofran and some fluids, okay?"

I nodded.

Jacob started prepping the IV and Briana pulled out a stethoscope and listened to my stomach. Checking for bowel sounds, I knew, looking for blockages. She finished and put the stethoscope around her neck. "Probably norovirus. A real nasty strain going around."

"Could be Taco Bell," Jacob said, giving his wife a playful eyebrow.

She gasped and gave him an amused look. "Well, now you have to take me there for dinner. See what you've done?"

He chuckled.

"Thanks for coming," Justin said from the foot of the bed, looking concerned.

Briana wrapped my arm with a tourniquet. "No problem. We got Benny and Jane to watch Ava. We'll probably turn it into a date night."

Justin chewed on the side of his thumb while she put my IV in, and I registered that he was really worried. Like, really *really* worried.

I started to feel better within half an hour. As soon as the nausea was under control, Briana gave me some Motrin for the headache. We had to do two bags of saline before the doctors were satisfied with my condition.

"Push fluids," Jacob said, packing up the duffel bag. "Food is less important than getting her hydrated. Tea, anything with electrolytes. Lots of rest."

"I'll call tomorrow to check in," Briana said. "Or call me if you have any other concerns, but I think she's looking good." She turned to me. "Justin says you're a nurse at Royaume. Come say hi to me the next time you're there. We can go get lunch."

"Thank you," I said, huskily. "I don't know what I would have done if you didn't come."

She nodded at Justin. "Thank him. You're better because *he* came."

She turned to go and paused. "Hey, do you know who your landlord is, by chance?"

"Neil?"

"That guy's an asshole. Just so you know."

I pulled my face back. "How long have you worked with him?" I asked.

"Too long, but that's not what I'm talking about. He used to date my best friend. For seven years. The guy's a dick. Just be careful."

I squeezed my eyes shut and blew out a tired breath. My brain was too dried up to think about this right now.

"Anyway, it was nice meeting you," she said, going on. "My husband's going to take me to get a chalupa."

Jacob smiled at his wife and put a hand around her waist as they walked out of the room.

"I'll be right back," Justin said, heading to follow them.

"Justin, you should go." My voice was raspy. "I'm fine now, and norovirus is super contagious."

"I'm not going anywhere." There was something final in his voice. "I'll be back in half an hour. Just get some rest."

I did. The second they were gone, I fell asleep out of sheer exhaustion. When I woke up, Justin was next to the bed with a bowl of soup and a Gatorade.

"I ordered food and groceries to the house so it was waiting when I dropped them off," he said. "I figured chicken noodle would be best, but I also got beef barley, minestrone, and this chickpea vegetable one they said was good. I got crackers and applesauce and some bananas too and I'm making you some tea."

He set the food on the nightstand while I scooted up gingerly to sit against the headboard, my sore stomach yelping.

"Where are the kids?" I asked.

"Sarah went to Josie's family's cabin for the week. Leigh took Alex and Chelsea to the ranch. I also got Imodium, Pepto, and some Kaopectate," he said. "Do you like honey in your tea?"

He waited for my answer with the sweetest, most concerned expression. He was so worried about me. It was in every line of his face.

I had to look awful. I hadn't brushed my hair and I'd been barfing for two days straight. I probably smelled terrible too, but I was too weak and exhausted to do anything about it.

But I was glad he was here. Not just because I'd needed help, but because I wanted to see him. His presence comforted me the way Maddy did, or Mom when she was taking care of me and not the other way around.

It was so rare that anyone took care of me.

It was rare I allowed it.

"Honey?" he asked again.

"Yes, thank you."

I ate the soup and drank the tea and fell asleep again. When I woke up, it was getting dark outside.

I got up wrapped in a blanket and wandered into the hallway. Justin was on the sofa on his laptop. Probably getting some work done. When he saw me, he put his computer on the coffee table. "Hey, you're up."

"Yeah." I nodded over my shoulder. "I just need to use the bathroom."

"Can I get you anything?"

I shook my head. "No. What time is it?"

He looked at his watch. "Seven fifteen. You were asleep for a few hours."

"You changed your clothes," I said.

He looked down at his white T-shirt. "I ran home and got my stuff."

I nodded again, too tired for more words.

I used the bathroom, happy I was hydrated enough to need to. Justin had cleaned. The room smelled faintly of bleach.

I decided to take a shower. My legs were wobbly, but I felt gross and slightly self-conscious with Justin here. When I looked in the mirror, it was worse than I thought. I looked like absolute hell. I was pale, I had deep black circles under my eyes. I was getting undressed and I lost my balance and fell a little into the wall. A second later Justin knocked on the door. "Are you all right in there? I heard a thump."

"Yeah." I steadied myself. "I'm just getting ready to take a shower."

"Okay." A pause. "Do you need any help or…?" I could hear the grin through the door.

He actually managed to draw a laugh out of me. "No, Justin. I think I've got it."

"All right, all right, I'm just trying to be useful."

He was being nice to me, but this was the first time in almost a week he'd been playful with me.

I knew I'd broken something between us that night on the lawn. It was the price for my honesty. I just hadn't anticipated how high it was or how much I would hate paying it.

Why did I think that he'd want casual sex with me? The idea seemed absurd to me now.

So maybe we couldn't be more than what we were. Our lifestyles didn't fit. But why did I want to cheapen the friendship that was there?

Because I didn't know how not to.

I didn't know how to be with someone that I had these complicated feelings for, I'd never done it.

He had every right to be upset.

When I came out of the shower, he'd stripped the bed and remade it with fresh sheets. He'd opened the window over the bench seat to air out the room. There was a new bottle of Gatorade on the nightstand. I stood in the doorway, watching him with his back to me, putting the last pillowcase on my pillow.

He looked over his shoulder and saw me standing there. "Oh, hey. Sorry, I tried to get it done before you got out."

"Thank you."

I was wrapped in a towel. I couldn't stomach putting on my dirty clothes again for the short walk to my room.

He set the pillow on the bed and smiled a little at me, and I felt myself blush.

I'd been fully ready to go home with him the other night. He'd had a boner pressed right into my stomach. But this was a different kind of intimacy than that and one I wasn't used to.

"How are you feeling?" he asked.

"Better. Still tired."

He looked away, like he wasn't sure he should be looking at me half-naked like this.

"I'll let you get some sleep then," he said.

"Justin?"

He glanced back at me. "Yeah?"

"Why?" I asked quietly.

"Why what?"

"Why did you come?"

"Because you needed me," he said simply. "I will always come when you call."

We stood there looking at each other. Then he seemed to remember himself and edged past me out of the room.

I got dressed and got under the covers, feeling good for the first time in days with clean clothes, clean sheets, clean body.

I passed out almost immediately. And when I did, I dreamed of him—being with him at a cafe on a date, walking his dog, going back to his house. I wanted to tell him something the whole time, but I didn't know what. I kept opening my mouth to talk to him and then nothing would come out and he'd just smile at me. It was weird how mundane the dream was, but how totally invested I felt in it. When I woke up, I was disappointed it was over and I was back on the island.

It was dark now. I felt for my phone and found it on the charger next to a perspiring glass of ice water that hadn't been there when I went to sleep. It was 3:00 a.m.

I got up and used the bathroom. Then I poked my head into the living room looking for him. He wasn't there. I checked Maddy's room. Not there either.

The disappointment swallowed me.

I don't know what I thought was going to happen. He had the kids, a dog. He had a job. I couldn't expect him to stay on this island just to hang out with me. He'd done more than enough coming here to begin with. But discovering he was gone did something to me.

I missed him.

I'd *been* missing him, I realized. At work. At home. I'd been wanting to see him every single day since the water park. I never got a break from it. It was burning a hole in me.

I stopped in the doorway of the living room and peered around the cottage in the dark. I could see the dishes washed and drying on the rack. A bowl full of fruit that hadn't been there yesterday. I padded over to the front door. It was closed and locked, but the frame was cracked. Had he kicked it in? He must have. And how did he even get here? Did Neil loan him the yacht? Did he hitchhike? Can you do that on a lake? I had questions that I'd been too out of it to ask when he was here.

I'd have to wait until a reasonable hour to call him. Though something told me that if I called him now and woke him up, he wouldn't mind. It was weird that I knew that. That if I needed him, he would be there and he wouldn't be bothered by it no matter how late or inconvenient the time. No...not just if I needed him. If I *wanted* him, he would be there. It didn't have to be important. He would be there for anything and any reason. And I knew that.

I took in a deep breath and let it out slowly. Then I turned for my bedroom—and that's where I discovered Justin, sleeping on the little bench beneath the window.

A soft smile spread across my face.

He'd stayed.

I gazed at him, wedged into that tiny nook, his long legs

tucked almost to his chest. The throw blanket from the couch covered him, and he was using a little decorative lake-life pillow. He must be so uncomfortable.

Why hadn't he slept in the living room on the sofa? Or Maddy's room for that matter? Why hadn't he gone home and slept in his *bed*? But then I knew why.

He wanted to be close to me. In case I needed him. And he didn't want to violate my space by sleeping in my bed without my permission, and he wouldn't wake me up to ask it. So he'd squished himself on a glorified cushioned windowsill instead.

Something happened in my chest. A flutter. Or a crack. I had to clutch it with a hand like a part of me was going to spill out.

I'm not sure why, but I knew I'd always remember this. The breeze rolling gently through the curtains on either side of him. The curve of his shoulder and the way he didn't make the room feel crowded even though anyone in my room who wasn't Maddy took up too much space.

I thought too about the other night on the lawn. His hands gliding up my rib cage. His mouth on my neck and the warm way he smelled and the feel of his kiss.

I drank in his gentle breathing sounds. The rise and fall of his chest. And something in me accepted him. Opened up and let him in. I felt the stirring of something in my belly so rare to me I could count the occurrences of it on one hand.

Justin was on the island.

Not the real one. The one in my soul.

My eyes teared up at the realization. I didn't know how to process it. It scared me, and I didn't know what it meant or what I should do now or how it would change things. But suddenly nothing was the same.

I made my way over to the window and shook him gently. "Justin."

He startled awake. "What happened? Are you okay?"

"I'm fine. Come to bed."

He stared up at me in the dark like he didn't believe what he'd heard.

"Come to bed," I said again. "Come on."

He peered at me another moment. Then he got up and came to bed.

When I got under the covers, I scooted over to snuggle up next to him. He wrapped his arms around me and tucked the blanket over my shoulder like this was the most natural thing in the world to him and we'd slept like this a thousand times before. I put a palm over his heart and lay there feeling the rhythmic beating under my hand.

I wanted to tell him how much I'd missed him. That I'd stared at pictures that had only fragments of him in them, how I'd dreamed about him and how I felt when he came to the cottage.

I didn't know why it was so hard to say what I was feeling. Maybe because it felt hard to feel what I was feeling.

"You didn't leave," I whispered.

"I will never leave you," he said tiredly. "I mean, unless you tell me to. I'm not a creep."

I laughed and my sore stomach hurt.

He pulled me closer and kissed the top of my head. And for the first time maybe ever, I felt like I belonged somewhere.

CHAPTER 33

JUSTIN

The next morning when Emma woke up and wandered out of her bedroom, I was in the kitchen.

"Hey, you're up," I said, over the stove. "I'm making you oatmeal," I said, nodding at the pot. "I figured it would be easy on your stomach. Maybe some bananas?"

She sat at the little table. "Thanks."

I let my eyes linger on her longer than they should. I liked the way she looked. Rumpled and sleepy like this was the morning after I'd stayed the night. I mean I *had* stayed the night, but not in the way I wanted to.

I probably never would.

It was funny how much I wished I had these small, normal things. To wake up next to her and make her breakfast. Make plans for the holidays, ask her what she needed from the store on my way home and have our shows that we wouldn't watch without each other.

I wouldn't get these experiences. Not with her.

It was a hard reality to accept. I'd been trying.

I looked back at the pot so she wouldn't see the expression on my face.

"How do you feel?" I asked.

"Like a human again."

I arched an eyebrow at her. "Not like a human who got bit by a zombie?"

She laughed a little.

"I was thinking we could watch a movie or something," I said. "If you're feeling up to it."

"You don't have to go home?"

"No. I mean, unless you want some alone time or—"

"No. I don't," she said quickly.

"Okay."

She peered over at me. "You're…you're not mad at me?"

I looked back down at the stove. "Why would I be mad at you?"

The words Because of What Happened Between Us the Other Day hung there.

"You haven't really been texting me," she said.

"You haven't really been texting *me*. I just figured you were feeling small after what happened with Amber and you needed your space."

She didn't reply.

"I missed you," I said, talking to her but looking at the oatmeal.

I don't know why I bothered to say it. She'd made her position on our relationship pretty clear. But for some reason I needed her to know it anyway. Maybe because her truth was hers, and mine was mine and I missed her and deserved to say it out loud.

There was a painfully long beat of silence. "I missed you too."

I looked up at her, my heart leaping with hope. I waited for her to say more but she didn't.

I'd realized something over the last week of almost complete radio silence. I knew now that if I didn't have the kids, I really would have followed her to the ends of the earth. The week apart had solidified that for me. I'd hoped the distance would make it easier to let her go. But it hadn't. It just made me miss her more. There was something so hopeless about it.

I reached for a bowl to serve her food to avoid the awkward silence. I cut up a half of a banana and sprinkled the oatmeal with brown sugar and cinnamon and slid it in front of her.

"You're not eating?" she asked.

I put the empty pot in the sink and ran water into it. "No, I'm not hungry for some reason."

She poked at the oatmeal. "What did you do this week?"

"Nothing. Took care of the kids. Worked."

"How have they been?"

It seemed weird to me that she'd ask about them. They were the reason she didn't want to stay. But still, I liked that she cared enough to ask.

"Good," I said. "They're adjusting. School starts soon."

"Have you talked to your mom?"

I pumped the dish soap and started scrubbing. "She's doing okay. I sent her a care package with some drawings Chelsea did and letters from Alex and Sarah."

Mom was still a mess, so I kept things light when I saw her. I told her about Mall of America and the trip Sarah was taking with Josie up to her family's cabin in northern Minnesota.

I didn't tell her that Chelsea had started crying for her at bedtime or how much Sarah was struggling or how Alex was less of his usual perky self. I didn't tell her that Emma and I wouldn't work out because my life had become something so complicated.

I think the hardest part to deal with was Emma admitting she felt this thing between us too and having to come to terms with the fact that she still didn't want it. This would end. She would go. And both of us would miss each other.

That was the tragedy.

"It's good you're sending her things," Emma said.

"Yeah, I—" My stomach gurgled and I stopped.

"What?" she asked.

"Nothing. I just thought I felt a little nauseous for a second there." I rolled my shoulders. "I'm good."

I went back to washing. Then I froze again. I stood there for a beat, turned off the water, and bolted past her to the bathroom.

CHAPTER 34

JUSTIN

Four hours later, we were in her bed. I had the bathroom trash can and we were watching a movie. When I'd start to retch, we'd pause it until I finished and then we'd start again.

She rubbed my back and shook her head. "Vomit, lice, drunks, the Toilet King. You really know how to show a girl a good time."

"Hey, this is your date, not mine," I croaked.

She barked out a laugh.

"Do you regret not leaving when I told you to?" she asked.

I spit into the can. "I regret nothing. In fact I kind of feel like we need to share all our infectious diseases."

"*Really?*"

"Yeah. What else ya got? Anything sexually transmitted?" *Spitting.* "That could be fun." I bounced my eyebrows weakly.

"I don't want to burst your bubble or anything, but now *you* look a little like a guy who got bit by a zombie and he's just about to turn."

"Oh WOW. Coming from patient zero that *hurts*."

"Am I the asshole?"

"Yes. You one hundred percent are."

She smiled and put a hand on my forehead, and I closed my eyes.

"No fever at least," she said. "Hopefully you got a milder case."

She rubbed her thumb tenderly on my cheek, and there was a very real part of me that would have gotten sick all over again for that one touch alone.

I coughed into the trash can and ruined the moment.

"I'm sorry you have to see this," I said, pitifully.

"There is nothing I haven't seen, I promise you. I'm just glad you're where I can take care of you."

I rested my head on my arm on the rim of the can. She was gazing at me with something I could have sworn was affection. Or I could be delirious. It was probably delirium.

"I think I've officially barfed out my entire skeleton," I said. "Even my mouth is sweating."

"Please don't make me laugh. It hurts," she said.

"God, we're a mess. Next time we barf at my place, okay?" I said. "We can get DoorDash there."

"What do you want from DoorDash?" she asked.

"That really good ice from Sonic."

"Yeeesss," she breathed.

"Cold Stone. And Yogurt Lab."

"I want ribs," she said. "Like, really tender ribs covered in barbecue sauce. And a baked potato with all the stuff on it. And bread. That brown bread from the Cheesecake Factory."

"I want Punch Pizza. I'll give you all the crusts."

"I want to order Thai food," she said. "And get so much of it the car will think it's a person in the front seat and the seat belt reminder will keep going off."

"If I live, I will take you anywhere you want to go."

She glanced at me. "What if you die? Can I have your dog?"

"Only if you promise to never change his name," I rasped.

She put a hand over her heart. "I will carry on all your petty vendettas."

I chuckled dryly and spit in the can again.

She put her chin on her knees. "Do you think this counts as our fourth date?" she asked.

My mood immediately dropped off.

I didn't want this to be our last date. "I don't think so, right?" I said. "It's not like we're having fun."

"Fun isn't really a prerequisite," she said. "I actually *am* kind of having fun though."

So was I. Sort of. Except for the puking thing.

"I mean, what makes a date a date?" she asked.

"We have to eat something together," I said.

"And do some sort of activity. Like watch a movie," she added. "We've done both of those things."

I felt the tiniest tic in my jaw.

"Yeah, I guess we did."

"So that's it then. We've had our four dates. You still haven't kissed me though," she pointed out.

"You want one now?"

She hit me with a pillow.

The pills I'd brought for her eventually started working. I was able to keep down food around hour six. We napped. Woke up and had soup. I took a shower and we'd just finished watching another movie and she'd gotten up to get me a cup of tea.

I looked around her room while I waited for her.

It wasn't really *her* room. She didn't pick the bedspread or the furniture. She didn't choose the lamp on the nightstand or the towels or any of it. I wondered if she ever got sick of not belonging anywhere or not owning anything that didn't fit in her two suitcases.

I wondered if she got tired of saying goodbye.

God knows I was sick and tired of saying goodbye. First Dad, then Mom. And eventually Emma too.

Goodbye was the bane of my existence. I hated it.

She came back in and handed me a cup of hot tea. I set the mug on the nightstand to let it cool.

Our knees were touching. We'd been touching a lot.

Maybe the fact that we were sick made the little intimacies less high stakes. We weren't going to do anything sexual when I was hugging a barf bucket to my chest, so what did it matter if her thigh pressed into mine, or she rubbed my back, or put her head on my shoulder?

But then I started feeling better and we didn't stop. Maybe we couldn't.

There was a Get It Out Of Your System energy hovering around us. But I couldn't get it out of my system. A one-night stand wouldn't make this feeling go away. It would only make me want more of what I couldn't have, and yet I still couldn't stop touching her. Not anymore. I couldn't trust myself not to take anything she offered me, no matter how temporary. It felt too good. So we cuddled while we watched movies and I held her while she slept and I breathed her in and savored every second of it. Even though I knew what it would cost me the day she left.

CHAPTER 35

EMMA

You're cheating," Justin said from his spot in the kitchen.

I gasped from behind the wall in the hallway. "I am not. I'm just better at this game than you."

"You can't just camp out and wait for me to come to you. It's not fair."

"Are you saying strategically I've bested you?"

He groaned.

We'd found Nerf guns in the storage bin on the side of the house, and since it was raining again, we were playing inside.

He darted out from behind the counter. I spun into the doorway, aimed, and shot him right in the chest. He stopped to watch the foam bullets bounce off and tumble to the ground. He gave me an exasperated look, then sprang for me while I shrieked, running into the bedroom laughing.

He caught me from behind, twirled me onto my back on the mattress, and pinned me under him by the wrists.

"You are *dead*," I said, wriggling. "I killed you fair and square. Those were fatal shots."

"I've come back to haunt you."

"Really?" I grinned. "You don't feel like an apparition to me..." I said, referring to the boner pressing into my hip.

He smiled at me wryly, but he didn't move. He slid his grip off my wrists and twined his fingers in mine and held me down by the hands.

It wouldn't go further than this. Just this tease.

This sexual undercurrent between us was like the elephant in the room.

He hadn't kissed me since that day on the lawn.

I mean, we'd both been sick. Yesterday was the first full day that neither of us threw up. We'd just hung out and watched TV and rehydrated. Cuddled and talked and slept holding each other.

There were erections and long lingering looks and tender touches—but he didn't kiss me. And I didn't think he was going to. And it wasn't my place to kiss *him* because he'd been the one to reject my last advances. So we just circled each other with tension so palpable you could cut it with scissors. We didn't talk about it and we didn't acknowledge it, because what was the point? I was still leaving. That hadn't changed.

Even if *I* had.

The shift in me was confusing. Like I was in some new territory and didn't know how to map it. Maddy wasn't here, so I couldn't talk to her about what I was feeling. And I couldn't talk to Justin about it either because I didn't know how. It was incredibly complex and also unbelievably simple.

I wanted to be near him.

I had to stay to do it. But that wasn't an option, because I didn't want the rest of it. The kids and the permanency and the commitment. I couldn't meet him where he was, and he couldn't leave. So we just did this instead. We skirted this line, alone on a bed, attracted to each other, wanting each other but at a standoff with no end in sight.

His eyes moved to my mouth for a split second. Then he let go of my hands and got off me.

I sat up on the bed and watched him pick up Nerf bullets in the hallway with his back to me.

When he was done, he set them on the dresser and then came back to the bed and sat down. He set his hand near mine and my pinky touched his. "When do you want me to leave?" he asked.

The question came out of nowhere. My heart bottomed out.

We hadn't brought up him going home. It was like both of us wanted to pretend that the time on this island was infinite and never had to come to a close.

I didn't reply.

"Emma?"

I answered him by climbing over him and straddling him. Then I pushed him back on the bed.

He put his hands on my thighs and looked up at me calmly.

"You can stay," I said. "You don't have to leave. Unless you have to get the kids. Or Brad."

"Leigh's fine with them. They're having fun. Sarah doesn't come back until Sunday. Brad's with his namesake. He's taken care of."

"Don't you miss him?"

"I'd miss you more."

My pulse picked up and I had to look away from him. Then I wrinkled my forehead. "How did you get here?" I asked, looking back at him. "Did someone give you a ride?"

"I paddled on the unicorn floatie."

I blinked at him. "Are you joking?"

"I am not joking."

"You paddled here," I deadpanned. "On the unicorn floatie."

He put a hand behind his head in a way that made his bicep bulge. "Are you impressed I have that kind of upper body strength?"

"Justin!"

It must have taken him forever. The wind and the waves and the—

He rolled onto his side and took me with him, hooking a hand behind my knee to keep my leg wrapped around him. He draped an arm over my waist and scooted closer until his forehead touched mine and he closed his eyes.

"I had to get here," he said. "Desperate times call for desperate measures."

We lay there, the air humid between us. Our mouths inches from touching.

I studied him up close while he wasn't looking. The cupid's bow at the top of his lip. The beard that had started to come in since he got here. I liked it. I put a palm to his cheek to feel it, and he smiled a little.

"What are you thinking?" I asked.

He didn't answer for a long moment. When he did, he did it with his eyes closed. "All I ever think about is you."

My heart pounded.

He opened his eyes. "What are we doing, Emma?"

Time stopped. Or I did. Reality smeared.

He put a gentle hand out to touch me. A thumb rubbed against my cheek to mirror the one I had on his.

"If this isn't magic, then what is?" he asked. "What does it feel like to be under a spell if this isn't it?"

His gaze held mine, and I couldn't break it. It *was* a spell. I didn't know how to answer him, and I didn't know how to push him away. I didn't know how to stay, and I didn't know how to leave.

I tried to imagine living here, I really did—signing a lease on an apartment. Getting a permanent position. Living in the same place for all the seasons. Making friends, growing roots. But the thoughts terrified me. *Why?* Why did anything with strings make me want to *run*?

His siblings were good kids. *Great* kids. I wouldn't have to live with them. I wouldn't have to do anything I didn't want to do because Justin wouldn't expect that of me. I had been through so much worse than sitting still, so why did the idea of staying feel so scary?

And then I knew. I *knew* why it was scary.

Because I *would* want to live with them. I *would* want to make those kids mine.

Staying meant I would fall in love.

I'd fall in love with this place. With him *and* his family. And that I didn't do.

My lack of permanence was my protection. I left people and places, so I didn't have to play. If I didn't play, I couldn't lose.

But if I left Justin, I would lose anyway.

The realization dawned before me. I'd been more affected by my upbringing than I'd been willing to admit. Because where else had I learned to live like this? Who else did I learn it from if not Mom, the woman who erased my past and never stopped moving? She'd trained me too well.

"I didn't want to beg you," he said. "But I don't give a shit about my pride anymore. Stay. *Please*. Just to see what happens. See where it goes. I'll take anything—a couple of months, a couple of weeks, whatever you'll give me. Meet me where I am because I can't go to you. I would if I could. I'd follow you anywhere if I was able to, but I *can't*. Please," he said again. "Stay."

I let out a puff of air.

His eyes pleaded with me, and I was drawn to him like he was magnetic. He had been from the moment I met him.

I could feel the gentle in and out of his chest pressed into mine. The warmth of his body through our clothes. We were our own little universe. The rain pounded on the roof and the white noise insulated us. There was nothing else outside of the electric space on this bed in this room on this island.

This island.

This impractical, crappy, lonely island that I was growing to hate.

I closed my eyes and put my cheek to his. I could feel his plea in every inch of his body. There was a desperation in the soft breath that unfurled in my ear and the tension in his muscles. I pulled away and he hovered above me, poised to kiss me.

I wondered if this was going to be another one of his teases, but I saw in his eyes the moment he gave up trying to stay away from me. His mouth came down and his tongue brushed against mine and I dissolved.

It was hard to imagine that this kiss was the same thing we'd casually agreed upon once. The checklist item he'd put onto a spreadsheet.

There are so many things in life that exist on a spectrum. Trust. Kisses.

Love.

You can love someone and still not be willing to give up your way of life for them. And then there are those you love who you'd take a bullet for. It's all the same emotion, just different levels. I'd lived on the low, safe side of everything. With the exception of Maddy, I kept my friendships at arm's length and my relationships even further away. I never fell for anyone. I never let anyone close enough to try.

I didn't let Justin close enough to try either, but he'd managed to get there anyway. Maybe there was never any other way it could have gone. He was always going to be this for me. And now we were in a kiss that was more than a kiss, and I didn't want him to kiss anyone else. Ever.

I didn't want to be kissed by anyone else. Ever.

Because how could it be better? How could I ever want someone so much again?

We stripped each other slowly. Selecting each piece of clothing to remove like we were revealing a sacred shrine. Exploring each other.

This is what my skin was for. To be touched like this. To feel this. Every nerve was for this sole purpose and I didn't even know it until now. To feel his strong hand slide up to cup my breast, his thumb circling my nipple. To feel his breath on my collarbone. I was made to experience *him.*

And he was right. It was magic.

I got up wrapped in a sheet to grab condoms from Maddy's stash in her room, and when I came back and he lifted the blanket to let me under, it felt like I was coming home again. The way he pulled me into him, warm and soft and hard and the rain on the roof and the thunder in the background.

Our breathing got heavier and his kisses got harder.

He raked down my thighs as he pulled off my underwear. Biting me gently on the way down and then pulling me to his mouth, fingers slipping inside of me, sucking and teasing until my back arched and I unraveled while he watched me from between the V of my legs.

He let me catch my breath and then I drew him down on top of me. When he slid inside of me, I had never felt closer to another person in my whole life.

I knew conceptually that sex was supposed to be like this. But for me it never was. It had always been one-dimensional, like a transaction.

This wasn't a transaction.

This wasn't like anything I'd ever known. I wanted him to hold me after. To wake up with me in the morning and eat cereal in my bed while we watched TV. I wanted to see his pajamas on Christmas morning and find out what he looked like with birthday candles lighting his face and snow in his hair. I wanted to be tangled in him, in all his limbs and all his strings.

I never wanted us to end.

And that's when I started crying.

He stopped immediately, pulling out of me.

"What happened?" he asked. "Did I hurt you?"

I shook my head.

I couldn't rein it in. The crying rolled into sobbing and I had to cover my mouth with a hand.

He started to look panicked. "Emma, what did I do? We can stop—"

"I don't want you to stop. I *never* want you to stop."

He waited for me to explain, hovered over me like a concerned, protective weighted blanket.

I blinked up at him through wet lashes. "Justin, I think something is wrong with me. Like there's something in me, in my heart, that doesn't work right."

He peered at me gently. "What doesn't work right?"

I pressed my lips together trying to keep the crying under control. "It's like there's a part of me that's always small," I whispered. "And I don't know why and I don't know what to do about it."

I started crying again and couldn't hold it back. I felt full of cracks all of a sudden. Deep, long, jagged cracks. And they'd always been there. I'd just learned to live with them so long I no longer noticed them. I'd hopped over them and built little bridges and taken other routes, but I never filled them. I never *fixed* them. I didn't even know how.

He put his forehead to mine and whispered and soothed me, even though he didn't know what I was crying about. But *I* did.

It was about love. I was falling in love.

Every fiber of my being had been fighting against it. It went against all the survival instincts that had kept me safe for the last twenty-eight years. My defenses fought the impulse without even letting me know there was a fight, the way your immune system knocks down infections you don't even know you've been exposed to. And the rest of me just went on, business as usual, planning to move to the next place like I always did because that was my normal. Normal was to keep moving, always leaving, never being anywhere long enough to give anyone or any place the chance to make me want to stay.

How many times had I done this?

How much love had I *missed*?

I started crying again.

"What can I do?" Justin whispered.

He brushed the hair away from my cheeks and looked at me with so much tenderness my heart ached. "What's wrong?" he asked. "Tell me what you're thinking."

I took a shuddering breath and tried to settle down.

"Tell me," he said.

I pulled in another deep, steadying inhale. "Justin, I like you more than I've ever liked anyone. And it scares me."

His eyes roamed my face. "I like you more than I've ever liked anyone too." He paused. "I like you more than like."

We held each other's gaze.

"I like you more than like too," I said quietly.

His face went soft. And then he leaned down and kissed me. It felt like a promise. A vow of some sort, even though I didn't know what it was for. I just know it made me feel safe. It made me feel calm and okay.

A few minutes later when we started to pick up where we'd left off, it was me who initiated it. I wanted his fast breath and the moan in the back of his throat and the gasp in mine. I wanted to forget. To be so lost in him I couldn't think about what scared me, or the cracks in my heart, or the things that didn't work right in my soul. I got lost in myself all the time. But I knew now that Justin was the only person in the world I could ever disappear into.

CHAPTER 36

JUSTIN

Someone knocked on the doorframe to Emma's room. We were snapped instantly out of the little bubble we'd been in for the last three hours.

It was Maddy.

"What in the hand, foot, and mouth is *this*?" she said from the doorway, grinning in at us.

I rolled off Emma under the covers and she scooted up. Luckily we'd only been kissing at this point, but if Maddy had been half an hour earlier she would have had quite the show.

"Maddy," Emma said, clutching the sheet to her neck. "You're back early."

"It's Friday," she said. "I'm back exactly when I'm supposed to be." She looked at me. "Heeey, Justin." She gave me a Cheshire Cat grin.

I waved, red-faced. "Hey."

"How'd you get here?" Emma asked. "You didn't call me to pick you up."

"Neil brought me."

"They're back?" she asked, surprised.

"Yeah. I ran into them at the airport. Got to ride home with them and everything, my own little chariot from hell."

She sat up straighter. "You saw Mom? How is she?"

Maddy shrugged. "Wearing a big-ass diamond bracelet and fawning all over him, so I'm gonna say okay." She turned to me. "So how long have *you* been here?"

I looked at Emma. "Three—no. Four days?"

Maddy nodded sagely. "I see."

"I got super sick," Emma explained. "He came to take care of me, and then he got sick."

"We basically spent the whole time barfing," I said. "Well. Not the *whole* time."

Maddy looked amused. "Clearly. Hey, Neil's waiting on the dock in case you want a lift back, Justin. We saw your car in front of the house. It's raining like a motherfucker through tomorrow so if you're planning on leaving today, I'd take the boat option with a roof."

I looked at Emma. I didn't want to go.

What had just happened between us was a big deal. We were post sex-for-the-first-time and had things to talk about. I wanted to be here, feel her out, know where she was with all this.

"You should go," Emma said.

My face fell. "Are you sure?"

"If you have a boat with a roof you should take it."

Then I realized that if I stayed, she'd have to drive me later in the rain on the pontoon. I didn't care about getting wet if I got to spend another few hours with her, but I cared about her boating in a storm.

"Yeah," I said. "Sure. I need to get my dog anyway. Get the kids."

"I'll tell Neil to wait," Maddy said, reaching for the doorknob. "I'll let you two get dressed." She bounced her eyebrows and left.

When the door closed, Emma didn't say anything. She just got up and started putting on clothes, so I got up and dressed too.

I kept looking over at her for any sign of what the past few hours meant. She didn't even glance at me.

I pulled my shirt over my head. "This was great, Emma. I really enjoyed our time together. When can I vomit with you again?"

She laughed a little while she hooked her bra, but she still wouldn't look at me.

The real question was under the joke. When would she see me again? *Would* she see me again?

I finished putting on my clothes and waited for her. When she pulled on her tank top, I came around the foot of the bed and drew her into my arms. I nuzzled the spot behind her ear. "Can I take you to dinner this week?" I whispered. "We can do the Thai food thing. Or the ribs and the brown bread from the Cheesecake Factory—"

She felt stiff. "I'll get back to you."

"I could bring it here…"

"Justin." She made some space between us and peered up at me. "I need to think. Okay?"

I studied her. I knew she liked me. She liked me more than like. But she'd also said it scared her. So what did that mean?

She gazed at me. "I wish you could come with me…" she said, almost too quiet for me to hear.

I held her eyes. Tried to decipher what that meant too.

The horn of a yacht blared outside.

"You should go," she said.

"Can I call you tonight?"

"I'll call you."

I swallowed. "Okay."

I kissed her. She did kiss me back, but by the way she was talking, I wondered if it was goodbye.

I grabbed my backpack and stood by the door to look at her one last time, then turned and made my way out. She watched me leave like she was getting a last look.

On the way back to the mainland, Neil was like Charon, the ferryman of Hades, taking a dead soul to shore.

I'd said what I could to Emma. I'd done all I could do.

My car felt foreign to me on the drive to Brad's to get my dog. For four short days, my whole world had been her and that island. Now it wasn't her. Maybe it never would be again. And now it was time to get back to real life.

I didn't *want* my real life.

I drove around collecting my dog and my kids, the car getting louder with every pickup. Chelsea was grumpy and whining, probably because she was overly tired and sore. She looked like she'd spent the whole four days on the back of a pony, which she probably had. She had dirt under her nails and was sunburnt and needed a bath.

While I appreciated that Leigh took her, I wasn't sure the trade-off was worth it if this was how I was going to get her back, and realizing that gave me a whole second wave of defeat because it meant I had one less viable option for overnight help.

Alex was going on animatedly about Leigh's and I was trying to act interested, but the whole thing just felt overstimulating and exhausting.

I came home to laundry and a mailbox full of bills and a long list of back-to-school bullshit. By the time I got Chelsea cleaned up, I had to make dinner. I wanted to DoorDash something, but then I remembered I was back in the real world and needed to start tightening my belt, which only put me in a worse mood. I was days behind at work, Alex was on me to get his school supplies and he wanted to go to Target, Brad was scratching again and probably needed a medicated bath and to go to the vet for another allergy shot, Sarah wasn't even back from Josie's family's cabin, so the stress wasn't even at full steam yet.

This was the price I paid for those four days. And I wouldn't have changed it for anything. Well, I might have changed the puking part. But not the rest of it.

I wanted to go back to the island.

I wanted to pretend to be young and child-free with a girl I was falling in love with, in a place where we could imagine it was all possible, because the further I got from those four days on the island, the more I realized it wasn't. And the reality check was sobering.

She could never meet me here.

Who would want to? Why would she give up a lucrative career and traveling the world with her best friend for *this*? Dinners of frozen dino nuggets, corn that tastes like the can it comes out of, soggy Band-Aids in the bathtub drain, and all the mundane shit that my life consisted of now.

I wasn't worth it. I didn't even blame her.

Maybe that's why she was crying. She liked me, but she didn't want everything that came with me, so she felt torn. I was the right guy at the wrong time.

And maybe she was the right girl at the wrong time for me too.

I couldn't think of a worse period in my life for this to be happening.

By 10:00 Emma didn't text, and it didn't even surprise me.

I got Chelsea in bed and I sat down at the desk in my room to try to get some work done. An hour into it she finally called.

I watched the phone ring for a few seconds. She was going to break things off with me. I knew it in my soul. I could *feel* it.

I hit the answer button. "Hey."

"Hey," she said. Her tone was apologetic. I pinched the bridge of my nose and braced for it.

"I was wondering if you wanted some company," she said.

I raised my head. "Huh?"

"I'm outside."

I froze for a solid five seconds. Then I bolted up and ran to the window. She was standing with an umbrella on the sidewalk under the streetlamp. She had the rosebush with her, sitting at her feet. The rain was falling softly and she peered up at me. I put my fingers on the glass.

"We'll try it," she said, into the phone. "I'll stay."

CHAPTER 37

EMMA

I woke up to my alarm at 5:30 in Justin's dark room.

He pulled me into a warm sleepy hug. "Don't go."

"I have to," I said quietly. "I don't want the kids to know I stayed the night."

He groaned and nuzzled into my neck.

This is how we'd been doing it for the last two weeks. Me, sneaking in after the kids went to bed and getting up to leave before they woke up. It was very exhausting and extremely inconvenient.

It was totally worth it.

Maddy and I extended our contract another six weeks at Royaume. Maddy said it was technically still my turn since I'd only asked for six weeks to begin with and a turn is usually three months long. So we were here now until late October.

We hadn't talked about what would happen next. Me and Maddy *or* me and Justin. I was a little afraid to.

I was already extremely outside my comfort zone. But at least I had six more weeks to feel this all out.

In the meantime, Maddy and I did need to decide on a new living situation. It was September now and we were officially over the island. Justin had offered his apartment for free for the few months he still had it. Maddy liked free, so we packed up and vacated the cottage, but the studio was unfurnished with only enough room for the one air mattress that Maddy and I had to share—*and* it had a giant toilet bowl outside. So we'd been looking at other rentals but hadn't found one we liked yet.

Mom hadn't even noticed I'd left. But then she'd barely cared when I was there, so that made sense.

Something was starting to shift inside of me with Mom. Maybe because I hadn't spent this much time adjacent to her in almost fifteen years, but I was realizing that even though I loved her, I wasn't sure I liked her.

Even thinking this felt wrong. She was my mom. But I didn't like what she did to Neil that day in the driveway. It put such a bad taste in my mouth, and she hadn't made any attempts to see me since then so the feeling lingered.

She never replied to any of my texts from the days I was sick. Didn't return one call. Never circled back to check on me. Even Maria had texted to ask how I was.

I looked at my watch.

Justin hugged me tighter. "Staaaaaay."

"You're seeing me later," I said. "I have to go. Maddy needs her car."

He shifted until he was half on top of me and his boner was pressed into my thigh. "Why don't you just take mine next time?" he said, peppering tiny kisses down my collarbone.

"I can't take your car."

"I have the van," he said, his hands wandering. "Alex can't drive it yet, so it's just sitting there. Uber the next time you come over and take my car home."

He slipped a hand into my underwear and I sucked in a breath of air. "What time does Alex get up for the bus?" I whispered, tipping my head back as he nibbled on my ear.

"Another forty-five minutes…"

Plenty of time.

"Let me brush my teeth."

We both got up and went to the bathroom. Justin stood there brushing his teeth over the sink, no shirt, bare perfectly defined chest, blue pajama bottoms with a hard outline in the front that I liked *very* much. I smiled around my toothbrush.

I could *not* get enough of him.

Opting for these sleepovers instead of actually sleeping was starting to affect my work. I'd been over here so much I'd only slept in the bed at the Toilet King studio three times since the first night I came over.

He made my lunch every day—enormous, chaotic bags of snacks and sandwiches. He always made one for Maddy too. He kept trying to get me to stay for one of his breakfasts, but that meant eating with the kids, so I never did. I bet they were good though.

I rinsed my toothbrush and trained my gaze on the front of his pants.

He spit. "Uh, my eyes are up here."

"Uh-huh," I said, not looking up.

"That's it. I'm cutting you off."

I gasped. "What? *Why?*"

He gave me a fake stern look. "You need to stop using me like a piece of meat. It's dehumanizing. I'm serious."

I cracked up and he crashed into me and walked me backward to the bed, laughing. He slid over me on the mattress and kissed me, his smile so big I could feel it against my mouth.

I loved this. Everything about it.

I loved that he always made me laugh. I loved that no matter what we were doing, it was fun. I loved that I slept so well when he was next to me, and I felt safe and cared for and wanted.

And I really, *really* loved the sex.

"I wish I didn't have to go," I breathed.

"Stay here. I'll hide you in my closet."

"Ha."

He nipped at my lip. "My secret girlfriend. Comes and goes under the cloak of darkness."

I snorted.

"We are trying this out to see if it works," I whispered. "Your siblings don't need to get attached to someone who might…"

He pulled away with an arched eyebrow. "Someone who might *what?*"

I gave him a look. "You know what I mean."

"I do not know what you mean," he said, smiling. "Because I like you more than like, so it doesn't matter if your people get attached to me. I'm not going anywhere." He caged me between his forearms and kissed under my chin. "If you came during normal business hours, I'd make you breakfast…"

I pretended to think about it. "I *do* like your food."

Wailing started a few bedrooms over. We both froze.

Chelsea.

And she was coming. The sound was floating down the hall.

"Shit," I whispered.

He dropped his head to my chest in defeat before he got up and dug in a drawer.

She'd been having nightmares.

"I have to go get her," he said, pulling on a shirt. He leaned down quickly and pecked me on the lips. "I don't know how long I'll be with her. If I don't come back before you have to leave, I'll see you tonight."

He slid out the door and closed it behind him. I could hear him scoop his baby sister up in the hallway. "Heeeey, what happened, huh? It's okay..."

"I wanna sleep with yoooou," she wailed.

"We can sleep in your room, okay?"

The crying went up a notch. She wanted to be in her mom's room. It was probably comforting for her.

Justin was trying to convince her to go with him back to her bed and she was crying and telling him no. The sobbing was hitting a crescendo. I got up.

I opened the door and popped out my head. He was holding her in the hallway, shushing her and rubbing her back. "Justin? Just bring her in," I whispered.

He turned and his little sister blinked at me through tears. Then she outstretched her arms and reached, opening and closing her fists.

My heart *melted*.

I stepped into the hallway and took her. She put her head on my shoulder, drew a deep breath, let it out shakily, and immediately calmed down.

I stared at Justin over the little girl in my arms and he smiled. We went back into his room and lay down with Chelsea between us. And he just gazed at me, head on the pillow, while his little sister fell back asleep.

An hour later, I was at breakfast, in my pajamas, in Justin's kitchen, with his whole family.

Justin was at the stove, flipping slices of ham in butter and making waffles.

The waffle maker beeped, and he plucked out the finished product with a fork and plated it, sliding it in front of Chelsea.

I started cutting it into bite-size pieces while he grabbed the coffeepot and filled my mug. When he was done, he kissed me on the cheek and went back to the sink.

Nobody batted an eye when I came downstairs. I just folded into the chaos of the morning while the coffee brewed and the kids got ready for school and the dog got let out. And it made me wonder why I hadn't just done this sooner.

I liked it.

I liked seeing this other side of him—this paternal version that signed permission slips and brushed a little girl's hair into pigtails and made breakfast in slippers and a hoodie and pajama bottoms.

"Who wants orange juice?" Justin asked.

"I do," Alex said.

Justin opened the fridge. "We're out. I'll check the garage." He turned off his burner and left the kitchen.

Sarah was eyeing me from across the table. "We know you stay the night."

I froze with my coffee cup halfway to my lips. "*What?*"

"We can hear you guys laughing."

Alex was nodding, a huge grin on his face.

"We don't care, you know. He's happier when you're here," she said. "You should stay whenever you want."

I was still blinking at them when Justin came back in with a carton of Tropicana. He set it on the table and went back to the stove.

"What's for dinner?" Alex asked, opening the carton and pouring himself a glass.

Justin put the frying pan in the sink. "Uh, I was thinking chicken fried rice maybe? I don't know. Emma, what do you want?"

I only paused for a second. "I like fried rice," I said.

He turned around to smile at me.

Alex pounded his juice and shoved a forkful of ham into his mouth. "I gotta go to school," he said, talking around it.

Sarah slung her backpack over her shoulder. "Can you dye my hair again?" she asked me. "Tonight when you come?"

"Sure."

She smiled and left through the garage for the bus stop. I got up and started clearing plates.

Only Chelsea was still at the table, eating a piece of waffle and wiggling like she had to go to the bathroom.

"Chels, go potty," Justin said.

His sister nodded and jumped from her chair and ran down the hall. I set the plates in the sink and as soon as my hands were free he grabbed me and pulled me into an embrace. "Alone, finally," he said.

I laughed. "For the next five seconds."

He tipped my chin up to kiss me but I pulled back. "You don't think we should lay off the PDA in front of the kids?" I whispered.

"I don't see any kids..." He smiled and leaned in but I stopped him again.

"You kissed me on the cheek earlier," I said.

He looked amused. "It's good for them to see that. This is what I got to see when I was growing up."

"Kissing in the kitchen?"

"A healthy relationship," he said. "Two people in love." He bent down and kissed me and I didn't stop him this time.

It was a casual comment. Not a huge declaration or even something he expected a response to. Just stating a fact.

We'd only ever said we like each other more than like. We'd never said that word.

I'd never said that word.

We'd been tiptoeing around it for weeks. He was still tiptoeing, really. I think he sensed that I wasn't ready for him to look me in the eye and say I love you, so he slipped it in this way instead.

He was right, I wasn't ready.

Even though I *did* love him.

How easy it was for him to acknowledge this monumental thing. To say it out loud without fear that the universe would take it from him now that it knew what he needed to live. That's what the universe always did to me. Took away the people I loved.

He still had his arms around my waist. Chelsea didn't pay it any attention as she climbed back onto her chair to eat her breakfast.

"Sarah knows I stay the night," I whispered. "Your brother too."

His eyes went wide. "They *do*?"

"Yup."

"Do you think we've been too loud?" he whispered.

"Yes. They hear us laughing."

He paused for a moment before cracking up. "Well, you do make me ridiculously happy. I can't help it." He rubbed his nose to mine.

Justin's heart was pressed to my heart.

He gazed into my eyes and I studied his face. The creases when he smiled. His messy hair, the little gold flecks in his irises. Something serious moved across his expression as he held me there, and the most overwhelming feeling came over me.

I felt like I could stay in this moment forever. Like it was timeless because of how absolutely perfect it was. And yet there was nothing perfect about it. Not in the traditional sense. We were in pajamas. We weren't on a date, standing under the moon. We were next to a sink full of dirty dishes and a crusty waffle iron. There wasn't music playing or candlelight or rose petals. But it *was* perfect. I wouldn't have changed a single thing about it.

He put a hand to my cheek. "Sometimes I feel like the seasons could come and go and come and go, a hundred years could pass, a thousand, the ground could collapse under us, this house could crumble and go back to the earth, and we would still be standing here frozen in time, because every *second* I'm with you is eternal. I've never felt anything like it."

The air stilled in my lungs. Words taken right out of my own mind and said back to me out loud.

If this isn't magic, then what is?

He didn't wait for me to reply. He just leaned down and kissed me again.

CHAPTER 38

EMMA

A week and a half later and I'd stayed over at Justin's every single night since the day we had waffles. Justin and the kids and I did everything together. I did driving hours with Alex, took Sarah to dance, folded laundry on the bed with Justin while we watched movies. I spent a full day and took care of his mom's plants in the yard, something he was stressed about. On Saturday Justin and I cooked dinner together and set up an ice cream sundae bar for dessert. We walked the dog holding hands, and I lay in bed watching him work after the kids went to school.

I don't think I realized how smart he was until I got to see him working. He was a lead engineer at a tech company. During his stand-up meetings with his team, it was like seeing a whole new side of him. And then he'd take off his headphones, log out, and climb into bed with me and be so soft and sweet and focused on me.

I liked taking care of him and his family. I liked bringing

Chelsea to school on my day off to give Justin time to go for a run and then going to Starbucks and surprising him with his favorite coffee. I liked rubbing his shoulders while he sat at his computer and hearing Sarah tell me about her day. But mostly I loved being there when he woke up. Not having to wait for a text. Seeing him the second I opened my eyes.

I'd planted the rosebush in his front yard and I liked seeing that too.

The summer was slipping into fall now. I'd picked up some mums for the front porch and I was just getting the last one out of the van when the phone rang. It was Maria.

I thought for a second she had maybe butt-dialed me? Or maybe a package had shown up at the house. I swiped open the call. "Maria—"

"Your mother has lost her mind! You have fifteen minutes to get here before I call the police!"

I froze. "What…what did she do?"

"She's throwing clothes on the lawn! The whole backyard is covered, I'm not cleaning this up!" She yelled something in Spanish. "She sleeps for days, then she's awake for a week straight, painting and painting her stupid wall all night long with the music blasting and she's leaving the front door open and the whole house is full of dead bugs. Now this—I am *done*. You come get her or I call the cops."

She disconnected.

Justin was in a meeting. I didn't want to interrupt him and I didn't have time. I just grabbed the keys, ran to the garage, and went and called Maddy on the way. When I got there, I threw the van in park and bolted around to the backyard to Maria just in time to see Mom chuck another armload over the railing.

I gaped at her. "MOM!"

She ignored me and went back in. A moment later she came out with more clothes.

"Mom, stop!"

Maria looked at me, exasperated. "I've had enough. I'm not a pinche babysitter. You deal with this, I'm leaving." She stormed off and I ran up the deck to the French doors in the kitchen. By the time I got upstairs, Mom had managed to toss most of Neil's clothes outside.

She was stalking back to his closet and I grabbed her wrist. "Mom! STOP!"

She yanked her arm free, spun, and crumpled into a sobbing heap on the floor.

I looked around, trying to catch my breath. The room was absolutely destroyed. Like a tornado had hit it.

There was a trail of men's clothes from the walk-in closet to the sliding glass door. Belts, shoes, ties, suits. A purple wet spot dripped down the wall with a shattered wineglass under it on the hardwood floor.

I looked back at my mother, heaving into her hands. She was in a stained white robe. Her hair was matted in the back like a messy bird's nest.

My stomach *sank*.

I hadn't seen her in weeks. She'd made zero effort to see me and I was so busy with Justin I decided not to care. But now I realized my mistake.

"Mom? What happened?" I said. "Tell me."

She was hiccupping and gasping. "He's kicking me out."

I blinked at her. "What? *Why?* What did he say?"

"He said it might be better if we take a little break," she said, putting her fingers in quotes.

"Did you guys have a fight?"

"He accused me of stealing."

I pulled my face back. "He accused you of *stealing*?"

"I guess some watches are gone and some cuff links. It's that maid. I know it. She hates me and they're always taking things."

I blew a breath through my nose.

I did not for one second think Maria took something.

"Mom…" I said, carefully. "Did you?" The question was tentative. But I had to ask it.

She glared at me. "What the fuck is that supposed to mean, Emma? You think *I* took it. Why would *I* take it?"

"It's just—"

"Are you kidding me? You know what? If you're here to talk to me about shit that happened twenty years ago, you can just go. Seriously. Go."

"Mom…you *do* take things. I'm sorry, but you have."

She pressed her lips together. "What the hell does he care? He has more money than he can spend. He can buy more."

I squeezed my eyes shut. And there it was.

"Why do you always *do* stuff like this?" I whispered.

"Like *what*?"

"Ruin things when they're *good*."

Memories pinged off me like little jagged barbs. This *exact* same situation, over and over when I was a kid. She'd have these eruptions, every time things were happy or we were somewhere stable. It was like she hated the calm and I didn't know why. Why did she always need this? This *chaos*?

Her chin started to tremble and the indignant expression dropped off, and she became the sobbing little girl again.

I didn't know what she was. But she was *not* okay.

I put a hand to my forehead and looked despondently around the room at the evidence of her decline. Empty wine bottles and glasses, garbage on the dresser, burned-out candles on the night-stand. There was no way Neil was sleeping in here. If I had to guess, he was sleeping in a guest room when he was home and he had been for a while. He'd never said a word of it to me at work. He was just trying to deal with it.

Guilt overcame me.

I hadn't been here. If I had, I would have seen she was strug-gling again. I could have gotten ahead of it. I could have saved him the grief.

"Mom, what time does Neil get home?" I asked.

"Who knows," she sniffed. "He can tell me ten and it ends up being two," she said, wiping her cheek with her sleeve. "He wants me committed, did you know that? He told me he'd pay for an inpatient program. It's either that or I leave. He thinks I need help."

"And you said *no*? You do need help!"

"I'm not crazy, Emma!"

"Well you're not okay either!" I snapped. "Look at this! Look what you did! We need to clean this up. You know that, right? We can't let him walk into this."

"Fuck him."

"Mom! What do you want? You want the cops to drag you out of here? You're stealing from him, and this is destruction of property. This isn't your house!"

She collapsed again into a heap and wailed.

I stared at her, feeling completely overwhelmed.

Maddy was right, I should have warned him.

I didn't know what to do.

Where would I take her if he kicked her out? She was back in one of her episodes, I couldn't leave her alone. She couldn't stay with me and Maddy. They wouldn't admit her at a hospital unless she was a danger to herself, which she'd never own up to, she turned down Neil's offer of help. So what? What do I do?

I get her off the floor.

I was an adult now, not an eight-year-old kid. If I could do this then, I could do it now. Just…get her off the floor. De-escalate her so she cooperates and stops making it worse.

"Mom," I said, trying to keep my voice steady. "Let's just take a warm bath. Get you out of these clothes. I'll make you some tea, okay?"

I ran the water and managed to put her in the tub. Lit one of her candles, then went downstairs to make her something to drink.

Maria was right about the house.

For all the long nights Maria said she'd worked on it, the rose wall wasn't even half done. It looked like Mom had painted over it and started again and the restart was sloppy. The herbs Mom had brought home all those weeks ago from the farmers' market were crispy on the windowsill. The house was full of decaying flowers. Vase after vase.

While I waited for the kettle to heat up, I wandered around collecting them. I dumped the water and tossed the wilted bouquets. Threw away the brittle herbs. Then I finished making her tea and brought it upstairs.

By the time I'd gotten back to the bathroom, Mom was calm, but she still looked awful. Her eyes were hollow. She was puffy, the way she got when she was drinking too much. But worst of all, the smell of her perfume was gone. There was nothing but the scent of rotting blossoms and stagnant water still in my nostrils and the smell of the candles she used to hide it all.

I set her mug on the tray over the tub and I leaned on the sink. "Mom?"

She stared glassy-eyed into the bathroom.

"Mom, have you still been seeing your therapist?"

She didn't answer.

"When's the last time you had a session?" I asked.

"Yesterday," she said finally. "Venus is in retrograde. I'm supposed to practice self-care. Opal should help."

"Okay." I nodded. "But what did your therapist say?"

"That *is* what my therapist said."

I stilled. "Why would your therapist talk to you about retrograde?" I asked carefully.

"What else would she talk to me about?"

My stomach bottomed out. *No...* "Mom, you said you had a *therapist*. A real one. You said—"

"She's a spiritual advisor, and she's helped me more than any doctor I've ever seen."

I stared at her. I didn't even know what to say.

Nothing was different.

It was all the same circle again and again. Maddy was right. Maddy was *always* right.

I felt sick. My breathing started to get shallow.

I had to leave before I had a panic attack. I got up and walked out of the bathroom without another word.

I felt like the house was spinning. I could barely make it down the stairs.

I knew what would happen now. The same things that always did: Mom, leaving in a blaze of glory. The police escorting her out if she wouldn't go, her making a scene, or them coming later to take a report of all the things missing when she slips out in the night.

Or maybe she'd just stop getting out of bed altogether and then Neil would call me to ask what he should do. I'd get her up and take her to the hospital with opals in her pockets and then three days later she'd check herself out against doctor's orders and vanish again.

I was devastated.

The inevitable hadn't happened yet, but it would. It had already started.

I felt defeated and stupid, and horrible for Neil, whose clothes were on the lawn and cuff links and watches were missing because I hadn't told him what Maddy said I should have told him from the very beginning.

And I couldn't even cry about it. I didn't have time. Because I would *not* let Neil come home to this mess, when it was all *my* fault for hoping and believing her when she said she was better. It was my fault she was even here.

I felt myself start to get small, the edges pulling in. The humiliation and disappointment making me want to isolate and disappear. I already knew I wouldn't go to Justin's tonight. I wouldn't want to see anyone, wouldn't want to socialize or be around the kids. It would be hard enough to see Maddy.

I grabbed a laundry basket and made my way outside, trying not to cry.

When I got to the lawn, Maddy was there. She was bagging up the clothes into trash bags.

"Hey," she said, grimacing at a pair of Neil's underwear that she'd picked up by the corner. "I didn't take him for a Hanes guy."

I was so relieved to see her, I almost broke down right then and there.

"You don't have to do this," I said.

"I know. I'm gonna anyway." She shoved the underwear into the bag.

My chin quivered.

She didn't want to help Amber. She didn't care what became of my mother. But Maddy knew I'd be the one cleaning up the mess because Neil would be the one injured if I didn't, and that would weigh on me more than any of it. So she came.

Maddy watched me look over the heaps of clothing, despair swallowing me.

"I wish I could not care," I whispered.

Maddy saw my face and dropped the bag and closed the distance between us and hugged me.

My best friend was a docking station. Same as Justin. And I cried right into her hair.

When I got it together enough to pull away from her, she put her hands on my shoulders. "I want you to know that your empathy is beautiful, Emma. I hope you *never* lose that. I do hope that one day you get some boundaries though."

I laughed a little but she didn't smile.

"You cannot keep caring about her more than you care about yourself."

When I didn't answer, she took a deep breath and let me go.

"Come on," she said, picking up the bag. "Let's get Neil's shit off the grass."

CHAPTER 39

JUSTIN

I got the text from Maddy right as I was getting out of my meeting. She told me briefly what happened, and I came immediately. I didn't even know Emma had left.

Maddy was alone in the yard putting button-down shirts into a laundry basket when I walked around the side of Neil's house.

I don't know how much was out there on the lawn to begin with, but it must have been a lot because it looked like a whole walk-in closet was still on the grass.

I shook my head over the mess. "What the hell happened?"

She pushed a loose hair off her forehead with the back of her hand. "Amber happened. I'm sorry you had to come. There's no way the two of us can clean this up. It's Emma's birthday tomorrow. If we don't help her get through this today she's going to be small for a week, and I will not let that woman ruin another important day for her."

"Yeah, of course," I said, looking over the clothes. "What can I help with?"

She handed me the basket. "Take this up. It's the last room at the top of the stairs. Emma's in the walk-in closet."

"All right." I turned for the house.

"Justin—"

I stopped and looked back at her.

"Do you know what to do when she gets small?"

I shook my head. "No."

"She's going to get really detached and distant. Give her space, but don't leave her alone. And whatever you do, *never* let her take off."

"Okay…"

"I'm serious," she said. "Keep her near you. Put her in a room, let her isolate, let her sleep, bring her food. Don't talk to her until she's ready to talk, give her time to come out of it. But don't let her leave."

I nodded. "All right. Why?"

"Because she won't come back."

By the matter-of-fact way she said it, I knew she meant it. And I wondered what she'd seen to make her believe this.

I realized that Maddy was probably one of the only people who'd ever taken care of Emma. She was probably the only person that Emma *allowed* to take care of her.

And now there was me too. And I would. However I needed to.

I carried the basket through the house to find Emma hanging things up in the closet of the master bedroom. When she saw me, her face went from surprise to crumpled in the course of two seconds flat. I set the basket down and wrapped her in my arms, and she burst into tears.

Protectiveness surged through me. I *hated* this.

I could feel how tired she was. It reminded me of the way Mom felt the day she left. An emotional exhaustion. Bone weariness.

Only love hurts this way. And the way that her pain hurt me was love too.

"How did you know?" she whispered.

"Maddy called me," I said, tucking her under my chin.

She nodded into my chest. "Thank you for coming."

"Just meeting you where you are. In a closet."

She laughed a little, and I tightened my grip around her.

"Where's Amber?" I asked.

"In the bathtub." She sniffled.

"What time does Neil come home?"

"I called Royaume. Hector says he'll be there until at least four."

"Okay," I said, pulling away to brush the hair off her forehead. "So we have some time. We'll get it all cleaned up, okay? Does he know?"

She shook her head solemnly. "No. But Maria will tell him."

"What do you think he'll do?"

She hugged her arms around herself. "Kick her out? That's what they usually do."

I drew my brows down. "Does she do this a lot?"

"She does this every time, Justin." She peered up at me, her eyes sad. "I don't know what's wrong with her." Her chin started to quiver.

I pulled her into me and held her again. "Maybe it's better if she leaves," I said, quietly. "Maybe it's better for you."

She shook her head. "When she's here, it's this. When she's not, I'm just braced for the call because she's doing this somewhere else where I don't know if she's safe." She paused. "There is no better for me."

We stood there, me holding her and her taking calming breaths in my arms. "We need to hurry," she said finally. "I don't want Neil to see this."

I spent the next hour carrying heavy baskets up the stairs like a pack mule. When we finally got everything off the lawn, the three of us blitzed the closet. About halfway through, Amber came dragging out of the bathroom. Emma tried to get her to help with the cleanup, but it was almost more work to get Amber moving than to just do it herself so she gave up.

It was obvious Amber was in some sort of meltdown. I knew I should probably look at her actions the way Emma did, with empathy and not anger, but I was angry anyway, because I was pretty sure Amber didn't do anything to try to help herself. I think she allowed Emma to mitigate the damage, and I think she'd been doing that since Emma was little. I could see now why Maddy hated her.

If this had been her childhood, Emma never got to be a kid. She didn't even get to be a carefree adult. And I didn't know how to help or what to even tell her. How would I feel if *my* mom were like this? How do you not care if someone you love is having a complete mental breakdown?

Amber felt like a curse.

I understood now why Emma wanted so badly for Amber to be working on herself and why Maddy didn't buy it and wanted her gone.

Maybe Neil would get her to agree to the inpatient program Emma told me he offered. Now I found *myself* hoping. Maybe Amber never had the means or the support to get the kind of help she needed. Hell, maybe Amber would do for Neil what she never did for her own kid and get her shit together. Maybe this would be the turning point. Because if it wasn't, when would this end?

By 3:30 we were done. Emma brushed out Amber's hair and put it in a French braid, then left her asleep in bed.

We came down the stairs to Maria in the kitchen. "You threw out the flowers," Maria said, pouring herself a glass of juice. "I wondered how long they were going to rot."

Emma stopped. "If you saw them rotting, why didn't you toss them?"

Maria scoffed. "Because she told me not to touch her stuff? So I don't touch."

"And what does Neil say about that?" I asked.

She shrugged. "If he wants to live with *trash*," she said, emphasizing the word, "that's none of my business."

Emma stared at her for a moment. I didn't know if she didn't defend Amber because she was too tired for the fight, or if she agreed with Maria's assessment of her mother, but she didn't reply. I led her out of the kitchen and took her hand as we came out to the backyard.

The second we were outside and the Amber ordeal was over, Emma was spent. It was like she funneled everything into fixing the mess, and when it was done there was nothing left of her. I could tell she was small. I'd never seen her like this before, but I recognized it on sight. She was quiet and withdrawn. Flat. Almost monotone. I was glad Maddy prepared me for it because I wouldn't have known what to think.

I checked my watch. "I have to go get Chelsea. Do you want to come home with me or have Maddy take you to the house so you can get in bed?"

"I think I need to stay home today," she said, tiredly. "I'll just go to the studio."

Maddy shook her head. "Go home with Justin. I'll come meet you tomorrow for your birthday lunch."

Emma looked blankly back and forth between us.

I put an arm around her shoulders. "Let's go home. I'll make you dinner, and you can stay in bed for the rest of the day. We'll watch movies, go to sleep early."

I was relieved when she nodded.

I drove us to pick up Chelsea, then put Emma upstairs while I helped Sarah with homework and got dinner started. I was stressed the whole time.

I'd missed almost a whole day of work today. I'd have to log in tonight after Emma went to sleep.

My job had always been flexible. I could pretty much do it whenever I wanted to, as long as I logged in for the morning stand-up and put in my hours. But now, if I didn't work while the kids were in school, I couldn't get anything done. I got up at 6:30 to get them out the door, made them a hot breakfast because that's what Mom always did, even though it meant cleanup and less time to sleep. I took Chelsea to preschool, worked from 9:00 to 4:30 basically nonstop. Then it was pick up Chelsea, homework with Sarah, activities, laundry, chores, dinner, bath time, and my whole day was gone.

I had no idea how single parents did this. I had no time for anything, let alone myself.

But for Emma, I would make time. It wasn't even a question. I would fit her into the complicated web that was my life. Because when you're in love, you do hard things.

And nothing about anything was easy right now.

CHAPTER 40

EMMA

Today was my birthday.

I felt better this morning. I'd been small for the rest of the day yesterday, but I was glad I came home with Justin.

He'd made dinner after picking up Chelsea, served me a plate, put me in bed, and I watched TV while he worked at his desk by the window with noise-canceling headphones on. I lay there and I mostly watched him instead of the show. It was grounding. It calmed me having him nearby. I felt my edges unravel again, the gradual untightening until I was almost back to normal.

It wasn't lost on me that Maddy pushed me to go with him instead of staying with her.

She would never let someone else take care of me unless she was sure they could do it. And he could. I hated that he had to, but he could.

Mom couldn't. She never had. It was very much the other way around and that had never been more clear to me than now.

Neil had to know by now what she'd done. Was I going to get a call to pick her up? Would she be standing on the curb with her bags, no money and nowhere to go? Or worse, would the call come from the police station when Neil reported the missing things she took?

I hated that this was what I got to think about today.

It's funny because I realized Maddy was right. Mom would forget it was my birthday. The only call I'd get this morning would be one where *she* needed something.

And Maddy was right about something else too—I did care more about Amber than I cared about myself. I needed to think about that. I had to unpack this situation with my mother. I didn't like the way I was living or the responsibility I'd assumed for her.

I wanted to block her. Even just for today. But this went against everything I'd spent my life doing.

All I ever did was wait for Amber. Sitting around hoping she'd come home or the phone would ring. But the calls were never good. They hardly ever brought me any sort of happiness—in fact, they usually did the opposite.

If I blocked her, it would feel like clocking out of a job that I'd been at with no breaks for the last twenty years. If I did it, it would not only keep her from calling, it would keep *me* from knowing if she didn't—and both things would protect my peace. And I hadn't felt peace in a really, really long time. But I couldn't. I couldn't leave her in the world with no one.

Even if she could do that to me.

So I settled for turning off my ringer instead and I got up to go find Justin.

I came downstairs still in my pajamas, following the smell of bacon, glad I was actually in the right headspace to eat with everyone. When the stair creaked as I made my way to the kitchen, Sarah poked her head out the door and saw me coming. "She's here!" She darted back the way she came.

I turned the corner just as Justin was lighting the candles on a stack of pancakes. Alex and Sarah flanked him on either side.

"Happy birfday!" Chelsea said. She ran and hugged my legs.

I hugged her back and beamed at the setup. He'd made me confetti pancakes. There was a HAPPY BIRTHDAY banner hanging from the light fixture and a present wrapped in colorful paper with a gold bow sitting in the middle of the table.

I didn't expect this. I didn't expect anything unless it was Maddy.

He pulled my chair out. "For the birthday girl."

I couldn't stop smiling. "Thank you."

I sat and he pushed my chair in and kissed the side of my head.

"All right, ready?" he said, rubbing his hands together. "One, two…"

They burst into the "Happy Birthday" song. Alex started belting it like an opera singer. Sarah glared at him, and Chelsea descended into giggles. Justin laughed through the last half and when it ended, I blew out the candles. Everyone cheered.

Justin set a Starbucks napkin next to my plate and sat next to me. "I hope you like what I got you."

"Do you want me to open it now?"

"Presents!" Chelsea said, bouncing a little.

"Open it! Open it!" Alex chanted.

Sarah looked annoyed at her siblings' enthusiasm, but by the way she was waiting, I could tell she wanted to see what it was.

"Okay." I pulled the box into my lap.

"Maddy helped me with it," Justin said.

"She did?"

"Yup."

I pulled the ribbon off and tore the paper. When I opened the lid, I had to dig through tissue to find it and when I did, I gasped. It was Stuffie.

He'd been cleaned and his eye sewn back on. His fur was brushed out and white again. His stuffing had been replaced, and he had a new mane. He looked like he used to.

I turned him around gently in my hands. "How...?"

"Maddy snuck it out for me. Faith did it," he said.

I brushed my fingers across the clean, soft fur on Stuffie's head, tears welling in my eyes.

He nodded at it. "She took a little of his old stuffing and put it in a fabric heart and put it back in his chest with his new filling."

I held the doll against me and looked over at him. "Thank you so much," I breathed.

He smiled and leaned in and kissed me. Alex hooted and Sarah moaned about it being gross, and Justin and I grinned against each other's lips.

Justin pulled the candles out of my breakfast and served me some bacon.

Alex grabbed a pancake and rolled it like a burrito and took a bite. "I gotta go to school," he said, chewing with his mouth open. "Happy birthday."

"Thank you." I smiled.

"Happy birthday," Sarah said, following him out.

Justin set a cut-up pancake in front of Chelsea and poured syrup over it and sat next to me.

"This is so sweet, Justin. Thank you."

He watched me take a bite of my breakfast. "Like it?"

I nodded, looking at the plate. "Why are you so good to me?" I whispered.

"Because you deserve it."

"No I don't."

"Yes," he said. "You do. You take care of everyone in this house. You do driving hours with Alex and you help Sarah with homework and you give Chelsea baths. You read her stories and you do laundry and you help in my never-ending quest to keep all the dishes out of my brother's room."

I laughed a little but his face went serious.

"You deserve to be appreciated, Emma."

"I think I'm just used to feeling like I'm asking too much when I need something. Unless it's Maddy. My mom—"

"You're not asking too much," he said. "You were just asking the wrong person. Ask me instead."

I peered at him, my eyes soft.

He kissed me again and I smiled after him as he got up to pour himself some coffee.

I did feel appreciated here. I liked being a part of this family. I liked Sarah's Snaps and the funny sarcastic texts she'd started to send me during the day. I liked that Chelsea seemed to need me, that she found me comforting for some reason, like maybe I was the kind of adult I'd needed once and I was making a difference for her while she was missing her mom. I liked Alex's Golden Retriever personality and how he was always happy, no matter what was going on. But most of all I liked that Justin was the leader of this band. A warm, capable patriarch who didn't realize how strong and incredible he was.

They were all very lucky to have him.

I was lucky to have him.

At noon Maddy showed up to take me to lunch.

"Happy birthday," she said, coming in the door sideways with an enormous gift bag while Brad yipped and jumped at her feet.

I shut the door behind her as Justin jogged down the stairs. "Hey."

"Hey," she said, handing me the empty bag. "For you."

I laughed. This was our tradition. She never got me anything other than a gift card because it wouldn't fit in my luggage. She always got me a certificate for a service or a restaurant and put it in the largest possible box or bag she could find. One year she used a refrigerator box she got behind a Best Buy.

We went to sit in the kitchen. Justin poured us iced teas and then took the seat next to me.

"So have you heard the Amber and Neil update?" Maddy asked, taking off her sweater.

I shook my head. "No."

Justin glanced at me.

"What happened?" I asked.

"They broke up."

"What?"

She nodded. "Yup."

"How do you know?" Justin asked.

"Maria told me. I called to check in this morning. She said Neil came home yesterday and Maria told him everything that happened. Saw the video footage of the whole thing, and he *still* didn't kick her out. I guess he had this come-to-Jesus with her, told her he'd help her and pay for whatever program she needed, and Amber got all pissed and said no. Then he told her if she wasn't gonna get treatment, she couldn't stay."

I sat back in my chair, defeat washing over me. I don't know why it surprised me. It didn't really.

I shook my head. "She doesn't have to pay rent, she doesn't have to work," I said. "He offered to take care of everything. I don't get it. It'll never be this easy again for her to get help."

"You can't help someone unless they want to be helped," Justin said.

"Neil told her she has a week to find someplace to go," Maddy said. "He's going to put a down payment on an apartment for her if she wants. Maria's like, super fucking happy."

I grabbed a Wendy's napkin off the table and folded it in half and then folded it in half again.

I already knew what came next.

She would vanish.

I squeezed my eyes shut and put my forehead into my hand. The roller coaster was never ending.

A part of me was relieved she was going to leave. The other part was scared for what would happen when she was gone. Because how long could she live like this? How long until her options ran out and she was too old to bounce from man to man and job to job? What would happen to her if she got injured or came down with a chronic illness or the games she used to manipulate people stopped working?

She would fall into *my* lap.

My whole life I was waiting for her to come back for me. And when she finally did, it wouldn't be for me at all. It would be for lack of other options. It would be for *her*.

She wouldn't try therapy. She wouldn't accept help even when it was paid for in full and being handed to her on a plate.

Resentment bloomed in my chest. I don't think it had ever

been so clear to me before that Mom was responsible for her own circumstances. I always gave her an out. I always argued in her favor. She had bad credit, she had no support, no money, no help.

Only this time she *did*. And she didn't *want* it.

"Did you ever get the results of the DNA test?" Maddy asked, breaking into my thoughts.

"Yeah," I said glumly.

"You did? What did it say?"

I sniffed and sat back again. "I'm Irish and German. A little of a lot of things."

"And relatives?"

"I didn't look," I said.

"Do you want to look?" she asked.

Justin peered at me.

I shrugged. "I don't know."

Maddy leaned in. "It's your birthday. I'd say today is a *great* day to let people know you exist."

"Mom always told me I wouldn't be wanted," I said.

"Oh yeah?" Maddy said. "She also lies a lot."

I let out a dry laugh. Then I looked at Justin. "What do you think?"

"I think it's a big decision," he said. "You can't undo it once you look. It's possible that it might cause problems for someone."

I sensed a but. "But?"

"But it's been twenty-nine years—almost thirty really, if you count the nine months she was pregnant. Chances are if she'd been seeing a guy who was married, they could be divorced, or one of them or both of them are dead. It's an old transgression. It happened a lifetime ago."

"But Mom said he didn't want kids."

"You're not a kid," Justin said. "You don't need raising. You don't need money. I think a lot of people who don't want kids don't want the responsibility. You're not a responsibility at this point."

I bobbed my head. "True."

"I think it would be worth looking to see if you have any siblings or cousins. To find out where you came from," he said. "I can't imagine not knowing who my dad was. Plus the health history is important. What if there's something that runs in the family that you should know about?"

I looked at Maddy. She nodded.

Any other day I probably wouldn't have had the courage. If I wasn't so exhausted from Mom's breakdown, I might have had more mental headspace to overthink it and chicken out. But today I didn't.

I took a deep breath. "Okay. I'll do it."

Maddy clapped her hands.

"Let's use my computer," Justin said. "The monitor's big enough for us all to see it."

"Good idea," Maddy said, getting up.

We went upstairs to Justin's room and pulled up the website and logged in. First I showed them my ancestry. Then I poked around and found the tab we'd come for. The one that said, "Participate to Find Relatives."

I hovered my finger over it for a long moment. Then I clicked it and the page started to load.

I thought the results would be more instant. Most pages don't take longer than a second to come up, but this one loaded for almost five minutes. Some colossal feat taking place on the other end.

My anxiety started to gnaw at me.

The extra time to think was making me second-guess my decision. I was about to make a joke about the website not being able to find any relatives for me when the page finished and the results finally popped up. My eyes landed instantly on two words, clear and in bold.

Amber Grant.

"Oh," I said, surprised. "She ran her DNA."

That was weird. She always told me she didn't know our ethnicity.

I looked at the next match. A little round purple icon with the initials DG, and next to it: Daniel Grant.

And under it: Half Brother, on your mother's side.

Maddy and Justin leaned in, reading it at the same time I did over my shoulder.

A half brother. On my mother's side?

"How would I have a brother on my mom's side?" I said, blinking at the screen. "She never had another baby."

I tapped on his name and his birth year came up. My stomach twisted.

"How old is Amber?" Justin asked.

"Forty-seven."

"According to the year he was born, she was only fifteen," Justin said.

"Okay," I said, licking my lips. "Okay, so she had a baby she gave up."

"But why didn't she ever tell you?" Maddy asked.

"Maybe it was painful and she didn't want to remember it? Maybe it was a closed adoption?" I said.

Maddy shook her head. "Then why does he have your last name though? I mean, that's weird, right?"

"Maybe a family member adopted him," Justin said.

I shook my head. "I don't have any family. Amber's an only child and my grandparents died young. She didn't have cousins, no aunts and uncles, nothing."

I clicked out of Daniel's profile and like the website was replying to what I just said, a list of names lined up under Daniel's.

```
Justine Copeland.
Aunt, on your mother's side.


Andrea Beaudry.
Aunt, on your mother's side.


Liz Beaudry.
1st cousin, on your mother's side.


Josh Copeland.
1st cousin, on your mother's side.
```

With every name, my heart pounded harder.

"What is happening?" I breathed.

Maddy looked at me and I could see it in her eyes.

"I'm going to message him," I said, clicking back on Daniel.

I started typing, but before I even hit send, a message from Daniel came through first. Four words that I felt my brain commit to memory forever.

Your mom is Amber?

My hands were shaking when I typed in "Yes."

His next message said "please call me" and there was a number.

"He wants me to call him," I said, looking up at Justin and Maddy.

Maddy gestured wildly to my phone. "Then call him!"

My heart was pounding in my ears. I didn't want to call him because I was suddenly extremely scared of what he was going to say.

"Emma. *Call*," Maddy said.

I looked at Justin. He was chewing on the side of his thumb. He gave me a small nod. I dialed.

"Hello?" a male voice said on the other line.

"Hi," I said. "I'm...it's Emma."

"I can't believe this," the man said. "I'm...I'm speechless. You're my *sister*," he said, almost in wonder. "Do you have any siblings? Are there more?"

"No, just me."

"Did you just find out who your mom was? Who adopted you?" he asked.

I shook my head like he could see me. "Nobody. Amber raised me."

There was a long pause. "She raised you," he said, like he didn't believe it.

"Yes. Who raised you?" I asked.

"My grandparents. She never mentioned you. Not one word—"

"Wait. You've talked to her?"

"Of course I've talked to her. She came down a couple times a year."

I'd never felt the blood drain from my face before. But I did now.

"What do you mean she…" I swallowed. "Did you say your grandparents raised you? On your dad's side?"

"No, Amber's parents. She had me when she was fifteen and left three years later."

"But…she said her parents were dead by the time I was born. They couldn't have raised you," I said.

The silence that followed felt like sap, it was so thick.

"Our grandparents died when I was twenty-three," Daniel said. "Eight years ago."

My breathing started to get labored. Justin's hand came down on my shoulder and squeezed.

Alive. They were alive until eight years ago…My grandparents had been alive until I was in my *twenties*.

It was all happening too fast. I couldn't process everything I was hearing. But one word kept repeating in my brain.

Lies. She'd been telling me lies.

So many. Too many to count.

I had a *brother*. A brother she saw, a brother she talked to. Parents she'd visited. Sisters. Nieces and nephews. And she'd hidden them from me.

She'd hidden *me* from *them*…

"I see Justine, Andrea, Liz, and Josh. Is there anyone else in our family?" I asked, almost hoping the answer was no. That the deception stopped here and there was nothing else. But there was.

"Tons," Daniel said. "Aunt Justine's got seven kids and a bunch of grandkids, Aunt Andrea's got five. Our cousin Liz lives down the street. I have a daughter, Victoria. She's two."

I sat there while he listed off family I wasn't supposed to have.

My mother's nieces and nephews, sisters she had told me didn't exist.

I felt shell-shocked. Like I was floating outside my body, looking down on myself.

Maddy nodded at the phone. "Where does he live?" she whispered.

I cleared my throat. "Where do you live?" I asked, my voice small.

"Minnesota. Wakan."

I repeated his words out loud.

"Two hours away," Justin said.

"I'm in Minnesota too," I told Daniel. "I'm in Minneapolis."

"Can we meet?" he asked.

"When?"

"As soon as you can. I could even do today."

I moved the phone away from my mouth. "He wants to meet me. Today."

Maddy was already getting up.

"Can I bring my boyfriend and my best friend?" I asked.

"Of course. I'll have my wife, Alexis, with me."

We exchanged information, and half an hour later we were on our way.

I felt like I was in some weird fever dream.

On the car ride down, I tried to repeat everything Daniel had said. My mind kept folding around this new information, and I grappled for any explanation to justify why she'd do this. Maybe they were horrible people. Maybe my grandparents were abusive. Maybe she was trying to protect me, and that's why she never told me.

As awful as it sounded, I wanted this to be true. But if it was true, if they were bad people, why leave Daniel there? Why visit them?

I couldn't think my way out of it.

Justin drove in silence most of the way, and Maddy didn't urge me to talk. Like they both knew I was overwhelmed and if they pushed me I'd get small.

My survival instinct wanted me to run. It wanted me to shrink and withdraw and never talk about this again. But something told me I needed to find out the truth.

*

The town we arrived in was picturesque. There were redbrick buildings with hanging flower baskets on the lampposts and ice cream and fudge shops on the main street and signs in the windows of the cafe and the family-run grocery store for a pumpkin-carving contest in October. All I could think was, this didn't look like a bad place to grow up. This didn't look like a place I needed saving from.

We pulled up to an old green Victorian with a wraparound porch decorated with pots of mums.

Justin put the car in park, and I stared out the windshield at the house.

"So this is where Daniel grew up?" Maddy asked. She was thinking the same thing I was, that this place didn't look like something to hide.

We got out of the car, and a man and woman came out the front door. She had shoulder-length red hair and was holding a baby. I knew my brother on sight because he looked exactly like me. He looked like our mother.

We both paused, staring at each other in disbelief. Like neither of us believed this could be real.

His wife must have sensed his paralysis because she stepped in. "Emma, I'm Alexis, Daniel's wife. This is our daughter, Victoria. Your niece."

The word "niece" made a lump bolt to my throat.

Maddy stepped around me. "I'm Maddy, and this is Justin."

Justin blinked at Alexis. "I know you. You're Briana's friend." Alexis seemed to remember him as soon as he said it. "Yes. It's good to see you again."

Daniel and I just stared at each other. Like we were looking at a strange mirror. Even with different fathers it didn't matter. We were both offshoots of Amber.

"I...I don't know what to say," I said. "I'm..."

Daniel snapped out of his daze. "Let's go inside. We can talk in there."

We came into the house and I peered around. I'd never been there, but there was something familiar about it anyway. Like maybe I'd seen bits and pieces of it through Mom, even though I didn't know what I'd been seeing.

Roses.

The house was *full* of roses. My brother had them tattooed on his arms. The stained-glass window on the landing was framed in red roses. A little girl in a pink dress took up the center of the design, holding a dragonfly on her palm. Roses were carved into the banister.

This is where Mom got the idea for her mural at Neil's.

"This is the family house," Daniel said. "It goes back six generations. Our great-great-great-grandfather built it. Our grandparents left it to Amber, actually."

My head whipped to look at him. "Her parents left her a *house?*"

"Yeah. I ran it as a B and B for her for almost six years. I bought it from her three years ago."

"You bought it from her," I deadpanned. She'd had property? "How much did you buy it for?" I asked.

"Five hundred thousand."

I blanched. "A half a million dollars..." I breathed.

I looked over at Maddy, and she was having a whole conversation with me in total silence. Beth and Janet had paid for my nursing school. They never got a dime from Amber.

This information saturated me. Soaked into my core.

And was this why I'd barely heard from her these last three years? Because she didn't need money?

Where was the money now? Was it gone?

But of course it was gone. That's why she'd come looking for me. That's why she'd latched on to Neil.

That's why she was stealing his watches and cuff links.

I felt dizzy. I had to grip the banister to keep from swaying. Justin sensed it and he came up behind me and put a gentle hand under my elbow. I was going to be sick.

I was about to ask for a bathroom when a man burst through the front door. He stopped in the foyer and stared at me. "Holy fucking shit..." He put his hands on his head. "Holy shi— She looks just like her. It's like Amber, twenty years ago."

Daniel cleared his throat. "This is Doug, my best friend."

"Fuck, sorry," Doug said. He put out a hand and I limply shook it. He introduced himself to Justin and then Maddy.

Alexis was watching me. Then she turned to Doug. "Doug, I think we should catch up later. This is probably pretty overwhelming for everyone."

"Shit, right," he said. "Yeah. Call me. Call me the second you want me to come back over."

He backed out the door, looking at me like I was a ghost.

I blinked around the house. There were black-and-white photos on the walls. The people had my face. My eyes. My nose.

"Is that her?" I asked. Daniel nodded.

There was a picture of Amber at the base of the staircase. I'd never seen a photo of her as a kid. I only knew it was her because she looked like me. She'd been twelve, maybe thirteen. She was sitting on the back of an old pickup truck with a bunch of other kids at a drive-in. She was smiling the way she did when she was okay.

"What would she do when she came here?" I asked, turning back to my brother.

Daniel shook his head. "Give Grandpa grief? Get money out of Grandma? Go on a bender? It was never good when she came."

"Do you have pictures of your grandparents?" I asked. "Our grandparents," I corrected.

"Yeah, lots. Come on."

We moved into a living room and he sat me on a sofa. Maddy and Justin took the two chairs, Alexis sat next to Daniel as he set a photo album on the coffee table.

He opened the cover. "This is William and Linda."

He flipped through to show me pictures of two people with kind eyes.

An old man, manning a barbeque with a GRILL MASTER apron on. A middle-aged woman, holding a little boy no older than Chelsea. The boy was laughing and she was hugging him on her lap. Daniel.

Pictures of the two of them standing next to an

eighteen-year-old Daniel at his high school graduation. Birthday parties and Daniel blowing out candles. Homemade Halloween costumes and William at some bar calling a Bingo game. Linda holding up a pie she made at Christmas with a Christmas tree behind her here, in this living room.

They seemed warm. Friendly.

I swallowed. "Did you have a good childhood?" I asked.

"Yeah," Daniel said. "It was a great childhood."

"Were they good people?"

I saw him study me. "They were the best people I've ever known."

We sat there in silence.

"Was your childhood good?" he asked.

It took me a long time to answer. "No."

I stared at the album. The picture on the page was kids. A lawn full of kids, playing in the sprinklers. My cousins. My brother.

I had been robbed. This life, this family, had been stolen from me.

This was my alternate universe, laid out in full color.

And then Daniel flipped to another page and there was a picture of a twentysomething Amber. Sitting in a lawn chair drinking one of her Bloody Marys.

She'd been here. But where was I?

"What year is this?" I asked. But I think inside I already knew.

Daniel turned the page and the date was scrapbooked onto the bottom.

The Fourth of July when I was eight.

Bile rose in my throat. The summer of the smoke alarm and the carrots. The first time I went into the system.

She'd left me alone and come *here*. She left me to starve and fend for myself while she came back to her secret family to eat burgers and pretend I didn't exist. It was the last thing I needed to see.

I got up. "I need to leave."

Daniel got up too. "Are you sure? I was—"

But I was already running for the foyer, a panic attack building. I had to get out of here.

I heard Maddy making excuses for me, and Justin came out on my heels, clicking the car locks off a second before I got to the door.

By the time Maddy got into the back seat I was sobbing.

Maddy leaned into the front. "Are you okay—"

"GO! GET ME OUT OF HERE!" I shouted.

Justin put the car in reverse and I watched through water-blurred eyes as my brother and his wife stood on the porch, shrinking in the distance as we backed out of the driveway.

I was breathing into my hands, trying not to hyperventilate.

"That fucking bitch," Maddy said from the back seat.

"Why the hell would she do this?" Justin asked, turning on the wipers. Dragonflies were all around the car. It was like a sudden swarm of locusts through the blur of my tears.

Maddy handed me tissues from her purse over the back of the seat. "Because she's a horrible human being."

"They seemed like nice people," Justin said. "I don't get it."

"They *are* nice people," Maddy said.

I couldn't stop crying. I had never in my life cried like this. I felt like my soul was leaving my body.

How could she have done this? How could anyone be this selfish? This cruel? And it wasn't just the people she kept me from, or the betrayal of knowing where she was when I was left behind. It was the depth of the deception. The layers upon layers of lies she told to keep me from ever knowing this existed.

If Amber could do this, what else was she capable of?

"I can't see," Justin said. "I have to pull over, there's too many bugs."

I felt the car drive onto the dirt.

"I can't breathe," I cried. "I can't breathe!"

As soon as Justin put the car in park he was unbuckling himself and getting out to come around to the passenger side. Then he opened my door and lifted me into his arms. "Breathe with me, okay?" he whispered. "In and out. Slow."

He held me there on the shoulder of the highway while I sobbed into his neck. He held me so tight, it felt like he was the only thing keeping me from falling apart.

"Tell me what I can do," he whispered.

"You can take me to her."

Maddy had been right all along. She'd always seen Amber for what she was: someone who destroyed everyone and everything in her path.

My childhood shifted forever in my mind.

My mother's neglect wasn't the product of mental illness, or lack of resources, or circumstances beyond her control, the inability to do better. My life was *chosen* for me.

It was chosen by *her*.

CHAPTER 41

EMMA

I walked right into Neil's mansion without waiting for someone to open the door.

Justin and Maddy were waiting in the pool house. They hadn't wanted to leave me, but I didn't want an audience.

I stood in the living room for a moment to stare at the incomplete rose wall that I now knew was the banister in Mom's childhood home. The re-creation of her pretty memories, distorted and beyond salvaging.

All the beautiful things she started, only to abandon.

I turned and went up the staircase to find her, opened the bedroom door without knocking.

The room was a mess again. Three empty wine bottles, along with takeout cups and containers, littered the floor. The bed was in disarray—except for Neil's side. That was perfectly made.

The bedroom was full of burning candles. At least two dozen. The air was so thick with their scent, it felt like I was breathing perfume. I heard water running in the bathroom and I came around the corner to find Mom in her robe over wrinkled pajamas, scrubbing a shirt in the sink. She glanced at me standing in the doorway. "What are you doing here?" she asked, barely looking up.

It was clear she was still in the depths of whatever crisis she was having. I didn't care. I had never cared less in my entire life.

I could see myself behind her in the mirror. My eyes were puffy. She didn't even ask what was wrong. It didn't even occur to her to see why *I'd* been crying. It didn't occur to her that today was my birthday and she'd forgotten, again. But now that seemed perfectly natural. Of course she'd forgotten.

Now I knew what I was worth to her. I truly, truly did. I'd been operating on the belief that I should be the most important thing in her life. How could I not be? I was her baby. I was all she had. So if she mistreated me, it was never for lack of love, because of course she loved me. How could she not? I spent my life excusing the very real evidence that I was nothing to her. I was a gerbil she kept in a too-small cage. A fish in a cup of water. Something to look at and entertain her when she was bored and wanted to play house.

"I met Daniel today," I said.

She didn't look at me. She kept scrubbing the shirt in the sink.

"Did you hear me? I said I met my brother."

"I'm fighting with Neil, I've got a headache, I don't have time for this."

My nostrils flared. "You will make time."

"Emma—"

"NOW!"

She tossed the shirt into the sink with a slap and turned to me. "I gave up a baby, Emma. I was fifteen."

"You said I had no family," I said, trying to contain my fury. "You lied to me my *whole* life."

She went back to the sink.

"You left me," I said. "You abandoned me. You let me go to strangers."

She didn't turn around. "You had a good family. Maddy's parents wanted to adopt you, but you didn't want it—"

"I wanted *you*! I was waiting for you to come back for me!"

She brushed a loose hair off her cheek with the back of her hand. "Well, I wasn't in a good place. You were better off there. You have a brother. Now you know. He's nice, you'll like him."

I stared at her back in disbelief. "That's all you have to say to me?"

She ignored me.

"My grandparents *died* before I ever got to meet them. I lost decades with people who would have loved me. Do you know what I lived through? The things that happened to me in foster care?"

"You think I was in any better place when you were in there?" she said.

I laughed incredulously. "Yeah, I do. I think you were in Wakan, sleeping it off."

Nothing.

"What other lies did you tell?" I demanded. "Was my dad really married? Do you even know who he is at all or was it just your mission in life to keep me from anyone who would have actually taken care of me."

She just focused on her washing. Didn't even look up.

And then I knew that's what it was. The truth roiled in my stomach. "Your parents would have wanted me, wouldn't they?" I said. "Like they wanted Daniel."

She whipped around. "You weren't theirs," she snapped. "They had no legal right to you—"

I burst into manic laughter. It was so fucked up, it was funny. She was the architect of the shattered life I'd lived. Of the life I *still* lived.

And she wasn't even sorry. That was the worst betrayal of all.

It was the death of the last innocent, naive version of myself. That Emma no longer existed. I was snuffed out like one of her candles.

And I was *done.*

That broken and damaged part of me that *she* made turned on her. The part of me that could leave anyone and any place behind and never look back activated just for her. My heart shut off. All attachments I had to her, every bond she'd ever been given was pulled from the root. My defenses wrapped around me like an impenetrable protective shield, and I felt myself go eerily calm. I knew this was the last time I'd ever see her. I wouldn't miss her. I wouldn't grieve her. I would never look for her. This is what I was capable of.

This was my gift.

This was my curse.

Not the silly thing I was trying to undo once with Justin. It was my ability to not love.

"I'm going to give you one chance to tell me why," I said steadily. "And then I'm never going to speak to you again."

She looked at me. For the first time since I walked in here, I saw something like fear flash across her face. But she didn't reply.

I turned and started for the door.

"Emma!"

I kept walking.

"Emma! Please!"

I stopped and turned back to her, my face flat. "Why?"

Her eyes were tearing up. "Because they would have kept you," she said. "They would have kept you like they kept Daniel. And I loved you too much to let you go."

I stared at her dispassionately.

"If you really loved me, you *would* have let me go."

Then I walked out the door and pushed her from my heart forever.

But I wasn't done.

I felt myself get small. I got so small, I vanished. It was catastrophic. A total decimation. A detachment like I'd never experienced.

I folded into myself tighter and tinier than I ever had, and when I was done, I got smaller still. There was no room for anyone. Not Maddy, not Justin. No one.

I didn't want anyone near me. I didn't want anyone to know me.

I wanted to be the island. I wanted to be alone and untouchable. To never rely on anyone or love anyone or let anyone love me, because *this* is what love gets you.

My heart shut off.

I called an Uber.

I knew it would hurt them when I disappeared, but I also knew the hurt I'd spare them because leaving was always in me. I was going to do it one day, I think I always knew that. My luggage would always be under the bed, waiting. As soon as Maddy didn't want to be on the road anymore, I would have continued on without her and left her behind. Or when times got hard with Justin, because life throws things at you and relationships aren't easy, I wouldn't stay and work on it. I'd withdraw. I'd sabotage us so I could have a reason to take off, the way Mom always did. I'd leave him before he rejected me or I'd leave him when I loved him and those kids so much it terrified me enough to flee to protect myself.

It already did.

This was always going to happen. I didn't know how to love anyone or let myself be loved. I couldn't even say the word.

I could admit to this flaw in me now.

I wasn't fit to be in a relationship. I wasn't fit to be a parent. I wasn't even fit to be a friend. I was full of cracks. And I didn't want Maddy and Justin to have to fix something they didn't break. I didn't want those kids to lose another person they cared about like I'd lost all the people *I'd* ever cared about. So I was going to be the island.

And this time nobody would be on it.

CHAPTER 42

JUSTIN

I looked at my watch. "Do you think we should go check on her? It's been an hour."

Maddy was bouncing her knee. "I don't know. Maybe give it five more minutes? This isn't good, Justin."

I raked a hand through my hair. "Yeah, no kidding."

"No, I don't think you get it." She looked at me. "This is going to bring up so much shit."

"She's strong," I said. "She'll get through it, she's gotten through worse."

"No." She shook her head. "No, she's strong but not with this. Amber does something to her. She always has, she's like her kryptonite." She chewed on her lip. "God, I fucking hate her so much."

"I hate her too."

"Good. Welcome to the club, we meet on Wednesdays and we bring pitchforks."

I snorted, despite myself.

She got up and paced, glancing every few minutes at her phone.

"I can't wait anymore," she said. "I'm going in." She started for the exit and I followed her. She stopped at the door and turned to me. "Justin, she's gonna get small. I need you to be ready for that."

I nodded. "Okay. I can handle it."

"She won't answer the phone, she won't want to see anyone. She's gonna get super withdrawn. It's gonna be bad. It might be the worst it's ever been. You just have to wait it out."

"All right. I'm ready."

She opened the door and immediately froze. "Do you smell smoke?"

I tilted my head and sniffed the air. "Yeah…What is that?"

She looked out into the yard and her eyes went wide. "There's smoke coming out of the house!"

We both bolted, running across the lawn toward the mansion.

The house was on fire. Smoke was pouring out of the primary bedroom. Maria stood on the grass by the pool, cursing in Spanish.

"Call 911!" I shouted.

"I already called!" Maria said. "Pinche pendeja, she did this! ¡Está loca!"

I didn't wait to hear who. Emma could be in there. I ran up to the French doors off the kitchen and rattled them. They were locked. I jumped off the deck and ran around the side of the garage, Maddy on my heels, and I crashed right into Neil in the driveway. He was standing there with his hands in his pockets looking up at the smoke billowing out of the top floor.

"Who's in the house?" I shouted.

"Nobody," he said calmly.

"Where's Emma? And Amber?" My heart was pounding.

"Gone. Amber just left in a taxi and Emma was getting into an Uber when I got home. Amber said they had a fight."

I bent over with my hands on my knees. "Thank God," I breathed.

I panted for a few moments, catching my breath before I pulled out my phone and called Emma. It went straight to voicemail. "Hey, where are you? Why'd you leave? Call me."

Maddy watched me hang up, then she walked away, typing into her screen.

Neil and I stepped onto the front lawn and he stood there, watching the tendrils of smoke curling out of the windows on the top floor. He was smiling.

I stared at him. "Are you okay?"

He looked over at me like the question surprised him. "What? Because of this?" He gestured to the burning house.

"Yeah. Yeah, your house is on fire."

He smiled up at it. "Yes. Yes, it is."

Sirens started blaring in the distance.

"She set it, you know," he said.

"Who did?" I asked.

"Amber. One of those soy candles she likes to burn. She threw it at me. My head actually. Really poor aim, I ducked it easily." He sighed happily at the smoke pouring now from the front door.

I blinked at him. "Are you *happy* about this?"

He gazed thoughtfully at his home.

"You might not know this, Justin," he said, "but I've done a lot of bad things in my life. I was a real asshole once. A few years ago, I lost the only woman I have ever loved because of it. I've been to a lot of therapy and worked hard on being a better person. Unlearning a lot of the toxic behavior I grew up seeing. Then Amber showed up. At first I thought this was my reward. I was a better man, so I was ready for a good woman. A nice, healthy relationship. But that's not why Amber was here." He looked over at me. "She was sent to test me. And I *never* wavered."

I shook my head at him. "She set your house on fire."

"I know." He peered up to the house. "And now my debt to the universe is paid. She has wiped my slate clean. That woman was an angel sent from God."

He looked at the flames licking out of the window over the garage and he started laughing. Pure joy.

I thought about what Emma said once. That framing is everything. That if you can frame the terrible things in the best possible way, that's where true happiness comes from. I guess in this case it was a good thing because his fucking house was burning down.

Fire trucks pulled up to the property just as Maddy came running over. "Emma's luggage is gone."

I looked at her, confused. "What?"

"She left, Justin."

"Yeah, she got in an Uber—"

She shook her head. "No, Justin. She left *left*. Like, in the bad way. Her luggage is moving, I've got AirTags on them. She picked them up a half an hour ago and she's heading to the airport."

My face fell. "What do we do?"

She was already tapping something into her phone. "You do nothing. Go home. Wait and I'll call you."

"Are you sure? I'll come with you—"

"I'm sure. Go home. If we're lucky we might just see her again."

CHAPTER 43

EMMA

I was sitting on the edge of the bed in my hotel room by the air-port staring at the wall. I couldn't say how long I'd been there. An hour. Maybe ten.

The momentum that catapulted me away from Neil's had lost its inertia. I had screeched to a halt and I sat where I stopped.

My brain was glitching. I was hungry and probably dehy-drated from crying. I hadn't eaten since the birthday breakfast Justin made me this morning. We'd never made it to my birthday lunch. That plan felt a thousand years away now. Pancakes felt like a fever dream. It was hard to believe it was even the same day. I'd turned twenty-nine and discovered a new family and a lifetime of lies and betrayal. Been to Wakan and back, met my brother and sister-in-law and niece. I'd seen my mother for the last time and I'd walked out on my entire life and everyone in it. All in the course of twelve hours.

I worked in a hospital. I knew the centuries that could take place in half a day. I knew the decades that could pass in a minute. I'd somehow aged more than that today. I'd lost eons and I'd never get them back.

It was scary how detached I felt. Like something had been unplugged. I knew objectively this was bad. A severe trauma response. A form of shock. But I was too disconnected to feel anything other than the void and I was too grateful for the void to want it to stop.

I replayed the day in my head like footage from a documentary. Like it had happened to someone else. The sweet things Justin said to me at breakfast, that I deserved to be appreciated. The gift he'd gotten me, so thoughtful. The way he held me on the side of the road, a docking station when I needed to dock. But thinking about it didn't bring me back. It pushed me further offshore. I just wanted to get away from it, put more space between me and him.

How do you recover from something like this? How do you walk around in the world after finding out your whole life was a lie? How do you wear mascara and buy stamps and go to the carwash and vacuum and do all the things that fully functional people do? I couldn't even stop staring at the wall. I'd been too shaken to pick a flight. The hotel was about all I was capable of. I needed to eat, but the thought of figuring it out was too exhausting. So I sat and I spiraled deeper into myself.

I thought things had been bad when I was sick and alone on the island. But it occurred to me that I might actually die here in this hotel room. This would be the thing to kill me. I would just wither away. Fail to thrive. I would lay down and not get up. And who would even know?

That's the nature of being on the island. That's the price. And it still cost less than the alternative.

Someone was calling my name. The sound drifted into my consciousness like a voice underwater.

Knocking on my door.

"Emma!"

It was Maddy.

"Emma, open the door. I know you're in there."

I didn't move.

"I know you're small, and you don't want to see anyone. I don't care, let me in."

Something instinctual got me to stand. I'd spent half my life taking orders from that voice. Even in my condition, I couldn't stop now. I dragged myself up and unbolted the door. My best friend stood on the other side.

"How did you find me?" I asked weakly.

"I put AirTags in your luggage." She edged past me into the hotel room. "I knew you'd leave me, but you'd never leave your bags."

She plopped her purse on the dresser and sat on the bed, hands folded in her lap.

I just stood there, looking at her dispassionately.

"Well, you finally did it," she said. "You went full AWOL."

I didn't respond.

"Were you even going to say goodbye to us?" she asked.

"No."

"You don't think that's a thing you should do?" she asked.

"I am the worst thing that could *ever* happen to either of you," I said.

She cocked her head. "Why? Because you have a flight response to stress? A messed-up attachment style from years of trauma and neglect?"

The truth hit me gently in the chest. Small futile soft thuds, like a child's fists banging on a brick wall.

"Is that what it is?" I asked, my voice flat.

She picked lint off her pants. "I mean, I'm not a therapist, but I've done a lot of reading about it. I've had my suspicions for a while. Avoidant attachment relationship style is my best guess."

I nodded and looked away from her. "Why didn't you tell me?"

"Would you have listened?"

I paused for a long moment. "No. Probably not."

She took in a breath through her nose and blew it out. "Sit. Go on, take the chair."

I took the order and dragged myself to the chair across from her. She got up and rummaged in her bag and pulled out a sandwich, a bag of salt and vinegar chips, and a bottle of apple juice. She unwrapped the sandwich and put it in my hand, opened the chips, and twisted the cap off the drink. Then she sat there and watched me eat.

I could barely taste the food, but my body responded like a wilted plant being watered. Some of the brain fog and misery dissipated as the sugar and nourishment hit my bloodstream.

The sandwich was what I always ordered.

She'd stopped to get this. She'd ordered it for *me*. She knew what kind of state I'd be in and she'd come prepared.

Maddy was like a first responder for my soul.

She always had been. And even when I quit her, she didn't quit me. This plucked at me. Tried to get in.

It did not.

She leaned forward with her elbows on her knees as I finished my food. "Better?"

I nodded. "Yes."

"Good. Now I'm going to tell you something, and I really need you to hear it," she said. "You can cut me off, cut Justin off, be so small no one can ever find you. Go ahead. Run like the wind, I won't chase you. But you can't escape yourself."

I just stared at her.

"You are *not* what happened to you. You are what you do next."

Something in her words finally got through, and I suddenly wanted to cry. A pinch of emotion in a dark, deep nothing.

"You turn around, you face it, and you *fix* it," she said. "Or you'll be running from what Amber did to you until the day you die."

My chin quivered and she held my gaze.

I swallowed the lump in my throat. "How?"

"Do you trust me to help you?" she asked. "You'll do whatever I say?"

"Yes," I said, my voice thick.

"Can you let Justin help too?" she asked.

"I can't," I whispered. "I want to, but I can't handle it."

It was funny that in my state I was able to articulate this. A brief moment of clarity. But it was true. I couldn't let Justin help me because he wasn't just Justin. He was the kids too. And they weren't mine. I couldn't handle any more unstable relationships or situations where someone I cared about could be taken from me. And neither could they.

They needed people in their lives who will stay. People they can count on. I was the furthest thing from that to ever exist—but he deserved to hear that from me, not to be left the way I almost did. And even that just thrust me deeper into my belief that I wasn't good for anyone. Not the way I currently was.

"I need to see him," I said. "Before we go. I have to tell him in person."

She nodded. "All right. We'll take you there tomorrow."

"And then what?"

"It's my turn to pick," she said. "I get to pick two times in a row. That was the deal."

I wiped under my eyes. "Okay. So where are we going?"

"Somewhere you always should have been."

CHAPTER 44

JUSTIN

I went home like Maddy said, and I waited. Emma texted me around 10:00 p.m. and told me she was coming to talk to me tomorrow morning.

I didn't sleep all night.

The kids kept asking where she was. I didn't know what to say.

She'd left her key on the credenza. I couldn't touch it. I couldn't move it. I felt like the second I acknowledged it was there, the reason why she'd left it would be real.

I kept thinking about what Maddy said, to never let her leave, because if she leaves, she won't come back.

I should have never let her out of my sight. I should have gone with her to talk to Amber. She was vulnerable and she wasn't okay, I should have seen that. And now even though she was coming home, I had a feeling she wasn't.

I wanted to be wrong. I pictured her showing up at the door with her bags and apologizing for leaving and I'd hug her and take her inside and life as we knew it would continue, and we'd never think about this blip again. She didn't take off on me and the kids because she intended to never come back, she was just freaked out. This was a knee-jerk reaction to what happened, understandable.

But when the morning came and she finally got here and I ran to the door and threw it open, it was just her. Nothing was with her. No luggage. And Maddy was parked behind her in front of the house with the car running.

My heart sank.

"Can we talk in the living room?" she asked, still standing in the doorway.

"We could go upstairs," I said. "We could sleep for a bit and talk when we feel better," I said hopefully. I felt like if I could get her to my room, I could derail this. Nestle her back down into the life we'd been living, remind her it was good and she wanted it.

"I think the living room is better."

I swallowed hard and let her take me to the sofa.

It didn't escape me that all the worst news I'd ever gotten in my life was delivered on this sofa. It was where I found out Dad had died. It's where Mom told me she was going to prison.

I had this almost out-of-body urge to ask if we could move to the kitchen instead, but I didn't want to taint the breakfast nook too.

She sat on the cushion next to me. Our knees touched. I wanted to grab her and take her off the cursed sofa and run away with her before she said what I thought she was going to say. I hated this. I didn't want it to keep going.

"Please stop," I said, before she even started.

She peered at me with a face that looked like heartbreak.

"Justin, you know I only want what's best for you, right?"

"Whatever you're about to do is not what's best for me," I said. "I don't want it."

She looked away. "Tell the kids I had to take a new assignment. Okay? Tell them it was an emergency and I had to go."

"No." I shook my head. "We're not doing this, Emma."

"Justin—"

"*No.* Whatever it is you're going through right now, we go through it together. That's what couples do."

"I am *not* okay." She came back to me and looked me in the eye. "I need you to hear me when I say this. I am not okay. I'm not someone who should be around the kids."

"Let *me* decide that."

"No." Her chin quivered. "Justin, do you know what I would never wish on anyone? The instability that *I* grew up with. That's what I am. I don't know how to be a normal human being. I don't know how to love without being terrified. I don't know how to fight with you without my first impulse to be to pack up and leave and never see you again. I don't know how to belong to a family who only belongs to me because I belong to *you*. I am not strong enough for it. And I am giving you the one thing Amber could never give to me and that's to be honest about it and let you go."

I felt the panic in my chest.

"Look at me, Emma. Look." I took her hands. "We can do this. I can help you."

"You *can't*. I promise you, you cannot undo twenty-nine years of conditioning. I don't even know if *I* can do it. I have cracks that I need to fill and I can't do that here. I can't do that with you, or them."

"How do you know?" I asked.

"Because the more I care about all of you, the more I want to run."

She held my gaze. "I almost left you last night without saying goodbye. Do you even know that? I would have disappeared on those kids just like Amber did to me. I almost left *Maddy*." She cracked on the last word.

The words lingered in the space between us.

"I have too much to unpack," she said. "I have triggers that I can't control."

I could see the pain on her face. I felt like I was looking in a mirror.

"Emma, I'm going to tell you something. And I don't need you to say anything, I just need you to hear it." I paused. "I'm in love with you. I've been in love with you since the moment I laid my eyes on you. And I know we haven't known each other long, but I don't care, because it's true and it's there, and it doesn't matter to me if it makes sense or not. I've been waiting my whole life to feel like this and I thought it was a curse that nobody else ever worked out. But it wasn't. It's just that they weren't you." I had to give myself a moment. "Please. Don't end this. I'm begging you."

She pressed her lips together, trying not to cry. "I have to deal with my issues before I can be a partner or a parent to anyone."

"And are you? Going to deal with your issues? Because I'll wait."

She shook her head. "No you *won't*. You are going to take care of those kids, and you're going to live your life and you're going to meet someone else. You are not going to sit around hoping that one day I'm whole enough to love you and them the way they deserve." The tears spilled down her cheeks. "I did that. I waited. I waited my entire life for her to be whole and she never was. I don't want that for you. Or them. I don't want to be their Amber."

This is what finally broke her. And then it broke me. Because

I knew there was nothing I could do to change it and I also knew she was right.

The kids did need stability. And she wasn't it. I knew in my heart she was making the right choice not only for herself but also for them. Maybe even for me too. Maybe she was doing now what she would have done anyway in a month, or two, or three and she was sparing all of us the pain of being that much more attached to someone and something we could never have.

But it didn't make it any less devastating.

I felt like my soul was being split down the middle and someone was about to leave with one half of it forever. And they were.

She would never come back. I think I was lucky she was even here now.

I thought about the rom-coms Mom used to watch when I was growing up. The dramatic grand gestures that keep them together at the end.

But that's not what real grown-up relationships are like. They're like this. Being mature enough to know your limits, and adult enough to accept when someone tells you what they are.

Even if it breaks your heart.

I hugged her like this was going to be the last time I ever saw her.

"What do you think she'll be like?" she whispered, after a moment.

"Who?" I said gently, holding her to my chest.

"The girl you'll meet after me. Your soulmate."

My heart shattered into a million pieces.

If you had asked me yesterday, I would have said it was her. Instead she'd end up being the one who got away. Not a soulmate, just the love of my life.

And unfortunately they're not the same thing.

CHAPTER 45

EMMA

SIX MONTHS LATER

Your blood pressure looks great," Maddy said to Pops, taking the cuff off his arm. "I think you're gonna outlive all of us."

The old man harrumphed and I smiled, helping him off the table. He was ninety-eight and sharp as a tack and one of our favorite townies.

I was living at the Grant House. I'd been here since the day I left Justin.

When Maddy called Daniel and Alexis, they said yes immediately. We got out of our contract at Royaume, citing an emergency situation, and we left for Wakan.

Alexis had hired us to work at Royaume's satellite clinic here. She was a general practitioner and the town doctor—and, as we came to discover, Briana's best friend and *Neil's* ex-girlfriend. That was an interesting revelation. And so was the update we got via Briana a couple of days after we arrived. Apparently the last thing Mom did before disappearing was to burn Neil's house down.

Briana said it was karma. She also said Neil didn't seem to be too upset about it, so at least there was that.

Alexis came in holding a coffee. "Are you two going to be home for dinner?" she asked. "Daniel wants to know how many veggie burgers to grill later."

"I'm going to the VFW with Doug," Maddy said.

"So you won't be home tonight." I gave her a wry smile.

"No, I won't be home," she said. "I'm going to let that tall drink of water slam me like a door."

Alexis sat in front of her charting computer. "I could have gone my entire life without that visual."

I was laughing when Doug popped his head in the room. "Hey, babe, ready for lunch?"

Maddy skipped over to him and stood on her toes to kiss him. She was a full foot and a half shorter than him. He wrapped his arms around her waist and kissed her back a little too enthusiastically, and Alexis and I shared an amused look.

Maddy broke away and grinned up at her boyfriend. "Let me run to the bathroom real quick."

Doug watched her go as I collected my purse. "So, when are you two moving in together?"

"I keep asking her," Doug said. "She tells me to shut up."

Alexis snorted.

"That woman scares the absolute shit out of me," he said, shaking his head. "I can't get enough of her."

"I think the feeling is mutual," I said. "She's only scary when she cares."

Alexis was laughing.

A minute later Maddy came back down the hall and Doug took off his jacket and put it around her shoulders before they walked out.

I'd never seen Maddy like this for a guy. And I realized now that was partially *my* fault.

It wasn't easy to have a relationship when you moved every few months. And I knew now that she'd done that for me more than for the adventure.

We'd had a lot of long talks since we'd come here.

She told me how much she'd worried about me over the years. How she had to stay with me because she knew if she let me go out on my own, I'd never come back.

She was right. I would have become Amber.

Only unlike Amber, self-preservation built me to be independent. So I never would have called for help or money. I just wouldn't have called at all.

I would have distanced myself from her until I was so small there was nothing left of me and her. She knew this. And she loved me enough to keep it from happening.

I used to never be able to say I love you. It was something I was working on in therapy. To say it meant to give someone power over me and the ability to hurt me.

But I could say, with my whole heart, that I loved Maddy. She was one of the great loves of my life. And the thought that I would have given that up because of what Amber made me was a cautionary tale that I would *never* let myself forget.

I hoped Maddy moved in with Doug when she was ready— that she knew *I* was ready to have a normal life now and it was okay to let me go a little because I wouldn't disappear when she did. I would never get that small again. I might fall back on old coping mechanisms from time to time. I would always have to work on it. The urge to isolate would always pop up when I got scared or stressed or hurt by someone. But I had the skills now and I knew what to do when I felt myself shrinking.

I'd done three months of CBT and I had a talk therapist I really liked who specialized in trauma. She had me do a once-a-week drive down to Rochester to meet her for EMDR treatments for my complex PTSD—another thing I hadn't known I'd been dealing with but made sense to me once I was diagnosed. I'd talked to Doug, who also dealt with it, and he'd said EMDR really helped him. So I'd tried it and it did help, tremendously. A few weeks into therapy I asked Daniel to put my luggage in the attic. I didn't want it under the bed ever again.

I felt stable for the first time in my life. Steady. Like I could stay somewhere, be someone who people got to know and depend on. I was capable of that now. It didn't scare me.

Well, it did. A little. But I was still ready for it. And that wouldn't have happened if I hadn't come to Wakan. Maddy had been right about that, like she was right about most things.

It was weird, but I'd gotten to know this place through my mother in little flashes my whole life. There had always been tiny pieces of Wakan in Amber. And it made sense. Daniel and Amber had been raised by the same people. I learned why Mom was so crafty. Grandpa had been a woodworker like Daniel, and Grandma was a seamstress. The whole family gardened, something Mom passed on to me. The little sayings she had, Daniel would say too. All of the good parts of Mom that I'd lost when I let her go weren't totally gone. A lot of the best of her was here. Wakan was an untarnished version of her. And I was glad Daniel bought Grant House. Mom would have ruined it. She wouldn't have cared what happened to it, the same way she didn't care what happened to me.

There were a few times over the last six months that my phone rang from a number I didn't know. For the first time in my life, I let it go to voicemail.

I was at peace with my decision to have no contact with my mom. I felt free in a way. I no longer worried where she was, or if she was okay. She wasn't my burden anymore and I hadn't even realized how heavy she'd been for me to carry because I'd done it for so long. I finally set her down. And that started with me forgiving her.

I chose to believe that she didn't want to be the villain in my life—even if she was. I didn't lose my beautiful empathy, as Maddy called it once. I still believed what I always had, that people are complex and nothing is black and white. I believed that now more than ever.

I knew from talking to my cousins and my aunts and my brother that Amber had shown warning signs of who she would become since she was a teenager. Manic and depressive episodes, acting out, drinking at thirteen, probably to self-medicate whatever she was dealing with. Maybe they hadn't known how to help her. No internet back then, and therapy was stigmatized. Maybe in this little town with no mental health services, they legitimately *couldn't* help her. Her mental state made her vulnerable. More prone to risky behavior and trauma inflicted because of it.

Cracks.

A baby at fifteen that she had to give up.

Cracks.

Tumultuous relationships with her parents and siblings— *cracks.* One leading to the next and she never learned to fill them.

She just tried to outrun them, and Maddy was right. You can't outrun yourself.

Being here, I understood her now, probably better than I ever had. And at the end, I just felt sorry for her.

Alexis was still at the computer when I grabbed my jacket. "You're cutting out early, right?" Alexis said, looking at her watch.

"Yeah," I said, putting on my coat. "I have an appointment. I'll see you at home later."

"Drive safe."

I zipped up my jacket and walked out to my car in the blustery March air. I didn't tell anyone where I was going today. Not even Maddy.

I was going to see Justin—and he didn't know that either.

I had a voicemail from him. He'd left it the day before we broke up.

"Hey, where are you? Why'd you leave? Call me."

I played it a lot just to hear his voice.

I wondered for a long time if he still wanted to know where I was. I wondered if he still wanted me to call. Because I wanted to.

I'd wanted to pick up the phone so many times. I missed him so much. But I didn't feel ready and I didn't want to give him false hope that I ever would be, or keep him from moving on. I had been small, dealing with everything that had happened and all the emotional fallout and trying to focus on my mental health and getting to know my family.

But I wasn't small anymore.

I told myself that if I could do the work, make strides in therapy, stay here for six months, be still in one place for the first time in my adult life, that I'd be ready enough to reach out to him and see if there was anything left of us—and I did it. Today was the six-month anniversary of my coming to Wakan. I'd been watching the date approach for weeks and it was finally here.

I timed the drive to his house so I'd get there while the kids were in school, after his stand-up meeting and with a few hours until anyone came home—assuming he'd want me to stay that long. I was going to meet him where *he* was for once. And I was terrified.

Nobody in this world still possessed the ability to break me like Justin did. Justin looking me in the eye and telling me he didn't love me anymore or didn't think I was someone he wanted around his family would destroy me. It would be worse than Mom. It was taking everything in me to be that brave and that vulnerable just to show up.

I didn't know where he was with his life. Maybe he'd moved on.

I never saw anything in Sarah's Snap stories that made me think he had a girlfriend—at least nobody serious enough to bring around the kids. But he might be dating. That was a very real possibility. Someone else's fingers tangled in his thick hair. Him laughing with his head on their pillow.

Forehead kisses.

This was somehow the worst image of all, him pressing his lips to someone else's head.

But even if that was the news I'd get when I got there, it was still worth trying, because I wanted to go home.

Grant House was where I lived, but it wasn't home. Justin was home. The kids were home.

Justin was right. Home wasn't a place, it was a person. For me it was a whole family.

I wanted to hold Chelsea. I wanted to help Sarah and Alex

grow up. I wanted to wake up next to Justin and plant things in his yard, stay in one place and let things take root. Make traditions. Have birthdays and Christmases with these people, even though they weren't mine. I was strong enough for that now, if he'd let me. For the first time in my life, I was capable of love—and the loss that came with it. I could handle it now. I'd healed enough for it.

So I got in my car and I started the journey back to him.

Toilet King billboards peppered the whole drive to his house like highway markers, letting me know I was headed in the right direction. I was less than half an hour away when out of nowhere, like I'd somehow gotten a signal on my phone that I hadn't gotten in the past six months, Sarah called.

I stared at the caller ID for a solid ten seconds before I hit the answer button. "Sarah?"

"Can you come get me?"

I wrinkled my forehead. "Come get you? From where?"

"School."

"Are you sick? Where's Justin?"

"I don't want him. The nurse says you're still on the emergency contact list, you can come pick me up, they'll let me go with you. Just come."

"You're going to need to give me a little more information than this," I said.

"I got my period, okay?"

Ahhhhhh…

"I'm not telling my brother to help me get pads. And I'm not calling Leigh. She'll throw me a period party. I'd rather die."

I laughed a little. Yes, Leigh would definitely do that.

I was close. I could be there in twenty minutes. But then the nervousness sank in.

For some reason seeing Sarah felt as hard as seeing Justin.

Harder.

I didn't just break up with Justin when I left. I broke up with all of them.

Alex would forgive me. He went with the flow and he'd probably be fine with whatever Justin decided. Chelsea was too small to know or hold a grudge. But Sarah...she would tell me *exactly* what she thought of me for leaving, and she wouldn't sugarcoat it. She probably wouldn't sugarcoat what Justin had been up to over the last six months either. Especially if it involved someone else. Just because she called me for help didn't mean Sarah wanted me back in their lives. She didn't forgive easily. She was hard on people and she didn't forget. It would be a tough conversation and I didn't have the bandwidth for it.

It took everything I had just to come and see *him*.

Also he wouldn't be alone now like I'd planned, we wouldn't have the privacy I'd hoped for if Sarah was there.

For a split second I thought of telling her I couldn't do it, to call her brother to pick her up and I'd try this talk with him another day. Turning around and going back to Wakan.

But I also remembered what it was like to get my first period without a mother to help me.

I'd been alone, I didn't know what to do. My cramps had me doubled over and I'd bled on my clothes. I didn't want Sarah to have any of the small traumas I'd been forced to endure because of an absentee mom. So I made my decision.

"I can be there in twenty minutes."

I came and I felt like an imposter when I signed her out of school. An adult she trusted enough to call in an emergency, but one who hadn't been here in half a year and had to answer for it.

"Does Justin know where you are?" I asked her as we came out to the parking lot.

"No."

"Okay, well we need to tell him. Text him right now."

"He's not gonna get a phone call or something telling him I'm gone. I'll just tell him when I get home, it's already embarrassing enough."

I opened the door on the driver's side and stood there to talk to her over the roof. "Sarah, I don't feel good about taking you from school unless your guardian knows I'm doing it."

She opened the passenger side and threw her backpack into the back seat. Then she leveled her eyes on me with the most annoyed teenager glare I'd ever seen. "He's not gonna care. It's *you*."

She got in and slammed the door.

I sighed. She was probably right, he wouldn't care. If he cared, he would have taken my name off the emergency contact list. Still.

I got in and started the car. There was no point in arguing with her. She wouldn't budge and *I* wouldn't be the one to text him. Six months of no contact and my first message to him was "hi, your sister got her period"? No.

I'd just explain it to him when I got there. And then I'd search every inch of his face looking for any sign that he didn't hate me.

I got Sarah her supplies. Then I took her to Culver's for burgers. I walked her through how to use everything while we ate in the parking lot in the front seat.

"Take this." I handed her two Motrin. "Take one to two every six hours starting the minute you get your period. You have to stay ahead of the pain, okay? It's harder to make the cramps stop once they start."

She took the pills with her Sprite.

"Hot baths help. You can also use a heating pad. And tell Justin he needs to wash anything with blood on cold, okay?"

"Justin doesn't do my laundry anymore. I do it," she said.

I looked at her, surprised. "Really? Since when?"

She shrugged. "A while. He taught me and Alex how to do it. We do a lot of stuff now."

The corners of my lips twitched up. "Like what?"

"I cook."

"You *cook*?"

"Yeah. With Justin."

"What else?" I asked.

She bit the tip off a fry. "We have a chore chart. Oh, and Alex drives. He's got the van." She wrinkled her nose.

I laughed a little. "And you? How have you been?"

She shrugged. "Pretty good. I won my dance competition. I painted my room. Taught Brad to roll over and shake."

"He never changed the name, huh?"

"Nope."

No, he wouldn't. And Human Brad probably still sent him every Toilet King thing he could get his hands on.

She went on about all the changes since I left. New traditions on holidays and funny stories about the other kids and plans they'd made for spring break.

I smiled softly.

I was so proud of them. They were okay—not that I thought they wouldn't be. But I think they really *were* okay.

They'd figured it out. Come together as a family, found normalcy and joy in the aftermath of everything they went through and everything, and everyone, that they'd lost. And Sarah had a maturity about her now that she didn't have before. And not the kind that comes from growing up too fast in the midst of trauma. The kind that comes from healthy parenting and coming of age. It made me happy.

It made me feel like I'd done the right thing leaving when I did. Because I would have done nothing but undo any progress they made when I would have inevitably left.

"Me and Justin made Mom's cookies," she said. "They came out good. He said you would have really liked them."

The sudden mention of him mentioning me made my heart flip.

I'd missed so much. Halloween, Thanksgiving, Christmas, his birthday, the kids' birthdays. They had to hate me. How could they not?

"We miss you, you know," she said.

The words caught me by surprise and I looked over at her.

"You do?"

She talked to the burger in her lap. "Everybody was like, really sad when you left."

I swallowed. "They were?"

"Yeah. Like, I know you're not, but it kind of felt like you were my big sister or something. You were our family." She looked at me.

I studied her. "I felt like that too. I didn't want to have to leave," I said.

"Then why did you?" she asked.

I turned away from her.

"Sometimes you leave because it's better to deal with your problems on your own."

"Did you?"

I came back to her. "Yeah. I did. And I'm really sorry if my leaving hurt you. The last thing I wanted was for you to feel abandoned. I know what that's like."

"I didn't feel abandoned," she said, looking me in the eye. "'Cause I knew if I ever called you, you'd come."

She said it so matter-of-factly. And it was funny, because the second she said it, I realized she was right. I would have.

Anytime over the last six months, I would have been there if she'd reached out.

I wasn't like Amber.

Even small, I was better than she was.

And then she did call and I *did* come.

I'd passed a test I didn't even know I'd been taking.

"When we get home, you should come inside," she said. "I bet he'd want to see you."

I had to muscle the lump down in my throat.

"Okay," I whispered. "I'll do that."

I just hoped she was right.

CHAPTER 46

JUSTIN

I missed her. It was an ache in my chest that never went away. After six months, I'd accepted that it never would.

The first few weeks after she left were the worst. I was depressed. There was no skirting around it, it was depression.

The kids kept getting sick from going back to school. It felt like I had someone home with a cold every day for two solid weeks. Then *I* got sick and had to take care of everyone else on top of it.

The house was always messy. Cleaning it was like shoveling in a snowstorm. Everyone needed me, all the time. Chelsea's separation anxiety from Mom and Emma hit a crescendo and she hung off me like a monkey when she was home and cried every time I dropped her off at school. I was touched out and overwhelmed and missing Emma so badly it was hard to breathe.

I lived my days going through the motions like a zombie. My life felt like a series of mundane tasks I had to tick off until

I die—meals, homework, laundry, doctor's visits, grocery runs. Rinse and repeat.

I hated everything. I was moody and tired all the time. I tried to fake that I was okay during our visits with Mom, but she saw through me. She kept pressing me for what happened and I couldn't talk about it and I'd leave feeling shitty because I could tell she was worried about me.

The guys tried their best to help. They tapped in. Took the kids to stuff. Sat with Alex at his games, Jane drove Sarah to dance for me a few times. They tried to get me out of the house, take me to lunch. But a light had gone out inside of me and nothing was going to turn that back on.

All of this was because of Emma. And I didn't blame her for one ounce of it.

If you can choose anger or empathy, always choose empathy. And I did.

A year ago I would have been mad at her for leaving. It was black and white back then. To me, love meant you stayed. But now I understood that love sometimes means you let someone go.

I appreciated the strength it required for her to come tell me she had to in person, even though it was hard.

I respected that she was self-aware enough to know what she was and wasn't capable of.

I saw the sacrifice it took to decide she wasn't going to repeat the same cycle with these kids that made her who she was.

And I didn't want to repeat the cycle either. So I let her go too. And the worst thing about that was it meant I could never let her come back, because I couldn't ever believe she'd stay.

I know she told me not to, but for a long time I *was* waiting for her. A very real part of me wanted to hope that she could change. Hold out for some miracle. But with distance I came to realize that wasn't reality. That the same thing that took her from me would be the thing that would keep her away—or make her leave again if she ever came home. And I couldn't put the kids through that. Not again.

I couldn't imagine what Emma could ever say to me to make me feel safe in that relationship after this. And this was the hardest part of all to deal with. The finality of it.

It was really over.

I let myself wallow for a few hard, miserable weeks. And then I looked around at my life and I realized that I was a guardian now and that me unraveling was no better than when Mom did it. I had kids to raise, an example to set. I didn't have the luxury of the meltdown I currently deserved. So I got my shit together. I did what I was good at. I pulled myself up by the bootstraps and I put systems in place.

I mapped out my day and took a good long look and I made changes.

I stopped making breakfast during the week. I liked doing it because Mom always did, but it was too much.

I took everyone to the store and let them pick out their favorite cereal and oatmeal. Alex's new job in the morning was to pour Cheerios in a bowl for Chelsea, who was already up by the time he was, and turn on her movie before he left for the bus. This took him two minutes and bought me another hour of sleep.

Once I started sleeping more, my energy and mood got better. I got a treadmill for under my desk so I could get my steps in while I worked. Got some weights and set up a little home gym to use after dropping Chelsea off at preschool.

Sarah liked to cook. I started asking her if she wanted to help me make dinners. She did. We bought that Sloan Monroe Crockpot cookbook and Sarah and I would meal prep and Alex cleaned up and suddenly dinner was fun again. A team-building activity I started to look forward to.

For Halloween Alex wanted to make the front lawn into a graveyard so we went to the Halloween store and bought a bunch of animatronic zombies. I spent way too much money, but it was the first project we all did together. We carved pumpkins and got Brad a dog costume. On Halloween night Sarah and I made a lasagna and hot chocolate and took Chelsea trick-or-treating. And I realized, when the kids were back at the house, sitting on the living room floor going through their candy, that I'd had a good day. It would have been better if *she* was here. But it was still good.

After that, the days kept getting better, a little at a time. Thanksgiving was hard without Mom, but we went to Leigh's and came home with lots of leftovers. A few days later we went to cut down a Christmas tree. We took pictures and the smiles were real. We spent a Saturday baking Mom's cookies and they came out perfect.

When the clock struck midnight on the TV on New Year's Eve, I missed Emma so much I had to leave the room. But by then I'd accepted this pain as part of my everyday life, and while it never got easier that she wasn't here, it did start to feel normal.

In January Alex turned sixteen and got his driver's license. I gave him the van. Now I had another driver in the house, which helped.

Little by little, we were figuring it out.

And there wasn't a day that went by that I didn't feel her absence like a void in my soul. I missed her like I missed the sun in the winter.

I'd realized something after being with her. A valuable lesson that I think all the best and most enduring romances have figured out.

The love stories sold us the wrong thing.

The best kind of love doesn't happen on moonlit walks and romantic vacations. It happens in between the folds of everyday life. It's not grand gestures that show how you feel, it's all the little secret things you do to make her life better that you never tell her about. Taking the end piece of the bread at breakfast so she can have the last middle piece for her sandwich when you pack her lunch. Making sure her car always has gas so she never has to stop at the pump. Telling her you're not cold and to take your jacket when you are in fact, very, very cold. It's watching TV on a rainy Sunday while you're doing laundry and turning her light off when she's fallen asleep reading. Sharing pizza crusts and laughing about something the kids did and taking care of each other when you're sick. It isn't glamorous, it isn't all butterflies and stars in your eyes. It's *real*. This is the kind of love that forever is made of. Because if it's this good when life is draining and mundane and hard, think of how wonderful it will be when the love songs are playing and the moon is out.

I *was* grateful that the life I'd been forced into taught me this lesson. I just wish I hadn't learned it with Emma. Because nothing and nobody else would ever compare. With anyone else, it's just folding socks on a sofa.

* * *

Chelsea was home today, she had a fever this morning.

I was just finishing up my last project of the day when I heard someone on the stairs, but the steps were too heavy to be hers. I leaned back in my chair to look down the hallway. "Chels?"

Sarah popped her head in the door.

"Hey," I said, blinking at her. "What are you doing home?"

"I got my period. You need to come downstairs."

"Who picked you up?"

She rolled her eyes. "Just come downstairs." Then she left.

I let out an exasperated breath. Alex probably brought her and he probably dinged the van or something on the way here. Great.

I got up and took off my headset.

Why'd the school let them leave without calling me? I made a mental note to suss that out. I mean, I know they let high schoolers walk off campus without a parent standing there, but I should have gotten a call about the missed classes at the very least.

I jogged down the steps. Sarah was standing in the mouth of the living room and I came up behind her. "Just please tell me Alex didn't damage any—" I froze.

Emma was on the sofa.

She had Chelsea cradled in her arms, bundled in her *Frozen* blanket, and she was talking softly to her. My dog had his head on her thigh, looking up at her.

It was like a still-life painting. Something a master had created out of the deepest recesses of my brain. I had to clutch a hand over my chest because it felt like it was going to split open.

Not a second had passed. It hadn't been six months since I'd seen her, it was a heartbeat. A flicker.

This is the thing nobody tells you about The One. How they're timeless. How the moment they pop up again you're right back in it, right where you left off. I was darted through the heart, hit by the truck, my brain taking the screenshot.

Her hair was in a loose bun. She had on this light blue sweater and these little gold dangling dragonfly earrings. And I couldn't even breathe looking at her.

She glanced up.

"She has a fever. Did you know?" she said.

I just stared. Mute.

When I didn't answer, she gazed back at my little sister and brushed the hair off her forehead. Chelsea was hugging her. She looked so content. Like a baby in the arms of someone she loves.

My mouth was dry. "I, uh. I gave her Tylenol two hours ago. She's been kind of pulling on her ear," I said.

Emma nodded. "I'll look at her eardrums."

The moment felt normal. Like she'd never left. Like I was just coming downstairs to get water in between meetings and she was home with me on her day off, helping with the kids.

I cleared my throat and turned to Sarah. "Can you—"

"Yup," she said, cutting me off. She took Chelsea from Emma and carried her out of the room. The second Chelsea was gone, Brad took the spot on Emma's lap. She put her hand on my dog's head and peered at me from the sofa. "Sarah called me to pick her up. She got her first period," she said.

I felt my heart sink. So she hadn't come to see me.

Not that I expected her to. She hadn't called me in six months. Still, it hurt.

"Can we go in the kitchen?" I asked.

I didn't know if I could have another depressing conversation on this sofa, I'd have to set it on fire.

We moved to the breakfast nook and I went straight to the fridge. Mostly to bury my face, to try and get my feelings together before I had to sit directly across from her. "Do you want something to drink?" I asked, talking to her but staring at a gallon of milk.

"No. Thank you."

I gave myself another few seconds. Then I closed the fridge door, walked over, and took the seat in front of her.

Brad hopped into her lap and frowned at me across the table while she peered around the room.

"I like the chore chart," she said.

"Thanks."

That's all I could muster. The disappointment was too sobering. What do you say after six months of nothing?

Sarah still followed her on Snap. Emma was living in Wakan. As far as I knew this was the longest time she'd stayed put in the last decade.

But she couldn't stay put for *me*.

For some reason, with her sitting in front of me, this felt like a slap.

They were her family. She was getting to know them, I *wanted* that for her. And I knew why she'd left, it had been a mutual decision. But she'd clearly put in some effort that she hadn't been willing or able to put in here, and seeing her opened the old wound like it had never closed. Or maybe it was a new injury altogether. Evidence that she'd been capable of more than she'd claimed.

If Emma had six months of staying in her, why couldn't she have given it to *us*?

Just two hours away.

She never visited, never called. And now she was only here because Sarah needed her.

I mean, I guess I should have been glad Emma at least cared enough to show up for that.

I sat back in my chair looking anywhere but at her.

All I wanted to do was look at her. Soak her up, store her away like I might never get another shot to do it. But I couldn't do it without the lump in my throat threatening to make me cry.

I missed her so much I just wanted to get up and grab her and hold her and kiss her, but I got to sit here instead, knowing her being here was only because my sister texted her. This was just a social call. Popping in to say hi. At least that's what it felt like. And did she drive two hours just to pick up Sarah? Because that didn't feel likely. It felt more plausible that she was already in the area and why would she be in the area?

Was she seeing someone?

The idea burst into my brain like an intrusive thought on steroids.

I'd managed not to think about this for the last six months and now that she was here in front of me this question felt like a swarm of hornets buzzing in my rib cage. The idea made me want to claw my chest open. I was so jealous at the thought of it, it felt cruel that she came here to remind me this possibility existed. Because if she *did* date, that meant someone else got the Emma who stayed still when she wouldn't stay still for *me*.

"How's your mom?" she asked.

I felt ill.

I gave her a one-shoulder shrug. "Fine. She's adjusted now. Has a few friends. We go see her once a month."

"I see you didn't rename the dog," she said.

"Nope."

Silence.

She cleared her throat. "So are you seeing anyone?" she asked out of nowhere. Her voice was a touch too high.

I glanced up at her to catch the tentative gaze she was giving me. My heart leapt at the question. Like maybe it was a sign she still cared.

I shook my head. "No. I haven't dated at all."

Something flickered across her expression.

"Are...are you?" I asked, terrified for the answer.

It was an excruciating moment before she replied. "No. I haven't."

There was a second of...something. But it didn't last. The conversation ended and we just sat there, quiet.

It was amazing how much this hurt.

It was like the universe wanted to let me know that no, I wasn't over it, and no, I didn't have it under control. No systems I could put in place could make this better. Nothing I did could change how absolutely shitty this felt.

"What are you thinking?" she asked.

I scoffed dryly. "Are you sure you want to know?"

She swallowed. "Yes."

I took in a deep breath. "I'm thinking that I'm happy to see you, but this just stirs up a lot for me."

She nodded slowly. "And?"

"And I kind of wish you didn't come."

I watched this hit her.

But I meant it. What was the point? I didn't want to catch up. I wanted what I couldn't have. What she wasn't capable of giving me. I didn't want her here on a technicality, I wanted everything.

She apologized. Then she got up to leave.

CHAPTER 47

EMMA

I came knowing he probably didn't want to see me, knowing I might not like what I found when I got here. I came knowing a door could be slammed in my face or not opened at all.

But I came anyway.

And now Justin was sitting back in his chair across from me, staring at the baseboards and he'd just told me he wished I hadn't come.

He was in a hoodie. His hair was messy, the way I liked. I'd almost forgotten how much I missed looking at him. How handsome he was. But his gentle brown eyes weren't happy to see me.

When I pulled up across the street from his house with Sarah, I sat there for a moment. I could see his bedroom window from where I was parked. The one he'd peered out at me from once when I showed up in the rain the night I'd decided to stay.

Home is something that's always there, I realized. No matter where you are in the world, you know it's where you left it, unchanged and waiting. Only now that I was here, I saw Justin was neither unchanged or waiting.

He was cold. Short with me. And not glad at all that I was here.

I'd planned to go right into what I'd come to say, but now I didn't even know how to start or even if I should.

It's one thing to go to therapy and learn skills. It's very different to have to use them in real life. And I did need to use them.

I'd felt myself start to get small the second I got here. My old coping mechanism triggered by his obvious unhappiness at seeing me. The plucking at the edges and the need to withdraw and turn inward. My old knee-jerk reaction begged me to get up and go before this did any more damage.

But I'd held my ground. I held it for as long as I needed to, right up until he told me he wished I hadn't come. And now it *was* time to go.

I wish I would have known that the last time he'd looked at me with love in his eyes was the last time. I would have savored it. It was so hard to see what I'd lost.

I missed everything.

The tender way he always touched me. My fingers circling the hair on his chest as I lay with my head on his shoulder while we talked. Hearing the rumbling of his voice under my ear. The way he'd wake up in the middle of the night and feel for me and pull me in. How his eyes used to light up when he saw me.

There was something faded there now.

All of what was good was gone.

My heart broke.

This was the price. The price of being better.

Because the old me would never have come here. The old me

would have left Minnesota six months ago, been in a different state by now. The old me wouldn't have gotten close enough to see if the love had disappeared from his eyes.

I was going to cry. And now I really did need to go. Not because I was running, but because this visit was over. I was sorry I'd come. I didn't want to stir anything up or hurt him or remind him of something he'd already put away. He clearly didn't want me here and there was nothing for me here either.

"I'm sorry. I'll go." I stood up and set the dog on the floor.

Justin looked at me but didn't say a word. A second later his chair scraped against the tile and he got up and started walking me out.

Brad was running at my feet, yipping and crying.

We got to the door and Justin opened it for me to a blast of chilly air. I saw the nose of my car across the street through the screen. Pictured the drive back to Wakan. The Toilet King billboards along the freeway until I got far enough outside of Justin's world that they disappeared. I would exit onto the windy road back to my side of Minnesota. Take the two-lane highway past the sign welcoming me to Wakan. Through Main Street, along the river. Back to Grant House.

Grant House. My family home.

But not *my* home.

My home was here. My home was *him*. The man saying goodbye to me. And he didn't even know it. I hadn't been strong enough to tell him then, back when it mattered.

But I was strong enough now.

I turned in the entry. "I have something to say to you before I go. I'm going to tell you what I'm thinking, even though you didn't ask." I braced myself. "I love you, Justin."

He blinked at me.

I took a deep breath. "I know that I hurt you when I left. And to be honest, I couldn't have done anything differently at that time. I was traumatized and dealing with PTSD. Back then, I couldn't even tell you how I felt about you. I didn't even want to admit it to *myself* because it scared me so much." I licked my lips. "I miss you. I miss the kids. I miss the dog. I think about you every day, I scour Sarah's Snap stories for little pieces of you and listen to the last voicemail you sent me, and it's sad and pathetic and I don't even care. I wanted to call you so many times, but I was trying to deal with what happened to me and I knew I wouldn't be good for you, so I decided to leave you alone. And some of that was me still being scared because with you the stakes are so high. I didn't know if I could recover if you didn't want me anymore. I needed to do more work on myself to be ready for that, and I have. I was coming here to see you today when Sarah called me. I was already in Minneapolis. And seeing her was hard too because I didn't know if she could forgive me either, and I went anyway. You might not understand what a big deal that is, but it's huge. It's progress and it's growth and I was brave and I showed up.

"I know it probably doesn't matter, but I could meet you where you are now. I can meet all of you. I've filled my cracks. I don't want to be an island. I want a village. I want lots of friends and lots of love in my life. I stayed somewhere for the first time without any plans to leave, I unpacked my luggage and I kept the stupid box to my new phone and I have way more than two suitcases' worth of stuff. I took a permanent job and I've been going to therapy. I'm learning to depend on people and ask for help. I'm trying to be vulnerable, even when I know I might end up getting hurt, and part of that is telling people how I feel." I took a deep breath. "I know I never said I love you. You have to understand how hard that word was for me. Everyone I have *ever* loved has been taken from me except for Maddy. And even with her I was always braced for it. So I just never let myself get close to anyone because that's the only way I ever felt safe. But with you…"

I peered at him, tearing up. His eyes were wide.

"I didn't have a choice with you," I said. "I couldn't keep you out. I want you to know that I loved you at first sight, Justin. It just took me a really long time to be able to tell you what I saw."

He let out a shaky puff of air.

"I love you," I said again. "I'm sorry it came so late. You deserved to hear it sooner. When it still mattered."

He was staring at me through tears. He didn't move and he didn't say anything. But I didn't regret telling him. I was proud of myself for coming here and telling him. The words were his and he should have them.

I pulled in a shuddering breath and turned for the door. Then I pivoted back around. "Also, I'm not leaving until I check Chelsea's ears. If you want to stop me, you're going to have to tackle me." I stepped around him and started for the stairs.

"Emma…"

Before I could process what was happening, he was spinning me into his chest. I blinked up at him in surprise.

"Not again," he breathed. His eyes pleaded with me. "Don't walk out on me again."

It took me a moment to comprehend what he was saying. It was such a change from the moment before. "*Please*," he begged.

"I would stay forever if you asked me," I whispered.

"Then *stay*."

I broke in half.

I peered up at him, at the open expression he wore. The dozens of emotions. Everything I thought I'd lost was suddenly flooding out of him.

He still loved me. He forgave me.

I knew in that moment that I would never run again. If he really did want me, I would dock for a lifetime. I would do it all. I would move in here and raise these kids with him and be still and big and present. I knew how to now.

I started crying. Sobbing.

He was crying too.

I don't know how long we stood there in the doorway wiping tears off each other's faces and whispering I love you. Long enough that the laughter of relief rolled in. The smiling and nodding and brushing hair off wet cheeks.

Alex came home and fist pumped in the doorway and then ran upstairs calling Sarah. Chelsea escaped her sister and came down holding her blanket and stood there hugging our legs. Sarah smiled from the top of the steps and didn't look the least bit grossed out by the scene.

And it was perfect.

All of it was perfect. An encapsulated moment.

Justin looked in my eyes. "You know," he said, "if the curse is true, the next person you date is going to be your soulmate."

I smiled. "The next person *you* date's going to be yours too."

He cupped my face in his palms. "I was wondering if you'd like to go out with me sometime," he whispered. "Four dates. A kiss. No breakup."

I laughed, the tears starting to well again. "Not just for the summer?"

"No. Forever this time."

EPILOGUE

AITA for proposing to my girlfriend on a Toilet King Billboard?

So I [31m] have been dating my live-in girlfriend [31F] for the last
two years.

We have this little inside joke about The Toilet King, that guy in
Minnesota with all the billboards everywhere? It's a long story, but
those billboards are how we met. They have sort of a special place in
our relationship because of it and we have a rule that we have to kiss
when we drive by one. One year she got me a Toilet King birthday
cake and then for her birthday I got her a birthday card with the Toilet
King jingle. We've won Toilet King coasters from a radio giveaway and
we have custom Toilet King stockings for Christmas—you get the idea.

Anyway, I've been wanting to ask her to marry me for some
time now. I currently have custody of my younger siblings and in
a few weeks my mom is coming home earlier than expected and
taking them back. My girlfriend and I are going to get our own
place nearby so we can stay close to the kids and we've started
looking at properties.

I had this idea to tell her that an apartment in my old building was up for lease and that we should go check it out. This apartment has a Toilet King Billboard directly outside the window and I thought it would be the perfect place to pop the question.

They have a really hard time finding tenants for it so it's currently empty. I contacted the landlord and he was open to renting it to me for a few days so I could execute this plan. The Toilet King said he'd be willing to replace the poop in the bowl on the billboard with "will you marry me?"

I was going to pretend that we were going to see an apartment, fill the studio with roses and twinkle lights, and then pull the blinds back where the Will You Marry Me? message would be outside on the billboard. Then I was going to drop to one knee and do the whole proposal thing with the ring. Afterwards a caterer would show up and our closest friends and family would come over for appetizers and drinks to celebrate with us.

I think it's a solid plan, but nobody else likes it. I sent out a survey to get everyone's opinion. My mom and aunt say it's disrespectful to ask her to marry me on a sign with poop-smeared toilet paper on it. My two best friends' wives also hate the idea. My girlfriend's moms were lukewarm on it, but to be fair I don't think they really get the whole Toilet King thing since they live out of state. Her best friend gives it two thumbs-up though and her husband Doug also thinks it's hilarious.

Thoughts? Should I just plan something else? But it won't have the same special meaning if I change it.

Edit: to answer your questions, yes, it's the one with the flies circling the bowl, no I won't make it less gross by taking out the plunger.

Update: I did it. She loved it. She said yes.

ACKNOWLEDGMENTS

Thank you to Sue Lammert, a licensed clinical counselor specializing in trauma; Dr. Julie Patten, licensed psychologist; and Dr. Karen Flood for helping me to depict the mental health aspects of this book with sensitivity and accuracy. As always, my disclaimer that any errors in this book are my own and are no fault of the people who advised me. Thank you to Olivia Kägel, registered practical nurse, and beta readers Kim Kao, Jeanette Theisen Jett, Kristin Curran, Terri Puffer Burrell, Amy Edwards Norman, Dawn Cooper, and sensitivity reader Leigh Kramer. Thank you, Valentina García-Guzio, for correcting the Spanish for me. A big thank-you to my agent who does way more than she has to—I'm very high maintenance, the poor woman's exhausted lol. Thank you to my editor Leah, who somehow makes sense of my long rambling word vomit on our plot calls. Estelle and Dana, thank you for coordinating all the wonderful media and publicity for my books. So many people discover them because of you. Thank you, Sarah Congdon, for the absolutely gorgeous cover! Thank you to Graham McCarthy, whose viral first-date questionnaire to Katrina Froese was the inspiration for Justin's surveys in the book. It's a great video by Katrina, go watch it!

P.S. They're still together ☺

YOUR BOOK CLUB RESOURCE

READING GROUP GUIDE

Q & A WITH ABBY JIMENEZ

1. The big question on everyone's mind—why bring Neil back?

Honestly? I wanted to burn his house down lol. Maddy makes a comment early in the book prophesizing this. It's fun to catch on a reread.

Both Neil and Amber were in *Part of Your World*, though Amber was almost completely off page. Neil was Alexis's ex, and Daniel was dealing with Amber's toxicity in his own way.

To explain why Neil was here, I need to explain why I brought back Amber.

I knew I wanted to write a book about trauma and the effects it has on relationships. I knew I wanted to feature a woman with a difficult mother, maybe someone a lot like Amber—and then I thought, why can't it actually *be* Amber? Daniel escaped so many hardships by being raised by his grandparents. What if there was a child who wasn't? What if he had a sister who was left to Amber's devices? What would her childhood be like and how would she have turned out?

Avoidant attachment relationship style is something

most of us have encountered in the dating wild, but chances are you didn't know there was a name for it. It's the person you hit it off with and everything is going great, you have incredible chemistry—and then they ghost you. Or they pick a fight with you out of nowhere and break up with you. They avoid deeper conversations and other opportunities to get closer to you. Maybe they cheat and sabotage the relationship and you can't understand why because things between you were so good.

Avoidants' relationships tend to be superficial and fleeting, because that's what they're comfortable with. It stems from childhood trauma, usually relating to an emotionally unavailable caretaker or unstable upbringing. They avoid emotional bonds and romantic relationships, they don't seek support from those around them, and they withdraw when someone tries to get to know them—which was honestly really difficult to write in a character as an author trying to tell a love story.

Emma was so aloof, it was challenging to create chemistry between her and Justin because she wasn't fully onboard. She wouldn't be, that's her issue. For much of the book Justin, who has a healthy, secure relationship style, is falling in love, while Emma is getting there, almost to her own surprise and against her will. She's drawn to Minnesota for the curse thing, liking Justin and signing up for the summer for the fun of it. She meets his family on a technicality and ends up getting close to them. Then she's forced to lean on Justin and confide in him due to the unexpected presence of her mother and a fight with Maddy. She's pressured to let him care for her when she gets sick and there's no other choice. Justin makes headway inches at a time until he finally breaks that wall and gets in—but once he's there, it can't last, because she hasn't addressed the trauma that's made her the person she is.

Enter Amber and Neil.

I wanted Amber to arrive and show us *exactly* what Emma grew up with.

Amber is not all bad. Almost nobody is. She can be extremely charismatic and charming and at times she was a doting mother. She was fun and eccentric and even protective in her own way. But Amber is prone to getting sucked into her toxic relationships and this started the neglect and abandonment that would shape who Emma becomes.

I wanted to show the progression of Amber's attachment style. How she gets so immersed in the relationship, it's all that matters.

I decided to have Amber attach herself to the man the two were renting from, and it was almost immediately obvious to me that the man should be Neil. We now have two antagonists from *Part of Your World* dating each other, and those who made the connection would spend the book braced for the shoe to drop. I loved this tension. And it made sense that these two would hit it off. Neil is working on himself. I think he was doing it in a very genuine way. But at the end of the day, Neil is still a narcissist, or at the very least still has narcissistic tendencies, and Amber very much feeds into that. Amber shows up showering him with praise and idolatry, and Neil doesn't even pause to question it because narcissists believe they deserve that kind of worship. He wouldn't suspect that maybe there's something wrong with Amber and her desire to attach herself to him so quickly.

Amber seeks male validation. She craves it. She becomes whatever she needs to be to please the man she's courting—but it can't last. It's not sustainable. She hasn't addressed the things that cause her problematic behaviors.

I purposely never explain what Amber's issues or diagnoses are—because that's real life. I know exactly what Amber has. I have to to write her authentically. I talked her over at length with my mental health advisor Karen Flood. But in the real world we don't always get answers for why people are the way they are. Even when we do get answers, they're often wrong or only part of the truth.

No two people are made the same. We all have different experiences and brain chemistry and abilities. Amber is complex and can't be summarized by a mental health condition or personality disorder. Nobody can. These things can overlap and evolve, wane and wax. They can be exacerbated by a multitude of factors, stress, and changing situations. I can say though that abandonment, or perceived abandonment, is very triggering for Amber. And unfortunately Neil is a workaholic with a job that makes him unavailable for long hours, and that was a recipe for disaster for them. Her fear of being left caused her to act out, putting a wedge between them. The wedge made her feel insecure, so she resorted to old habits like stealing since she was financially unstable and was afraid Neil was going to leave her. It also starts her on a mental health spiral that causes Neil to further question the relationship. Ultimately Amber's behavior creates a self-fulfilling prophecy where she is in fact broken up with. She will repeat this cycle again and again because she won't seek treatment to learn the skills to change it, because unlike Emma, Amber lacks the self-awareness to admit something is wrong with her.

It's this same deep-seated fear of abandonment that leads to Amber hiding Emma from her family. Even though Emma ends up separated from Amber for a lot of her childhood, that separation is still on Amber's terms and it's less permanent than giving Emma to her parents. Amber can always pluck Emma out of foster care, but her parents would never give her back. Instead of Amber examining why her life is so tumultuous, she continues to chase relationships that will fail, seeking the stability of someone who will never leave her because she draws her self-worth from whatever man she's dating.

Neil, to his credit, tried to navigate this using the skills he developed in therapy. In an earlier version of the book, I made a mention of Neil being in a healthy relationship at the end with someone after Amber, and my beta readers expressed disappointment that Neil was given a happy ever after, so I took that out. Apparently even putting him through Amber and burning his house down wasn't enough for readers to forgive Neil for what he did to Alexis in her book—and that's fine. We don't necessarily need to see Neil be happy. That wasn't the point in having him in this book. I needed him as a device to display the behavior Emma grew up seeing from her mother and I also needed someone who could offer Amber every resource she needs to be better, to show that she would turn it down. Emma needed this for her own closure.

2. Why did you choose to have the women stay on the island?

I'd gone on a summer boating trip with a friend and we ended up on Big Island on Lake Minnetonka. I'd never been out there and I was fascinated by it. The summer homes were both novel and sort of impractical. I could absolutely see the draw of owning one, but also the downsides. I loved the thought of Emma being drawn into the romantic idea of it, and then slowly realizing that it's not all it's made out to be. That the isolation and seasonal nature of it was less than ideal. I liked that the island was very much a metaphor for her own way of living, and we see the decline in the quality of the experience as the story goes on. The house looks great at first glance. It's in a beautiful setting, it's adorable inside. But we begin to realize that it's poorly maintained and falling apart. It's uncomfortable and even proves to be a little dangerous when Emma gets sick with no way to get help. And I love that we see Justin get on the island, literally and figuratively, by painstakingly clawing—or paddling—his way there.

The island isn't the only symbolism in this book. Stuffie the unicorn is the token of Emma's innocence and childhood. He's one of the last things she attaches to before she loses the ability to attach at all. Justin cleans up Stuffie as a gift to her because he knows how unsentimental she is about things and he wants to honor the things she cherishes. He also uses a unicorn floatie to get to her when she needs him, a symbol of her vulnerability, to scale the insurmountable challenge of breaching her defenses and finally reaching her.

There's also the ongoing role that roses play in the book.

The roses that Amber brings to the story are always fleeting and temporary. Perfume that fades, flowers that she gives Emma that wilt and die, a painting on a wall that she never finishes. Justin gives her roses that need planting. He wants her to put roots down.

The roses in Grant House, however, never die or change. They're on Daniel's arms as tattoos and carved into the banister and they represent the stability and permanence of the family home. This is where Emma eventually finds herself and takes control of her life and trauma.

The changing stained-glass window of Grant House makes its third appearance in this book, and it depicts a young Emma, surrounded by roses, celebrating her return home.

I also bring back the dragonflies from *Part of Your World*, a symbol that change is coming.

3. Any other Easter eggs? We know how much you love them!

Yes! Of course there's the obvious ones. Mentions of Jaxon Waters, the Sloan Monroe slow cooker cookbook that Justin and Sarah use, Josh Copeland coming up as a relative of Emma—did you catch that Easter egg in *Part of Your World*? Daniel Grant is cousins with Josh from *The Friend Zone*!

There's a lot of foreshadowing for the Maddy-and-Doug thing. Maddy is a vegetarian. So is Doug. Her favorite song is "More Than Words" by Extreme, the only song Doug knows how to play on the guitar (badly). Maddy is also someone who deeply understands PTSD, which Doug has. Maddy would know how to love and support Doug through his own challenges with his mental health because we've seen her do it with Emma. Also Doug needs someone to tell him to shut up lol.

Another Easter egg/inside joke to anyone who lives in Minnesota is the subtle nod to the Kris Lindahl real estate billboards that are everywhere here. I got the idea for Justin's studio after seeing a viral TikTok where someone showed an apartment with a Kris Lindahl billboard directly outside their window.

At first I strongly considered using actual Kris Lindahl billboards in the book. I reached out to Mr. Lindahl to ask his permission and he very generously agreed. But I decided being able to create a fictional billboard would give me more flexibility to make it funnier, and also make it more universal to the readers who won't get the joke, so Toilet King it is.

There's lots of other Easter eggs—including a deeply buried one that takes us back to my first book. But I'll let you find those yourself.

BOOK CLUB QUESTIONS

1. If you could live anywhere just for the summer, where would you live?
2. Have you ever met someone who acts like Amber? How did that relationship end up?
3. Do you think Emma leaving to work on herself was brave or selfish?
4. What do you think about Emma and Maddy's lifestyle? Would you like traveling and changing states every three months?
5. Have you ever felt small like Emma?
6. Justin's mom did something really out of character while dealing with her grief. What are some of the things you've seen grief do to someone?
7. Would you ever put a wild baby animal in your shirt?
8. Is Justin the asshole?